SINGULARITY

ALSO BY THE AUTHOR

THE STARSTRUCK SAGA

Starstruck

Alienation

Traveler

Celestial

Starbound

Earthstuck

Inalienable

Wanderer

Head over Heels (Starstruck Halloween Short)

Lasers and Tiaras (Starstruck Short)

Into the Sallyverse (Starstruck Side Story)

AIX MARKS THE SPOT

OVER THE MOON

NOVELLAS AND SHORT STORIES

Miss Planet Earth

Miss Planet Earth and the Amulet of Beb Sha Na

The Horrible Habits of Humans

Study Night at the Museum

Smells like Teen Virgin (Being Ace Anthology, Page Street)

BOOK TEN OF THE STARSTRUCK SAGA

SINGULARITY

S.E. ANDERSON

BOLIDE

SINGULARITY

First published in 2024 by Bolide Publishing Limited
Bolidepublishing.com

ISBN: 978-1-912996-79-7

FOR ALL OF US
WHO MADE IT HERE

WE MADE IT.

ONE

IN CASE OF BREAKUP, REFRAIN FROM TIME TRAVEL STALKING

IT IS A COMMON MISCONCEPTION THAT THE coldest thing in the universe is the void of space. It's not: it's the absolute zero of loneliness. So, if you find yourself lost in the universe, just remember, it's not the lack of heat that will get you, it's the crushing weight of existential dread.

Life is luck. Existence is luck. That's all it is. And if you happen to find someone who makes your journey through this cosmic chaos more bearable, cling to them like a starved leech in a blood bank. After all, there's more empty space in the universe than anything else — but with someone to share it with, it might just be a little less cold and a smidgen less bleak.

Once again, I'm ignoring my own advice. Or more accurately, coming up with said life advice in retrospect, pretending I can go back and offer it to a younger self.

Which, honestly, I probably could, but the ethical ramifications are tying my brain into knots.

"Do you see that star there?" Zander simultaneously *had* said and *was* saying, so beautifully, so plainly, that my mind had simply gushed out of my head. At least, I remember it had when *I* had been the one floating in the lake with him, being romanced, rather than creepily watching from a distance with a pair of binoculars and a bucket of ice cream shoved under my arm.

They say you shouldn't revisit the past during a breakup. But here I was, doing just that. I don't know if being literal makes this better or worse.

Zander kept his lips in a tight line, as he so often did when he was in deep thought. Oh, for that beautiful voice, borderline musical when he was excited about something, when he was discovering or rediscovering the beauty of the universe. If only I could snatch that voice away and gift it to a more deserving spaceperson.

Asshole doesn't deserve it. I took another bite of ice cream, relishing the taste of successfully reached deadlines. The 26th century was incredible at capturing the flavor of emotions, and I was eating it up.

I watched myself reply that *yes, I was pretty sure we were looking at the same one.* Seeing as how "that star there" was more accurately a sun at this point, as large as the nail of my pinky in the sky, while most other stars had been mere pinpricks, but you know, semantics.

"Right now, this planet is making a choice," he continued in that melodious tone of his. "By some bizarre cosmic hiccup, that star spun into this system, got tangled up with the local sun, and now the planets are forced to pick which star they are to orbit. And this one is about to make that decision."

"Why not both?" I had muttered as I floated, serene, on the crystal clear waters of the lake, rocked by the gentle waves and the occasional brush of his shoulder against mine, like two celestial bodies lost in space.

"Yeah, Zander, why not both?" I grumbled, taking a large spoonful and shoving it in my mouth. *Cold.* The relief of not having to think about old projects anymore washed over me, even as the ice cream melted down my chin. "Binary systems are a thing."

"Interstellar accidents are rare enough as they are," he had replied. "Things just… happen. And the rest of the universe has to accommodate, without complaint."

"I've never heard of a planet complaining before," past-me had mused.

Who are you trying to impress? Grow a backbone, Sally, jeez.

Zander had only clutched my hand tighter. "Neither have I. Isn't it nice how well behaved they are?"

Well, they didn't have to deal with existential dread now, did they? Nor did they have to deal with anything, being inanimate piles of rubble and rock. Like everything in the universe, there was no choice, only chance. The universe always got what it wanted in the end.

I sighed as my spoon hit cardboard. My last mouthful of ice cream melted away along with the bittersweet nostalgia and the auto-dissolve pot. Which was good, considering I didn't have a bad to carry anything back with me. My trusty duffel had been unceremoniously forgotten on the *Traveler* when I'd made my hasty exit. I'd have to go back for it, but right now, I wasn't ready to face anyone onboard.

You might think that being able to watch your own past with the clarity of an omniscient narrator would offer some profound insight or comfort. But all it really did was remind me that, in this vast, absurd universe, we were all just trying to find a little warmth among the stars. And sometimes, even that was too much to ask for.

I put down my binoculars as I stood up. I didn't want to watch what happened next. It was hard enough seeing myself so happy, so blissfully ignorant of who I had by my side. Stars, how naïve I had been. It wasn't that I didn't know who and what Zander was. I literally just thought his… *issues* wouldn't apply to me. That I was special somehow.

I closed my eyes, hoping to shut out the weight of the universe for just a moment longer. But when I opened them, the choice had been made. The second star was nothing more than a pinprick now, a distant memory. All I was left with was the warmth of a new sun on my face —

not enough to counteract the crushing cold of the body missing by my side — and the weight of the universe on my shoulders.

"Move!"

I stumbled back as a runner flew past me. A runner with about a dozen legs and twice as many arms, most pinwheeling around uselessly while only four legs did any actual work. I didn't have enough time to gape at him before another runner slammed against my shoulder, mumbling a curse as they rushed past. Shit— *running*. Never a good sign. I didn't waste any time, gritted my teeth, and rushed after them.

Oh, Frash. Somewhere between the ice cream and self-pity party I had become unstuck from time. I guess that's what happens when your intergalactic boyfriend kills your not-actually-dead brother and accuses him of future genocide. Most people don't have to deal with this crap after a breakup, do they?

The planet had changed radically in the time it had taken me to blink: the new star was small but nurturing, and an entire jungle had sprung up around me, lush and vibrant with life. The three of us raced down a road, zigzagging around puddles of teal gelatinous goo. Behind us, screams filled the air, a loud, constant barrage of sound.

And footsteps. Hundreds of footsteps.

"Ahhh!" The runner in the lead, the one with a few too many limbs than they knew what to do with, had tried to leap over a puddle, only to fumble his landing and fall back. Only the goo seemed to wrap around him, cradling him; the runner thrashed against it, but the stronger they fought, the stronger the goo seemed to get.

SINGULARITY

The other runner kept going, ignoring the other's cry for help. The forest, however, burst open, and a team of people in bright neon jumpsuits hurried over to extract the fallen racer, so completely unfazed that I had to wonder if this was a daily occurrence.

The world around me was chaos. The once-crystal clear waters of the lake were now a chaotic mess of splashes as hundreds of people slipped, slid, and belly-flopped across the surface, turning what had been such a serene location into an absurd, definitely unromantic carnival.

Was this some kind of competition? I took a step back, deeper into the foliage, lest I get dragged further into this mess. It was exactly the kind of scenario Zander loved: show up somewhere, accidentally get pulled into a marathon, win the thing, become a local legend, befriend everyone in the process. It was a small relief I didn't have to pretend to like that anymore. Zander wasn't your typical extrovert. He took socializing to a whole other level — an extraterrovert.

I dug my nails into my palms. *He would have laughed at that.*

Somewhere in the back of my mind, I felt the awe of understanding. This bizarre, gooey substance must have been some naturally occurring non-Newtonian fluid, the sort of stuff that behaves like a solid when you apply pressure but flows like a liquid when left alone. I could imagine the locals had spent countless eons trying to make sense of this peculiar fluid, only to incorporate it into their sporting events.

The spectacle was a far cry from the quiet, intimate moment I had shared with Zander all those years ago. It seemed almost fitting that the universe would choose this particular spot to host such a ridiculous event, as if to mock the memories that still haunted me. Was this really what it had in store for me? An endless parade of absurd scenarios, each one more bizarre than the last, all meant to remind me of how small and insignificant I truly was in the grand scheme of things?

As if to answer yes, ten competitors — sharing the same number, I suppose multiforms do only count as one — hit the puddle closest to my hiding spot, throwing a wave of gooey scum into the air, where it promptly crashed all over me. Thankfully I wasn't wearing anything particularly nice — I mean, what do you wear to stalk your past self, other than pj's and a robe? — but still, I won't let myself get covered with goop like this unless I've won the kids' choice awards, and that's not happening anytime soon.

I closed my eyes and focused on my shower at home, concentrating on the familiar, comforting details of my bathroom: the worn bathmat, the bleached tiles, the sand you couldn't get rid of no matter how hard you tried. On the place where my towel was hanging, warm and welcoming. I could almost feel the steamy warmth of the water on my skin and hear the gentle patter of droplets against the tiles. With a deep breath, I willed myself to be there, out of my quickly tarnishing romantic memory. I reached out for a towel and grabbed nothing but air.

I shivered at the sudden chill, blinking down at my bare feet, which now stood on a lovely hardwood floor. Slowly, I lifted my gaze to the silent room before me. A few dozen gentlemen in black coats and starchy white ascots stood, staring at me with a mixture of shock and curiosity. Human? At least they looked human.

The room itself seemed to be some old meeting hall, complete with a massive piece of parchment sprawled across a large table. A man was hunched over the document, quill gripped tightly in his fingers, his jaw hanging open at my sudden appearance.

"Oh dear," one of the wigged men uttered, his tone teetering between shock and amusement. The others remained silent, perhaps too dumbfounded to speak. "Would someone kindly procure the poor lady a towel?"

My cheeks flushed with embarrassment as I realized that I had not only missed my intended destination but had materialized in the presence of strangers — and rather distinguished-looking ones at that — in my sopping wet pj's.

But before I could react, the jump snapped back into place, and with a sensation akin to being pulled through a straw, I found myself standing in my parents bathroom, where I was meant to be.

My breath came fast and hard. Shit. *Shit shit shit.* The scene was straight off the back of a dollar bill. Those had been the founding fathers, unless history really did repeat itself. And they saw me. They *saw* me.

I had botched my mark. Not just once, but twice.

This. Did. Not. Happen.

The knot in my stomach writhed once more. Heartbreak, stress, and shock made for a rather ghastly recipe when attempting such strenuous endeavors as galaxy-hopping. I would need to find better ways of coping; maybe I should take up yoga. Marcy had raved about it — though that had been before she had moved in with the Empress of the Alliance and gotten pregnant, so maybe she had better methods of coping now. I would have to ask her when I was done avoiding her.

Ok. Get a grip, Sally Webber. First take a shower, then check if the world is still as you left it.

The shower was definitely the right idea. I scrubbed off the goop from the alien race, watching tendrils of teal slither down the drain. I dried myself off and slipped on some proper clothes — a different pair of old *Star Wars* pj's — and ran a towel through my hair in a feeble attempt to tame it, but of course it was of no use whatsoever, and left me with more knots than when I had begun.

But who cared? No one was going to see.

I stepped out of the bathroom, flicked off the switch, and sauntered downstairs to the kitchen. The tea I had left on the counter was cold. *Crap.* I had planned my return for the precise moment when the tea should have been warm, yet just shy of scalding. I frowned. It seemed the universe had conspired against my perfectly timed tea consumption. I took a reluctant swig and trudged to the curtains, which I ripped open, squinting into the darkness.

Well, the beach was still there. Nothing looked like the weird middle section of *Back to the Future II*.

My parents' house was just as I left it. That meant the USA was most likely just as I left it, which suggested I hadn't inadvertently annihilated the American Revolution by botching my jump. Further proof that what I do doesn't faze the universe in the slightest.

I slumped onto the couch and seized the remote, zapping the television to life on a random channel. I watched dully as a woefully subpar sitcom trudged through the depths of its rerun marathon, the laugh track making me question the very fabric of human creativity. I was in no mood to binge-watch anything, but then again, I was in no mood to do anything right now. My phone was clogged with messages and emails, most marked urgent, none of which I had the energy for.

The most infuriating thing about time travel is knowing that all things will pass, but still having to sit through them. Time heals all wounds, but wounds still take time. I needed space, but I had too much of it at my fingertips.

So, I came here, to wait time out, at home. Well, at least to this house, with the comfort of my family. Nothing really felt like home anymore, except for them.

But it took less than a day for me to realize that it had been a catastrophically awful idea.

I couldn't tell anyone about what had just happened.

I couldn't tell anyone about John.

My parents had mourned his loss for years, were still grieving him, just as I was. Telling them that he had decidedly *not* died, only for Zander to have killed him, for reasons impossible to believe? That would be like reopening the old wounds only to fill them with acid before sewing them back shut again.

I couldn't put them through that.

It was a strange kind of isolation, being surrounded by loved ones and not being able to tell them exactly what kind of personal hell I was going through. The one person I would have confided in, who would have understood my pain, was the very person who had caused it.

"How can you stand that trash?"

A hand came out of nowhere, ripping the remote from my grasp. "Stars, is there anything good in what you call entertainment? Or is this a capitalist plot to fry your brain cells?"

The living room was now occupied by the formidable figure of Blayde, clad in a silver catsuit, looking slightly bemused at the TV screen. Her rainbow hair had been cropped into jagged, inky spikes, looking for all intents and purposes like the event horizon of a poorly rendered black hole.

Breakups have the peculiar side effect of behaving like a divorce court, divvying up friendships in a manner not unlike an Alliance bureaucrat deciding which paperwork to approve and which to annihilate. As is typical, siblings become the unwitting casualties of this interstellar custody battle, so this was the first time I'd seen Blayde since Planet Nope. While it had been a week for me, how long had it been for her? A day, a month, a year? How long had she waited to speak to me? Had she waited at all? Knowing her, she might have just skipped ahead until now.

She gave me a half grin. "What, aren't you happy to see me? I thought my sparkling presence would be a beacon of light in your darkness."

I couldn't think of a witty answer. Whatever I tried to say just came out as a groan.

"Oh, relax, Sal. You should be thanking me for saving you from that awful reality show about… competitive nose picking?" She plopped down on the armchair beside me. "Besides, I brought you a present."

"A present?" I scoffed. "The best gift you can give me right now is an empty living room."

I had learned a thing or two from this woman, setting my boundaries being one of them. Unfortunately, the teacher still surpassed the student in many ways and rotated in the armchair so that her legs dangled over one of the arms, ignoring my request.

"Your beef's with Zander, not with me." She sunk deeper into the plush chair. "I honestly wouldn't advise my brother to kill his girlfriend's brother; from what I had heard, he was a good man, your John. No, I'm not here on Zander's behalf; I'm not here to ask for your forgiveness for him. I'm here as a friend, and, as a friend, it is my duty to see how you are doing. I myself am doing very well. I just had a city named after me in the Andromeda galaxy. And you?"

I rolled my eyes and collapsed back onto the sofa, resigning myself to the force of gravity. I had expected to despise her, but now that she was here, I experienced the same emotions that overwhelmed me when I devoured that ice cream that defied all known laws of flavor.

"I don't want anything to do with you," I insisted. "I think I made it very clear that I was done with the two of you."

"Not really. You kinda…" She made a *poof* gesture with her fingers. "Stormed off. I assumed you wanted some time, not to become a hermit."

"Is it clear now?"

"Crystal," she sighed, scanning her gaze over the living room, looking anywhere but at me. "What if you need us, though?"

"I won't. Not unless you're back here with Felling alive and well."

Her face fell. "That's cold, Sally. You know I'm working on that."

"So you say."

"That's your plan, then?" she challenged, her glare piercing. "Live here on Earth until people realize you're too young for your age, break all ties, move to some other planet and repeat it all over again, alone for the rest of your days like some tragic space nomad?"

"I haven't figured it all out yet," I admitted. "But for now, I have this extraordinary planet to explore. Infinite beauty, and all that." I waved my hand, gesturing around at my world.

"Sounds like a party," she snorted. Galli, the family dog, trotted lazily up to her, giving her a solid sniff before hopping up on the couch beside me. "A lonely, sad party. But it's your party."

"Maybe that's what I'm looking for right now, my own brand of solitude."

"So you leave *me* with the moping immortal that's just had his heart shattered by the woman of his life — no, his eternity. Thanks a lot."

"We hadn't even made it to the one year mark." I sighed. "He'll get over me. Falling in love is not exactly a once-in-a-lifetime event for him. And I'm sure you can deal with his moping. It's not *his* brother who was just *murdered*."

I shuddered at the image of Zander snapping John's neck. I had to watch my brother die twice over; not something that would ever leave me.

Her skin lost all its color. "I fought Provis the Destroyer. Trillions of people died under his reign of terror. Zander and I were helpless to stop him. By doing what he did, Zander may have saved the universe. You should be thanking him."

"Thanking him?" I didn't notice I had stood. Even looming over Blayde, I felt small. "He killed my brother! Shouldn't the fact you both remember fighting this

Provis guy prove it wasn't him? By killing him now, none of those things should ever have happened — yet you remember. *We can't change time.*"

I ground my teeth so hard that the fine enamel formed a powder on my tongue, bitter and chalky. I paid barely any attention to it. John could never become the person they believed he would be: he was a good man, a good brother, a kind and gentle soul. Nimien's dying wish wouldn't have been to ruin all our lives like this — would it have?

Blayde sighed yet again, more fervent than before, a sigh of annoyance, aggravation, and sadness, all rolled into one like an emotion burrito.

"I don't know what to tell you. It *was* the same man. I would never forget that face. Zander wouldn't have either, if it wasn't for his memory mishap. Kissing your brother triggered a total recall. Now he knows, and he's having a tough time dealing with that, the murder, and the breakup, all at once."

"That lying son of a…!" I bit my tongue. "He told me the memories had been back since Miro's planet!" I wanted to explode, to scream, but a sense of decorum was essential in front of Blayde, even now, so instead I drank my tepid tea and breathed through my nose. "And what the hell… did you say they *kissed?*"

Blayde threw her hands up. "I thought you knew all this. He's going through a lot right now, and—"

I slapped my leg, making her jump. "There you are, making more excuses for him. Does he know you're here?"

She shook her head. "He was punching a volcano last I saw him. Not a live one, not that he knows. I could be gone for weeks without him noticing I was missing. As I said, he's a little messed up with it all."

I rolled my eyes. "I take it he's not processing the multiple lifetimes' worth of memories very well?"

"No," she said. "He's a little self-destructive right now. But other than that, I think he's going to pull out of it — eventually. If he doesn't get annihilated for messing with the fabric of space-time, first. What about you?"

"Time heals all wounds, doesn't it?" I shrugged. "It's too bad we destroyed Nimien's labyrinth. I could sure use a memory wipe right about now."

"I'd rather we not joke about that." Blayde frowned. "But I did bring you something that might help."

She reached into her pocket and pulled out a small, silvery keychain which she lobbed my way. It was shaped a little like a Tamagotchi, though it had a single round friendly button on its surface instead of a screen, practically begging me to push.

"What is this?" I asked.

"Press it," she said, standing up. "You won't regret it."

My thumb hovered over the button. We stared at each other across the living room, engaged in a silent battle of wills. Finally, Blayde shrugged, her forced smile betraying the tension around us.

"I guess I'd best be on my way."

"You do that."

"So… this is goodbye?"

"Yup," I replied, coolly. "I'm surprised you're not happier. The first time around, you couldn't wait to put as much distance between us as you could."

"That was before I knew you," she said calmly. "Now, I'd rather you come along."

I shook my head *no*. Before I could blink, she was gone. That was the way she was — no time for drawn-out goodbyes.

A wave of loss washed over me as I realized that was the last I would see of her. At the same time, I had never really known her. The only reason she had come back was to get me to return her brother to her, to help her deal with the new him. No matter what she said, I wasn't her friend. I was a tool to keep her brother sane and, in turn, keep her sane as well. A glorified babysitter for a murderous man-child.

The new era of me — a me that would never age or die, a me that was alone through all this — had just begun. It was time to make some changes. Adapt.

And no baggage was coming along with me into this new chapter.

Well, except for the giant panda that burst into existence right in front of my eyes.

TWO

THE UNBEARABLE LIGHTNESS OF BEING A PANDA

I'D NEVER SEEN A PANDA BEFORE IN REAL LIFE, but even so I'm pretty sure they shouldn't be eight feet tall and glowing blue. Yet somehow, this was the most panda thing I had ever seen in all its fluffy, monochromatic glory. With its big, soulful eyes and fluffy, star-speckled fur, it was both adorable and mildly disconcerting.

I blinked in disbelief, releasing the key chain I'd inadvertently squeezed. Was this some kind of joke? I was trying to deal with heartbreak here, a potential historical catastrophe, and the loss of my brother, and Blayde had sent me... a pandagram?

The space panda spoke in a surprisingly high-pitched voice that was equal parts charming and grating. "Greetings, Sally!" it exclaimed with unbridled enthusiasm. "I am Clyde, your Emotional Support

Companion! I have been sent to you by *identity unknown* and the Interstellar Wellbeing Consortium to provide comfort and solace in your time of distress!"

I groaned, internally or externally I couldn't tell you. I suppose this meant Blayde did care about me, though not enough to finish personalizing the gizmo. Was this the kind of gadget you got in a medical office by prescription only, or for a buck at any ol' asteroid rest stop?

"You're a panda," was the only thing I managed to blurt out. Nothing constructive in the slightest.

"Indeed I am." Clyde smirked. Could pandas smirk? "Not just any panda, though. I am a highly sophisticated artificial intelligence, designed to help you navigate the emotional roller coaster that is your life."

"But you're a panda." I shook my head. I was much too tired for this — any of this. I needed space and I needed sleep. "It's a little patronizing. I already have a therapist."

Oh, shit, did I? Had I remembered to text Doctor Schumann after I came back from my three-year time hiccup? It was going to take forever to find a new one I could get along with.

Wait a minute. I'm a freaking space-time traveler. I could probably find the perfect therapist, one who knows exactly how to deal with exactly what I'm going through.

Unless… was this the best the universe had to offer? I looked up at the panda, feeling my eyes stretch in their sockets. What had Blayde gotten me into?

"Let us reframe that," said Clyde. "I'm a panda because… why not? Pandas are cute, right? I am what your mind wanted me to be, so if I am patronizing to you, what does that say about your current state of mind, *Sally Webber?*"

I dropped my head between my knees, willing myself to take deep, deep breaths. This was all too much right now. I wasn't going to let myself get psychoanalyzed by a key chain.

Not like mister emotional support over here was doing much supporting.

"So you're here to, what, exactly?" I pulled my head back up to study him. He hadn't moved since he'd appeared from the key chain. "What do I do with you?"

"Consider me your personal therapist." Clyde smiled widely. "I am here to be your friend. To support you. Emotionally."

"Right, that's enough of that." I grabbed the key chain and squeezed the button, ready to send Clyde back into the digital depths. But Clyde stood unwavering in front of me, his smile slowly replacing itself with a frown.

"I do not function that way," he said, seemingly sad. "I am here to help. You cannot just shut me off. I will not deactivate until you no longer need me."

My groan was loud enough to shake the entire house. "My God, I'm a Sim, aren't I? I've got the social bunny or something."

"I do not understand the reference, but I can assure you I am no curse, *Sally Webber.*"

A small warmth flowed through me. Maybe Blayde had spent five minutes setting this thing up. Come to think of it, she had never really given me a gift before, had she?

"Alright, Clyde." I sighed, deciding to humor him for the moment. "You said you're here to help. What's your advice for dealing with the mess that is my life? And you can call me Sally, not Sally Webber."

"Parameters adjusted." Clyde tilted his head. "Well, Sally, I believe that it is essential to acknowledge and validate your emotions first. It is alright to feel angry, hurt, and confused. These feelings are natural reactions to the experiences you have had."

"Alright, that's not terrible advice." I raised an eyebrow. "Not particularly personalized, but I can deal."

"Perhaps if I knew a little more about your situation, I would be able to calibrate my responses to better suit your exact needs?"

I took a deep breath, steeling myself. This was it. I was going to spill my entire alien-laden, impossible life story to an artificial panda genie who sprouted from a key chain. This was definitely a new low, even for me.

"Once upon a time, a young girl followed a spaceman to the stars, and found her heart along the way." The words tumbled out before I could stop them. Clyde flickered in apparent surprise, but I plowed on. "Then she discovered he should never have been trusted with it in the first place — because he broke it."

Clyde paused a moment, as if assessing if I was going to continue, before he replied. "Well, Sally, using third person to talk about yourself, that is… interesting. You sound like you are reading from a space opera. But remember, it is *your* story. You are the one calling the shots, not some spaceman."

I gave an exaggerated eye roll. "Clyde, it's not a space opera. It's my life." A heavy silence lay upon the room. "The thing is, it's not just about some broken heart. The spaceman — God, why did I call him that? Zander — killed my brother, who I thought was long dead. My brother was apparently supposed to become a space tyrant or something, and Zander... he stopped it from happening. Only now I *know* that time is fixed. Nothing we do can change the future. So, he didn't prevent anything. He just... killed him."

Clyde's response was a gentle, "Oh, Sally..."

"John, my brother... I'd thought he was dead for years." My fingers tightened around the edge of the table, my grip white-knuckled and trembling.

Clyde was silent for a moment. I could see him digesting the information, processing it, trying to compute the best way to provide emotional support for such an outlandish and complicated situation. "That is a heavy burden to bear, Sally."

"That's not all. Now, I've lost the only other two immortals I knew in the universe, Zander and Blayde. They were the only ones who understood... who knew what I was going through. And Zander... he'd been lying to me about his mental health for months." The hot sting of tears made themselves known at the corners of my eyes, but I stubbornly blinked them back.

"And to top it all off, I just learned Zander kissed John! John... I just... I can't..." The words dissolved into a strangled sob as the enormity of everything came crashing down.

Clyde remained silent for a moment longer before speaking. "I see, Sally. This is indeed a considerable amount to process. We have many elements at play here: deception, loss, betrayal... But remember, we can take this one step at a time. We will navigate through this together. Would you like me to start with techniques on managing stress or perhaps coping with grief?" His soft voice brought a small comfort, a faint beacon of hope amidst the chaos.

"But how do I move on from this? I've lost my brother *again*, my heart's been shattered, and I'm dealing with..." The weight of the past few years pressed down on me.

Clyde's eyes seemed to twinkle. "One step at a time, Sally. Healing is a journey, not a destination. It is important to surround yourself with supportive friends and to engage in activities that bring you joy. Perhaps we could start by exploring your interests and finding new ways to connect with others."

"Right, because nothing says 'I'm a well-adjusted adult' like an eight-foot-tall, glowing panda therapist."

Not that any of my old friends were still in touch. My stint as a criminal had seen to that. My only true bestie was light years away, growing a baby and saving a civilization from itself. She didn't need any extra stress right now.

Clyde's expression shifted to one of mock indignation. "I would have you know that I am still in the process of... learning. I am constantly updating my database to provide the best possible support. I put the intelligence back in AI, and I am committed to helping you navigate through these challenges."

Right, so a machine in the process of machine learning. Not strange at all.

"Well, this planet isn't exactly ready for holograms yet." I held up the key chain. "So I can't have you hovering around me all the time."

"I am not some genie for you to shove back into a bottle," Clyde scoffed. Huh local mythos: he may actually know a thing or two about Earth. "You need not worry about my appearance. You are the only one that can see me."

Right. This was exactly what my mental health needed: an imaginary friend.

"So you're saying I'm stuck with you."

"I would not put it that way, but yes." He smiled. "The Interstellar Wellbeing Consortium believes that your mental health should be your own problem. Lest it ruin someone else's mental health, you see."

"*Riiiight.*" I shook my head in disbelief. "Ok, Clyde. Let's give this a shot. Just promise me one thing — you'll work on upgrading your canned responses, okay? I need a therapist, not a fortune cookie."

Like I have a say in the matter.

Clyde's grin returned, and he gave a playful salute. "Promise, Sally. Together, we will face the roller coaster of life, one loop at a time."

I snorted. "You sound like a Hallmark card."

"What is a Hallmark?"

This was going to go great. I stood up, stretching, feeling the knots of tension in every muscle of my body. Clyde was right about the roller coaster my life had become. I needed a break from throwing my hands up in the air and screaming.

"Mind if I go to bed? It's been a long day."

"Of course not." Clyde's voice took on a more soothing tone. "Rest is crucial for emotional well-being. I will be here when you need me, and I will be working on refining my responses to better suit your needs."

I rolled my eyes, but there was something almost endearing about Clyde's earnestness.

My parents had set me up in their office, a cozy little space on their pullout couch. Exactly what I needed while I got back on my feet. As I entered the dimly lit room, Clyde followed closely behind, his blue glow casting a soft light on the shelves and desk.

I slid between the bed sheets. "Well, it's been great getting to know you. Good night, Clyde."

"Good night, Sally. Sleep well."

I leaned my head against the pillow and closed my eyes. The back of my eyelids remained a light blue.

I flicked one eye open. Clyde was still there, as big and blue as ever.

"Good night, Clyde," I repeated, a little more forcefully this time.

"Good night, Sally!" Clyde replied, still beaming.

"Can you… I don't know, also go to bed? It's a little hard to sleep with you there."

"I'm here to provide emotional support. I will not leave you isolated and alone while you still require it."

"Right now, the best thing you can do for me is let me sleep. Rest is crucial for emotional well-being, and all that, remember?"

"Indeed. And I will watch over you as you rest."

I groaned. It was beginning to become a habit of mine. "Clyde, I really can't sleep with you glowing like a neon sign. Can you at least dim the lights or something?"

"I'm afraid I cannot control my luminosity, Sally. My apologies for any inconvenience."

"Great," I muttered. "Maybe there's a sleep mask in here somewhere."

Giving up on sleep for the moment, I got up and started searching my parents' office for anything to block out Clyde's persistent glow. To his credit, he did attempt to help, his holographic paws awkwardly clasping at the air. "You know, Sally, sometimes the answers we seek are hidden in plain sight."

I snorted, still digging through the mess of papers and knickknacks. "Not helpful, Clyde."

I pulled open an unusually hefty drawer and almost screamed in shock.

A green orb about the size and shape of a crystal ball rolled at the bottom of it, glowing with a dim light that revealed the swirling mist within. A green orb I hadn't seen since the previous worst day of my life.

James.

I slammed the drawer shut, breathing so hard I was borderline heaving. I fell to the floor, dropping my head back between my knees again. No, she couldn't be here: Blayde had said she'd placed her somewhere safe, somewhere she was sure she wouldn't be disturbed as Blayde searched the universe for a solution to James Felling's physical death. She'd promised to save her. She'd promised…

My chest refused to expand. I couldn't breathe. Images of James's lifeless body flashed before my eyes. I was in the temple again, in the chamber. I was suffocating. This couldn't be happening. Not again.

"I am sensing heightened levels of stress, Sally," said Clyde, drifting nearer.

"You think?" I snapped, looking up at the panda.

The level of stupidity in his sentence brought a roll of laughter to my lips. What the absolute hell had my life become? Finding my friend's soul in my parents' bottom desk drawer was probably the least unexpected thing to happen today, but it was the straw that broke the camel's back. I laughed so hard that I hardly felt the tears roll down my cheeks, didn't notice the snot popping in my nose.

No panic attack tonight. Not with an oblivious panda watching over me.

"You want to help me, right? You want me to feel better?" I took a deep breath. "In that drawer is an orb containing the mind of my friend, James Felling. She was killed saving my life. Blayde and I placed her consciousness in that orb until we could find her a new body. Blayde swore she'd put the orb somewhere safe, that she'd figure out a solution."

Clyde's eyes widened. He rubbed his fluffy paws together, as if unsure of what to do with them. "That is quite the predicament. I can understand how seeing the orb might have brought up intense emotions."

I nodded. I took a deep breath, turned around, and dove back in. This time I was ready for it: ready for the orb to slide around like loose change as I opened the drawer, ready for the green glow to pulse when exposed to the rest of the room, almost like it was happy to see me.

I bit my bottom lip. It is an orb containing James, it is not James herself. I can't let myself feel that way.

I reached into the drawer and picked it up.

The sphere did nothing as my hands wrapped around it. Cold glass met my fingertips. Cold. Had it been cold, when Miro had placed James in it? Why couldn't I remember? In my mind, it should have been warm, warm like James, warm like life.

I missed her more than words could contain.

I clutched the sphere in my lap, sitting on the floor, my back to the desk and my front to the panda.

"You know what? Maybe trying to save James would be a good way for me to cope with the breakup. Yeah. I could focus on something positive, something to keep me busy."

Clyde considered my suggestion before responding. "While that is a noble pursuit, it may only serve as a distraction rather than a means of dealing with your emotional pain. The loss of your brother, your heartbreak... these are issues that must be faced head-on, not avoided."

"Having a hobby is supposed to be good for mental health, right? What if this is my hobby? Helping James, finding a solution to save her. It's something productive. Something worthwhile."

Clyde hesitated, then gave a resigned nod. "Alright, Sally. If you believe this will help you heal, then I will support you in this endeavor. Just remember that facing your emotions is also an important part of the healing process."

I sighed. The relief that washed over me was oddly warm, like a blanket. "Thanks, Clyde. She's… this gives me something to hold onto, and right now, that's what I need."

Strangely, the green glow of the orb didn't bother me half as much as Clyde's blue glare. I slept with James in my arms, clutching her like my life depended on it. Like her life depended on it, like somehow deep inside she could feel my love and my warmth.

We were going to get through this.

THREE

MO' COFFEE, MO' PROBLEMS

IT'S IMPOSSIBLE TO EAT A GOOD HEARTY BREAKFAST when your lips have unionized into a firm line of disgruntlement and your teeth seem to have taken up the daily grind. Hunched over in the breakfast nook, I cradled James's orb on my knees under the table, while a bowl of untouched Special K loomed before me, cast in Clyde's gentle blue light. I hadn't gotten much sleep with him glowing like the beacons of Gondor last night, which had seriously soured me to the idea of working with him. Maybe if I kept ignoring him, he'd realize he had knocked on the wrong mental door and leave.

Dad appeared at the kitchen door, eyes going soft as he saw me.

"Morning, kiddo," he said, plonking down next to me with his bowl of fiber-filled disappointment. He seemed blissfully ignorant of Clyde, so at least the panda hadn't been wrong about being invisible. "Sleep okay?"

"Mmm," I grunted noncommittally.

Beside me, Clyde crossed his arms and shook his head. "Use your words," he suggested.

Why didn't this guy come with a mute button?

"The answering machine is getting clogged up," Dad added. "Can you please listen to those messages? Are they really from the White House?"

The White House? I groaned. That explained the mountain of texts on my phone. I guess the planet was in danger again, and only my special friends could save the day. What would I tell them? *Oh, sorry, the defenders of the planet are on the wrong side of this breakup?*

"Are they really looking into Black Knight satellite?" Dad leaned closer, whispering conspiratorially. "Were the forums really onto something?"

"Really, Dad?" I tried to keep the sarcasm out of my voice. "I'd rather stay away from the mess. You should too."

"Speaking of, the computer's been struggling for about a month now," he continued nonchalantly. "Do you think you could look it over? Maybe give it a boost with some of your fancy space gizmos?"

"Don't pester her," Mom said as she took her seat, her body distorting Clyde's pixels, though he seemed unperturbed. "Can't you see she's been through enough?"

"Dumping an interdimensional drifter strikes me as a cause for celebration," Dad retorted.

"Hal!"

"What? I'm just trying to lighten the mood!" He turned to me, plastering a smile on his face. "You were too good for him, sweetie. He didn't deserve you."

Before the rising tide of emotion turned into a tsunami, I took a calming breath, letting the orb's chill wash over my clenched palms. My mind was a cyclone of questions. Did they even know what this thing was?

"You didn't mention you had another admirer," Dad said, his eyes twinkling mischievously.

I was starting to feel something I thought would be gone from my life forever: a headache. "Sorry... what now?"

"Some flowers were left on our doorstep this morning," Mom chimed in, her tone cautious. "I wasn't going to tell you, considering your 'no-Zander zone' policy..."

"But they weren't from Zander," Dad interrupted, barely containing a grin that was too wide for his face. "They were from a certain... Spurlock?"

"Hal! You weren't supposed to pry!" Mom scolded.

Dad defended himself with a shrug. "I was performing a civic duty. Otherwise, those flowers would've ended up in the trash, and Sally would've been none the wiser."

My stomach did a wobbly summersault. Spurlock Magnesar had sent me flowers? I couldn't picture myself dating an interstellar rock star, but then again, I couldn't picture myself dating anyone ever again. Infinity was a long time, though.

"Did you see that Glen called?" Mom asked, her focus entirely on my dad. "It seems they did find the suitcase they were looking for, only it wasn't the right size in the end."

Feeling the orb's weight press into my thighs, it was almost as if James herself was nudging me to confess. My parents' small talk was making my skin crawl. My inner pressure gauge was shooting towards the red zone, ready to blow any second.

Deep breaths, Sally, deep breaths. You don't need your panda to remind you.

"I could have told him that," Dad scoffed. "Airlines are always looking for a way to scam you. They're in cahoots with the luggage companies, always changing the acceptable suitcases sizes so they can catch you with the wrong one and charge you more."

My hands were shaking, and without even realizing it, I found myself gripping the orb even tighter, clinging to it like a life raft. Despite its cool, glassy surface, the sphere seemed to hum in sync with the frantic rhythm of my pulse. Enough was enough.

"Your stress levels are dangerously elevated, Sally," said Clyde. "Would you like some relaxing meditation music?"

I lowered my head so I could mutter in peace. "Maybe. If it's gentle."

"What's that, honey?" Mom asked.

Before I could answer, Clyde began to chant "Om" in a slow, low voice. Mom stared at me too intently for me to say anything about it, so he must have taken that as encouragement to go on because every "Om" got stronger.

With a deep breath, I gripped the orb, lifted it off my lap and slammed it down on the table. The plates and utensils rattled, the cereal in my bowl jumped and splashed, tiny vibrations quivered on the surface of our coffees. The sound was like a thunderclap, echoing throughout the room and silencing everything.

My parents' eyes went wide, their jaws dropping as they stared at the orb. Its glow cast a surreal, otherworldly light on their faces, highlighting their shock and confusion. The air in the room felt electric, charged with the energy of my outburst and the significance of the object before us.

In that stretched-out moment, time held its breath. My gaze locked onto the orb, my emotions a whirlpool of anger, sorrow, and determination. This was James — my friend — and I was hell-bent on pulling her out of whatever cosmic rabbit hole she was trapped in. No matter what.

"What's this?" asked Dad, staring first at the orb and then at me.

"What's this doing here?" I asked, trying as hard as I could to contain the rage that was bubbling inside of me.

"Oh, that?" Dad shrugged, a mask of nonchalance he might as well have borrowed from a poor poker player. "We, uh, found it on our morning walk. You know how people sometimes leave random things out by the curb? Thought it might make a nice paperweight or something."

Mom nodded her head like a bobblehead in an earthquake. "Yes, that's right. We had no idea it had anything to do with... well, anything important. Did you go snooping again?"

I shot them a glare that could've melted lead. "You seriously expect me to swallow that? This isn't just some tchotchke! It's James Felling's very essence! Her soul! And you're covering for Blayde? She entrusted *you* for her safekeeping and you're really going to sit there and pretend you don't know what this is?"

Their faces fell, guilt written all over them. But the guilt was quickly overwritten with shock.

"*That's* Agent Felling?" Mom stood up, leaning over to examine the orb up close. "Your friend who died? How is she in there?"

My teeth were at risk of grinding themselves to nubs. My parents, guardians of a life essence they didn't even comprehend, and Blayde forgot to include a manual. I clenched my fists, my nails digging into my palms. Blayde, queen of omissions. She was incorrigible.

Clyde chimed in. "Ah, the classic family dynamics at play. You know, according to a study I once read — or maybe it was an AI-generated psychology paper, who can keep track — open communication is key in dealing with delicate matters such as these. Nothing like a good old-fashioned honesty circle to air out grievances."

"Not now, Clyde!" I hissed under my breath, thanking the stars that my parents were too fixated on the enchanting green disco ball to notice my nonexistent ventriloquism skills.

"Sally, we had no idea." Mom frowned, defeated. "If Blayde had told us... you really think this would have been in a desk drawer all month if we'd known it was your friend?"

"All *month*?"

Dad broke his stunned silence. "How does one cram a whole person into a bowling ball? What kind of Star Trek techno-wizardry are we dealing with here?"

"Honestly, I'm still confused about that part." I reached for James and pulled her orb close. "But why you? Blayde said she left her at the safest place she could think of."

The color returned to Mom's cheeks. "Well, I can't say I'm not flattered."

"Could also have a little something to do with the Big Brother-style Alliance surveillance we live under," Dad grumbled. "Isn't your friend Marcy some sort of space empress?"

With a groan, I facepalmed, which, considering I was clutching an orb, meant I headbutted James's orb. A collective wince echoed around the table.

I blinked back the stars dancing in my vision, feeling a cocktail of vindication and betrayal. "So you've been lying to me this whole time? Keeping this secret right under my nose?"

"Secret?" Dad scoffed. "Listen to her, Laurie. *We're* the ones keeping secrets!"

"Well, if there is one thing we've learned from all this, it is that honesty is always the best policy, right?" Clyde stated, with all the subtlety of a foghorn.

I focused on my parents. "Why didn't you tell me Blayde left this here?"

"Ah, the old adage, 'Ignorance is bliss.' Or in our unique circumstance, 'Ignorance ensures breakfasts that are mildly less like a soap opera,'" Clyde quipped.

"She told us not to tell anyone," said Mom. "Said she trusted us. We trust her, too."

The three of us stared at the orb in silence. Were their thoughts swirling as tightly as mine? I couldn't breathe. Which is a weird feeling to have, since technically I don't need to anymore. I took a comforting gulp of air.

"She conveniently skipped over this part," I said, my voice barely a whisper. "She showed up, practically begging me to get back with Zander because his inability to handle a breakup is too much for her, and not once did she mention that the person whose life she was meant to be saving was stored right here."

"She was here?" Dad stammered, overlapping with Mom's "You've seen her? When?"

"Last night," I confessed, avoiding their probing gazes. I felt like a teenager who'd been caught sneaking out to a late-night party.

"Why didn't you tell us?" Mom's glare was hot as lasers. "You can't scold us about honesty when you're not being open with us."

"I highly recommend an honesty circle right now," Clyde continued with enthusiasm. "Everyone takes turns sharing their thoughts and feelings, and we all listen attentively and non-judgmentally. Did I mention that a study found that families who participate in honesty circles have a 37.2% increase in trust and a 24.6% decrease in cereal consumption? Fascinating, right?"

"Shut up, Clyde!" I slammed my hand on the table, making the food jump again. The orb rolled lazily towards Dad's cereal bowl, colliding and drenching his lap with soggy flakes. He didn't react; his eyes were fixated on me, wide with shock.

"Sally…" he gaped. "There's no one else here."

"Well, tell that to Blayde's latest parting gift." I passed him my napkin, which he accepted while maintaining a petrified stare. "Say hello to Clyde, my new… emotional support AI. Basically a sentient stress ball."

The room fell into a silence so dense it could have swallowed a black hole.

"Sally." Mom's hand found mine, her grip soft, soothing. "Is Clyde in the room with us right now?"

"Yeah, he's sitting right between us." When her frown tightened, it hit me that maybe I wasn't being as transparent as Clyde was. "Right, he's a hologram. That only I can see. Some kind of biotech I suppose."

"Very nice to meet you, Hal, Laurie," Clyde said politely from his seat. "Now, back to the matter at hand. I believe we were discussing the complex intricacies of interdimensional soul-transference and the perplexing nature of trust in intergalactic relationships."

"You *just* told me they can't see or hear you," I said.

"You can speak up on my behalf. It is part of taking responsibility."

My parents exchanged glances across the table. A glance I'd seen before. A glance that said *How do we suggest therapy without sounding like we're suggesting therapy?*

Seeing the pain in their faces was too much. Keeping the truth about Zander and John from them was too much. It was all too much.

"Your father is just concerned," Mom said, "that you're piling too much on your plate right now. Why not try something a little… down-to-earth? Like taking a course at community college. Or a pottery class."

"I can't go about my life as if nothing's happened," I insisted. "I can't just go back to work. What would I even do? I'm still a college dropout, and the longest I worked anywhere was as a sales clerk. I'm not qualified to do anything but evade the law, and you can't exactly put space-vagabond on a resumé."

"But you know our galaxy better than Neil deGrasse Tyson on a caffeine high," said Dad, beaming.

"Sure, I can tell you where the closest black hole is," I replied, "but it doesn't mean I know the math that makes it… do hole things. And it doesn't mean I can just bust into universities claiming to know the secrets of the universe."

"You can fly spaceships, for heaven's sake!"

"Um, no. Not without autopilot," I muttered. "So unless SpaceX is recruiting for Button Pushers, I'm out of luck."

Dad's eyes twinkled. "How about the space force?"

"You really want your daughter in combat?" I asked. "You want the US government controlling me zap-zapping around the world and the rest of the galaxy?"

He shook his head, looking down at the mess on the table.

"I worry about that on a daily basis," I added. "The government knows about me, and if our answering machine is any indication, they want to talk. The only reason they haven't taken strides to either ensnare me or eradicate me is because the Agency thinks I'm still in cahoots with Zander and Blayde and ordered a hands-off. When they find out I'm not with *them* anymore, it's going to be a free for all. The government wants me. The Agency thinks I'm their pawn. I need to decide my own narrative before they write it for me."

"So, a life incognito it is," Dad finally said, finishing off his juice as if it were a shot of something much stronger.

"I'm still just me, with special added space powers." I cringed — Blayde was right, it did sound cheap.

Dad's eyes softened. "You don't need powers to be special, Sally. Never did."

His words hit me like a beam of sunlight breaking through a cloudy sky. For a moment, I allowed myself to bask in them, feeling a warmth I hadn't felt in ages.

Mom sighed, brushing a stray strand of hair from my forehead. "So why not take this time to do what makes you happy? I'm sure the universe can wait."

I looked between them. "Maybe that's it. Maybe I don't have to save the universe today, but I can start with one person. James. I don't think I could commit to anything else, knowing she's in here and not doing anything about it. Blayde let her down. I refuse to do the same. I'm going to find her a body. Make her whole again."

Their eyes widened. Dad was the first one to recover. "Finding a body. For your dead Men in Black friend. With your holographic panda therapist. *That* will keep you grounded?"

"Well, when you put it that way," I said, "it does sound a little... eccentric. And for the record, she wasn't part of the Men in Black."

"That you know of," Dad retorted.

I rolled my eyes. "Look, the point is, I'm going to save James. I need something that'll anchor me in this chaos, and rescuing a friend seems like a pretty good start."

Mom's brows furrowed. "But... how do you even start with that?"

I bit my lip, feeling a knot tighten in my chest. "I think I might know someone who can help. A friend of mine. Meedian."

If anyone could navigate the murky waters of a body black market, it was him. Whether he'd be willing to lend a hand was a different story. The last time we crossed paths, fire-breathing cats in military-grade exoskeletons were torching his house and business. Our future selves had set up a new base of operations for him, instead of, you know, doing the logical thing and setting his house up *not* to get burned down by flame kitties.

I breathed out between pursed lips. What would happen, now that I was not a part of that future?

"Who's that?" Mom asked. "We haven't heard of him before."

"He... he's from Malaysia," I explained, fumbling with my words. "He's into some weird tech stuff. If anyone can help me with this, it's him. He recently moved, and I need to find him."

They exchanged worried glances.

"Clyde will be with me," I added. "He's like my guardian angel or something. "

"But Sally, we..." Dad started, his words drying up as I did not interrupt where he expected me to, leaving us all in a confused silence.

"I need to do this," I told them, firmly. "I can't stand by and do nothing. She saved my life. I owe her this much."

There was a silence in the room as they both stared at me. I bit my lip. It wasn't like I needed their approval: I could head off to the bathroom, jump away, and jump right back to the exact same moment as soon as everything was said and done.

But I needed them. I needed… validation. More than what Clyde could give. I wasn't the perfect daughter. I know it wasn't in their hopes and dreams to have their little girl go off on dangerous space adventures. But I could still do right by them. I would love them, quite literally, forever.

"Alright," Mom finally said, her voice just above a whisper. "But promise us, Sally, you'll be safe."

I nodded, feeling a strange mix of relief and determination washing over me. "I promise."

"That was a wonderful display of open communication, Sally!" Clyde began with an excited clap. "You advocated for yourself with confidence and respect. I must say, the clear articulation of your thoughts and intentions was quite impressive. Indeed, I would go so far as to say it was textbook quality! The entire conversation could be transcribed and used as a reference point for effective communication tutorials. In fact, I believe I will make a note of it."

I sighed, rubbing my temples as Clyde prattled on, his enthusiasm hardly dimmed by my lack of response. He continued with his praise, analyzing the interaction like a sporting event.

"And the way you expressed your desires while still validating your parents' concerns, that was an excellent use of assertive communication. Not to mention your flawless integration of empathy and tact. I would rate this conversation a solid 9.2 out of 10!"

"Appreciate it, Clyde," I said.

I looked down at the orb in my hands and felt a new surge of resolve. I was going to save James. No matter what it took.

Then again, I wasn't even sure how I was going to go about finding my — possibly former — friend. If Meedian was even on Earth anymore. If the future our future selves had set up for him would still be his future if they no longer existed.

My phone buzzed. I pulled it out of my pocket and laid it on the table, expecting another urgent message to ignore, except this time…

Customer support: Location shared with you (fifteen minutes).

Customer Support? Support from what? Who? My eyes crossed, staring at the notification, which made less and less sense the longer I stared. Was it my phone company, finally catching up with me with a bill from here to the moon? I tapped the message and a map popped up. For a moment, it seemed to hone in on my location, but then it veered off to drop a pin less than 100 miles away.

I stared up at Clyde. "Did you do this?"

He threw up his paws. "I am not even sure what you are accusing me of."

"Never mind."

Bizarre. Was this Meedian, reaching out somehow? If so, how did he know I was talking about him? A chill ran down my spine as I glanced around the room. Had he bugged my home? Or maybe this was the Alliance's work. Or simply the Agency's. The same question remained: was someone listening in?

I shivered. Not a nice thought.

Maybe, more likely, this was just a coincidence. Those do happen sometimes. Not often, but sometimes.

In any case, what would be the harm in checking it out?

I looked up at my parents. "I know where I need to go. And you'll be happy to know I'm not going far. I'm not even leaving the state."

Their frowns turned to smiles. The feeling was infectious.

"Will you be back for dinner?" Mom asked. "Maybe your friend can join us. It'd be nice to meet some of the people in your life."

I smiled at the image of Meedian making small talk with my parents. My mom's tacky seaside décor. My dad's elaborate conspiracy theories. Actually, he would probably love it here.

"I'll let you know," I said, scooting out from the breakfast nook, past her.

"Will you be taking the car?" asked Dad.

"With these gas prices?"

"Then at the very least, take this," he said, sliding out of the breakfast nook and rushing off into the house. He came back a minute later with an old bowling bag, its leather surface worn but still intact.

"Here," he said, handing it over. "You came home empty handed. Maybe you could use this for your... journey."

"A bowling bag, Dad?" I glanced down at the bag, and then back at him. He'd noticed I'd come home without my duffel. I hadn't thought he paid that much attention to the details of my life.

He chuckled, turning the bag so that I could see his monogrammed initials on the side. "Ah, this isn't just any bag. I won my first tournament with it. It's lucky."

Then again, maybe I didn't, either. A smile crossed my lips. I hadn't known he was a bowler. It was strange to learn something new about someone I'd known my entire life. "Thanks, Dad. I could use some luck right about now."

He looked at me earnestly, a strange blend of pride and worry on his face. "You always make your own luck, sweetie. But a little extra never hurt anyone."

With that, I placed James carefully into the bag. The sphere fit perfectly as if it was meant to be there. I missed my duffel dearly, but this... this would do nicely.

"Keep it safe," he whispered, almost as an afterthought.

"I will," I promised, feeling the weight of the bag, both literal and metaphorical, as I slung it over my shoulder.

Clyde followed me into the living room, away from their gaze. I checked my phone again — yup: Orlando, Florida. Not far at all. Maybe I would see if I could sneak into Disneyworld on the way back. Grab some ice cream.

The location marker, though, was a puzzler. Who had it come from? Was it really Meedian who was waiting for me there? Or could it be a trap? The uncertainty gnawed at me, but it would only get worse if I didn't find answers.

I closed my eyes, letting the memory of the red pin on the map guide me. A short jump, nothing too far.

So why was I suddenly in the dark?

FOUR

UNEXPECTED GUEST AT THE REPTILIAN FEST

GONE ARE THE DAYS WHEN THE WORST THING about Florida was its unpredictable weather and the odd alligator in your swimming pool. Now we had to worry about those alligators turning bipedal and throwing parties in secret caverns.

The cacophony of hissing jolted my senses awake. I was surrounded by a thunderous crowd, stomping with an intensity that quaked the earth beneath my feet. The crowd hissed and clapped in a rhythm that was both alien and oddly catchy. I found myself joining in, tapping my foot despite myself.

I didn't know where I was, but it was dripping with exotic vines and a congregation of bipedal reptiles adorned in what I could only assume was their finest attire. Their scales shimmered in shades of green and blue, reflecting the light from the glowing orbs suspended above, the only source of light in the oversized cave. Even the smell was foreign and fierce — murky water, dark plants, earth.

In the middle of the cavern, some sort of ceremony was in full swing. Two reptiles, both sporting impressively long tails and crowns made of shimmering crystals, stood waist-deep in a glowing pool. An older creature — though who am I to assume it was old, maybe wrinkles were for the young here — I could only describe as the Gandalf of the reptile world, if Gandalf had decided that robes embroidered with the entire Milky Way were this season's must-have, seemed to be officiating the event in grand, sweeping gestures.

So much for sunshine and oranges.

A knot of anxiety lodged itself in my gut. I had to get away before becoming part of the wedding album. I focused on the pin again; on the place I was meant to be going — but nothing happened. Was this the same thing that had happened yesterday, with the founding fathers? My teeth ground together. I was somehow stuck in this strange mid-jump limbo. The user manual on universe-hopping had glaringly omitted this bug. It was as if I was caught riding the time-space express subway and was now stuck at a stop thanks to an interstellar leaf on the line, with no way to understand why because the PA system was as comprehensible as a drunk whispering secrets in ancient Sumerian.

"Clyde, this is *not* Florida," I hissed, trying to blend in with the wall, which, to my dismay, was covered in slimy moss that squelched under my touch. "If this is your idea of therapy, we need to have a serious talk."

"Do not look at me, Sally, I am incapable of affecting your ambulatory systems." Clyde's voice was clear despite the ruckus around me. "Now, why are we at a traditional mating ceremony of the Saurian species? I do not believe this is where we discussed our next trip to be."

"I, um, have no idea what we're doing here," I muttered under my breath. My gaze shifted to a pair of young reptilian onlookers who seemed fascinated by my non-scaly appearance. They poked at my jeans with clawed fingers, emitting chirps that sounded suspiciously like snickers.

At that moment, the rhythm of the music hiccupped, and the entire cavern turned to face me. A particularly ornate reptile in the ceremonial pool, who I guessed was one of the spouses given its sparkly headgear, fixed me with a glare that could curdle milk. It didn't take a universal translator to know I'd just committed a major faux pas.

"Sally, your current situation is statistically improbable and culturally... problematic," Clyde intoned, the digital concern heavy in his voice. "In Saurian terms, uninvited guests often double as the buffet."

I didn't need Clyde's crash course in Saurian etiquette to sense the mounting tension. The reptilian guests advanced on me, their hisses a symphony of displeasure. Then, the other lizard-person from the pool, one with a crown of fiery red spines, emerged from the throng. His eyes bore into mine, and I half expected him to unleash a torrent of flame from his gaping maw.

"Oh, this isn't the Vance-Lapin wedding!" I raised my hands in a universal — guesstimating here — gesture of peace. "Look, big misunderstanding. I'm just going to, uh, see myself out."

My attempt at diplomacy was cut short when I backed right into a scaly wall. Turning around, I came face-to-face with a hulking reptilian bouncer. His jaw unhinged, revealing a row of sharp teeth.

I gulped. "If you do want to eat me, can it wait until after the reception?"

At once, the cavern exploded into a hissy fit. Around me, the throng of reptilian guests tightened, backing me up towards the cavern wall, their hisses and growls building into what I assumed was the Saurian equivalent of "cut the cake."

I spun around took off in a run, desperately scanning the cavern for any sign of an exit, or at least a less toothy audience. My escape was less a graceful exit and more a clumsy salsa through a minefield of reptilian extremities, dodging claws and talons alike.

"Suggestion: Avoid stepping on any tails," said Clyde. "It is considered a grave insult in Saurian culture."

Too late for that. Spotting a sliver of darkness that hinted at a tunnel entrance, I made a dash for it, doing my best to dodge the swishing tails and clawed feet as I made a beeline for what I hoped was an exit.

"Excuse me, pardon me!" I called over my shoulder, ducking as a well-aimed glob of what I hoped was just saliva whizzed past my head. "Lovely ceremony by the way! Your scales are shimmering magnificently today!"

My compliments seemed to fall on deaf ears — or whatever auditory organs Saurians used — as the crowd's agitation only grew, louder and louder until I couldn't even hear myself think. The cavern was a labyrinth of irate reptiles, and my attempts at being polite were doing little to quell the uproar.

I plunged into the relative safety of the tunnel without hesitation. My footsteps echoed in the tight space, a percussive reminder that I was still very much in a race against potentially becoming someone's wedding feast.

"Sally, your stress levels are registering higher than recommended for healthy human functioning," Clyde remarked.

"Yes, Clyde, I am well aware!" I snapped back, my breath heavy. "This is not exactly a stroll through the park!"

"You made a promise to your family to stay safe."

"Yeah, well, I took a wrong turn. That happens, right? A girl can make mistakes."

What had I even done, exactly? Last night's jump had also gone awry. I had to be doing screwing up jumping, but how?

"Sally, I don't think—"

"You there!"

My head jerked around. For a fleeting moment, my eyes locked onto a human man in the same fancy dress as the reptiles, standing silhouetted in the tunnel. The dim light cast a shadow over his features, but his posture, the tilt of his head, the way the hair reached for the ceiling like gravity was merely a suggestion, it was uncannily familiar — Zander?

"Is that you?" I called out. The figure didn't respond, didn't move, just a silhouette against the faint glow from the wedding cavern. Could it really be him? My mind raced. How could Zander be here, in this bizarre place, at this exact moment?

Before I could take another step, reality shifted, the rest of my jump finally snapping back into place. The figure and the tunnel blurred as if being wiped away by an invisible hand, replaced by a speeding motorcycle. The roaring engine ripped through my momentary illusion, hurling me back into a new reality — a raging highway under a hot summer sun.

My first instinct was primal, born of sheer adrenaline and panic — *run*. Again. Car horns blared in the disapproving rush of modernity, rubber screeching against asphalt as drivers swerved to avoid hitting the woman sprinting across four lanes like a rabbit.

After what felt like an eternity but was probably no more than seven would-be-heart-stopping seconds, I found myself on the other side. My legs gave way, and I collapsed onto the grassy verge, gasping for breath. The scent of exhaust fumes and fast food replaced the lingering reptilian musk in my nostrils.

"Clyde," I panted. "Something is seriously off."

What the frash was wrong with me? My jumps weren't just deviating, they were dragging me to dangerous places. If my jumping was off, who knew what else was…

"Indeed," he replied, looming over me, not a holographic hair out of place. "Your current navigational choices — first bringing us to a Saurian wedding, then to a rapid transportation flow — suggest a rather tumultuous emotional landscape. I must inquire: Are we experiencing a metaphorical journey reflective of your internal turmoil, or is this simply your unique approach to sightseeing? Either way, it might be beneficial to investigate this."

As much as I wanted to dish out a snappy reply, the truth was, I was scared out of my mind. I should probably tell him but putting my problem into words seemed out of my reach right now.

I fumbled for my phone in my pocket. The screen flickered to life, displaying a map with a blinking dot indicating my current location. Thank heavens for small miracles and durable tech. A mile away, the mysterious pin marked the destination I had been chasing. The goal that had set this whole, twisted adventure in motion.

"At least I'm not far from the pin." I slipped the phone back in my pocket. "Maybe we'll finally get some answers."

Clyde's voice held a note of caution. "Will you re-attempt teleportation?"

My eyes narrowed. The temptation was there, a siren's call, urging me to just vanish from Point A and reappear at Point B. So easy, so simple. And yet, so spectacularly disastrous given my recent track record.

"I think not." I said, shaking my head, hoping to jolt my brain into more reliable thinking. "The last couple of jumps have had… unsettling detours. If this were an Uber rating for jumping, I'd be at a one-star, facing deactivation."

Clyde nodded gently. "Perhaps this is your body's way of suggesting a more... grounded approach to problem-solving, Sally. Remember, physical movement can be quite therapeutic."

I pulled myself to my feet and dusted off my clothes. "Therapeutic or not, my feet are on the ground, and they're staying there. At least until we figure out why I keep taking unexpected side trips."

The sun hung high in the sky, though its light barely reached through the trees as I followed the map on my phone. The red pin seemed to be mocking me as it remained just out of reach.

All the while, thoughts of that cavern tumbled around my head like clothes in a dryer. I couldn't shake the vision of Zander, dressed as a wedding guest, shouting as if he didn't know me. Before I could explore that existential black hole, I reached the edge of a fence — chain link, topped with barbed wire, bringing the trees to a halt.

"We seem to have reached an obstacle," Clyde observed.

"I can see that," I muttered, inspecting the fence. My eyes wandered upward, and a structure loomed in the distance — loop-de-loops. A roller coaster? We were miles from Disney or Universal. What was this place?

"Are you thinking of climbing it?" Clyde asked, a hint of judgment — or was it caution? — in his tone. "I should warn you that it constitutes as trespassing."

"But then again," I reasoned, shoving down a sudden flush of uncertainty, "this pin is leading me here for a reason. Maybe it's an invitation."

Clyde took a moment to process this. His pause confirmed what I'd been thinking. "I cannot endorse illegal activity. From what I can ascertain from your media, your law enforcement is not patient when it comes to mental wellbeing."

"Then we don't call law enforcement."

Taking a deep breath, I gripped the chain-link. Each metallic step rattled through the empty forest as I hoisted myself up. The barbed wire was not ideal, but the cuts closed quickly— at least that part of me was still working.

"Sally, be careful," said Clyde, sounding borderline anxious as he drifted through the fence. "I would prefer you to remain in one piece."

"Aren't you sweet," I said as I landed on the other side, my eyes still fixed on the distant structure. "Let's find out what this roller coaster is doing in the middle of nowhere."

I made my way through the underbrush until the plants gave way to a gravel lot. My eyes were trained on the mysterious loops growing larger in the distance. Construction materials were scattered haphazardly throughout the area. Stacks of iron beams lay like dormant giants waiting for their moment to rise, covered in tarps that rustled softly in the breeze. Piles of bricks and concrete blocks sat next to wooden pallets, as if prepped for some large-scale game of Tetris. Plywood barriers, some of them splashed with paint samples of various colors, cordoned off zones that seemed intended for future attractions. Even the ground was uneven, with patches of newly laid asphalt interrupted by stretches of gravel or exposed dirt.

It was a surreal sight, like stumbling upon the secret lair of some mad carnival planner. All these building blocks for fun and excitement, yet no one around to bring the dream to life.

As I maneuvered around the obstacles, avoiding rogue nails and sharp edges, the skeletal frame of the roller coaster grew clearer. Like a monument to human ambition, its steel tracks spiraling skyward, then twisting and plunging into yet-to-be-completed loops. Beside it were the frames for other rides, all distinctively futuristic in design. Metallic grays and neon colors stood out starkly against the green of the surrounding forest.

This wasn't just one ride, but an entire theme park—or at least the promise of one, still under construction. All seemingly connected by a theme.

"Is that... a spaceship?" I asked, captivated by a half-built intergalactic cruiser, complete with mock laser cannons and solar panels.

Clyde's voice broke my reverie. "Ah. Your world is pre-contact. How adorably quaint."

I ignored him, my eyes widening as I took in the other elements of the park. There was a sign staked in front of what appeared to be a retaining pond, declaring it "The Black Hole of Despair" while another section seemed prepped for a twist on classic bumper cars, judging by the stenciled lettering on a sign that read, "Meteor Showers: Collide at Your Own Risk!" — I couldn't decide if it was a warning or an invitation for chaos. Next to that was another attraction ominously named "Alien Encounter," and from what I could gather through the window, it featured a variety of extraterrestrial animatronics — at least, I hoped. An enormous inflatable planet near the roller coaster was labeled "Not Earth" in big, bold letters. As if that wasn't clear enough, someone had felt the need to add a smaller sign below that read, "Really, it's not Earth. Please adjust your expectations accordingly."

SINGULARITY

This place was the amusement park equivalent of a fever dream, like diving headfirst into a Salvador Dali painting if he'd been friends with George Lucas. The sort of place where reality seemed to have called in sick and let absurdity run the show.

I was going to love it here. This park felt like it was made just for me, minus the creepy emptiness of it all. That part was… more than unsettling. No construction crews, no engineers. No sounds of drills, hammers, or the cursing of overworked builders. Just silence.

"The place is deserted," I mumbled. "I mean, why would someone go through all the trouble of starting a project like this and just... abandon it?"

Clyde seemed thoughtful, his pause a bit longer than usual. "There could be numerous explanations, Sally. Economic downturns, planning disputes, or perhaps they ran into something... unexpected."

That last suggestion sent a shiver down my spine. "Unexpected? You think there's something more to this place?"

"There is a distinct possibility," Clyde replied. "Given our current adventure, I wouldn't rule anything out."

I glanced down at my phone. "Well, in any case, we're here. Whatever *here* is. The pin is right at that... space tower thing over there. "

Treading carefully, I approached the unfinished tower that looked like it belonged in a sci-fi movie set. As I got closer, I couldn't shake off the feeling that there was something familiar about it. The shape of it, at the very least.

The door creaked open as I nudged it, causing my heart to leap into my throat. I hesitated for a split second, half expecting something to jump out at me. Instead, the first thing I heard was a startled yelp, followed by my own reflexive shriek.

"SALLY?!"

"MEEDIAN?!"

For a moment, we just screamed at each other, our screams of disbelief turning into relieved laughter. Then he rushed over and hugged me tightly, lifting me off my feet for a brief second.

"Meedian, it's really you!" I exclaimed, pulling away to look at him. "I've missed you!"

He looked much better than the last time I'd seen him, though back then the Dread had drained him as badly as the rest of us. He'd filled back out, his round face a warm pink, his rotund skin suit comforting as the arms wrapped around me. Gone were the flowing robes I remembered: In their place, he wore a checkered flannel shirt, faded jeans, and had topped it all off with a Stetson hat. He was embracing a whole new local stereotype.

"And I've missed you, Sally," he replied, smiling.

"Is this..." I scanned the tower's interior, relieved to see what had formerly been the back end of his ship shop. The controls on the walls flashed a comforting blue. "Have you been here since the..."

"Since the cats burned down my life's work?" he said. My face went cold, and he laughed again. "No hard feelings. Blayde was right, you all came through. I can't thank you enough. Where is she, by the way?"

"It's a… long story," I said, clutching his shoulders tight. Clyde slowly glided back into my field of vision, and I shook the sight of him away. "I wish I could take some credit, but I haven't done anything yet. What… what exactly is this place?"

"You don't know?" Meedian frowned. "Then… how… how did you know where I was?"

I held up my phone. "I got a location pin. It wasn't you?"

His eyes widened, radiating genuine surprise. "Sally, I don't even have your number."

My stomach churned. I glanced at the message again, though the pin was no longer live. *Customer Support* glared back at me. "It must've been Blayde."

Meedian's eyebrows shot up. "Blayde can text now?"

"Apparently." I sighed, pinching the bridge of my nose. Here I had thought I was tracking down clues, but I was still being led. If it even *was* Blayde. Should I have been more cautious? Probably. But when you're floating untethered, even a mystery text feels like a lifeline. "So, where are we exactly?"

"Ah," he replied. "Well, somehow, future you set up this land decades ago, along with a substantial bank account and all the interests therein. All the permits I need to build a new compound were signed and sealed away before the state of Florida even knew what a theme park was. Thanks to you, I'm legit on paper, and it's a great way to keep my offworlder clientele hidden in plain sight."

My head spun. A future me did what now? Set up an alien sanctuary — in Florida? But that was a riddle for another time. For now, the unsolved mystery of who had sent me this location weighed on me, nudging me further into an enigma I wasn't sure I was ready to solve.

I shook my head in amazement. "Only you could turn a theme park into a front for an extraterrestrial black market."

Meedian chuckled. "Not just a front, my dear, a thriving business in its own right! Do you know how much Earthlings love roller coasters? And funnel cake?"

"Fair point. Though I suppose Blayde could have handed over the reins with a little more… finish." I gestured back towards the park, at the empty construction site. "The place feels like a ghost town."

"It's Sunday," he said, frowning oh so slightly. "Everything here is all above board. I'm strictly following Earth's labor laws, so builders get weekends off, social benefits, you know how it is. Universal healthcare in both senses of the term."

"You're amazing, Meedian," I replied, shaking my head, smiling despite the fact I had completely forgotten what day of the week it was. Had I left my parents' house on a Sunday?

"So, what brings you to my little corner of the universe?" He gestured for us to step back outside.

"Other than a mysterious text sharing your location with me?" I hesitated, choosing my words carefully. "Long story. I guess you could say I've been doing some soul-searching. Or, technically… the opposite."

I unzipped the bowling bag with the delicacy generally reserved for disarming nuclear warheads. A ghostly green glow sprang forth, doing strange and poetic things to Meedian's face — sort of like watching a sunset, if the sun were a radioactive lime.

Meedian's eyes went wide; his jovial demeanor evaporated in an instant. "Well… shit," he muttered, almost under his breath, as he ran his fingers nervously across his scalp. "Is that James's orb?"

The words hung heavily in the air, like a dark cloud threatening to burst. A range of emotions played across his face: confusion, understanding, and finally, regret.

I snapped the bag shut, cutting off the unsettling illumination.

"You've seen it before?" I found myself pressing him.

Meedian took a deep, labored breath. His eyes met mine. "You and Blayde aren't on speaking terms, I take it? Because if you were, she might've warned you that this quest of yours might be in vain."

His words hit me like a ton of bricks, each syllable adding to a weight that I already found difficult to carry. "What do you mean, 'in vain'?"

He looked away, his gaze settling on a distant construction crane silhouetted against the sky, as though searching for the right words — or perhaps the strength to utter them.

"Blayde came here," he finally said, his eyes meeting mine with an intensity that was almost unbearable. "She was looking for me to help her with the James problem. And I'll tell you what I told her." He paused, letting the silence stretch painfully between us. "It's too late, Sally. That orb is empty."

FIVE

EVEN MY BIKINI HANGS BY MORE THREAD THAN THIS PARADOX

EMPTY.

About how I felt right now as well.

My feet dangled off the edge of the inflatable unicorn into the cool water of a colossal pool. The sky stretched languidly above; an expanse of powder blue smudged with Pixar-perfect clouds. Beside me, Clyde floated along on the water; so long as I did the same, he assumed I was relaxing, and he left me alone.

The pool was part of Meedian's first completed resort-hotel, a place where even the air seemed to sigh with the knowledge of entropy — nature's eternal promise that things will always find new and exciting ways to fall apart. A comforting thought, really. If existence was all downhill from here, at least I could take solace in the fact that the universe, too, was in a perpetual state of decline. Ah, the poetic justice of cosmic disarray.

Still, it was really nice of Meedian to let me stay here free of charge.

The resort was a portrait of otherworldly elegance. I could see tourists, still a rarity in Meedian's half-finished theme park, lounging on deck chairs. No, not tourists — *offworlders*. Making deals with Meedian, relaxing. Living.

Beside me, an inflatable pool donut bobbed in the water. Clasped in its plastic embrace was James's orb, shimmering with a faint green light even in the daytime. Perhaps the orb was enjoying its little vacation. Or perhaps it was as empty and adrift as Meedian had said, and as I felt.

"The orb's internal lattice has decayed," Meedian had explained. "Blayde came to me about a month ago. Had James still been in there, I have ways — contacts — that could've given her a new body, made it possible for her consciousness to move. But she's *not* in there. No one is in there."

My teeth clenched. Of course. That explained the text. Leave it to Blayde to shift the burden of discovery onto me, making me confront the harsh truths she didn't have the courage to tell me herself. Coward.

"The l-lattice… d-decayed," I had stammered. "So we broke it. We broke her."

"No, it hasn't broken," he continued. "It's just… empty. The decay comes from the fact it's unoccupied. Think of it like the shell of a hermit crab; James has moved on to somewhere else, there's no one left to maintain the place."

"Somewhere else? Where?"

Meedian couldn't answer that.

None of it made sense. I reached over and patted the floating orb. It sure felt alive, slightly humming even while its surface was cold. Why would James have left? And where was she now?

"Emotional vacuums are a funny thing," Clyde said gently, drifting by on some imagined current. "They are filled quicker by questions than answers."

"Reassure me, you can't read my thoughts, can you?"

"No. Though, it would make my job easier."

I let myself try to unravel the problem while baking under the Florida sun. I'd purchased a red bikini from the resort's gift shop — the gift shop being the only completed part of the complex. My skin roasted without any sunscreen on, but continued to repair itself, so I was in a constant state of fresh sunburn. It was oddly cleansing.

"Mind if I join you?" A somewhat familiar voice broke through my introspection.

The man standing on the side of the pool held a towel over one arm and wore sunglasses so large they could have qualified as a solar panel. I blinked away the sunlight, taking in his brown skin and wide smile. It took me a second to recognize him, having only met him once before — months ago.

"Sunan? Is that you behind those lenses?" I couldn't help but smile. Meedian's right hand man was — would become — a friend of mine, somewhere down the line, though he'd already known my future self for quite a while. He'd thankfully been absent when the cats torched the last compound.

"Yeah, it's me." He laughed, settling down on the edge of the pool, his legs dipping into the crystal clear water. "You seemed lost in thought. Contemplating the meaning of life, the universe, and everything?"

"More like contemplating the meaninglessness of it all."

His expression turned serious. "Heard about the James situation. Tough break. You always talked so highly of her."

My gut sank to the bottom of the pool. "So it's true, then. You know future me, but not future her. It's the end of the line."

I'd been trying so hard to keep my emotions in check that the tears breaking out of my eyes felt like a personal failure. That was it: confirmation. James was well and truly dead. I had spent so long convincing myself we'd saved her, when all I'd been doing was deepening my denial.

James died. Because of me.

Clyde glanced at me with a comforting expression. "Do not suppress your emotions; they are valid indicators of what matters to you."

I gritted my teeth. I could get through this. I was going to get through this.

I was going to survive Clyde.

Sunan's eyebrows rose from behind his glasses. "Um, actually, you told me she couldn't handle time travel. Honestly, I'm as surprised as you are about this: your future self acts like she's alive."

I sprung upright on the unicorn, so quickly that I nearly tipped it over. Water splashed around me as I caught my balance. "Wait, what did you just say?"

Sunan nodded, pushing his glasses up the bridge of his nose. "I mean, whenever your future self talks about James, she always speaks in the present tense. Like, 'James would love to see this,' or 'James always says that.' No past tense. You did tell me once she was temporally challenged, but I never asked for details."

My gut had dropped and climbed again so quickly it was like it was riding its own unfinished roller coaster. I clutched my hand over it, trying to calm the intestinal whiplash. Hope flared inside me, a tiny spark in the darkness. It was irrational, maybe foolish, but I couldn't help it. Could it really be possible that James was alive somewhere, in some form? That I hadn't failed her entirely?

"So, you're saying there's a chance? Even with everything Meedian told me?"

Sunan nodded again. "Technically, I'm not supposed to tell you any of this. Blayde would be so mad."

I collapsed back on the inflatable unicorn, letting out a sigh of hot air.

"Except that future is gone," I said, struggling to hold in the tears yet again. They had come out so fast I didn't know if they were there for the good news or the bad again. "Zander changed it. So James isn't alive in our new timeline."

"New timeline?" I could hear Sunan squirm on the side of the pool. "What do you mean?"

"When Zander murdered my brother," I explained, "it changed history. Either John was destined to become a genocidal tyrant, and Zander stopped that timeline from happening; or more likely, he was wrong, and got him confused with someone else. Either way, Zander and I are no longer together, which means our future selves couldn't meet you in your past. Ipso facto, that future no longer exists."

A shadow cast across my face. I turned to see Sunan sitting there, blocking the sun, his face scrunched up in confusion.

"Except," he said, "that your future already happened to me. I know you because we've already spent time together. Us… and Zander."

"But how is that possible?"

My eyes narrowed, wrestling with the paradox that unfolded before me. "If Zander's action changed our future, then that change should reverberate backward *and* forward, right? Erasing the you who knows us."

"I'm no expert." Sunan adjusted his sunglasses and sighed. "But time is rarely a straight line. Right?"

"Only it has been… until now," I said. "Time was always a closed loop, a self-paradox-resolving unit. I never had to worry about stepping on butterflies;

Nimien showed me that, in his own twisted way." When he'd kidnapped me and forced me to decide between action and inaction, between saving my timeline or forcing it to change. It had been so clear how impossible it had been to do anything differently.

Sunan's frown deepened. "Something's not adding up."

I propped myself up on my elbows, feeling the inflatable unicorn shift beneath me. "So let's say there are multiple timelines, just for argument's sake. You meeting us in a different timeline shouldn't impact this one. There shouldn't be memory overlap."

"Exactly," Sunan agreed. "Unless—"

"—Zander broke time. By killing John, Zander broke time itself."

I looked at Sunan, both of us absorbing the weight of that idea. "I was going to say the multiverse is real," he said, "but yeah, time breaking is probably more likely."

For a moment, we both just sat there, the weight of a fractured universe settling on our shoulders. Sunan collapsed back on the tiles.

"I came here for a wellness check, not a crash course in temporal mechanics," he groaned.

"Believe me, this is beyond me, especially for a Sunday," I said, unable to keep the exasperation out of my voice.

I fell back, staring up at the sun in silence, letting the blue sky drown me. So much better than drifting in an empty alien lagoon with a lying jerk of a spaceman beside me.

Stupid assface. Thinks he can get away with everything, including breaking time. Why does he get to screw with the timeline, and I don't?

"That's it," I gasped, sitting up straight again, sending water sprawling. Call it a genius idea or maybe heatstroke, but I knew what I needed to do. "Meedian said if James's orb was still intact, he could get her a body. I'm going to change James's fate."

Sunan sighed, shaking his head. "Sally, if Zander broke time, you're suggesting you do what — break it again?"

"Why not? If time is a shattered mirror, then one more crack won't hurt," I said, seized with a sudden, exhilarating thought. "I can go back and fix this. Save James."

"You're talking about editing reality like it's a Google Doc. Sally, that's not how this works — or at least, it shouldn't be."

"But what's the worst that could happen? Zander played God and got away with it. If he can, why can't I?"

Sunan paused, the gravitas of the moment sinking in. "Just because he did something irresponsible doesn't make it ethical for you to do the same."

"But what about justice? What about setting things right? Why does my brother deserve to die, while James doesn't deserve to live?"

"Justice according to whom? You? Me? Zander?" Sunan seemed to grow more philosophical, or perhaps he was just stalling. "We can't be sure what the consequences would be, Sally. By going back to fix things, you might cause more harm than good."

I rolled my eyes. "Oh, come on. How much worse could it get?"

"Do you really want an answer to that? Because I have a pretty active imagination, you know."

I laughed despite myself. "So, what? I should sit back and let Zander get away with ruining multiple lives? Let him be the only one to scribble with the ink of fate?"

"Time travel ethics are more complex than that," Clyde warned. He'd been silent for so long, I'd almost forgotten he was there.

"What do you know about time travel ethics?" I muttered under my breath.

"Only that you need to take a myriad of elements into account when considering even the simplest of changes," he continued. "There is the butterfly effect, and then there is the actual structure of time and space itself. The Pythanoreans—"

"Those people that look like they're wearing rubber unicorn masks?" I recognized the name. Blayde and I had accidentally visited the dreaded party of Pythanous Five, filled with seventh-dimensional beings contemplating ascension, when we'd been trying to find the source of the Dread. "Since when do they have a say in this?"

"Sally?" Sunan asked.

"Sorry. Talking to my emotional support hologram." I turned back to Clyde, who was still floating on his back in the pool. "Clyde. What do you know about the unicorns?"

"Only that they operate in higher dimensions where — to them — all of time and space exists as a single, unified field," he replied. "These beings see time differently than we do. You should know that paradoxes can't exist for long in our universe. The Pythanoreans view the timeline as a precious artifact — something that belongs to them. If you alter it in any way, they will act to preserve its integrity."

"Hold on, you have an emotional support hologram now?" asked Sunan, his words overlapping with Clyde's monologue. I held up a finger, urging him to wait.

"So they'll erase me? Us? What?" Anxiety filled my voice.

"It is not about erasing," said Clyde. "It is about corrective action. They may intervene to restore the timeline to its original state. You might find that your actions get nixed or, in the worst case, catastrophic events might be triggered to counterbalance the paradox."

"So you're saying if I change things, these beings are going to come and un-change them? They'll reset the timeline?" My eyes darted between Clyde and Sunan. "So why haven't they fixed what Zander did?"

"There's no telling what corrective action they might take. The universe does not like to be tampered with, and those who do often face dire consequences."

"But it's not like the universe has a preferred timeline. It's that a few unicorns think their way goes."

"Is it not a comforting thought?" said Clyde, practically beaming. "You do not need to worry, the timeline will always sort itself out — dimensionally speaking, it already has."

"What's your hologram saying?" Sunan glanced over to the spot in the pool I had been staring intently at for at least five minutes. "What was that about a unicorn?"

"Then what should I do? Just accept that James is gone? That the universe sucks and that's it?" I was nearly shouting now, frustration bubbling into fury.

"Life is full of choices," said Clyde. "And each one takes you down a different path. The key is not in finding a way to go backward, but to navigate the road ahead as ethically and responsibly as you can."

"Predetermined paths. But Zander changed the timeline, massively from what it sounds like. And no one's fixed that yet!" I swung my legs around so I could face him and Sunan. "I won't be doing anything nearly as dramatic. I go back in time a month, to the moment Blayde gave my parents James's orb. I swap it out for the empty one" — I patted the orb floating beside me— "and bring her forward to now, where Meedian can find her a suitable body. Come to think of it, there's no sign I haven't already done that; maybe that's why the orb is empty now."

Sunan groaned again, this time dragging his fingers down his cheeks. "I hate the concept of time travel."

"I've sat back long enough." I grabbed James's orb from the pool donut. "Zander changed the future, maybe even broke time, and he's not facing any consequences. I can't live knowing that he gets a free pass while James, and who knows how many others, suffer. Especially if James was meant to be alive in the timeline he destroyed."

"Fine." Sunan sighed, as if acknowledging an argument he couldn't win. "Let's say you go through with this. You're talking about altering time itself, a fabric you admit you don't fully understand. How do you plan on doing it?"

I glanced at the orb, still humming and glowing faintly beside me. "If the orb is empty because James moved on, then I have to go back to before she did — before her consciousness left. I'll have to find a way to stop it from happening. And if Meedian's right and her lattice is still intact, then I should be able to bring her back. With a new body and everything."

Sunan looked as though he were about to object again but then seemed to change his mind. "Well, it's your choice. Just remember that you're playing with forces that none of us fully understand."

"And that's exactly why I have to try. Someone has to. If I don't, then what's to stop the next Zander — or worse — from doing whatever they want?"

"I suppose that's one way to look at it," Sunan conceded.

"And if those higher-dimensional unicorns have a problem with it, let them come. I'm not afraid."

"Maybe you should be," said Clyde, uncharacteristically hushed.

I shook his voice out of my head. What did he know? He was trained and programmed on psychology, not moral philosophy.

"So…" I turned to the orb, which seemed to pulse as if in anticipation. "Are you ready to see some temporal precision surgery?"

I didn't think, I only jumped. Whether it was bravery or foolishness, I no longer cared. For James, for justice, for a universe where right and wrong still had meaning, I was willing to risk it all.

Because if Zander could break time, then so could I. And maybe, just maybe, I could fix it too.

But here I forgot I was already broken.

SIX

WHEN BENNY MET SALLY

THE COLONIAL TOWN STARED BACK AT ME WITH a judgement so tangible it was just shy of holding up a sign saying *I told you so*. Cobblestone streets crisscrossed the terrain, the brickwork of the huge buildings exuding an earthy red hue, offset by the whitewashed wooden shutters that framed their windows. The air was an olfactory fiesta of freshly tilled earth, the unspeakable aftermath of horses, and the welcoming scent of bread that almost made you forget the aforementioned horse business.

At least this wasn't a Saurian wedding. Small mercies.

No one seemed to have seen me appear in the middle of the street. It must have still been rather early in the morning, judging from the lack of people milling about. A chill wind snaked through the streets, whispering like it was gossiping about me already. It wasn't entirely different from the time I'd visited Jamestown, though it was a heck of a lot colder.

"Sally." Clyde, whose hue of blue had managed to become even more obnoxious, floated beside me. "It appears you have traveled significantly further back in time than you intended."

"Thank you so much for that." I rolled my eyes. "I thought the manure was decorative, and for a second there I was disappointed that my tax money was so utterly wasted."

"My sarcasm module is currently in beta testing. I'll add your input to the data." Clyde's tone didn't change. "However, my point remains valid. Having already discussed the ethical implications of altering timelines, I thought it valuable to remind you of your current temporal struggles."

He was — insufferably — right. The cold nipped at my exposed belly, as if the streets themselves were offering a well-curated critique of my lack of planning, all without uttering a single word. I hadn't dressed for the 18th century. Heck, I hadn't dressed for *any* century. I was still in my bikini.

Oh shit. I was still in my bikini.

I threw myself between two buildings, crouching low. Dirt clung to my wet legs. Of all the moments not to be dressed appropriately, this topped the charts. Why hadn't I given myself time to get dressed?

"Sally, may I point out that you insisted you would alter time with surgical precision, yet you neglected to make any kind of preparations for this trip, even knowing the risks of time travel?" Clyde droned on. "Planning is crucial in managing risks. The absence of planning typically denotes impulsivity, which can lead to unforeseen consequences."

Maybe he's right. Maybe I am being impulsive.

He doesn't have to rub it in.

"Can you be quiet for a second? I need to think," I snapped.

"Very well. But when you're ready, we should discuss this pattern of impulsivity." Clyde dimmed a little, falling into a merciful silence. "Thinking time initiated."

As if it was a pattern for me to end up shivering and stuck in an era where women wore more layers than an onion. Talk about being out of place. Like with the other times this had happened, I'd just have to sit this out until the rest of the jump kicked in. It shouldn't take long. Then I could get back to ignoring Clyde's nagging analysis.

James's orb was solid against my chest, its smooth surface cool to the touch but teeming with a dormant energy. It was the only piece of my time — of my reality — that I could hold onto. My whole reason for being in this intertemporal pit stop, if even accidentally. My grip tightened around it as if it were an anchor.

"You have found an adequate place to hide," said Clyde, shattering my fragile silence. "This would be the perfect time for us to discuss your sudden bout of impulsivity."

"Not *now*! Can we not turn every crisis into a therapy session?"

"If you continue to repress the issue, then no progress can be made," he insisted. "You cannot avoid the problem forever."

"I said not now!"

"Good heavens, woman!"

My head spun around, making eye contact with a face I'd seen every time I'd been lucky enough to handle a 100 dollar bill. A rotund figure with a balding pate and spectacles, clutching papers under his arm. He instantly turned his gaze skyward.

"S-sorry!" I stammered, hugging the orb as if it could magically clothe me. "This isn't what it looks like."

Oh, stars. Of all the colonials to see me, it had to be one of the founding-freaking-fathers. Thank the heavens time was already broken.

"Emotional distress detected," said Clyde. "Would you like a summary of potential coping strategies?"

"No, Clyde, I don't need a summary," I muttered. "Right now, I'd pay you not to talk, and you're not even on salary."

"Are you quite alright?" Benjamin Franklin — Benjamin *freaking* Franklin — asked, his eyes still riveted on the opposite building. "Are you in trouble? Injured? Has someone stolen your clothes?"

His tone was oddly modern, throwing me for a loop. So much for my expectations of "thee" and "thou."

Bless the overpowered translator for sparing me from linguistic gymnastics.

"Just a slight mishap with the latest Parisian trend," I replied, struggling to keep my voice steady. My heels dug into the soil as I sank even deeper into the alley, like an ostrich burying its head in the sand. As if by sinking far enough into the ground, I could dissolve, becoming one with the earth and escaping this nightmare. My face felt like a furnace, and for a moment, I could see my body heat melting the brick wall behind me. "Um, fashion thieves. You know? Please, kind sir, continue on your way. Pretend you stumbled upon an exotic bird, or better yet, a figment of your imagination. It will be as if nothing has happened."

He hesitated. "I cannot simply walk by when someone is in need of aid." His eyes flicked to my face, then skyward again, then, regretfully, back to me. He was doing that awkward dance people do when they're trying to be polite but also can't help being curious. I tightened my grip around the orb, covering myself as best as I could, my fingers almost fusing with it. "Good heavens, it— it *is* you! The strange apparition from the meeting hall! The woman in undergarments!"

Shit, he remembered.

Of course he remembered. You frashing appeared and disappeared from the middle of a room, dripping alien puddle water all over the hardwood floor. Who could have forgotten that?

History. History did. History had amnesia.

Relief washed over me. This wasn't *my* Benjamin Franklin, no. This was Benjamin Franklin from the broken timeline, a version of history that evidently allowed for bizarre interruptions like mine without causing ripples. If our history books made no mention of my temporal accident, then the unicorns, or whoever the temporal custodians were, had done their job. So well, in fact, I'd always assumed time was perfectly linear.

Realization flushed through me like a shot of adrenaline. If time wasn't a fragile glass sculpture but rather a rubber band, snapping back into shape no matter how far it was stretched, then wasn't I, in essence, free to be as reckless as I wanted? Whatever happened here today was a free for all.

Time was already broken either way.

"Err, yes, that was me," I admitted. "Another fashion mishap. You could say I have a habit of popping up unexpectedly."

And in that moment, hiding in an 18th-century alleyway in my modern-day bikini, clutching an orb like it was the last relic of sanity, facing one of the most iconic figures in history, I felt a wild thrill run up my spine. Maybe this hiccup in time was turning out to be more of an opportunity than a disaster. I was about to have a heart-to-heart with Benjamin Franklin, for crying out loud. Or at least as much of a heart-to-heart one can have while mostly naked in the street.

"Indeed, it appears so," Franklin said, still respectfully averting his eyes but looking less like he'd seen a ghost. It was slightly sweet, the way he spoke so naturally about something that should have probably terrified him. Like I was — well, an alien. But then he chuckled. "I'll have you know, Madam, modesty is a virtue — though I, too, have been known to question societal norms now and again."

Or… maybe it was the lack of clothing. I cringed, a full-body cringe that felt like every muscle was pulling in different directions. I mean, this guy was a founding father and all, but he was old enough to be my grandfather.

Before my mind could travel down any further on that repugnant road, Franklin seemed to catch himself. "Come, let me get you inside, away from the cold."

With practiced grace, Franklin slid out of his long coat. He extended it towards me like a flag of truce. Or decency. His eyes stayed fixed on a spot somewhere over my shoulder. "Here, take this. It might not be a perfect fit, but it will provide at least a modicum of coverage and warmth."

"Thank you, Mr. Franklin." I took the coat with one hand while still clutching the orb with the other, hurriedly wrapping it around myself. It smelled like tobacco, ink, and a faint undertone of old books. A wave of relief washed over me. This garment that had likely been part of so many historical events. I was literally wrapping myself in a piece of history.

"You know my name?" he gaped.

"Let's just say your kite experiment really takes off." I avoided his gaze. "I'll explain where prying ears can't hear."

"My kite…" Franklin frowned, meeting my eyes again, as if my partial coverage had renewed our social contract. "This way, please."

He led us to a nondescript back door, rummaging through his pockets for a set of archaic keys. Clyde floated behind, staring so hard at my neck that it was palpable.

"Here we are," said Franklin, unlocking the door. "Better than sneaking you through the front and causing a scandal, wouldn't you agree?"

"I couldn't agree more." He held open the door for me, and I stepped into the modest antechamber. It was private but not intimidating, with delicate curtains drawn mostly shut, leaving just a sliver for me to glimpse the street outside.

Franklin turned to me, his curiosity now piqued beyond polite concern. "Who are you, truly? Calling you merely 'the apparition' is amusing but hardly satisfying."

Here goes nothing. I was stuck out of time, and this man was one of the greatest scientists of his era. *Let's do this.*

Taking a deep breath, I braced myself. "My name is Sally — Sally Webber, and I am from your future."

"Excuse me?" Franklin's eyebrows shot up so high they almost got lost in the receding line of his forehead.

"I am a time traveler," I blurted, my words trembling in the air between us. If anyone could understand, if anyone could wrap their head around this bonkers situation, it had to be him. "I keep getting pulled back to this time and place — or at least somewhere close — and I need to figure out why."

"A… time traveler," he repeated, letting the phrase settle in the room like a dense fog. His eyes studied me warily, as if trying to discern whether I was a lunatic or a messenger from the great beyond. "*And* you know who I am?"

"You're more than just a name in a history book where I come from," I replied. "I am afraid of how much I can divulge about your own future — there's no handbook on the etiquette of time travel, unfortunately, and discussing your legacy feels a bit like spoiling the end of a good book. But I am an American woman, born in Virginia. Meeting you is an honor, Mr. Franklin."

For a moment, Franklin's eyes widened as if grappling with the weight of my words. I held my breath, my grip on the orb tightening. No going back now.

"Say I believe you." Franklin finally spoke, his voice barely above a whisper. "And I'm not saying I do, because this challenges every rational fiber in me. However, I have already witnessed you vanish from this realm. So let us entertain the notion that I believe you. What is your purpose here? Are you sent to warn me of some impending doom?"

His questions were fired rapidly, each one imbued with a sense of urgent curiosity. Taking a deep breath, I tried to squash the rising panic in my gut. The decision tree of every word I uttered seemed to sprout new branches at an alarming rate. What information was safe to reveal?

What did it even matter?

"I'm not here to change your future, Mr. Franklin." I chose my words as carefully as a person disarming a bomb. "I'm here by accident. Twice now I have been redirected to your era, like a moth inexplicably drawn to a flame. If I can figure that out, maybe I can go home."

"Well, I have not brought you here." He shook his head. "No. I did not call you here, not that I would know how. Unless it is a side effect of some of my research? Who knows… but you are certain it is *me* you keep coming back to?"

"No. I'm unsure whether you are the beacon I'm drawn to or simply this time period, but twice in these… temporal malfunctions… I have seen you — by chance, not by choice."

"Perhaps you are here to help me with my inventions? To give me a stroke of genius? Or perhaps to help in this war? You say you are an… American?"

"I am." I nodded, keeping my answers moderately vague. "From the 21st century. Believe me, I do not wish to muddle with the flow of history."

His brow furrowed. "So, time travel's a common pastime in your era?"

"Hardly. It's more of a 'don't try this at home' kind of hobby. A few of us are... Let's just say we're... testing out the invention."

"And the invention's malfunction seems to be around... me?" Franklin said, taking slow strides across the room, visibly deep in thought. "How very... peculiar. Tell me, you did not intend on barging into the hall wearing your..."

"My sleepwear," I clarified, face going hot again. "I must apologize for my attire. The time travel... device seems to modify my clothing based on its own inexplicable criteria. It's another variable that defies logic. My goal is to remain as inconspicuous as possible, to avoid disturbing history."

"Ah, and yet you've done just the opposite," he said, chuckling gently. "We'd initially considered the possibility that we were all suffering from the same mass hallucination. I confess, part of me wonders if I've slipped into madness."

"I can assure you, you're as sane as one can be given the circumstances. And potentially the only person knowledgeable enough to help me out of this predicament. I'm in desperate need of a scientific perspective."

"Ah, the challenges of inventing, unpredictable outcomes and unintended effects. Sounds familiar, doesn't it?"

"It's nice to know some aspects of scientific endeavor remain constant across time," I admitted, a smile playing across my lips.

He paused and looked at me. "You're aware of my future — my fate, my contributions. Do you... do you know my work?"

"In my timeline, you're a towering figure in science and politics," I responded, oh-so cautiously. "But as I said, I'm keen on not altering history. Even a hint could create ripples."

His face fell slightly, but he quickly masked it with a gentle smile. "Very well, I respect the bounds of your unique ethics. A scientist's responsibility transcends time."

"Quite literally, in my case," I agreed, feeling the weight of that responsibility ever so acutely.

Franklin looked up, locking eyes with me, his face illuminated by an unspoken understanding. "It seems, Miss Webber, that we have an unprecedented scientific quandary on our hands. Shall we dare to unravel it?"

I grinned. "Let us dare."

Despite the potential pitfalls of revealing too much, the gamble seemed to be paying off. Franklin was engaged, not dismissive or fearful. He grasped the severity of my situation, seemed curious about it. We shared a brief pause, united in a newfound camaraderie that bridged the centuries separating us. The room felt charged with the possibilities of what two minds from different eras might achieve together. And for the first time since this ordeal began, I felt a glimmer of hope that maybe I could figure out what was happening to me.

"Given the complexity of your situation," he said, "I surmise that figuring this out won't be a matter of mere tinkering or adjustments. No, it would require a true leap of insight — a paradigm shift, if you will."

"That's what I've been struggling to find," I admitted, still cautious but a little less alone. "I've attempted… recalibrating the time coordinates, but despite the adjustments, here I am. Again."

"Recalibrating time coordinates, you say," he murmured, almost to himself. "This device you're holding, this… orb. It wouldn't happen to be the instrument of your time travels, would it?"

I'd been clutching James's orb tightly to my chest this whole time. "It's… related, let's say. But not the time machine itself."

Franklin's eyebrows arched, a knowing smile playing on his lips. "Ah, but surely, a closer examination could yield some insights. Perhaps I could offer my expertise in natural philosophy to assist in your… recalibration efforts."

His eagerness was palpable, and I couldn't help but laugh. "Mr. Franklin, I'm afraid it's not as simple as that…"

Franklin's eagerness, however, was undeterred. His hand inched closer to the orb with the stealth of a cat stalking its prey. "Just a peek, Miss Webber," he cajoled, his voice laced with the kind of persuasive charm that he was famous for. "For science, you understand."

I instinctively twisted away, securing the orb out of his reach with a maneuver that would have made a quarterback proud, but my gaze accidentally swept past the window. The sight that greeted me froze me mid-turn. My breath hitched.

There he was, as out of place as a smartphone at a Renaissance fair yet blending into the 18th-century streetscape with an ease that belied the absurdity of his presence. His movements were unmistakable, a stride I'd recognize anywhere — the confident walk, the casual tilt of his head. And that uniform: well, isn't this a scene straight out of Hamilton, minus the catchy tunes. But how? How could he be here?

"Warning: elevated stress levels detected. Recommend immediate de-escalation procedures," Clyde piped up.

My mind was a hurricane of thoughts and emotions, a chaotic tempest I couldn't even begin to navigate. My fingers clenched into fists, nails biting into my palms as I tried to process what was unfolding before me. It was impossible. He shouldn't — couldn't — be here.

"Miss Webber?" Franklin's voice broke through my internal cacophony. "You look as if you have seen a ghost."

"That man, there." I pointed, words stumbling out before I could catch them. "Was he in the hall when I... appeared?"

"Captain Gamout?" Franklin followed my gaze. "Yes, I do believe he was. Why?"

The color drained from my face. He was in the room where it happened? Part of Earth's history? This was even worse than I'd imagined. What was he playing at?

"I don't know how to explain it without sounding even more outlandish," I finally managed to utter. "But yes, he is *very* consequential. Incredibly so. And the fact that he's here, now, could spell disaster on an unimaginable scale."

"Do you mean to say that he is also from your time?" Franklin gasped. "Two anomalies in the same era? Extraordinary."

"Unimaginable is more like it." My voice was barely above a whisper as a sickening twist of realization coiled in my gut. "This changes everything."

Franklin frowned. "Ah, so I may not be the one bringing you here."

"Yup." I nodded, my eyes still locked onto the window, even though the man was now long gone. "I'm pretty sure he's the one."

"Do you know him?"

"Intimately," I hissed, the word laced with a venom I barely recognized in myself.

In the next instant, I was yanked from the room, the walls and Franklin's astonished face melting into a blur of color and light, and I was swept away to my intended destination, Zander's new name echoing in my mind like a curse.

SEVEN

THE FATHER, THE DAUGHTER, AND THE GREAT ORB SWITCHEROO

I STUMBLED INTO EXISTENCE ABOVE THE TOILET IN my parents' bathroom, my knees nearly buckling beneath me as I stumbled forward. The walls closed in as I gripped the porcelain sink for balance, my free arm clutched around James's orb, gulps of modern air filling my lungs but doing little to stave off the hyperventilation that overwhelmed me.

I was supposed to arrive in the office, not the bathroom. These small mistakes were adding up.

"Warning," said Clyde, "*extremely* elevated stress levels detected."

"Yeah, no shit." I was struggling to get my bearings, my mind still back in 1776.

Zander was there. Zander was the reason I kept getting rerouted. Like some kind of reverse stalker, rather than following me through time he was somehow making me come to him. The thought made my blood boil. First, he uproots my life. Then, he kills my brother. And now, this? He can't leave well enough alone.

"Immediate de-escalation procedures engaged," said Clyde. "Would you like assistance with breathing exercises?"

I was about to dismiss his canned attempt to comfort me with a witty retort when I caught my reflection in the bathroom mirror. I looked like a specter, eyes wide with terror. I dropped James's orb into the sink.

Clyde, seemingly sensing the slight ease in my tension, softly chimed in, "Let's do this together. Inhale for four seconds, hold for seven, exhale for eight."

I hesitated. Up to this point, Clyde had been nothing more than a sounding board with the emotional acuity of a kitchen appliance. But in that moment, I didn't have the brain power to process anything else. For reasons I couldn't fully articulate, I clutched the sink and followed his instructions.

Inhale, hold, exhale. Inhale, hold, exhale.

The tension in my chest eased slightly, the tightness around my lungs giving way just enough for me to exhale. Ironic, for someone who didn't need to breathe, that this one, slow, human thing would be what drew me back to myself.

Inhale, hold, exhale.

"Good, Sally," Clyde encouraged. "You're doing well. You have control over this moment."

Inhale, hold, exhale.

SINGULARITY

I dug my hands into the edges of the sink, letting its coolness ground me. For the first time since I first met Clyde, I felt as if the AI had reached through the layers of algorithms and actually found what I truly needed.

Or maybe… it was the first time I had actually listened.

Inhale, hold, exhale.

"Thank you," I finally said.

I took one last deep breath. The glitches in my time travel, the unexpected detours, the impossibly dangerous anomaly of Zander — or should I say, Captain Gamout — in history; these were issues too pressing to ignore.

Clyde's voice resonated in my ear, almost contemplative. "You're welcome, Sally. Wherever you go, remember, you are not alone."

Tears burned at the corners of my eyes, blurring my vision. I blinked them back. Ugh. Weak, weak. For an immortal I fell apart so easily. "Not alone," Clyde had said, but the irony was bitter; the comforting voice was just a string of code, algorithms mimicking empathy.

"Shall we examine the emotional context of your recent experiences?" Clyde asked.

"Precision surgery. That's what I told myself, right?" I sighed, my words heavy with defeat. "Instead, it's like I took a goddamn sledgehammer to the fabric of existence. But why should I care, huh? My house still stands, my life is intact, my parents are downstairs, blissfully unaware. Nothing I do even makes a ripple."

I let out a hollow laugh, a jarring sound that even I didn't recognize. "You know what's messed up? All my life, even long before I got entangled with… *them*, I've walked on eggshells. Worried about every word I'd say, every look I'd give. Terrified that one false move would be a landmine, blowing up my life and the lives of those I care about. I know anxiety… depression… they aren't rational, but my own mind wouldn't let me accept that. And then Zander happened, and time travel, and suddenly there was this big, massive thing to distract me. I was helping people. Making a difference. And it made sense, because if the timeline was linear, then I had *always* been making a difference. I was meant to help. But that's not how time works, now, is it?"

Clyde remained quiet for a moment, as if contemplating the right response. Finally, he spoke. "Existential concerns are a normal part of human cognitive development—"

"Existential concerns?" I cut him off, a hysterical laugh bubbling up inside me. "Clyde, I just learned that nothing really matters. Time does not care. I can dance in front of Benjamin Franklin in a bikini while telling him about the wonders of the 21st century, and the universe just... carries on. As if I'm not even there. As if I never mattered."

"If it is any consolation, you matter to the people you interact with." Clyde's voice softened. "Besides, it is likely the Pythanoreans came through and cleaned up the damage, as they always do."

"Yeah, well, I wish that were as comforting as you make it sound," I snapped, wiping away a rogue tear that had managed to escape. "If the Pythan — the unicorns fix the timeline to their liking, is John alive, or dead?"

"It is entirely possible that he is both," said Clyde. "Quantum superposition dictates…"

"Quantum superposition? Are you kidding me? We're talking about a person's life, Clyde, not Schrödinger's cat! My brother is either dead because Zander killed him, or he's alive and a genocidal warlord. Those are mutually exclusive states of being!"

"In quantum mechanics, particles can exist in multiple states until observed. It is not outside the realm of possibility that timelines work in similar ways," Clyde reasoned, his voice still unnervingly calm.

Since when had he become an expert on quantum mechanics? Was that part of every emotional support AI's programming?

"That's a cold comfort, don't you think?" I gritted my teeth. "So what, we're just supposed to accept that the universe — or some higher-dimensional beings — decide which version of my brother gets to exist? What about free will? What about the choices we make? Don't they count for anything?"

"Free will is an important variable, certainly. But it functions within the parameters set by the larger cosmic forces. It's not a contradiction but a coexistence."

"A coexistence that allows for manipulation," I retorted. "If these unicorns are editing the timeline, who's to say they're doing it right? Why do they get to decide?"

Clyde paused, as though his algorithms were rolling through all the ethical implications. "The Pythanoreans are not moral arbiters. They are more like custodians of temporal integrity. Their actions aim to maintain the stability of time, not to pass judgment on individual lives."

"Maintaining stability at what cost? My sanity? My brother's life? This isn't some kind of cosmic housekeeping, Clyde; it's playing God. And I don't know about you, but I find the idea of my life being tidied up by mythical creatures both disturbing and offensive."

"By your primitive civilization's definition, they *are* God." Clyde's next words came slower. "Sally, the complexities of existence, the uncertainties of time, the moral quagmires — they are all part of the human condition. You're asking questions that philosophers, theologians, and scientists have wrestled with for centuries. There may be no definitive answers."

"I'm sick of uncertainties," I confessed. I had nothing left in my emotional batteries. "I want something I can hold onto, something real and unchangeable."

"Then perhaps focus on what you can control, on the choices you make within the tapestry of existence. In a universe fraught with variables, you are your own constant."

"But I'm not even that, now." I looked up into the mirror, meeting my own gaze. "I can't even jump right.

Zander freaking too-good-for-a-last-name keeps drawing me back to himself for no reason. All I can do now is prepare myself for the next accidental pit stop on the way back home. Heck of a detour."

"One problem at a time. Perhaps you should concentrate on *one* thing you can control."

I nodded. "As long as those higher-dimensional unicorns aren't floating around here to 'tidy' things up, I can still save James."

"Exactly," Clyde confirmed, sounding oddly earnest for a machine. "Your purpose here remains unaltered."

A knock on the door jarred me back to reality. "Sally, you in there?"

It was my dad's voice. Which made sense, considering this was his house. From his perspective, assuming I'd nailed the timeline, Zander and I had jetted off on our galactic gallivanting just yesterday, the day after Blayde had gone looking for a new body for James. That was also a day after we'd filled my parents in on the family's newly complicated W-2 forms: Zander, extraterrestrial; Sally, botched space-time tourist.

"Uh, yeah, Dad. Just a moment," I stammered.

I looked down at myself: the red bikini stared back. What a relief, Franklin's coat had stayed in the past where it belonged. I grabbed James and plonked her orb in the bathtub, pulling the curtain before grabbing a towel for myself. Drawing in a deep breath, I unlocked the door and pulled it open, offering my dad a forced smile.

"Hey," he said, looking shocked and slightly embarrassed at the sight of me in a towel. "Thought you'd left."

I glanced back at the bathroom mirror, then at my dad. At that moment, I realized that, in the grand scheme of things, whether I was a time-hopping mess, or a confused young woman didn't matter. To my dad, I was just Sally. And right now, that was the only role I needed to play.

"I forgot my bathing suit," I replied. "I could have bought a new one, but between the alien currency and weird interstellar body standards, it was just easier to grab the one I already had."

"I can see how that would be a pain. When shopping for trousers, I find even Earth's gravitational variations give me enough of a headache," he said, sounding casual except for the small hitch in his throat.

"It's exactly like that, but with more tentacles."

Dad looked at me, smiling. "It's, uh, good to see you," he said softly.

"Good to see you too, Dad," I said, though technically neither of us had been missing the other for that long.

He looked at me for a moment, his eyes misty. "Be careful out there, okay? I know you and Zander are off doing... whatever it is you do, and I'm proud of you. Really, I am."

I felt a lump in my throat. "Thanks, Dad. I do a lot less than you think, though."

He shook his head. "Doesn't matter how much or how little you do, Sally. I'm just so happy there's someone out there who cares."

I hugged him tightly, fighting back tears. I couldn't tell him about the unicorns or the timeline fixes or the fact that my actions might not matter in the grand scheme of things. I couldn't lay that on him. But for the first time in a long time, the weight of my responsibilities didn't feel like a crushing force, but a purpose. And as I pulled away from the hug and looked into my dad's eyes, I knew that, even if the universe didn't care about my actions, there were people who did.

"Thanks, Dad," I said softly. "I'll see you soon, okay?"

He smiled. "I'll hold you to that."

As the door clicked shut, a sense of normalcy returned, if only for a moment.

"Your heart-to-heart with your father was touching, Sally." Clyde's voice returned, tinted with what I could only interpret as machine-made warmth. "Though, might I suggest a bit more candor in future conversations? Authenticity can be quite liberating."

I nodded, only half listening. "Noted. But we have other concerns right now."

With purpose in my step, I made my way to the office. It was amazing how much simpler things became when you didn't have to skulk around like a cat burglar in your own home. No tiptoeing, no ducking behind furniture — just a straightforward walk to the home office with interdimensional implications. How refreshingly mundane. Still, something about it felt like trespassing.

I slid open the desk drawer where the orb was stashed. There it was, glowing like a green interstellar pearl — or watermelon, considering the size. I made the swap, feeling a bit like a magician who'd pulled off a particularly tricky illusion. A smile crept across my face. Despite everything — the existential crises, the time loop madness, the unicorns — I was getting rather good at this. I closed the drawer, another mission completed.

The orb looked the same as the one I'd replaced it with. Felt the same, thrummed the same. How Meedian could tell one soul-filled sphere from an empty one was beyond me.

"I hope you're still in there," I whispered to the orb, before turning back to Clyde. "Right. Let's get back to the present."

"I would like to remind you that due to the temporal anomalies we've been experiencing, there's a substantial chance of another unintentional stopover in the year 1776."

"Yes, 1776 has an unhealthy obsession with me." My eyes rolled towards the ceiling. "I'm ready."

"My sarcasm module may be in early development, but I know that it is unnecessary here." Clyde almost sounded a touch offended. "I only wished to remind you of your current state of dress."

"You're right," I said, my mouth going dry. Shame rolled over me like a wave, dragging me under for a second.

Everything that hadn't fit into my duffel bag had been left in this room, so it made changing clothes easy. Not that I had anything 18th-century appropriate. I did my best with what I had, grabbing a baggy button-down and long summer skirt from my suitcase. I slipped the clothes over my bathing suit.

Now I had to brace myself for the inevitable: Another detour. Zander's persistence ensured that I couldn't escape the past, no matter how hard I tried. I gritted my teeth, ready for the universe to shove me somewhere else I had no intention to be.

The one thing this place had going for it was that I wasn't crashing a wedding or the administrative phase of a revolution. No, whatever I was crashing, none of the guests seemed sober enough to notice.

I blinked in the dim space that was less like a room and more like a scene from a screensaver. Colorful multi-colored lights pulsated from the walls, accompanied by the thumping bass of some cosmic beat. In front of me, a wild assortment of beings bobbed and weaved to the rhythm, some with shimmering tentacles that reflected the cyberpunk lighting, others with multiple heads that somehow moved in perfect harmony, even one that seemed to be made entirely of floating orbs, each glowing in time with the music. Another group was engaged in what I could only describe as zero-gravity Twister — I hoped — their limbs intertwining in a way that defied physics and made me slightly dizzy and oddly tantalized.

"Is this your intended destination?" asked Clyde.

I shook my head. "Another detour. Any idea where we are?"

"The décor, music, and assortment of intergalactic species suggest a celebratory gathering, commonly known as a party. However, the exact location is... uncertain."

Right, nothing more than I could have deduced myself. A party. I sniffed the air — no, this was nothing like the loathsome party of Pythanous Five, full of its higher-dimensional smoke and equally awful music. This was more like a house party, by the looks of the small, cramped space. I nodded in time with the beat, trying to blend in, or at least not stick out. A couple of beings with antenna-like appendages and eyes on stalks sipped a bubbling beverage from a levitating punch bowl. The drink changed colors as it rose, an oversized lava lamp.

In the corner, two orbs were pressed against the wall, changing colors faster than a strobe light. I quickly turned the other way.

"Hey, you're new!"

The voice made me turn, anxiety screaming in my head that I was about to be thrown out, before being replaced by a voice asking why I even cared. The being striding towards me was entirely silver from head to toe, smooth and shimmery and corrugated like a washboard on two legs. They moved with a kind of fluid grace that was hypnotic, each step seemingly choreographed to the pulsating beats of the music. They smiled at me, and I offered a smile back.

"Yeah, sorry, I took a wrong turn," I replied, trying to sound casual. "This isn't exactly the party I had in mind."

Their laughter was light and musical, like chimes in a gentle breeze. "Well, fate has a funny way of bringing us where we need to be! I'm Xylar. Can I interest you in some punch?"

What was the protocol about not accepting drinks from strangers here, wherever this was?

"Oh, I can't stay long," I said, shaking my head. "I need to get back to where I need to be."

"Come on, stay, have some fun!" Their silvery face dimpled in seven different places, only for an instant. "We throw the best parties on campus, no one will blame you."

Campus? I scanned the room, trying to absorb the mismatched furniture, the flimsy artwork on the walls, the pulse of people — oh, this might have been a frat party of some kind. I'd missed out on those in my own short-lived college life, but it seemed the experience was universal.

"I appreciate the offer, Xylar, but I really shouldn't," I said, trying to sound polite yet firm. "I've got places to be, people to... well, you know. Um, designated driver?"

"Sally," said Clyde, "it is imperative that we find a way to return home. This environment is unpredictable."

"Tell me about it," I muttered under my breath. "But it's not like I can just snap my fingers and—"

Xylar leaned in closer, their eyes gleaming. "Ah, come on! Stay a while, let loose!"

I opened my mouth to answer, then slammed it shut again. There, amidst the sea of gyrating alien forms and flashing lights, I saw him.

Zander.

He was dressed in loose-fitting clothes, a shimmery tunic thrown over bright orange pants. It was obviously him: his soft brown hair, determined to break gravity; his bright, silver-green eyes that could see right through me. Yet, something was seriously wrong. He just… stood there, a lone figure in the chaos, his unmistakable presence sending a chill down my spine.

What was he doing here? Was this just another bizarre coincidence, or something more?

I had to go.

Come on, Time, bring me home, I begged of the universe. *Get me out of here.* But if Zander was behind my temporal rerouting, who knew how long I would be stuck.

"Please excuse me," I muttered to Xylar, before making a beeline for the exit.

"Hey, where are you going?" they called out, but I was already too far to hear them over the music.

I was wrong, it wasn't the exit. I dipped into the corridor, the thumping bass muffling into a distant echo.

I found myself navigating a maze of corridors, sinking deeper and deeper into the bizarre space. The walls were adorned with what looked like tapestries depicting battles and celestial celebrations, though they could have been movie posters for all I knew. I squeezed past a creature with six eyes offering me a suspicious-looking drink, another with glowing antennae that started whistling the Indiana Jones theme when I got close.

Clyde's voice was clear over the din. "Sally, confronting your feelings towards Zander could lead to significant emotional catharsis. It's a fundamental concept in human psychology, often leading to—"

"Clyde, not now." I wasn't in the mood for a psychology lesson. I needed to escape, to process everything far away from Zander and his infuriating ability to distract me at the worst possible times.

Rounding a corner, I almost collided with a group of what appeared to be levitating jellyfish, their tentacles rhythmically swaying to the distant beat. I offered a quick apology and continued on, turning and slamming full force into a solid chest.

I looked up, heart figuratively sinking. Because looking back down at me, lips a thin line and eyebrow slightly raised, was Zander.

EIGHT

THE ONE WHERE I CRASH MY PRE-EX'S FRAT PARTY

THERE'S NOTHING MORE AWKWARD THAN running into your ex at an alien frat party. Especially when your ex isn't a *pre* yet.

"You?" Zander squinted at me. "I've seen you before."

"Um, I think you've got me confused with someone else," I replied, my voice betraying my nervousness. I glanced at Clyde for some kind of help. "Now, if you'll excuse me, I was trying to find the punch bowl."

He held out his glass in a gesture. "No, it's more than that. You keep turning up randomly like some tarnished currency. You were at Shav'ha'rah's mating ceremony weren't you? In the caves?"

"I have no idea what you're talking about." I tried to slip away from his reach, but I was pinned in — to my side, gelatinous beings were doing more than just dancing.

Gross. Get me out of here get me out of here gemme outta here…

"And you were at Liberty Hall, when we were trying to liberate the Terran colonies?" he insisted. "The clothes, I remember thinking the clothes matched another woman, one who interrupted a puddle-hop I had raced in years before, but you *are* the same person, aren't you?"

Why wasn't I jumping out of here? I couldn't say anything, not when he had everything so spot on. And that memory — how could he remember so much detail? The Zander I knew could barely juggle the few memories he still had in his head.

"You have me mistaken for someone else." I tried to step away, but the gelatinous beings beside me had started embracing in such a frenzy that they might have been dissolving into the floor, and I didn't know the etiquette about stepping on people when they were in a liquid state.

Clyde's voice rose above the rest. "Sally, emotional confrontations can lead to catharsis, but they can also escalate tensions. Caution is advised."

I ignored him, focusing on Zander. "Look, I just came here for a good time, not to be grilled. I need some air."

Zander's eyes narrowed slightly. I seized the moment to sidestep the amorphous couple and made a break for it, hoping to lose myself in the crowd once more.

"You jumped!" he exclaimed, grabbing my arm. "Each time you were there, then suddenly gone, just like... the same way it looks when Blayde jumps in front of me. Please, please, tell me who you really are."

His features, once so familiar, seemed to belong to a stranger now. Was he playing a game? Was he the puppeteer behind my erratic jumps, feigning ignorance? I scanned his face, looking for any sign of deceit.

"Are we really doing this?" Standing before him, all the pent-up anger and grief I had been holding in came bubbling to the surface. I had so many questions, yet the sight of him, alive and well, reignited the pain of loss. He was responsible for my brother's death, and here he was, seeking answers from *me*.

He killed John. He killed my brother.

"You're... like me," he said, his eyes wide, dare I say, hopeful.

"Fair deduction," I replied, my voice tight. I didn't have much wiggle room here. If this Zander truly didn't know me, this was either his future — or his past. If this was his future, then it was a disappointing one at that: another mind wipe, something he swore he wouldn't do again. If this was his past, which loop through was it?

His posture stiffened. "Are you from the Institute?"

Institute, institute... I didn't know any institutes. Then again, if this was a more closed- off Zander, would he have shared his lack of a homeworld with a complete stranger like me? The eggshells I was walking on crunched all around me.

"No," I replied. "I don't know who or what you're talking about."

"So how were you made?" he asked, tilting his head. "If you're like me?"

"That's incredibly personal. Wait, what do you mean, *made*? Someone made you like this?"

"Yeah, genetic experimentation. Probably highly illegal, but I haven't been back to 22nd-century Earth since my escape." He let out a sigh. "You were *born* this way?"

I gritted my teeth. The truth of Zander's origins, the huge mystery that had been driving him before I'd even met him, tossed out like a curse. This was what he'd been struggling to remember, after his failed memory retrieval: no homeworld filled with others like him. No loving family missing him and his sister. Just some institute on earth where he was a lab rat.

My heart broke for him.

"No," I replied, raising my voice slightly over the din. Around us, the party continued in full swing, a cacophony of laughter and chattering, the partiers oblivious to the weight of our conversation. "It's too long to explain. Where exactly does this moment fit in your life's convoluted puzzle?"

"What do you mean?" Zander's voice was tinged with a hint of defensiveness as he took a swig from his luminous drink. The bass music throbbed around us.

It's hard to measure a life lived non-linearly. "How are things with Blayde?"

For a moment, Zander's facade slipped, his eyes betraying a flicker of surprise. "My relationship with her is just fine. Why do you ask?"

I scanned him over. Young Zander was less adept at masking his feelings. Nervous fidgets, uncomfortable shifts in posture — it was like watching a novice bluffing in a high-stakes poker game.

But one thing was clear: Even if this was the Zander from before all the betrayals, he was already a damn good liar — just not good enough. Yet.

"You're lying," I stated. "This is it, isn't it? The rift with Blayde, the big fallout you two had?"

"How would you even know about that?" The pitch of his voice rose slightly. "Who in the universe are you?"

"I am Sally Webber," I said, attempting to assert some semblance of control over the conversation.

"But to me," he pressed, his eyes narrowing, "who are you?"

A friend, a foe, a ghost from a future not yet realized.

I struggled to find the right words.

Someone who had mattered, once.

"A friend," I finally settled on, forcing a smile that felt hollow. How do you reconcile a friendship with someone who, in a timeline yet to unfold for him, *killed your brother?*

Zander scoffed. "A friend, huh? That's as convincing as a politician's promise. If you really know me, you'd also be aware of my... let's say, less savory capabilities. So, who are you? Truly? If you know my past, or future..."

His attempt at intimidation would have been laughable if it weren't for the context. Coming from this half-formed, undercooked Zander, it sounded utterly ridiculous. I could have laughed if it wasn't so… sad.

"Don't try to threaten me." My patience was wearing thin. "Believe it or not, I am your friend, or I will be. We haven't met yet from your perspective, but I do know you, the person you're going to grow into. So, can we skip the menacing act and get to the point?"

"What point?"

"You! Deviating my jumps!" I retorted, feeling more than a little out of place among the gyrating aliens. "I can barely *do* anything without being rerouted to *you*."

"That's not my doing." Zander's smirk flickered, barely noticeable under the neon lights. "Perhaps you're drawn to my irresistible charm?"

"In your dreams," I spat. His self-assured attitude was grating, to say the least. My Zander had warned me about the person he'd once been, the man he'd seen in Blayde's memories. It wasn't any more fun to witness it up close and personal. "Your ego's bigger than this whole party. I've got my own knot of problems to unravel. The last thing I need is to keep getting sidetracked. Don't get me wrong, meeting Ben Franklin was a neat surprise, but I have much more pressing things to do. So if you'd please…"

"Likewise," he said, his smile morphing into something unsettling, an eerie mirage that sent a shiver down my spine. This version of Zander was a far cry from the man I knew. He was like a doppelgänger, a twisted reflection that captured the outline but none of the essence. He leaned in closer, his voice a conspiratorial whisper. "The future can wait. You're not even my type."

He bit the edge of his lip in a way I'd seen him do many times before, with much better results. This time, the groan was not internal.

"Nice one, Casanova. Is this what passes for flirting for you? Negging?"

"Can't blame a man for trying. Well, hot chick, party, time travel — that's a sexy combination."

This was going nowhere. "Forget it. I'm going to get some air."

He nodded, seeming relieved at the change of subject, though it wasn't an invitation. We made our way through the throng of partygoers, dodging dancing tentacles and avoiding the more inebriated attendees who seemed to have lost control of their anti-gravity fields. I grabbed a punch from the tray by the door and stepped outside.

Except there was no outside. The exit door to the frat house led me to a dark hallway, one which also glowed blue and smelled of some kind of burning grass. I groaned, shoving my hands deep into the pockets of my outdated clothes, and kept walking.

"Did you and future me ever…" asked Zander.

This current Zander was a never-ending groan-fest. "I thought you said I wasn't your type?"

"I must be dreadfully mundane in the future," Zander quipped, smirking again. "How's my future-self faring? Still kicking?"

"As if your ego would let you die," I spat.

Whatever trace of warmth existed in him evaporated instantly. His features tightened, locking into an icy facade. Clearly, I had stepped over an invisible line — a line more elusive than a decent Wi-Fi signal in a black hole.

"This is about the rift, now, isn't it?" I said, suddenly aware of a gap in my understanding wide enough to drive a truck through.

"If my future self hasn't already told you, there's probably a good reason."

"I never asked him. He wasn't ready then. Maybe you are now. Between you and your sister…"

"Sister?" His eyebrows furrowed. "I have a sister?"

"Blayde?"

"She's not my sister," he said, the confusion settling into a grim realization. "Huh. Then, I guess we do reconcile, eventually."

I bit my lip, a wave of unexplainable sadness washing over me. The famous Siblings, not actually siblings. I guess they'd believed for so long it had eventually become their truth.

The hallway opened into a cavernous room, and I gasped. The space looked like a shopping mall, complete with escalators and oversized indoor plants, but the glass ceiling glowed with the gaseous filaments of a nebula. Gentle white lights lit the empty promenade.

I dropped onto a bench, unable to take my eyes off the sights above. I dropped James' orb onto my lap. Zander fell down beside me, sighing deeply.

"How long have you been immortal, Sally?"

"About a year," I replied, matching his gravity. "Though I'm not sure exactly."

"No one should live as long as I have." His words weighed down the air. "After you've seen everything, twice, ten times — you become a phantom, endlessly traversing time, yearning for an end. Eternity becomes a cage. It's only natural one should want to escape."

My breath caught in my throat. I knew what he was about to say, yet I dreaded hearing it. I couldn't speak, I couldn't stop him, couldn't find the right words to offer comfort. Even Clyde, wellspring of canned advice that he was, wasn't adding to the conversation. From the way he stood motionless by the escalator, I wondered if this conversation had broken his circuitry.

Zander's head dropped as he continued. "I've plunged into the heart of a star, hoping to be disintegrated by its nuclear furnace. I let myself be stretched to my atomic limits in a black hole, and it rejected me."

My hand flew to my mouth. "You can't mean—"

"I even tried to sever my jump midway, leaving myself in the void between universes. Ended up crashing a surreal soiree, let me tell you. I've aimed for the end of time itself, only to find myself back at the universe's first tick. I must've witnessed the Big Bang at least fifty times. Enough for it to get a bit dull."

The words hung in the air like a haunting melody, a testament to an agony so vast it spanned millennia, so profound it defied the laws of the universe. The chasm between our experiences, his lifetime and mine, became almost palpable.

And this was only his *first* lifetime.

"Please, I don't…" I stammered, my voice quivering. Tears blurred my vision. But he continued, his gaze fixed on the ground — neither proud nor ashamed, just laying out his life.

"Each attempt to reclaim my mortality only landed me somewhere else, fully intact. Blayde would find me every time, urging me to give eternity another shot — another second, third, or infinite number of chances. But I didn't want chances. I wanted the finality, the peace, the next stage — be it heaven, hell, or oblivion."

"The rift," I breathed, the pieces finally snapping into place. "*This* is what caused your rift."

"We had a fight," he continued, his voice breaking for the first time. His head dropped into his hands. "She told me how much my death wish was tormenting her, and that she couldn't stand by and watch me self-destruct. So she gave me an ultimatum — shape up, or go it alone. She left, and here I am, wrestling with the existential nausea that comes with a never-ending life. So there you have it. That's the rift."

I was at a loss for words. It was as if a vacuum had sucked all sound from the space, leaving only the raw, heavy weight of his confession. Zander's hands were trembling now, as they struggled to support his head.

In that moment, he resembled a man resigned to his own execution but impatiently waiting for the executioner who was running late. And it wasn't fear or apprehension that clouded his eyes: it was frustration, a quiet resentment towards the universe that wouldn't even grant him the courtesy of a straightforward exit. Keeping him around for its own unknowable reasons.

"This is the moment where you're supposed to console me," he rasped. "You know, talk about my redeeming qualities, the people who care about me. That sort of thing."

"I would. But what could I say that hasn't already been said? If even Blayde couldn't break through to you, what hope do I have?"

My eyes dropped to my hands, staring at the way they fidgeted on my lap.

He looked at me, his eyes pleading for something more — but I couldn't give it. This man had willingly unleashed chaos; he had crafted his own Pandora's box and laughed while opening it on himself. A part of me ached to feel sympathy for him, but another part — the bigger part — resisted. I couldn't, *I shouldn't*, feel bad for who he was, who he would become.

Yeah. Easier said than done. Especially when there's that call deep within you, to ensure life keeps on living. One that grew stronger every time you fought that fight yourself.

"Who even are you?" he demanded. "Why am I spilling my darkest secrets to you?"

"I've already told you. I'm a friend."

"A friend who seems uncannily good at letting me talk without interruption. You must know me quite well in my future. And you know Blayde, so we must eventually make peace, and I must go on — living this life, as one might loosely term it. To be honest, I don't think I can stand another minute with myself, let alone an eternity."

My silence stretched on, filling the room like an uninvited guest. He sighed, exasperated.

"Smart choice," he acknowledged. "Why waste comfort on a killer? I'm sick of wars, yet they're inescapable. It's like the universe uses me as its own personal chess piece, directing the outcome of conflict after conflict. Countless millennia of death and destruction takes its toll, you know. Being alone with the monster I've become is a torture I wouldn't wish on my worst enemy. So, if you really are a friend from the future, could you try, just try, to make this wretched existence feel a bit more bearable?"

The air was thick with the magnitude of his request. He wasn't just asking for consolation; he was asking for a reason to endure his never-ending life — a life that had, by his own admission, gone off the rails. What could I even say to that?

The desperation in his voice was palpable, stripping away the layers of the battle-hardened soldier, the unfeeling killer, to reveal the fragile core of a man. A man who had been riding the cosmic roller coaster for an eternity, each loop-de-loop unraveling him more, each climb and fall tearing at his soul.

"I know you," I said softly, but firmly. "Or at least, I know a future version of you. He revels in the novelty of new worlds, cherishes the little things. He and Blayde have reconciled. At the very least, let me share with you that hope."

"Hope?" His eyes went wide. "It sounds as if I've been lobotomized."

"Don't trivialize it," I snapped. "That future you — that's resilience. That's change. The road ahead is neither short nor smooth, but I can assure you it's there. A future where you're… happier."

"You sound far from convincing." He eyed me warily. "And there's something else — something that's making you hold back. What is it? What have I done?"

"You took a life," I said.

He sighed, exasperated. "Of course, I did. My romantic history reads like a Trajurian tragedy. The last person I was involved with was out to avenge their father's death, and guess who they found out was responsible? Me. And that wasn't even the first time that happened to me. So, who did I kill in your life?"

The weight of his words hung heavily between us. This wasn't just a man who had fought wars; this was a man who had become a war, wreaking havoc on everyone who dared love him. The enormity of his flawed existence filled the room, becoming almost a third presence, pressing down on both of us. Would the future version of this man be worth all this pain? Could he ever truly change? I was running out of answers, but the questions were piling up.

"My brother, John." My mind raced — what would he say? What *could* he say? Could he truly understand the depth of what this meant to me? "Though you knew him as Provis."

His voice came out in a shuddering exhale. "Your brother is Provis, destroyer of worlds? The Butcher of the Qua'atzi quadrant, the Reaper of Coxilihan?"

I let out a low breath. So he hadn't been lying about that. I stared down at my lap, at James' orb glowing its gentle green.

"My brother is John Webber," I muttered, each word heavy. "He never did any of those things. Yet you sure seemed certain he would, when you snapped his neck."

"Would...?" Zander's eyes remained wide, unblinking. "It took years to finally end him, excruciating years. He was intelligent and pitiless, a machine programmed for annihilation. Why would anyone mourn him? Who would lament the end of a man bent on genocide?"

"He was bent on nothing. All he wanted was to go home." The words, so cold and factual, tore at me. "He'd been abducted as a teen, forced into the Alliance's child hire program. We had just saved him from Planet Nope. We brought down the Sters. He was ready to come home to Earth. And you killed him."

As I spoke, Zander's eyes widened, as though he were seeing something in me he hadn't noticed before.

"Impossible. If I killed him… then how do *I* remember killing him?"

I wanted to rip out my hair. "I was about to ask you the same question. If timelines are immutable, then how do we both have memories of events that contradict each other? It's a paradox."

Zander's face paled. "No," he whispered. "This is impossible. Do you realize what this means? My future self has done something incomprehensible, something fundamentally against the very fabric of existence. I have broken time itself. The Pythanoreans—"

He flew to his feet, hands flying to his cradle his head, panting as if he'd run a marathon.

"Yeah, them," I interrupted, but he seemed to have slipped into a full-blown panic. "I know, I know, they're supposed to clean up the mess. But if we still remember everything, then they haven't acted yet, now have they?"

"The Pythanoreans," he practically shouted, his eyes wild with terror. "Guardians of the cosmic fabric, keepers of the timelines. They're going to come after me!"

"You're *scared* of them?"

He gripped his hair, his knuckles white. "The cosmic entities that safeguard the integrity of time and space?

You can't fathom what they're capable of! We're talking about beings that can erase you from existence, eliminate entire timelines—"

"So you're finally acknowledging there's a problem. It's about time."

"You don't understand. If I've caused a paradox, it's wrinkled their perfect little universe. They will—"

"If you're that worried about justice, what about the wrong you've done to others? What about my brother? If you're so scared of breaking time, what about breaking lives?"

"They're going to *exile me from Time!*"

Silence fell over us like a dropped sheet. I stared at him, at this younger Zander. I knew this man so intimately, yet not at all. And in both versions of this man, I had never once seen him so terrified.

"Sally," he said. "Seventh-dimensional beings don't mess around. The only reason they've left me alone so far is that I don't cause ripples. I don't look at the timeline. I don't use time to change my actions. I provide the occasional craft liquor for their never-ending party. If my future self was dumb enough to create a paradox, none of that matters. I will be ripped out of the universe and my existence smoothed over."

"Right. The party," I muttered incredulously, as though that were the most improbable part of his rambling. But then again, we were talking about cosmic unicorns. I pinched the bridge of my nose, trying to wrap my head around it.

"Why aren't you panicking? Everything I've ever done or will do — gone! And it's not going to be a party with champagne and balloons. It'll be nothingness, void. End of story, end of Zander. Do you get that?" His voice wavered, teetering on the edge of a complete breakdown.

I barked out a laugh, one devoid of real humor. "You've just spent the last ten minutes telling me how you wished you'd never existed, how your life is a constant loop of regret. Isn't this what you wanted? Won't they be doing you a favor?"

The muscles in his jaw tightened, and I saw something in his eyes flicker. Not anger, not quite that, but an ember of something deeply human.

"You don't get it, Sally. There's a difference between wanting an end to your existence and wanting to have never existed at all. I made a difference, once, in lives that mattered. I tried to leave the universe in a better state than when I found it. I can't leave Blayde to escape from the Institute alone. I can't…"

His voice cracked on the last sentence, and it stopped me dead in my tracks. I looked at him, really looked, and realized just how incredibly complex this man was. A walking paradox, a jumble of contradictions — and yet, in that moment, it all made sense.

His words hung heavy in the air, like a dense fog that neither of us could navigate through. My mind began to churn, conjuring up a universe without Zander. No more trips to distant galaxies where we set right what was once wrong. No more instances of him charming some alien council into avoiding a devastating war. I saw the faces of countless beings who'd been touched by his interventions, the communities we'd aided, the civilizations we'd nudged away from the brink. I remembered the stories I'd heard, stories that painted him as a roving cosmic hero, a man who came from the stars to make every planet he touched a little brighter.

I remembered what it felt like to admire him, to look up to him, and yes — to love him. That love, which had been eroded by anger, bitterness, and betrayal, rose like a tidal wave, catching me unprepared. For the first time, I allowed myself to feel the full force of it. And it was overwhelming.

My eyes blurred, and tears slipped down my cheeks before I could stop them. I felt a hand on my shoulder and looked up to see Zander's face, his eyes searching, alarmed. But it wasn't about him, not really. It was about the love that had been stifled, shoved into the corner of my heart, a love that had been so powerful, so overwhelming, that it had become unbearable.

In that moment, I missed him. I missed us. I missed the man he was and the woman I had been when I was with him. The ache of it, so acute, filled the air between us, and for a second, it felt like he had already been erased, like he was already gone. Like he had died, and I was left grappling with a void so enormous it could consume me.

I turned away, pressing my hands against my face, trying to get a grip on the torrent of emotions. But my voice betrayed me, coming out as a whisper, choked and raw. "It feels like you've already been erased, like you've already died. And I don't know how to exist in a world where you never lived."

My mouth filled with chlorine as I spoke the words to a resort swimming pool.

NINE

BEHIND THE MUSIC:
UNPLUGGED AND UNDERWATER

MY SCREAM FIZZLED OUT LIKE A WET FIREWORK as I tried to evict the water that had taken a detour into my lungs. The chlorine assaulted my nostrils, threatening a hostile takeover of my brain, and I made a mental note to always jump to and from solid ground from now on.

Out of nowhere I was swept out of the pool and into a splashy, dramatic rescue by a set of muscular arms straight out of a glam rock music video. With a wet thunk, I dropped the orb onto the sunbaked tiles, watching it roll off like a petulant child avoiding bath time.

"Breathe, Sally, breathe!" The voice was urgent, tinged with a melodramatic flair that could only belong to one person.

I pushed against the hands that were all but performing a drum solo on my chest. "I'm okay, I'm okay!" I spluttered, still coughing up the last remnants of pool water. I blinked the water from my eyes. "Magnesar?"

I hadn't immediately recognized my rescuer through the haze of chlorine, but there was no mistaking that hair, that mane of green with ski-slope striping, though the last time I'd seen him it had been shorn to the scalp. He was climbing out of his crouch, soaking wet from head to toe, as Sunan stared, hands on his hips.

"You alright there?" Sunan looked concerned, though the effect was somewhat hampered by his oversized aviators. Honestly, I was half convinced he wore those sunglasses just to hide the fact that he was often as clueless as the rest of us.

Magnesar flicked his damp hair back with a dramatic flourish. "Asks the man who almost let her drown." He shook off the water droplets from his extravagant bubblegum pink coat, which seemed to defy the rules of both fashion and practicality given the heat.

"She *can't* drown!" Sunan groaned. "There's no need to play the hero."

Ignoring him, Magnesar sashayed over to me, arms spread wide like he was about to start a concert. "Sally!" he exclaimed, his voice a melody of excitement and dramatic flair. "How good it is to see you! I was trying to plan the perfect reunion when you fell into the water."

I couldn't help but smile as he helped me to my feet. "Magnesar, what are you doing here on Earth? Not that it's not amazing to see you, but... Earth?"

"I've come for you, Sally cakes," he beamed, his teeth sparkling almost as much as his hair. "You vanished before the grand celebration. I simply had to make sure you were groovy."

I shuffled uncomfortably. "I had... things to sort out. But it's amazing to see you, Magnesar—"

"Spurlock, please." He corrected me gently, a mischievous twinkle in his eye. "After all we've been through, we're past formalities, aren't we?"

"Right, Spurlock." I nodded. He was right, but it felt strangely intimate, stepping out of his persona and into something more... personal. "Your hair? How?"

He laughed, a sound that was music in itself. "You *know* the moment I returned to Pyrina my stylist team was on a mission to restore my signature look. Needed something familiar after all that chaos." He shook his head, sending his striped, green locks cascading around his shoulders.

The initial surprise of seeing Spurlock here on Earth slowly morphed into a warm fuzzy feeling. Despite the oddity of it all, it was genuinely good to see him.

Sunan cleared his throat. "So? Was your mission a success?"

"I did it," I declared with exhausted triumph. "I switched them out. James should be okay."

"You did?" Sunan lifted his head to look off in the direction the orb had rolled. "Just now? That explains the sudden apparition of clothes."

He hadn't even noticed I'd been missing. Sure, I was getting sidetracked by the American Revolution and interstellar frat parties, but other than that my aim was extremely good. Falling into the pool had been dumb on my part, but not a miscalculation.

It was only then that I realized the glowing blue panda hovering over the pool hadn't reacted to any of this.

"Clyde?" I called out, waving my hands as if he were a distant ship I was trying to signal. "Earth to Clyde, come in, Clyde!"

His silence was eerie. He was normally so chatty, especially when I didn't want him to be. He hadn't said a word since I'd left the frat party with Zander. Since when did Clyde have an off switch?

"There's no one there, Sally…" Magnesar said carefully, turning to stare at the spot where Clyde was floating. "Unless… frash. Are they invisible to the human eye? Hello! Sorry to have been rude!"

"Sorta," I replied, my eyes fixed on Clyde. He looked fresh out of the box, so to speak: emotionless, staring straight ahead, all his limbs pressed close to his body. "Clyde is — was? — my emotional support AI. I'm the only one who can see him. But I think I broke him."

"No way, Sally cakes, you got a Gryniokiian AI?" Magnesar whistled. "Those things are programmed to handle just about anything, how did yours crash? You introduce them to teen drama?"

I cringed: little did he know.

Sunan scratched his head, clearly out of his depth. "If he's an AI, maybe he's processing something? Or... do AIs meditate? Or on strike! Do you think AIs form unions?"

I shook my head. "I don't think it's any of those things. Clyde's never acted like this before. It's like he's completely shut down." Shame rolled over me as it hit me just how much crap I must have put him through to have shorted his motherboard.

But I had more pressing things to worry about than Clyde. The safety of James's orb trumped all else. I pivoted, my gaze locking onto the gleaming object resting on the manicured lawn. It had come to a gentle stop, so ordinary, almost as if it hadn't just been the epicenter of a not-exactly surgical time maneuver.

Out of the corner of my eye, I could see Clyde follow, but instead of his usual panda-like gambol, he was floating eerily along. It felt like having a balloon tethered to me, gliding just above the ground, silently trailing in my wake. Except far less festive.

I nestled the orb delicately against my chest, feeling its faint pulse. It was alive, in its own unique way, and the weight of responsibility sat heavy in my arms.

"What is that?" asked Spurlock, eyes growing wide.

"This is my friend James." I shifted the orb over a little. It wasn't the easiest thing to carry. "Or at least, it should be. I've got to bring her to Meedian. If anyone's got a lead on how to untangle this mess and help get James into a physical body, it's him."

Spurlock let out a low whistle. "Frash, Sally cakes. You don't take a break, do ya?"

My face felt red. He wasn't wrong. I'm sure if Clyde was active, he would have said something about this, too. "Rest is for people who have time on their side. Unfortunately, time and I have a complicated relationship."

"Right then!" Spurlock nodded. "Let's not dawdle. I may not be much help with the technical stuff, but where there's a will, there's a way. Onward!"

He spun on his heels and marched away from the pool. He might have been out of his element, but his willingness to dive headfirst into the unknown was oddly comforting.

"I bet you're busy," I said to Sunan. "Don't worry about me, ok?"

Sunan rolled his eyes, a smirk pulling at the corner of his mouth. "Oh, absolutely. Because, obviously, there's a lot on my calendar that trumps rescuing a sentient being from an extraterrestrial storage device." He glanced at me up and down, shaking his head. "But, priority numero uno: procuring a towel. Trust me, once you hit AC, you'll turn into an icicle."

· · · · · · · · ● · · · · · · · · ·

"I NEVER THOUGHT I'D GET THE CHANCE TO SAY this to someone, but do you know how dangerous it is to mess with time?"

SINGULARITY

We were in Meedian's office, several shades darker — and I'm not just talking about the décor — than his public-facing office or even for his offworlder public. This wasn't the kind of room for greeting visiting dignitaries or engaging in diplomatic niceties. It had the aesthetic of a cross between a space-age bunker and your grandma's moth-infested attic. Brimming with gadgets and gizmos, many pulsating with ethereal lights and enough lens flares to be worthy of a JJ Abrams movie, this space was meant for deals darker than a black hole. His inner sanctum.

I'd changed back into my clothes, ditching the wet skirt and bikini for something warmer, something that could hold me together when I felt I might shatter from the inside out.

"And what is he doing here?" Meedian continued without looking up. Sunan, Spurlock, and I occupied a plush bench behind him that seemed to adapt to our forms, offering comfort on a cellular level. Clyde hovered in the back corner of the room, always slightly northwest of me no matter what I did or where I went. His silence was simultaneously a relief and terribly eerie.

However, this coziness did little to diminished our shared sense of waiting in the kitchen for our mother to reprimand us. Said mother being Meedian, fretting not over a hot stove, but over the green orb that I hoped contained an uncorrupted James Felling. As he tinkered with the artifact using instruments that seemed more magic than science, he made soothing hums and gentle mutterings, as if coaxing the orb to reveal its secrets.

"Spurlock?" I asked, since nobody else was talking. "He's a friend. Long story short, we were trapped as human hamsters for a while. It wasn't pretty. Anyway, he's decided to come Earthside for a visit."

"But our trauma bond is strong. And I owe Sally a power ballad." Magnesar beamed at Meedian, who only offered him a cursory glance. "I'm honestly surprised you haven't heard of me. Come on, I won nineteen Ziggies! I know Earth is a pre-contact world, but my music transcends interstellar vacuums."

My fingers interlaced in a tight clasp, almost white-knuckled. Deep inside of me, I knew that the split second I looked away, I'd miss something.

Keeping my eyes locked on the orb, I responded, injecting as much assurance into my tone as I could muster. "Look, I didn't rewrite time or anything. I kept everything as it was. No one, not a single soul, noticed a thing." Unless you counted Zander and Benjamin Franklin, but that was a problem for another day. "If I hadn't, would we even be having this conversation?"

Meedian let out a deep, throaty harrumph, his patience fraying at the edges. "How many times must we even *have* this conversation? Time is—"

"Still unclear!" I threw my hands up in the air. "No unicorns yet, right? If they're even bothered."

Meedian dropped his tools and turned, staring me square in the eyes, his gaze so cold it turned my spine to ice. "Don't tempt the Pythanoreans," he sneered. "It's best not to poke the bear. Or in this case, the horned equine gods. They don't appreciate being underestimated. It's nothing to them and everything to you, and that's the whole point."

"Gods again?" I scoffed. "Please. Everyone's giving them too much credit."

"They're as good as," he replied, coolly.

Sunan cleared his throat. "Look, we've managed to avoid unicorn Armageddon so far—"

"I may have come at a bad time—" Spurlock squeaked.

"—which means Sally's touch on time has been... let's say, delicate enough. We have James's orb. Let's keep the timeline untouched, and everyone's happy, right?"

"Yes, and no." Meedian dropped his tools and let out a heavy sigh. "I'm sorry, Sally, but the orb... it's already started to decay."

My heart sank through the floor, though the very core of the Earth, back out the other side, and still kept going.

"It... no, it can't be." I rushed to the orb as if it was James sleeping on the table, as if I could see her body again, as if it was her in the cave in the heart of Miro's temple dying in my arms all over again. "I got it just after Blayde dropped it off. Just after the funeral. Her mind couldn't have been in there for more than a week, tops. It can't already be empty!"

And yet, in the back of my mind, I remembered Miro warning us this could happen. That the orb wasn't meant to hold a human, someone who wasn't a part of their hive mind. I choked back a sob, fists clenched so tightly that the nails dug into my palms, leaving crescent moon imprints. *Well, shit.*

Sunan furrowed his brow. "You know, this might actually simplify the whole paradox mess. I've been wracking my brain. If you exchanged the deteriorating orb for a pristine one, then when did the original actually start to decay? To be consistent, it would've had to start breaking down outside your intervention. Otherwise, it's like the chicken and egg scenario: which came first? The decay would have had to start outside of your loop, in order for all this to make sense."

I groaned, rubbing my temples. Dabbling in the intricacies of time was like trying to untangle the world's most complicated knot with both hands tied behind your back. And this? This was supposed to be a simple swap.

Just… to save my friend.

"Sunan… not now," said Meedian, calmer than I'd ever heard him.

I was starting to wish Clyde was here with his reassuring procedurally generated nonsense, but no, he was still stuck in limbo. My fingers grazed the cool surface of the workbench, eyes locked onto the orb's shimmering green hue. I half hoped that I might see a hint of James within, like some animated heroine might use sheer willpower to summon a trapped spirit. Spurlock put a warm arm around me, and I found myself leaning into it. This was the same arm that comforted me as we escaped the sweat farm, and the relief was strong and familiar. The scent of him — a peppery musk barely masked by the synthetic freshness of high-tech fabric — filled my senses. It was the smell of safety.

"When you say it's started to decay," I began, "is there enough of James in there to mount a rescue mission? What about those shadowy associates of yours, with their black market tech? Can they do anything?"

Meedian sighed deeply, like a deflating balloon if that balloon had seen too many things. "It's... tricky. The lattice is vacant, but it's not a total write-off. Some whiz kid with the right tools might be able to reverse engineer whatever essence James left behind. The real question is whether my contacts are feeling charitable... or if they've just had a good lunch."

"So you're saying there's a chance." Spurlock spoke when I could not.

I raised my eyes to Meedian's, attempting my best intense, unwavering gaze. "I don't care who you need to call or what price I need to pay. I'll find a way to make it happen."

He looked like he was about to interject, perhaps with a reminder about the dangers of underworld dealings or to question my commitment to future offspring. But then, the most mundane noise interrupted the weight of the moment — my phone buzzed. A little ding in a room that seemed too advanced to recognize such a sound. It could've been a message about a shoe sale or a meme from a friend, but given Meedian's suddenly sharpened focus, I doubted it.

"This room is more sealed off than a paranoid squirrel's nut stash," he muttered. "How on this or any other planet do you still have a signal?"

Figuring out why my phone retained its peculiar habit of working in places and times it had no business functioning in was a lot like trying to explain why I prefer mismatched socks or how I once mistook a ferret for a very fluffy snake: It's complicated, and I didn't even know myself. So, instead of diving into a monologue, I simply cleared my throat, looked at Meedian, then Sunan, then Spurlock, and with an eloquent "uh..." I shifted my attention to the unexpected message.

Customer support. Them again? The text was straightforward, devoid of emojis or the kind of flair one might expect from, say, a technologically adept millennial: just another pin.

"An address in Portland?" Squinting, I read it aloud, hesitating as if the address might spontaneously transform into a comprehensible sentence upon repetition. Alas, it did not. I turned the screen towards Meedian. "Recognize this place at all?"

"Port land? An entire land of ports?" Spurlock's eyes practically sparkled. "This planet is full of wonders!"

Meedian leaned in, ignoring the rockstar, adjusted the monocle he wasn't wearing, and frowned. "Can't say that I do. Then again, my Earth geography stops being reliable around 1969."

"That's... illuminating." I placed the phone beside the orb, which, now that I thought about it, was like parking a bicycle next to a spaceship. "This is my second mystery text of the day. The first one sent me right to… well, you."

Sunan sidled up, scrutinizing the text. "So it could equally be a friend… or a trap."

Stepping out of the shielded confines of the room, I hastily fired up the Google app. After pecking in the address, the virtual curtain lifted to reveal... *Repairium*, an electronics supply and repair shop. The digital facade boasted a commendable four-star rating and a smattering of reviews ranging from "My toaster is reborn!" to "The cashier gives solid relationship advice." Nothing overtly offworlder about them at first glance. Well, that, or they were as talented at hiding their offworld identity as they were at electronics repair.

Huh. Maybe this had all been a complicated advertisement for an elaborate customer service.

"I'll investigate," I declared, securing James's orb within the embrace of Dad's faded bowling bag. Customer Support had sent me to Meedian when I needed him most: who's to say they weren't sending me to the very person who could fix James? Or maybe… I glanced back at Clyde, frozen in the corner of my eye.

Maybe this was a Clyde thing? Either way, it was worth a shot.

"Again, Sally, it might be a trap," said Sunan, his eyes boring into mine.

I raised an eyebrow. "Those texts... they've been pretty accurate so far, haven't they?"

"You got *one* good one. Who's to say this one is even from the same person?"

"No one good should be handing out my address," said Meedian, arms crossed. "No one should know I'm even here."

"Look, if this is some long con, it's a weirdly detailed one," I countered. "They should at least bank on a few positive experiences to lull me into a false sense of security, right? In any case… I've got to know. Either it's help or it's a trap. And I've faced traps before." I inhaled deeply, like a puffer fish psyching itself up for a showdown. "Well, it's been lovely seeing you all again. I'll keep you in the loop about any progress."

"Sally, you're not thinking of leaving without backup, are you?" Spurlock turned to look back at Meedian and Sunan, searching for his own flavor of backup. "How many times must everyone remind you this could be, and most likely is, a trap?"

Ready to leap into action — or more aptly, away from this intervention — I paused, gritting my teeth so hard I could almost hear my enamel filing a complaint for workplace harassment. I had been ready to jump away even before he'd started to try and convince me otherwise, but a more pressing problem came to mind — *Zander*. Or more accurately, my accidental detours to visit with the colonial era version of him.

Shit. Jumping to Portland was off the table.

"I wouldn't let any of you offer to throw yourselves into that kind of danger for me," I said, glancing from one to the other.

"I'm not offering." Meedian threw his hands up. "I have much more important work here. A theme park doesn't build itself."

"I'm offering," said Sunan. "I mean, if you don't mind."

"I don't mind," I shot back quicker than a hiccup. "I'd like the company, actually. Especially if we're road tripping."

"Road tripping?" Meedian raised an eyebrow. "You. *Driving.* Why in the great black abyss would you waste your carbon footprint like that?"

"Currently a little jumping impaired," I said, trying to shrug it off like it was nothing. "I'll rent a car. Or we can fly! I haven't been on a plane in ages. Easy peasy."

Meedian crossed his arms over his chest. "Sunan, I do need you here."

"Even for Sally?" Now it was Sunan's turn to cross his arms.

Meedian shook his head and gestured at Spurlock. "You there. You said you were visiting Earth, right? What better way than to road trip with your friend? Long conversations! So many landscapes!"

"That sounds incredible!" Spurlock clapped his hands with apparent glee. "Adventure! This time, without monsters at our heels. I like the sound of that." I wasn't quite sure how I liked the sound, but it was Spurlock, and it was better than going into the unknown completely alone.

Sunan nudged Meedian in the ribs, apparently hard enough to reach through the costume to his real body below, as he emitted a noise somewhere between a grunt and a whimper.

"No. Not going to happen. Those are for official employees only," he said to Sunan.

"Aren't *I* an official employee?"

"But this isn't official park business, is it?" Meedian's tone was gruff.

Sunan frowned like a child told his pet unicorn was actually a donkey with a party hat. "Sally is family. That's as official as it gets, right?"

Mumbling and muttering, Meedian retreated like a grizzly bear into the cozy den of his back office. I exchanged a glance with Sunan, hoping for an explanation, but he only smiled, waiting, arms crossed the whole time.

Finally, Meedian emerged, flinging a small, silvery object at Sunan with the disgruntled finesse of a cat knocking over a water glass. "Here. But if she breaks it, you're buying it — that's coming out of your salary."

"Will somebody tell me what's going on here?" I asked.

SINGULARITY

Sunan, with the flourish of a magician revealing his final trick, held aloft the small silvery object — car keys that glittered with the promise of untold adventures. "Ladies and gentlemen, we've got ourselves a chariot."

TEN

WHEN THE BUS IS A ROCKIN', IT'S PROBABLY ABOUT TO TAKE OFF

CALLING IT A CHARIOT WAS AS GENEROUS AS A billionaire donating a single pair of socks to charity: ambitious yet glaringly off the mark. Our VW bus bore a striking resemblance to the Mystery Machine — if Scooby-Doo and the gang had ever decided to trade in psychedelic for practical. The van's once-vibrant hues were like a tie-dyed shirt that had been washed too many times, now just shy of pastel. It squatted behind Meedian's half-built resort with the grace of a retro gargoyle amongst a haphazard parade of modern sedans and motorbikes that seemed to be smirking at the bus's old age.

"Wish I could be going with you." Sunan brandished the keys, the metal jingling a clumsy melody that cut through the air as his steps grew bouncier. "This baby is a dream to drive."

"Sunan," I said, biting my lip. The modesty of our vehicle did little to reassure me. It was hard to picture driving this thing cross-country, let alone it staying intact the entire trip. "I don't know… is that thing roadworthy?"

"Not really." He let out a laugh. "But spaceworthy, for sure."

"*Space*?" I was unable to contain my snort. "This old thing? This is a spaceship?"

"Sally, I think I love your planet," said Magnesar, rushing to the bus as if to give it a hug. "Even your shuttles are groovy."

"Just this one, I think," said Sunan. "The indigenous ones are a lot more streamlined."

"So the company car is a VW… spaceship." I tried to keep my voice level. "What was Meedian planning on doing, offering space flights along with free continental breakfast?"

I clambered into the bus, warmth blooming in my cheeks as the claustrophobic cocoon of retro vibes wrapped around me. The interior was decked out like a hippie's daydream — shag rug that had seen better days, a bean bag chair that slouched with the wisdom of the '60s, and a faint smell of incense mixed with motor oil that probably counted as a feature.

"It started off as a personal project, actually," said Sunan as I explored. "The previous owner thought he'd stumbled on a vintage fixer-upper for hipster road-trippers. Little did he know that it was less about fixing rust and more about recalibrating the flux capacitor."

"Flux capacitor?" I echoed skeptically.

"Figuratively speaking. Though I wouldn't be surprised if this thing ran on good vibes and '60s folk music."

My eyes roamed over the interior, the beanbag chair, the psychedelic shag carpet which vibrated along with the hum of extraterrestrial technology. It made slightly more sense than a blue police box. "I guess back then, if your van was rocking, it might just be because you were literally taking off."

"Exactly." He laughed. "It was apparently a great time for offworlder tourism, thanks to the natural camouflage the hippies offered and the many similarities between the two communities. Love for the cosmos, communal living, experimental... botany."

I raised an eyebrow. "Is that why it smells faintly of... incense in here?"

Sunan laughed again.

"In any case," he said, leaning through the driver's door and pointing to the dashboard. He tapped a button, frowned, and slammed the dash hard with his fist. A whole new control panel dropped out the bottom. "Please let me say this, because I always wanted to — Sally, where you're going, you don't need roads."

I scanned the new dashboard, anxiety rising in my chest as I took in the multiple buttons and controls I had never needed to use in a car before. Thankfully, cruise control smiled up at me in nice, friendly letters. Sunan gestured to a dock for my phone; seems navigation would be as easy as opening a map app.

"What about landing, though?" I asked, turning to Sunan. "I mean, it's not every day a VW bus descends from the heavens in Portland."

"Actually, from what I've heard about Portland, they'll probably think it's performance art." He shrugged. "We just have to hope the sky's blue enough. Thankfully, governments don't care about objects this size. We're just a blip on a radar. Not even worth investigating."

"That explains the paint job," I muttered, feigning a calm I did not feel.

"That's your takeaway?" Sunan patted the driver's seat. "I really wish I could come with you, but duty calls. Take good care of this thing, though. And... of yourself."

"Will do, Sunan." Our gazes locked. "You know, you've been an unexpected rock in all this chaos." My hands tightened reflexively around the steering wheel.

He chuckled lightly, the sound buoying my heart. "Isn't that what friends are for?" His shades obscured his eyes, but I could almost picture the teasing glint in them as he cocked his head playfully, hinting at a wink.

A flush of warmth bloomed across my cheeks. "It's just... odd, you know?" My words tumbled out more candidly than intended. "I knew it, in my head, that you and my future self would get to know each other. But it's one thing to know it and another thing to feel it. It's bizarre, realizing there's a version of me out there, in some lost chapter, that knows you just as well."

Sunan paused, a shadow of something more profound flickering across his features. He extended a hand, a gesture of comfort, perhaps, but let it fall shy of contact, respecting the space between us. "Take it as a sign that you haven't destroyed time yet. This friendship withstands the test of timelines."

A laugh, short and sharp, escaped me. "I can't wrap my head around half of what's happening, but that? That I'll take."

He slapped the roof twice. "Just take it easy, Sally. You've got this."

I buckled up out of habit, placing the bowling bag behind my seat. As I straightened back up, I shuddered — Clyde. He was floating there, the same two meters away as he had been since I'd fallen into that stupid pool, just… drifting. Always slightly northwest of me, his expression blank.

One problem at a time, Sally. I adjusted the rearview mirror to block him out as best I could.

"Right," I said. "Spurlock, front seat, buckle up."

"You got it, Captain Sally!" He fastened his seatbelt with an exaggerated click. "I am only slightly disappointed I won't see the delightful scenery of your world."

I turned the key in the ignition, bringing the engine to life in a symphony of coughs and sputters — a mechanical beast awakening from a long slumber. It read my phone, then beeped cheerfully. Before I could react, it was already driving out of the parking lot, leaving Sunan to wave goodbye.

It didn't take us to the highway, instead it traveled deeper into the construction area. Then, in a move that scoffed in the face of physics, the VW spaceship floored its gas pedal. The world tilted on its axis, and suddenly, we were not driving; we were soaring. The landscape below shrank into a patchwork quilt. My fingers clutched the seat, knuckles whiter than the clouds we were now acquaintances with.

I settled back, the thrum of the VW spaceship lulling me into a sense of adventure. I tried to relax in it, to look up at the blue sky rather than at the rapidly shrinking land beneath us. But it was easier said than done, as the blue sky was no longer the soft blue but a darker shade, threatening to drown me whole.

Deep breaths, Sally Webber. You've been through worse. This time, you have a car.

Well, a car from the 1960s. Which was also a spaceship from the 1960s. What was the mileage on this thing?

"Outta Atmo!" Spurlock let out a low whistle. "You alright there, Sally cakes?"

I took a deep breath. "Just a little…"

If only my emotional support AI was here to help me through this uncomfortable situation. Except he was, but still hovering out of the corner of my eye, expressionless and silent outside in the big blue sky.

"Afraid of heights?" Spurlock asked, closing his eyes sympathetically. "I know that feeling. I myself fear empty rooms."

"No, no, it's ok." *Exhale. Deep, calming breaths.* "It's just that most of the times I've been in shuttles this size, they've ended up crashing."

"Ah. Well, now you've reminded me of a phobia I should be nurturing," he said with a shudder.

The bus pressed on. The retro interior was oddly comforting despite the abyss outside the windows.

Focus on the beanbags, Sally. Focus on the beanbags. The autopilot can handle the rest.

"Spurlock, what are you really doing here?" I asked, unable to steep in silence any longer. "You're not just on vacation, are you?"

Spurlock shifted in his seat, his gaze flickering to the passing scenery. "Ah, Sally," he began, "who doesn't need a vacation after what we've just been through?"

I, for one, didn't. "Come on, Spurlock. Out with it."

He let out a long breath, his shoulders slumping in resignation. "Sally, darling, when you bolted from Planet Nope before the celebrations even kicked off, I knew something was up. You should have been the life of the party! Or at least, the after-party."

Shit. I hadn't thought about the aftermath — or -party. The Siblings always jumped away once their job was done to avoid awkward questions. I hadn't considered we might actually get a hero's treatment this time.

"It was just too much." The words came out way quieter than I wanted them to. "Everything happened so fast, and then suddenly, it was over. I needed... space."

Spurlock nodded. "Space, you say? Well, now you've got the literal kind!" He gestured grandly to the world rushing by outside our windows. "But in all seriousness, I'm here for you, Sally Cakes. Plus, I relish the opportunity to visit Earth. It's not every day you get to be anonymous, especially not when you're as famous as I am."

I chuckled, despite the tension knotting in my stomach. When I'd first met Magnesar, I'd found his ego grating: now, I could see his confidence was honest and earned. "Well, with your hair, this won't be as low key as you were hoping for, I'm sure."

Spurlock laughed, running a hand through his vibrant locks. "Ah, my dear Sally, you underestimate the power of a good hat! But yes, anonymity might be a bit of a stretch. However, I'm more interested in the cultural exchange. Earth music has always fascinated me. So raw, so... emotive. It's like everyone's singing about their ex or their dog or their... truck?"

"That's a rather... narrow view of Earth music." I raised an eyebrow. "Where are you getting this information?"

He shrugged. "I've been studying up! Did you know there's a whole genre dedicated to people strumming on a piece of wood and wailing about heartbreak? And another where they talk really fast over beats about how many credits they have?"

I bit my lip to hold back a laugh. "Those would be country and… hip-hop, I think?"

"And don't get me started on your so-called classical music," Spurlock continued, his voice rising. "Hours upon hours of intricate compositions played by people dressed as birds! And the fans just sit there, quietly stewing. It's so… quiet! How can the musicians know if they're successfully evoking emotion if nothing is expressed?"

I snorted outright now. "Maybe so that the audience can properly hear the very thing that's meant to be giving them emotions?"

Spurlock grinned. "But truly, Sally, Earth's cultural landscape is rich and varied. I'm eager to dive in, absorb it all. Who knows, maybe I'll find inspiration for my next album. 'Spurlock, Earthside' — it has a nice ring to it, don't you think?"

"Sure does," I agreed. "Though didn't you want to write a rock opera about our experience on Planet Nope? How's that coming along?"

His shoulders slumped again. "It's coming."

"This trip isn't a distraction from writer's block, is it?" Do musicians get writer's block? Or is it called something else?

"It's missing… something," he said, nodding to himself. "Just like the heroic rescue."

He glanced over at me, and I felt a gentle accusation there. Nothing cruel, but a definite insistence that I should have been there. I warmed, slightly.

The VW hummed along as we chatted and laughed, our daunting mission momentarily forgotten. Earth music, with all its genres and quirks, seemed to have provided the perfect distraction for both of us. The closer we got to our destination, the more I felt a little lighter. A little more ready to face whatever was waiting for us there.

A little.

The bus beeped, and we began our descent, the blue sky reclaiming its territory from the darkness of space, the air growing thick around us. The world tilted once more, gravity embracing us in a familiar hug as the VW settled behind a grove of trees. From there it was just a hop and a skip onto the main road, the highway, and Portland.

The repair shop was part of a strip mall — the location the mysterious pin had led us to. It was a nondescript building, one that seemed to promise more than toasters and washing machines. I stepped out into the parking lot, my legs shaky from the transition between space and Earth. The air was humid, a stark contrast to the controlled atmosphere of the bus.

Spurlock joined me, stretching his limbs with a grin. "The final stretch," he said. "Ready to meet the elusive repairman of Portland?"

I nodded, readjusting the bowling bag over my shoulder. "Lead the way!"

We moved forward, the safely parked bus behind us, Clyde floating silently beside me, and the repair shop ahead — a beacon pulling us towards answers and, undoubtedly, towards more questions.

The Repairium shop front was as nondescript as they came — old-timey, crammed with the ghosts of gadgetry past. It was the kind of normal that screamed *trap* to my jittery senses. The neon sign flickered, the letters buzzing like an insistent whisper. They matched with Clyde, who was still, *still* drifting beside me. This was going to get tiring fast.

Spurlock made a noncommittal hum, his gaze fixed on the display of secondhand appliances that crowded the window. "It's too quiet. Too normal," he said.

"Like most shops." I gestured at the other ones that lined the street. It looked like any strip mall in North America, the Repairium nestled between a Jamba Juice and a pet store. Too bad the pin hadn't been a few meters to the right; I would be investigating adorable puppies right now.

The door jingled cheerily as we entered. Inside, it was like a museum of appliance history, the air tinged by the smell of dust and old rubber. Washers and dryers sat like ancient totems, microwaves lined up like books on a shelf, their cords trailing onto the floor like bookmarks.

"Can I help you?" The voice was unexpectedly gentle, almost lost amid the hum of a refrigerator showcasing its unwavering work ethic.

SINGULARITY

My eyes flicked to the clerk, and my feet froze in place. She was turned away, her stature unassuming, her attire blending with the rows of secondhand electronics. Then she turned, and for a second, I was sure my heart woke up just to skip a beat.

A face I hadn't seen in three years. A face covered with pimples-that-were-not-pimples, a face with too many eyes for a skin suit to contain. A face I hadn't seen since we'd drunkenly made crop circles together, the night before my best friend's wedding.

"Rochelle?" The name came out as half whisper, half disbelief. And by the look on her face, I wasn't wrong.

There was a beat, where only the buzzing of the neon sign filled the space between us. Her brown eyes met mine, and the skin suit did its best to keep up, hiding the extraocular hints. Her mouth opened, but nothing came out, so she shut it again. The two of us stared at each other, communicating like fish, with Spurlock watching in silence by the door.

"Sally. It's been a while." She cleared her throat. "I heard you were… no matter. What are you doing here?"

Rochelle had been one of Robin's friends, back when they'd been Taylor, before they'd dumped me and left me to fend for myself in the middle of the ocean during an alien invasion. No matter, that wasn't Rochelle's problem: she was just another offworlder, a part of their expat friend group, just trying to fit in on Earth.

"It's been a while. Oh, um, this is Spurlock," I said, the introduction slipping out awkwardly as I gestured towards my silent companion. His hand raised in a half wave, met with a polite nod from Rochelle, her many hidden eyes assessing him in a blink.

"A pleasure," said Spurlock, brandishing a wide grin.

"Any friend of Sally's…" Her voice trailed off. Maybe she realized that perhaps we weren't exactly friends anymore. Not in the traditional sense, anyway.

"I need your help with something," I said, licking my lips, which had suddenly turned to parchment. James's orb felt like a leaden weight in the bowling bag that was threatening to slip from my sweat-slicked shoulder. "I, um…"

She raised an eyebrow. "Your AI's throwing a tantrum, huh?"

I did a double take, staring at Clyde then back at her. "How could you tell?"

Her lips curved into a half smile. "This isn't my first tech support call. You've been giving that empty corner of the shop the side-eye like it's full of ghosts. Give me the emitter?"

Reluctantly, I handed her the innocuous key chain. She inspected it, her fingertips dancing over its surface, and then — she squeezed it, tight. After a handful of awkward seconds, Clyde flickered out of existence.

"Thank you," I exhaled, a deluge of relief washing over me. It wasn't merely the absence of Clyde's intrusive neon blue aura; it was the ease with which Rochelle slipped back into the role of the friend I once knew, capable and kind.

Then guilt stabbed at me, deep and sharp. Did she just... *extinguish* Clyde? Despite his synthetic existence, he'd felt unnervingly real. A lump formed in my throat.

"Of course," Rochelle said nonchalantly, returning the now dormant device. "Sounds like you had him running on marathon mode. Next time he goes haywire, press and hold the power for ten seconds for a hard reset. Don't make a habit of it, though. Do it too much and you might find his personality... changing." She punctuated her words with a shrug. "It should be good now. Just flick it back on when you're ready."

My eyes widened as I stared at the key chain in my palm. "He has an off switch?"

Her laughter was a bright sound in the dim room. "Is this really what you came all the way to see me for? An off switch for your AI?"

I bit my lip, scanning the store. "Is it safe to talk here?" I murmured, half expecting to hear the walls whisper back.

She gestured towards a corner where a coffee pot sat like a proud, outdated sentinel. "Old walls keep secrets better than new ones," she assured.

She motioned for us to follow her behind a counter where the true heart of the shop beat — a workshop cluttered with tools and the guts of machines in various states of disassembly. It was here, amidst the innards of Earth's technology, that Rochelle's disguise as an appliance repair person was entirely credible.

"*Novalicious,*" Magnesar exhaled.

As we settled onto mismatched stools, Rochelle's expression turned serious. The silence stretched on as she studied me, a flicker of something unreadable in her eyes — eyes that had once gazed up at the stars from a crop circle, while we drunkenly lay beside each other, pondering the cosmos. Eyes that hadn't looked for me since, not until this unexpected reunion in a place reeking of metal and lost time.

"So *you're* customer support?" I ventured into the stillness, my voice barely audible above the hum of an ancient air conditioner.

"Suppose I could be?" She frowned. "Though that's a funny way of putting it."

"So you didn't send me the text?"

"A text?" The skin suit stretched tight over her pimples as her frown deepened. "I didn't even know you were on this planet, Sally. The last I heard, you were... well, that's ancient history now, isn't it? All pardoned and what not."

I nodded, feeling a pang of something akin to regret. The history between us felt like a chasm now, one that neither of us had time to bridge.

Worse than that, *she hadn't sent the text*. That would have been easy, a safe and wonderful answer to this mystery. But if she hadn't sent it, then who had? And why bring us back together?

My throat tickled, and I coughed, clearing it. "We're here because someone calling themselves Customer

Support sent us this address. We thought it was a lead… or a trap."

Rochelle's lips quirked up at that, a wry, knowing smile. "And you still walked in," she observed, her tone laced with something that sounded like respect. "Brave or foolish, I can't decide which."

"Both, probably." I allowed myself a short laugh.

"You never seemed the type to follow mysterious texts if you didn't know who sent them," she added. It was disarming how quickly the familiar banter came back, as if the years had been mere minutes.

"I'm a little desperate." I held up the bowling bag, placing it delicately on the workbench in front of me. She said nothing as I unzipped it, her eyes flashing wide as she took in the green, glowing glory. "I need your help saving James."

"James?" She reached for the orb, pulling back her hands at the last second. "*Our* James is in that thing?"

Right, she had known James. Not well, of course. James couldn't know Rochelle was alien, else things would get complicated. No, James was *Taylor's* friend, the brilliant agent trying to make sense of extraterrestrial activity on Earth, ignorant to the Agency pulling strings.

"She… I tried to save her," I explained. Once again the tears threatened to well up and break through, but I was getting more adept now at keeping them back.

Rochelle's hands hovered hesitantly over the orb's luminescent surface, the multiple concealed eyes on her face blinking in a rapid, rhythmic dance of concern. "How did James end up... like this?"

"It's a long story." I let out a breath, stopping myself from diving into the mess. "But the short version is that the orb was all we had on hand when... things got messy."

Her brow furrowed. "This is meant to carry a *hive mind*. To allow the multiple memories to reintegrate and merge. A single human mind would surely drown... unless..." She trailed off, her mind clearly racing through possibilities and probabilities that I couldn't hope to comprehend.

"Yeah, *unless* has become a regular part of my vocabulary these days." My fingers absentmindedly traced the cool, hard surface of the bag before I realized what I was doing and pulled back to let her work. "The hive mind made room for her. It should be just her in there, but the lattice decayed, and we don't know why. We need to get her out. To put her in a body."

That must have been why the mystery text sent us here. A repair shop, when I was holding the one thing that I couldn't bear to keep broken. My biggest failure.

Rochelle took a deep breath, the pimples on her face dimming and then brightening. With a resolute nod, she extended her ringed fingers and let them gently caress the orb. A hum filled the room, the kind of sound you feel in your bones rather than hear with your ears.

"Woah," said Spurlock. "Sorry. But that... did you feel that?"

The orb responded, its glow pulsating like a heartbeat syncing with Rochelle's touch. "I'm going to try and interface with it," she announced, her voice taking on a new edge of determination. "If there's a shred of James's consciousness in here, I might be able to communicate, or at least... assess the situation."

My eyes locked onto the orb, watching the play of light that seemed to dance between Rochelle's hands and the sphere. I thought of James, trapped somewhere within that small cosmos. Rochelle had to bring her back. She had to.

Rochelle's posture stiffened, her focus so intense it was almost tangible. Minutes stretched into an eternity as she worked in silence, save for the occasional whispered tone that seemed to harmonize with whatever the orb was giving off.

Suddenly, she snatched her hands back as if scorched. Her many eyes cringed in unison.

"She's gone," she gasped. "She's gone."

The room tilted as if reality itself had skewed. The ambient noise of the shop seemed to fall away, leaving only her words hanging in the air.

"No!" The word burst from my lips. My palms struck the table with a force that echoed my fracturing composure. Spurlock jumped in surprise. "That's not possible! The orb is meant to hold a whole damn hive mind, you said it yourself. A human mind would be nothing for it."

Rochelle's many eyes narrowed, and I could see the strain on her face. "Sally, you don't understand: James isn't just gone — she *left*. Of her own free will."

The words hit me harder than any physical blow could. "She what?" Shock knotted my throat. How could James choose to leave, to abandon... What had driven her to do such a thing? To give up on her chance at life?

Spurlock's hand on my shoulder grounded me in the chaos of my thoughts, his touch a reminder to breathe, to stay anchored despite the torrent of emotions threatening to unmoor me.

"She left, Sally," Rochelle continued, her voice a steady thread, but I could barely hear her over my own rapid breaths. "The lattice is empty, decaying, but only from neglect. The ghost pattern of the previous hive mind is still etched within, and the space James occupied is unmistakable, but it's vacant now. Not erased, not damaged. She simply... chose to leave."

A cold shiver ran through me. "She left? But how?" The question clawed its way out, raw and unshielded. "Where could she possibly go from inside an orb?"

For a heartbeat, Rochelle and I just stared at each other, her many eyes searching for the right words, a solace that could bridge the chasm of my understanding.

When she finally spoke, her voice was soft but carrying an undercurrent of something I couldn't quite read.

"Sally, I think I need to buy you a drink."

ELEVEN

DANCE LIKE NOBODY'S SOBER (EXCEPT YOU)

THEY SAY YOU CAN NEVER FIND AN ANSWER AT the bottom of a bottle, but sometimes if you squint hard enough, the small print starts to look like encouragement. In the low hum and clinking glasses of the bar, that's exactly what I was doing — squinting for hope in the condensation on my half-empty beer.

The bar's murmur enveloped us, the sound a soft blanket that couldn't quite smother the cold dread in my stomach. Light pooled on the table, liquid gold that spilled over our glasses. My bottle was half gone, a feeble attempt to drown the gnawing inside my chest — stupid, really, considering alcohol barely fazed me anymore.

"What's the point?" The question slipped out, quiet and heavy. I wasn't really expecting an answer. It was more a plea to the cosmos, a 'why' tossed into the void.

If I couldn't pull James back, couldn't even touch the edges of her new existence, then what were we even fighting for?

Rochelle offered me a half smile. "James left for a reason, Sally. A reason we have to trust was important." Her words were steady, a lighthouse in the fog of my despair.

"But where did she go? Where is she now?" I could hear the crack in my voice, the splintering of a hope I'd held onto without realizing it.

"There are more things in the universe than our science can grasp, Sally," Spurlock offered, his words a lifeline I wasn't sure I could grab. "Your friend James might have found a passage we can't comprehend, a path to a place beyond."

The idea of James somewhere out there, alone, hurt me in a way I couldn't put into words. I would find her, no matter where she was; but the universe was huge and infinite, and tonight I felt so very small.

I shivered, Spurlock's warmth a silent comfort as our shoulders touched lightly in the booth.

"To James," he said, raising his glass. "She might not have known the secrets of the cosmos, but she fought for them, all the same."

"To James," we echoed, the fizzy beer going down with a bitterness that had nothing to do with hops. I should have ordered something stronger.

SINGULARITY

The silence stretched, taut and suffocating, until I couldn't stand it any longer. "Your shop looks good," I said to Rochelle, desperate for any other topic.

"It's been good to me." Rochelle's drink swirled in her hand, a miniature galaxy of ice and liquor. "Earth tech is child's play, but it's fun, like solving puzzles for toddlers. And every now and then, if I'm lucky, I get to tinker with something that's not from around here."

I smiled, imagining Rochelle hunched over a table laden with gadgets from planets I'd only heard stories of. "Sounds perfect for you."

"Yeah, it's... it's nice to work with my hands again," she admitted. "But enough about me. Last I heard, you were on the run with Zander and Blayde, the infamous Siblings. Then you turned hero for saving the president of the Alliance? How did that happen?"

A wry smile tugged at my lips. "Oh, you know. Play the hero once, and suddenly you're shaking hands with one half of the galaxy and dodging blasters from the other. We earned that pardon the hard way."

"And Zander?" Rochelle's question was soft, treading lightly around the edges of a wound still fresh.

I looked down, tracing a ring of condensation on the table. "He crossed a line he shouldn't have, and I couldn't... just couldn't anymore."

There was a gentle touch on my arm. Not Rochelle, but Spurlock. Spurlock, who didn't know the whole story yet, either. "I'm sorry, Sally."

"It's for the best, really." I shook my head, dismissing it. "Spurlock, I don't know whether to thank you or apologize for dragging you into this."

"Thank me after we find her," he said, his hand giving mine a reassuring squeeze. "And no apologies necessary. After all, what's life without a little unplanned adventure? Dull, dull, abysmally dull, that's what."

Rochelle glanced at Spurlock, then back at me. "And you two...?" She asked, quirking a smile.

Spurlock's hands snapped right back to his lap. I felt the heat rise to my cheeks. "No, we're not... It's not like that. We're just..."

"Friends," Spurlock concluded, nodding solemnly at Rochelle and me in turn.

"You know what?" The arch of her eyebrow was a silent dare, her eyes a playful spark in the dim light. "For a night like this, a drink isn't enough. We should go dancing. I could use some terrible Earth music to cleanse my palate."

I laughed, a real, unguarded sound, a release valve to the pressure building within me. There was an undeniable appeal to the idea, a chance to get lost in a sea of beats and bodies, to be just another soul in the throng, no destinies or decisions weighing me down.

"Let's do it." I tilted the bottle, watching the last of the beer swirl before meeting its end. "To James, to terrible music, and to finding answers on the dance floor."

"To all of that," Rochelle toasted. She turned to Spurlock, a conspiratorial glint in her eyes. "Spurlock?"

"There are clubs… here?" Spurlock's question was hesitant. I tried not to feel insulted for my planet.

"I'm not saying they're good," said Rochelle, throwing her hands up defensively. "But after a few drinks, you don't really care anymore."

We slid out of the booth, Rochelle looping her arm through mine, and together we stepped out into the neon-lit night, the cool air sweeping away the remnants of the bar's warmth. Tonight, we'd dance for James, for ourselves, and for the tiny spark of hope that refused to die, the one that said maybe the universe was kinder than it seemed.

And as for Zander? I'd dance right through the memory of him, each step a defiant stomp, each spin a clear, resolute turn away from the past. Tonight, I would be unmistakably, unapologetically human.

Downtown was bathed in the warm light of streetlights, their glow combating the encroaching chill — a chill that had Rochelle zipping up a jacket with an almost theatrical shiver. Spurlock, in stark contrast, seemed as impervious to the cold as a penguin in an ice bath.

The first club Rochelle led us to, was a nondescript hole-in-the-wall, its entrance lit by a neon sign flickering "Open" with lazy indifference. It was the kind of place that didn't promise much, which paid off because it didn't disappoint. The music was a pulsing heartbeat, less a melody and more a summons. The drinks were swift and potent, the kind that slipped down your throat with deceptive ease, wearing velvet gloves over their iron fists.

Rochelle and Spurlock dove into the fray of dancers, a blur of limbs and laughter. There was a primal part of me, a vestige of the old Sally, that wanted to leap in after them. The thought of dancing felt like stepping back into a world that had spun on without me. It wasn't like riding a bike — there was no muscle memory for the rhythm of the reckless.

Still, with a drink fizzing — as gently as it was —I took the plunge. I danced, not with any grace to speak of, but with an enthusiasm that felt strangely alien and yet familiar. The buzz was there, humming beneath my skin.

Yes. This is what I want. This is what I need. Dance until I forget why I'm dancing.

This was all fine and good until Rochelle shook her head, leading us outside again, muttering about how even she had standards when it came to Earth music. Club number two loomed like a behemoth, its walls throbbing with the bass. The crowd inside was a sea, a tidal wave of bodies in motion. Here, in the pulsating heart of the night, I found myself swept up in a group whose laughter was as loud as their outfits were bright. Drinks appeared and disappeared like magic, a sleight of hand performed by tipsy conjurers with bottomless pockets.

I downed another and another and another. The drinks poured in, but the numbness remained a mirage. I was chasing the high tide with a kiddie bucket.

"Woah there, Sally cakes," said Spurlock, as I reached for a bottle. Not sure what, not quite sure where. "We have all evening."

"I have frashing infinity," I said, taking it anyway. "Eternity and an infinite supply of livers."

He didn't reply — or maybe he did, but I tuned him out. There was a recklessness nipping at my heels, urging me to dive headlong into the night, to let it swallow me whole. To get so irretrievably lost in the intoxicating maze that the exit would become a mere afterthought. It was a reckless itch, one that whispered seductively of a morning amnesia I'd wake to with open arms.

But I couldn't reach that, not anymore. I felt nothing more than a buzz.

Go on, Sally, forget he ever existed. But as I drowned in a sea of bodies, lost in the bass throb of the music, I realized the buzz I was feeling was less tipsy giddiness and more slightly over-caffeinated. I was trying to summon a whirlwind of inebriation, and my body was failing me — utterly uncooperative, like a herded cat.

For every drink passed around, I took two, feeling nothing. My skin tingled slightly, and I found myself with an incredible urge to eat tater tots, but nothing more. I should've been swinging from the chandeliers by now, or at the very least, mistaking the bathroom sign for a philosophical question. But no. I wanted oblivion and got a buzz that couldn't even lull a kitten to sleep.

My friends were having the time of their lives, and I was as sober as a judge at happy hour, remembering that maybe I'd never *really* been a party girl. It was a sobering thought — pun absolutely intended. I was stuck in Club Limbo, where the music pounded, the lights blinded, and I stood, the most sober soul on the dance floor, surrounded by revelers who had happily checked their dignity at the door.

I sidestepped the human whirlpool and made a beeline for sanctuary — a vacant booth, sticky with the ghosts of spilled cocktails past. I slumped down, welcoming the reprieve from the thumping bass that seemed intent on becoming my new pulse.

Rochelle, noticing my tactical retreat, waddled over with all the grace of a happy penguin and slid into the seat beside me. "You're not..." she began, voice laced with concern and three too many vodka cranberries. "You're not okay, are you?"

I gave her a half smile, a shrug. "I'm just out of practice. It's like my party gears are stuck in neutral."

Easier than explaining that my liver was healing faster than I could damage it, and that alcohol slid through me as easily as Diet Coke. At this point I probably had enough alcohol running through my veins to be considered a cocktail myself.

"Pfft, gears, schmears." Rochelle dismissed me with a wave of her hand that nearly took out a passing server.

"You need an oil change. And I know just the mechanic."

Before I could ask what she meant, she was on her feet, a mischievous glint in her eye that was equal parts alarming and infectious. She scanned the crowd and then, with a shout that could only mean impending trouble or unexpected pizza, she beckoned to someone — or someones — in the distance.

Shanshan and Finn emerged from the crowd, unmistakable and unchanging.

I flew to my feet, propriety dropped on the floor as I rushed to catch Shanshan's embrace. She squealed excitedly into my ear. Incredible, considering the last time I'd seen her, I'd weirded her out with knowledge about her planet which, it turns out, hadn't yet happened.

"Oh my stars!" she exclaimed, shaking me like a doll. "I saw you on the news every day, Sally! I couldn't believe you were on the run with the frashing *Siblings!*"

"It's so good to see you safe and sound, Sally," said Finn, who could have been the love child of James Dean and every sci-fi captain who'd ever dashed across the galaxy.

A smile crept onto my face, genuine and wide. "What are you guys doing here?"

"Rochelle sent out an SOS," Finn quipped, sliding into the booth with the ease of someone who was used to cramped spaceship quarters.

"Yeah, she said you needed to be reminded how to lose yourself without actually losing yourself," Shanshan chimed in, her tone as bright as her skin.

I prickled with a touch of embarrassment and gratitude. "I guess I do at that."

"What are you thinking, bringing Sally here?" Shanshan turned to Rochelle. "The Space Bar is way better."

Just as I was about to respond, a shadow loomed over us, casting a rock star-sized silhouette across the table. Shanshan's eyes widened, while Finn started fidgeting like a fan about to meet their idol.

"Spurlock-frashing-Magnesar," Shanshan breathed out in awe and disbelief.

Spurlock laughed, a rich, genuine sound that filled the space around us. "Indeed I am! And who might you two be? Fans, friends, or a bit of both?"

Shanshan whipped out her phone, her fingers trembling slightly. "Could we, maybe, get a selfie with you?"

"Of course!" Spurlock leaned in, his smile camera-ready as he wrapped an arm around each of them. The flash went off.

Finn, recovering from his initial shock, grinned wide. "Thanks, man. We're big fans of your work. Your last concert on Cygnus IV was mind-blowing."

Spurlock waved a hand modestly. "Ah, that old show? I'm just glad you enjoyed it. But let's focus on the star of tonight, shall we?" He turned to me, his expression softening. "Sally needs us right now, more than ever."

I felt a warm rush of affection for Spurlock and a surge of gratitude for my friends, old and new. It was strange, surreal even, to be here, surrounded by those who cared, with an intergalactic celebrity by my side, yet it felt right.

"Now we definitely have to go to the Space Bar!" Shanshan grabbed my hand, dragging me towards the door. "Come on, I'll drive! My truck's got autopilot."

We all piled into Shanshan's truck, which hummed like a kitten — a really big, space-faring kitten. The dashboard looked like it could solve calculus problems or pilot us to Mars, whichever came first. Spurlock strapped himself in like he was preparing for liftoff, eyes wide at the alien tech wrapped up in vintage Ford styling.

The Space Bar was tucked away in an alley. Stepping through the door felt like passing through a portal — on the other side was a carnival of the cosmos. The décor was a love letter to the universe, complete with a nebula-cloud ceiling and tables that hovered a few inches off the ground.

Aliens of all shades and shapes milled around, some with the luminous elegance of astral deities and others who looked like they'd be right at home in a space swamp. It was people-watching on an intergalactic scale, and I was here for it.

"Welcome to our melting pot," Finn announced, leading us to the bar with the swagger of a seasoned astronaut.

Rochelle leaned in, her voice low. "Just don't order anything that looks like it has its own ecosystem."

We perched on stools that felt suspiciously like they were breathing — another quirky alien tech that I decided not to question. The bartender, a being with eyes like swirling galaxies, slid us a menu. Everything was written in an elegant script that looked suspiciously like Wingdings gone haute couture.

"Recommendations?" I asked, feeling utterly out of my league.

Spurlock's finger danced down the list, stopping on something called "Cosmic Fizz." "This one comes with a warning label," he said with a grin that didn't quite reach his eyes. "It's like a supernova for your taste buds."

I shrugged, all in. "Hit me with the Big Bang."

Moments later, a glass of shimmering liquid arrived, fizzing and popping like a carbonated comet. The first sip was a starburst, flavor exploding in my mouth, and I couldn't help but let out a delighted laugh. The second sip was a little less poetic — my head spun like I'd just done three rounds with a gravitational anomaly.

And then it hit me. All at once, like a meteor shower to my cerebral cortex, the buzz I'd been chasing all night crashed through my system. The world turned a delightful shade of tipsy.

"Why is everyone luminescing?" I squeaked, and someone laughed.

Rochelle and Shanshan, however, were a spectacle. If drunkenness was an Olympic sport, they'd be on the podium wearing gold. Every ten minutes, they burst into what could generously be called a duet, which usually devolved into a stand-up comedy routine without the stand-up — or the routine.

"Watch this, Sal," Rochelle slurred, as she started another round of what was probably meant to be Bohemian Rhapsody but sounded more like Bohemian Rhapsnotty. Two lines in, and she'd already rewritten the lyrics to include something about a "poor boy needing spaghetti" — a culinary twist Freddie Mercury definitely missed. Finn tried to follow her lead but couldn't keep up with the lyrical gymnastics. Instead, he provided a sort of interpretative dance, which mostly involved him wobbling on the spot like a jellyfish in a wind tunnel.

It was the best thing I had ever seen in my life.

The dance floor beckoned, a riot of movement and music where even the most tentacled of beings were busting moves that defied physics. I grabbed Spurlock's hand — steady, solid Spurlock — and we joined the fray, letting the pulsating beats of a thousand distant worlds carry us away.

Laughter bubbled up from somewhere deep inside, pure and unfiltered. My feet moved of their own accord, finding the rhythm of a song that felt like it could have been the pulse of the universe itself. I glanced at Spurlock, and he just smiled, the kind of smile that screamed "we're in too deep, but who cares?"

And right then, for just a moment, I felt it — the sheer, unadulterated joy of being utterly, awkwardly human in a place where everyone was at least a little bit alien. I let loose on the dance floor like I was the center of a very confused solar system, arms and legs orbiting to the synthetic beats until my own gravity gave out.

Spurlock extended his hand to me, an invitation back to stability, or perhaps to something entirely new. His fingers were steady. A lifeline in the swirling sea. I took it, feeling the strange pull of impulse and the warm buzz of intergalactic alcohol urging me to just go with it.

Why the hell not? I thought, breathless from the dancing and the night's relentless surprises.

Throwing caution to the stars, I surrendered to the magnetic pull of desire, and our lips met in a fervent clash that set the world ablaze. His kiss was intense, a storm of sensation that consumed all thought, promising a depth of passion and warmth I hadn't known I was seeking.

For a timeless moment, I was engulfed in the inferno, every sense heightened, every nerve alight with the fire of his presence. The desire to dissolve into that embrace, to chase the flame to whatever destiny awaited, was irresistible.

Frash, I was kissing Spurlock Magnesar.

For a moment, I was lost in it, lost in him — a sweet anchor in the tumult of my world. The urge to melt into that heat, to follow the feeling into whatever madness or normalcy it led, was overwhelming. I could have stayed there, could have let everything else fade away.

But then the reality of where we were and who I was, crashed back down on me. I broke the kiss, my breaths coming in little puffs of shock.

"I'll... uh, I'm gonna get another drink."

Spurlock's brow creased, a silent question in his eyes, but he nodded, letting me go. I turned away, my legs carrying me towards the bar. I needed a moment to think, to breathe, to figure out why a simple kiss had felt like another step into uncharted space.

I stumbled to the bar and leaned heavily against it.

"Hey." I raised my hand high despite the fact that the bartender was standing right in front of me. They might have been transparent, but their gaze was piercing. "Can I get the strongest cocktail you've got? I'm craving something that could make my head spin faster than the planets."

They nodded. "One Warp Drive. Coming right up."

I peered through the translucent bartender — seriously, it was like looking through a living, breathing Jell-O mold — as they marched down the bar to make my drink, and did a double take.

There was someone else perched at the bar, exuding an aura of cosmic mystery that even my booze-addled brain couldn't ignore. That, and a conveniently placed latex unicorn mask on the bar in front of them.

"'Scuse me," I slurred, sliding down the bar and plopping onto a stool beside the pale figure.

"Do I know you?" the being inquired, squinting at me as if I were a puzzle missing a few too many pieces.

"Uh, maybe?" I drawled. "Were you at that rager on Pythanous Five?"

Their eyes popped open like saucers, and suddenly they were crying a river, beating the bar with a hand so pale it could've been a prop from a ghost movie. From zero to weeping willow in three seconds flat.

"Oh, uh, my bad," I stammered.

"I failed," they blurted between sobs, each word punctuated with a smack of their hand on the bar.

The bartender deposited my drink in front of me, saying nothing as they avoided the stranger's tears and bar slaps. I gingerly picked it up, only slightly disappointed at its complete lack of color. The taste was sweet, but not out of this world. I guess I'd set my bar too high.

"Failed at what?" I leaned in, curiosity piquing, eager for distraction.

They jabbed a finger at the unicorn mask, now adorned with dramatic streaks of red paint that looked suspiciously like a preschooler's attempt at abstract art.

I squinted at it. "Sorry, you lost me. I don't get the whole tragic unicorn vibe here."

"I was on a transcendental quest," he declared, exhaling a sigh so heavy it could've sunk a ship. "I attended that party to finally ascend to the seventh dimension. You know, master of time and space, immortal-ish stuff. But I flunked out. Breathed in their cosmic kale salad of drugs and found nothing waiting for me on the other side. Booted from Pythanous, persona non grata in the higher planes."

Awkwardness wrapped around me like a too-tight sweater. "That's rough, my dude," I managed, glancing at the latex unicorn mask that was giving me the stink eye.

"But hey, I met you, right?" They perked up suddenly. "You're Sally Webber, aren't you?"

And then it hit me, and I choked on my drink. "You're the apple guy? That's where I know you from!" Memories of that bizarre encounter fluttered in my mind like a confused moth. "How the heck did you wind up here?"

He shrugged; a gesture so nonchalant it could've been a shrug-off competition. "Stumbled out of the party, and voilà, here I am. Weird, right? My readings were as foggy as my head back then. Too much spirit gas, not enough grounding. But I remember reading you."

"You do?"

"Yeah, you had this aura, all bright and shiny. Like… a disco ball in a coal mine. You've been marked by higher planes, etched by their cosmic Etch A Sketch." They gazed upward, getting lost in the ceiling tiles like they held the secrets of the universe. "You're in cahoots with *them*, aren't you?" he blurted out, snapping back to the present.

"With who now?" I asked, my brain trying to connect the dots in this intergalactic dot-to-dot.

"Them," he insisted, as if that cleared everything up. "The real deal ones."

"Real deal whats?" My confusion was now doing the cha-cha with my inebriation.

"The Pythanoreans," he recited, like he was reading from an interdimensional brochure, "are the high-and-mighty seventh dimension residents. We can only interact with them at the cosmic party they throw, where space-time gets more twisted than a pretzel. But Zander, and Blayde, oh, they're like cosmic nomads. They don't play by anyone's rules. They hop dimensions like I flip channels. They're true immortals."

"Wait, the Pythanoreans aren't?" I prodded.

He sighed, the kind of sigh that had seen too many dimensions. "My masters, the higher-ups, they're forever, yeah. But they ditched the whole flesh-and-blood gig. Eventually, they'll just kinda... fade out. Like a ghost with bad reception. I bailed 'cause I realized I was chasing after a ghostly forever. I wanted mine with more... substance. Turns out, I was chasing a dream with the substance of a soap bubble."

So the Pythanoreans were... a state of mind? My eyebrows tried to kiss despite my interference. This wasn't a species, it was some kind of... cult?

I nodded, sagely or drunkenly, hard to say. "Well, maybe that's for the best. Eternity's overrated."

The alcohol was really taking effect now. The former unicorn was getting fuzzy, blurring as they fell back onto the bar. And the bartender was getting woozy, reaching for my drink as I put the empty glass down.

"I know you, don't I?" the bartender asked, raising an eyebrow.

"Maybe you do, maybe you don't." I winked. Or, well, I think I winked, because it got dark for a second.

"The president is…"

"Annoying." I laughed. "Trust me. We've met. Our country could do better."

"The Alliance will—" They tried again, but I was having none of it.

"Look, unless this Alliance has a secret cocktail recipe, let's save the world-saving for sober Sally," I interrupted, waving a hand dismissively.

"Right this way, Miss Webber," said a man in a suit, who appeared seemingly out of nowhere.

"Commander Buzzkill, I presume?" I flashed a grin. "I asked for a drink that'll knock me off my feet, not a guy in a tie. Unless you're here to tango?"

He didn't crack a smile, just nodded towards the back of the club. I shrugged and followed him, throwing a wink over my shoulder at the bartender. "If I'm not back in five, tell my friends I've been abducted by Men in Black!"

I probably should have been worried. But then again, I was freaking immortal, and I had finally cracked the code to being drunk despite it all, so I was blissfully content with whatever came my way.

The door slammed shut behind me with a thud that felt ominously final. The atmosphere in this new club was charged, a cocktail of determination and dissent that was worlds away from the frivolous rebellion of dance and drink I'd just left. The room hummed not with bass, but with the low murmurs of many species united by a cause. A cause, it seemed, I'd stumbled into with the grace of a newborn giraffe on roller skates.

I blinked, taking in the sea of diversity that would have given the cantina at Mos Eisley a run for its galactic credits. Beings of all shapes and sizes mingled. Some floated where gravity seemed optional, their forms a soft glow of bioluminescence. Others chatted in the corner, mandibles clacking and feathers ruffling in what appeared to be heated debate.

The walls were plastered with posters, all bearing slogans that screamed rebellion: "Shatter the Stars!" "Unite for the Universe!" "Alliance against the Alliance!" It was a veritable smorgasbord of subversion, and here I was, smack dab in the middle of it. The last place I wanted to see or be seen.

"Oh crap," I whispered, the words escaping me like traitors.

This was quite the opposite of an Alliance meetup.

It was the resistance.

TWELVE

REBEL WITHOUT A CLUE

I WAS SUPPOSED TO BE DRINKING MY SORROWS away, not inadvertently joining an interstellar uprising. An uprising against my best friend and her wife, no less.

A hush fell over the room as all eyes settled on me. The offworlders — a trail mix of humanoid figures and truly alien ones, in varying degrees of skin wraps — were watching me with an expectation that felt heavier than the densest star in the cosmos. I was prepared to face many things after the breakup — pity, loneliness, maybe the odd rebound if I was lucky. But becoming an intergalactic mascot of dissent was not on my bingo card.

"Oh great Void." A rubbery-looking life-form that seemed somehow silicone based clapped a dozen or so tentacles together. "It's her! She's here! How is she here?"

I had to get out of here.

"This isn't the door for the bathroom!" I squeaked. "Is there a bathroom nearby?"

"And she has a sense of humor!" The being slapped me hard on the back, almost knocking me over. "It is good to have you among our ranks!"

Just as my inner panic reached its peak, the anticipation in the room shifted, pooling towards a rather unassuming bucket in the center. I squinted, my vision still a bit blurred from the kiss of alien liquor, as the bucket stirred. Yes, the bucket. A murmur of respect rustled through the crowd.

"Sally Webber," it vibrated, the voice echoing strangely as if it came from the bottom of a well — or a bucket. "Your presence is the sign we've been waiting for."

I stared, regretting reaching that alcoholic daze I'd been chasing. It was as if the surface of the bucket was rippling in reverse. The gelatinous entity pulsed with colors that had no business existing outside of a psychedelic poster. Its presence commanded the room, even without a face.

My heart sputtered like a faulty engine. "Sign? Wait, no, there's been a mistake. I'm not—"

But the bucket's contents rumbled, and the room stilled somehow even further. "Your actions, the way you've evaded the Alliance, have inspired us. You, Sally Webber, are the symbol of resistance."

I gawked, both at the idea of being a face of anything for this jiggly pile of resistance and at the absurdity of this bucket-bound revolutionary. Me? A symbol? I glanced back at the door, half expecting it to burst open with my friends, with Spurlock's wry smile and Rochelle's infectious laughter. But it remained closed, as silent as the stares that pinned me in place.

"I'm not…" I stammered, teetering on my wobbly legs. "How do you know who I am?"

"Everyone knows your face," the gelatin said. "You were public enemy number one of the Alliance for a while."

"Number three," I muttered. "And I'm really not supposed to be here."

But as the eyes of the resistance looked upon me with something akin to hope, I felt the night's drinks finally hit. Not with a buzz, but with the gravity of a black hole.

"I just came for the cocktails," I finally managed to say, the truth slurring out. But it was too late; the room erupted into laughter, a cacophony of clicks, whistles, and alien applause.

But the liquid in the bucket remained serene, its colors shifting in thoughtful patterns. "Every great movement has started with less," it oozed philosophically. "And we are honored to carry you into this battle, as you have carried the spirits of many."

I blinked, trying to process the situation. Around me, creatures of all shapes and appendages nodded and clicked in agreement. There was no escaping it — I had fallen into the role of interstellar insurrectionist by virtue of just showing up.

"So… this is an offworlder social, huh?" I blurted out, trying to find my footing in the conversation. "A spot where everyone can bond over their mutual dislike of the Alliance?"

"And to mingle," piped up a being that looked like a secretary bird had a fling with an old-school librarian. "It's a great place to meet singles." They shot me a look that I think was supposed to be a wink — if you could call it that given their lack of visible eyelids.

"I think there's been a huge misunderstanding." I tried to inject a firm note into my voice, but it quivered like a violin string under the gaze of a dozen unblinking alien eyes. "I'm not who you think I am."

The gelatinous leader, now oozing with what I assumed was anticipation, sent ripples through its mass. "Sally Webber," it hummed. "Even if you did not intend to become a beacon of hope, that does not negate the light you shine upon our cause."

The silicone-based creature with more tentacles than I could count leaned in, its voice a sibilant whisper that sent shivers down my spine. "The Alliance has wronged many of us. Your defiance, even accidental, is a spark that can ignite the fire of change."

I swallowed hard, the reality of my situation setting in. I was surrounded by beings who had every reason to dislike, even hate, the Alliance — my best friend's Alliance. Saying the wrong thing could be disastrous. Yet, my loyalty to Marcy and Dany prickled at my conscience, reminding me that these beings saw them as tyrants.

My phone buzzed in my pocket, and I dazedly picked it up, checking the text I had just received. My hands trembled as my eyes struggled to make out the words, reading them at a snail's pace.

Get out of there now.

Customer support was back.

The being made of silicone and the entity of gelatin stared at me awkwardly. The bucket could have been as well, but without eyes, who could tell. I clutched my phone tight in my sweaty palm. Was this the same mysterious customer support that had been sending me the pins? It hadn't steered me wrong yet.

"Well, it was really nice getting to meet you all," I said. "But my friends are wondering where I got to."

The bucket-entity's hues swirled faster. "Sally, you, your friends — do they not understand what is at stake? We do not wish to keep you against your will but consider the power of your influence. Even the smallest asteroid can destroy great civilizations."

"We only ask that you hear our pleas," The silicone being chimed in, its voice a soothing melody that contrasted with the tension in the room. "Too long have we lived in the shadows of the Alliance's decisions."

I inched towards the door, the weight of their stares almost tangible. "I hear you, I really do," I said, voice trembling. "But revolutions and... resistance... Look, I meant it when I said I didn't plan to get involved in anything tonight. Just ask your bartender how much I had to drink, okay?"

The secretary bird-librarian creature ruffled its feathers, stepping closer. "You never seemed the type to stand by while injustice thrives."

Suddenly, a small, four-armed figure darted through the crowd, clutching a device that looked part tablet, part alien flora. "She must stay! She must see!" it squeaked, eyes wide and earnest.

Before I could object, the tablet-flower hybrid sprang to life, casting holographic images that danced in the air between us. Scenes of Alliance forces clashing with protesters, of planets stripped of resources, of families torn apart by policies and power plays — all flickered before my eyes.

My breath caught in my throat as I absorbed the stark reality of the Alliance's rule, so far removed from the glossy facade presented to its citizens. I knew there were atrocities in the Alliance's wake, had seen it for myself, had stood up to them, even. But Dany was trying to make things better... wasn't she?

"Sally, you've always been one to stand up for what's right," said the bucket again. Strange that everyone here knew my name and I didn't know any of theirs. "Fate has brought you here tonight!"

Always? I wanted to laugh. I'd tried, sure, but these people didn't know me. They'd seen me in their media, on the run from one thing or another, the third wheel to the well-oiled Sibling machine.

My phone buzzed again, breaking me out of my spiraling thoughts.

Turn around, and walk away, Customer Support said again.

Normally it would be hard to decide whether or not to follow cryptic messages from a mysterious source, but seeing as how getting out was already a top priority for me, it didn't need to tell me twice.

"Honestly, if it really was fate, I'd be sober," I replied, forcing a jovial smile. "Let's schedule a nice chat when we're all dry, how's that? That way I can see, um, what you…"

"The anti-Alliance alliance!" the silicone being announced proudly.

"Right, that way I can see how the anti-Alliance alliance can really benefit from my help." I took a tentative step back towards the door, keeping my eye on everyone assembled. Nice and easy, nice and easy.

My phone buzzed once again. I picked it up, startled to read the words on the screen.

Get out of there. They are coming. Good luck.

The black letters stared up at me like daggers through my clouded eyes.

I'd gotten this same message before. But it couldn't be — that phone call, minutes before some shady government goons had tried to kidnap me from my apartment.

The exact same message.

But it couldn't be. Because that warning had come from James Felling, and James Felling was dead.

Unless… I looked at the text on the screen, unable to process the words. James had left the orb, but where was she now?

Was she… in my phone?

"My friends are looking for me," I said casually. I managed a wobbly smile, keeping my voice as steady as I could. "I'll just go grab them. They'd love to hear about the anti-Alliance alliance firsthand, you know? They're big on causes."

The crowd parted slightly, an aisle of expectant faces. The bucket-entity's colors pulsated, shifting from the urgent hues to something softer, perhaps disappointment — or calculation. The silicone being's tentacles writhed in what I hoped was contemplation rather than preparation to stop me.

"They should indeed hear of our plight," it murmured, the many voices harmonizing into one. "But they should come to us. It is safer in numbers, is it not?"

"Oh, absolutely," I agreed quickly, too quickly, "but you know, they're a skeptical bunch. They'd want to see that I'm okay with their own eyes." I chuckled, my laughter sounding brittle in my own ears. "You know how friends are."

The room seemed to breathe a collective sigh, an eerie sound of sliding scales and soft whispers. The four-armed creature with the tablet-flora device nodded earnestly, its eyes glistening with a fervor that bordered on fanaticism. "We will prepare for their arrival then," it chirped.

"Yes, prepare away," I said, inching further towards the exit. "I'll be back before you know it with a whole crew ready to... to... get involved."

I took another step back, my hand reaching behind me for the door handle. My fingers brushed against the cool metal, and I almost sighed with relief. Just a turn and a step, and I would be free.

"Remember," the gelatinous being in the bucket intoned, its colors now a calm sea of blues and greens, "the path of righteousness is often laden with peril, Sally Webber. But it is a path that must be walked."

I nodded, my mind screaming for me to flee. "Paths, yes, peril, absolutely. Walking, best done with friends."

With a swift motion, I turned the handle and slipped through the door, pulling it shut behind me with a soft click. The sweet symphony of escape.

The hallway was empty, dimly lit with the same ambient lighting that seemed to permeate the whole place. My phone was still clutched in my hand, the screen now dark. James Felling was dead, but the messages... the timing was too impeccable. I shook my head. I couldn't afford to spiral into conspiracy theories — not now.

I needed to get out, to find Spurlock and Rochelle, Shanshan and Finn, to get somewhere safe and try to make sense of it all. I shoved the phone into my pocket and pushed off from the door, my legs carrying me swiftly and silently down the hallway.

As I turned the corner, a chill crept down my spine. There was a thrumming in the air, a vibration that I felt more than heard. *They were coming.* Whoever they were, whatever they wanted, I knew instinctively that the message hadn't been a trick.

I broke into a run.

The club seemed impossibly normal since I'd left. I blinked hard, trying to steady my vision and my nerves as I navigated through the thrumming mass of bodies on the dance floor. The music was a thumping bass line that seemed to echo the rush of blood in my ears.

I spotted them near the pulsating neon lights — Spurlock, Rochelle, Shanshan, and Finn, the latter two now sporting identical braids that somehow glowed under the club's lights. Shanshan was demonstrating a series of moves that looked like a cross between martial arts and interpretive dance, while Finn attempted to mimic her with less grace and more flailing.

"Guys!" I yelled, but my voice was swallowed by the music. I pushed through, my hands grabbing and moving past shoulders, and offering apologetic smiles until I reached my friends.

"Sally!" said Rochelle excitedly, reaching for me. "Where did you go off to? Moligua?"

I wanted to shout "run," but it was up to me to keep calm, to be steady in all of this. Not to panic my drunken friends. "There's, uh, something like a rebel hive in the back... and they kind of think I'm their mascot or something."

Rochelle, sweat glistening on her brow, laughed and leaned in. "What, like a queen bee?"

"More like a... confused butterfly? But listen, they're serious, and I'm getting these weird messages..."

Spurlock edged nearer, his face tight with worry. "What messages?"

"The 'we're in danger' sort. The 'they're coming for us' sort."

At that, Finn's dance faltered, a marionette with strings cut. "Who's 'they'?"

Wish I knew. The words stuck, but my eyes flickered to the exit, signaling urgency. "Doesn't matter. We have to go. Now."

Shanshan's laughter peeled out, naïve to the edge of night. "The night's still young, Sally!"

Without waiting for more questions, I grabbed Spurlock's hand, feeling a jolt that wasn't just from the urgency of the moment, and weaved through the crowd. Rochelle, Finn, and Shanshan followed close behind. We spilled out into the cool night, the air a sharp contrast to the heat of the club.

"Now what?" asked Rochelle, her words forming little clouds of steam in front of her mouth.

"If they're after anyone, it would be me," I said. "You three should head somewhere safe in Shanshan's truck. Spurlock and I will get the hell out of dodge."

They looked at me curiously, until Shanshan laughed, a cold, humorless laugh. "Ha! I got that one."

As they scurried to the truck, their levity abandoned, I was left with a gnawing desire to join them, to disappear until the threat subsided. But life had other plans.

My phone vibrated.

I pulled it out, and a map appeared on the screen, a glowing line tracing a path through the city. Spurlock peered over my shoulder.

"You're not actually thinking of following that, are you?"

I didn't answer, my eyes fixed on the line, the dots connecting in my head. It had to be from her. From James. Or at least, someone connected to her.

"I have to."

Spurlock's hand was warm on my arm, a stark contrast to the cold dread that was creeping into my bones. "Sally, this could be a trap."

I knew he was right. But James had never steered me wrong. And if there was even a chance she was out there...

"If it's a trap, then I'll deal with it. I can't ignore this."

Spurlock's lips pressed into a thin line, the hint of a frown.

As we walked, the night felt heavier, the city more ominous. The kiss we had shared earlier hung in the air between us, unspoken but as palpable as the tension from the messages. I was acutely aware of his hand occasionally brushing against mine, and each time it felt like a static shock to my system, a jolt that insisted "remember this." The kiss was there, in every glance, every accidental touch. I was torn between the desire to confront it and the need to focus on the path unfolding before me. But with each step we took, the weight of that unspoken moment grew heavier, like a secret we were both trying to dance around, even as we left the music far behind.

"The bus!" Spurlock exclaimed. It seemed a mundane miracle, the humble chariot parked under the stark white light of the streetlamp. "I didn't think we'd parked here."

"The map still has a ways for us to go," I said, awkwardly, as Spurlock rushed across the street, throwing open his door and reaching over to open mine.

"So? We'll drive there. It'll be warmer." He closed his door, adjusting his mirrors.

Resistance was futile, and truth be told, unnecessary. I slid into the seat, clicking the seatbelt home. "Should you be driving, though?" I asked, watching Spurlock fumble with his own buckle.

"Adrenaline's sobering," he insisted, his words stumbling over each other. "Plus, you threw back way more than me."

"Yeah, but my liver's already back to peak health," I said, reaching for the wheel, realizing only after that it was still a pretty drunken move.

"I've got it," he said, making a terrible display of trying to insert the key. But it wouldn't turn over. "I…" He froze, turning back to look at me with wide eyes wide. "This isn't a ship."

"What?" I sputtered.

"Um… no dashboard."

"So we're in someone else's VW bus."

"One with all the same décor?" He poked buttons this way and that, as if hoping he was somehow wrong, and our ship was somehow still under the layers of camouflage. "Seems our star-cruiser's been replaced with a grounded doppelgänger."

"Just drive, Spurlock!" I sputtered. "Get this thing moving!"

"The key isn't right!" he protested, his hands flailing theatrically around the steering column. "And I can't drive ground-based vehicles!"

That's when the night turned to day, a glaring spotlight enveloping us. It blasted through the glass, transforming the windshield into a glowing canvas of blinding white, forcing me to shield my eyes with a forearm.

The van lurched; the world outside swung into a dizzying waltz. We were airborne, the ground's embrace a memory beneath us.

"Oh, great." Spurlock sounded oddly detached, as if remarking on the weather rather than our current predicament. "We are being abducted."

"Abducted? By whom?" I asked, voice rising with each word.

"How should I know? You're the one getting the mysterious messages! I told you this could be a trap!"

I bit my tongue, refusing to remind him that the text hadn't led us to the bus; that was his own detour. I gave up on the steering wheel — what's the use of driving if there aren't any roads? — And staggered to the back of the van, throwing open the doors to see Portland falling away from me, the light drifting downwards as we swung through the air. I pulled the doors closed quickly as the rushing wind sucked the pressure from our small craft. Vertigo activated then deflated just as quickly, giving me jelly legs frozen in place.

"Spurlock, think!" I gasped. "We need an escape plan."

He scratched his head. "You could… I don't know, teleport us out of here?"

"Can't," I said, shaking my head. "Navigation's off, we could crash the American Revolution."

"Who cares!" He threw his hands up in the air. "Anywhere is better than here!"

"Spurlock, we could end up impaled by cannonballs. Not a very nice death."

"Would any death be? Besides, is that such a bad thing right now? I mean, compared to being space-napped? Do we have any other options?"

I stared at him, the seriousness of our predicament pressing down on us like the gravity we'd left behind. We needed a plan, and fast, before the unknown intentions of our captors became an unwelcome reality.

"What about parachutes?" I ventured.

"We don't have parachutes! This isn't our bus!"

I scrambled through the retro interior. "What if we empty the beanbag, maybe we can use it as one!"

"Not enough drag, not even for one of us," he said, shuddering. "We're trapped."

I gritted my teeth. Maybe I could jump us away — but could I risk dropping Spurlock in the middle of the unknown?

"Right," I said, sobering up quite suddenly. "Spurlock, I need you to get the doors."

"What are you planning?" he asked, grabbing for the handles.

"We need to size up our hosts. Hold on to me."

With Spurlock's hands gripping my belt, I braced myself and yanked the door open.

The vista before us was a mesmerizing canvas of deep blues and the ever-distant curvature of Earth, retreating from our sight. In a whirl of instinct and panic, I yanked back on the doors. The van's interior felt claustrophobic after the vastness of space, and my lungs buzzed with a weird fizzing, like a carbonated drink had been poured into my chest instead of air.

"We're not being transported to somewhere on Earth," I muttered. "We're going up."

"Up." Magnesar nodded, rubbing his windpipe. "I think they're Alliance."

"That's a relief." I rolled my eyes.

"Seriously?"

"At least I've dealt with them before. At least I know what they want. Or, at least, I can make a pretty educated guess. But if they're taking us to the Agency…"

"Air…" Spurlock shot up, launching himself to the sliding door, running his hand over the joints. "This van is far from airtight."

"So we're close to where they're taking us. They have nothing against any of us, they're not going to attempt anything…"

Our conversation was cut short as the once-blinding light dimmed to a twilight glow, allowing us to gaze out of the windshield. A behemoth vessel materialized before us, its presence monstrous and all-consuming. It advanced towards our insignificant van, looming larger with our every breath until it engulfed us whole within the cavernous maw of its docking bay.

My fingers worked instinctively, smoothing the fabric of my clothes, an attempt to regain some semblance of composure. These were the very people I loathed to negotiate with — the sort who played chess with living pawns. And as the darkness of the ship swallowed us, I steeled myself for the game that lay ahead.

THIRTEEN

THE FREQUENT FLYER'S GUIDE TO ALIEN ABDUCTIONS

NOW I KNEW WHAT IT FELT LIKE TO BE THE ONE others turned to during moments of absolute panic, and I wasn't feeling it. Spurlock stared at me, his head tilted, eyes wide with that blend of confusion and curiosity typically reserved for pups out of their depth. Meanwhile, I was trying to anchor my attention on anything that might offer a tactical advantage, but no dice: everything outside the windows was washed out by the harsh, unyielding glare of lights of the mysterious docking bay.

Right. We didn't run out of air, so we didn't go far: this was probably the same type of ship that took us from the beach before the whole Dread incident. Which meant...

"Is Stook still director?" I asked Spurlock, who only tilted his head the other way. Kinda endearing, if it wasn't for the precarious nature of this instance. "Of the Agency?"

He straightened, and the vulnerable curiosity was replaced by a hardening of his stance, a withdrawal. "First-name terms with the Agency aren't in my repertoire," he said, a brittle edge to his words. I could feel him tense up, which made me realize how close we were standing. *Oh.*

"Fan-freaking-tastic. You didn't plan your Earth vacay through the official channels, did you?" I took a step back, along with a steadying breath. I'd faced off against the Agency before, but Spurlock... he was famous. Famous, and not playing by the Agency's rules. "Ok, Spurlock, how do you feel about dating?"

"Are you asking me out?" His lips quirked into a smile.

Ugh. Not the right time for this. "As a cover, Spurlock," I said, the sharpness in my voice slicing neatly through the air, heavy with the scent of metal and machinery. "Play the part, and maybe you'll be invisible to them. Maybe."

The rhythm of approaching footsteps served as a stark reminder of the ticking clock. I'd let precious minutes slip by, frittering away our chance at concocting a viable escape strategy.

"I was under the impression that you were somewhat of a hero to the Agency," Spurlock remarked as a distant door groaned shut, the clatter sending a shudder through my heart. The stark shipboard illumination softened to a deceptive calm. "After everything you've done — saving the universe — and us too, more recently — they owe you, don't they?"

"One would think," I murmured with a wry twist of my lips. I glanced down at my phone, at the triple digits of red notifications in my inbox. "But here we are."

And then — a knock. *Tap tap tap* on the VW's door.

Huh. They were being polite. This was... unexpected. But not altogether unpleasant.

Masking my trepidation with unearned bravado, I flung the van doors open wide. There, filling the frame with her towering presence, stood Foollegg. Nine feet of meticulously reptilian stature and that *neck*; her uniform without a crease, a stark contrast to the chaotic dishevelment from our last encounter amid the Dread debacle. New silvery adornments graced her elongated neck, delicate metal cobwebs that somehow managed to bridge the gap between her broad shoulders and her head, perched like an afterthought. She was flanked by four guards, which even I could tell was probably overkill. Maybe she was expecting someone else to be standing in this van tonight.

Her large doe eyes flicked between us, and I held her gaze — or rather, the unassuming slits of her nose. Mimicking her, I offered a nod, firm but not unfriendly.

She dipped her head in a bow, a gesture of respect — or was it mockery? Spurlock and I returned the motion, mirroring the formality. She opened her mouth to speak, but the words that echoed through the bay came from behind her, another stealing them right from her mouth.

"Ms. Webber!" Stook's voice thrummed with an enthusiasm I couldn't trust. His smile was as wide as it was unwarranted. Foollegg tensed up instantly. "How fortuitous of you to come!"

I hadn't seen him since the signing of the accords between the Alliance and, well, me. The agreement we'd had to make to give us the power to deal with the Dread. He looked entirely the same, except maybe his bowling-ball scalp was a tinge more dry.

"You never gave me much of an option," I said, stepping lightly out of the van. "Fortuitous isn't the term I'd choose, but semantics aside, next time let's opt for the full limo service, shall we? It's only proper for an abduction of this caliber."

The cool, hard metal beneath my boots was a welcome relief compared to the lurching uncertainty of the bus. The space we'd docked into was vast, a cavernous room that made our scrappy little bus look like a toy dropped into a sterile, futuristic landscape, all industrial chic and likely not designed with rust buckets like ours in mind. It was probably the same ship from the beach escapade, now that I was giving it a second glance, and feeling the same grittiness underfoot.

Stook's eyes roamed over Spurlock, a visual pat down that bordered on the edge of creepy, too close to subway gawkers for comfort. I couldn't help but link my hand with his, an instinctive move. His hand was unexpectedly steady in mine, betraying none of the nerves I felt thrumming through me.

"Keep your eyes off him," I said, the snap in my voice a clear warning. A young woman's scorn had a kind of weight to it, I figured. Love, or the appearance of it, was as good as armor in some cases.

Stook's smirk widened, an inch shy of friendly but miles from kind. "So, the gossip is true? Your relationship with Zander is no more?"

I clenched my jaw. "My personal life isn't on the docket for discussion," I shot back, trying to draw his focus away from Spurlock. But he was already well within Stook's sights, and he was sizing him up like a werewolf at a buffet.

"Now, where are my manners?" Stook finally bowed. "I am Director Stook, of the Earth Agency. You may have already heard of us."

"And I am Assistant Director Foollegg," added Foollegg hastily.

"Flash," interjected Spurlock, thrusting out a hand with a showman's flair. Stook examined the hand like it was an unidentifiable object, choosing to ignore it, while Foollegg, perhaps out of a sense of duty or awkwardness, shook it vigorously. "Flash Terran… son. Terranson. I'm an… entertainment specialist. From Portland, city of ports."

His confidence was so overdone it might as well have come with a side of theatrical flair. Stook's enormous eyes twitched ever so slightly, a flicker of disbelief. Foollegg didn't react either way.

"And you," Spurlock continued with an apologetic smile that didn't quite reach his eyes, "have interrupted our date night. Sally was just showing me the stars when you so gracefully swooped in." His tone was pitch-perfect polite, a masterpiece of feigned annoyance. I almost believed him myself.

"Date night," Foollegg repeated, her voice flat like soda left out overnight, eyes shifting between us with calculating coldness. "How... quaint."

I stifled a grimace. "Quaint" was one step away from "insignificant" in the Agency's book of underhanded compliments. Yet, despite the obvious skepticism, Foollegg's expression softened just a fraction — either charmed by Spurlock's audacity or amused by his efforts. Her eyes flicked back to him, my existence momentarily forgotten. Well, two can play at that game, and I was about to up the ante.

"Yes, well," I interjected, "we all have our roles to play, *Assistant Director*. When did that happen?"

Foollegg's chest puffed out, her sinew shimmering with a sheen of pride. "Oh, a stroke of fortune," she crowed. "Our new president found my... resourcefulness during the Dread incident rather commendable. Post-crisis, she decided a game of musical chairs was in order for the Earth Agency." She paused, a wry smirk curling her lips. "How does your Earth saying go? The cream rises to the crop?"

Stook's face slowly gained a few shades of red as she spoke. *Oh.* So there was more here than just a field promotion. Was Foollegg being groomed for his role against his will? Had she been promoted to keep him in line? Either way, he wasn't pleased having her here, which meant I probably should enjoy it.

"I suppose congratulations are in order, then," I said. Whether the rift was an intentional good cop, bad cop, or naturally occurring, I'd do anything to widen it. "Assistant Director Foollegg. I like the sound of that."

"So do I," she replied, a hint of a smile playing on her lips. "And it means I no longer need to wear that constrictive skin suit, so I consider that the greater win."

I laughed, delighting in Stook's discomfort. His gaze lingered on Spurlock and our intertwined hands for a moment. With an imperious flick of his long neck, he spun around, signaling our cue to fall in step behind him.

Foollegg signed before ushering us forward. "Quickly now. No dawdling. My schedule doesn't include babysitting duties."

I gave Spurlock's hand a reassuring squeeze. Then, with all the dignity I could muster, I tugged him along, guiding us into the sterile, metallic bowels of the ship that somehow felt more intimidating than any Dread-infested beach ever could.

At least they hadn't taken our phones away. I reached for mine, willing it to buzz, for a new mysterious text message to come in. To save us. Rescue us. To confirm that it really was James Felling, somewhere out there, looking out for me. But my phone, with its impossible data plan, remained stubbornly silent.

"Freaking Omenkin," Spurlock muttered under his breath, casting a wary glance over his shoulder at the guards trailing us. Their eyes were sharp and unyielding, watching our every move with unsettling precision.

"Omenkin?" I echoed, raising an eyebrow. Those muscles were sure getting an unnecessary workout today.

He nodded towards our escort with a subtle tilt of his head. "Yeah, them. Their kind can't tolerate harmonies, sets them on edge. Can you imagine? A universe without fans or groupies. It's my personal version of a horror show. Plus, there's something about that stoic stare that gives me the creeps."

"I know what you mean." I nodded. "They've been studying my planet for years, know so much about our species, and yet I don't know anything about them. Makes you wonder what they truly see when they look at us."

Spurlock smiled lightly, lifting only the corner of his lip, and for a split second I saw Zander in his place, looking at me with excitement in his eyes, ready for another adventure. But just as quickly, the image was broken, as Spurlock chortled and stuck out his tongue, squashing his chin into his chest for a split second. It was all I could do to keep my snort silent.

Stook's office was a testament to indulgence, sprawling and grandiose, a veritable cathedral to command and control. It seemed as though half the space onboard the craft had been dedicated just to these quarters, from the large bay windows and oversized wooden desks to the plush sofas and modern twisted chairs. My blue planet rotated slowly outside the window, Madagascar appearing on one side of the window and slowly making its way to the other as the director welcomed us in. A large portrait of Dany took up almost an entire wall, a surreal reminder of who she'd become.

"Sally Webber," Stook boomed, a thrum of pride in his voice as he gestured to the gaudy room. "Your presence graces us. May I offer refreshments? Mexican Cola, perhaps? Water sourced from the pristine isles of Fiji?" His wave encompassed an array of bottles and glasses on a sideboard that glistened with opulence. "Delicacies from your world, as I understand it."

"No, thank you.", My tone was as crisp as the air in the room.

"Do make yourselves comfortable," Foollegg insisted, indicating the seating with a magnanimous sweep of her arm.

I caught the slight hesitation in Spurlock's posture, his eyes flicking to me for direction. Being the de facto decision-maker wasn't a coat I wore often, but it seemed to fit in these odd circumstances. "We'll remain standing, if it's all the same," I said, planting my feet with subtle resolve.

Stook's smile didn't waver. "Very well, I too prefer the formality of standing."

Spurlock, mimicking our host's example, stood stock-still, his casual vigilance betraying the tension in his frame. Meanwhile, my own muscles coiled instinctively, adopting a readiness that was more reflex than intention. Foollegg stood to the side, her hands crossed behind her back.

"What is this about, Stook?" I asked, once more. "The Alliance has a branch made specifically for contacting us, if you weren't aware."

"I am aware, thank you very much," he replied. Had his neck somehow gotten longer? "But that is the office for *Sibling* liaison, and you aren't either of them. No. We made a pact, you and I and your government."

The hair on my arms and the back of my neck slowly rose to attention. Something definitely wasn't right here. I wasn't foolish enough to assume the Agency wouldn't notice I was on Earth without my usual Sibling escort, but I didn't think they'd jump on me so quickly. I thought I had at least a few days to respond to their barrage of texts.

"Even so, I have a phone, you know."

"One you haven't been answering."

"I've been back on Earth three days, Stook." I spat. "I have my own life to live, and it doesn't involve cleaning up your messes every five minutes. So why have you brought me here?"

"I didn't," he replied with a casual flip of his hand. "You appropriated my vintage transport. I could press charges."

I resisted the urge to face-palm. "I'm not playing games with you, Stook. I was having a great night until you interrupted it."

His defensive posture softened somewhat, though his hands remained raised as if to fend off the accusation. "Technically, the car you took was mine. One typically avoids commandeering property that doesn't belong to them," he said with a tone that suggested he was explaining this concept to a toddler.

"So you set a trap for me? How very Looney Toons." It was taking all my energy to keep cool, to act like this was rolling off my back instead of crushing me into the floor.

Stook's face contorted. "Where are your friends?"

So no more beating around the proverbial bush tonight. "They're dealing with matters that don't involve being kidnapped for impromptu meetings," I retorted. The banter was wearing thin. I could still play dumb, though. Be the simple Earthling he assumed I was. "You're deflecting. What do you want?"

"Well, my dear, if you must know" — Stook's expression morphed into a grimace though it could have been an attempt at a smile — "we would like to offer you a job."

That threw me. "A job?" The words felt like a puzzle, each syllable a piece not quite fitting. "You want to hire me? Let me guess, the cosmos is in peril once more, and it's up to me and the gang to save the day? What's the calamity du jour? An interstellar spaghetti monster looking to turn the galaxy into its personal meatball buffet? Or perhaps the great handkerchief is finally *en route?* Do the whales need a good talking-to?"

Stook's scoff was as dry as the vacuum of space. "Your whales?" He shook his head with an air of amused disdain. "No, Miss Webber, we're offering a bona fide nine-to-five position, complete with the kind of benefits that would make your Earthbound insurance brokers weep."

"The Agency wants to hire *me?*" I couldn't help but let out a bemused snort, my eyebrow arching high enough to threaten my hairline. "What's the gig? Chief coffee fetcher? Head of extraterrestrial payroll calculations?"

"Special relations," Foollegg clarified, her voice taking on the cadence of someone who had rehearsed this pitch. "Your country's president is becoming inconveniently well-informed. He's starting to peel back curtains we'd rather keep closed. We require a liaison between him and the Agency."

Was that why the White House had been trying to call me? I leaned back slightly, arms crossing as Spurlock fiddled with a loose thread on the hem of his jacket, an absent-minded gesture that didn't quite mask his unease. "So I would be… the red telephone? Or rather the gray one?"

"Precisely." Foollegg's lips curled into something that might be considered a smile if one squinted. "He has questions, he goes through you. We have instructions, we relay them through you."

"Why would you want that?" My question was laced with skepticism. "Since when do you actually play by terrestrial rules? Not to mention, we have a UN."

"For diplomacy's sake," Stook replied, the lines on his face softening into a diplomat's practiced concern. "He's a curious one, your American president. And since we can't have him... eliminated — trust me, that approach is old hat and never ends well — we need a Terran to guide his gaze elsewhere. Someone who can feed his curiosity without indulging it."

Spurlock, who had been tracing patterns on the plush carpet with the toe of his shoe, glanced up. He didn't need to be here. He could be safe, on Earth right now. Having him by my side put him at risk. Just being seen with me had painted a massive target on his back. How much of his life had I ruined because I hadn't thought this night through?

"Why not dispatch one of your own?" I pressed on, curious despite myself. "Why am I, of all people, the voice you want?"

Stook leaned forward, his eyes narrowing with a hint of respect. "Miss Webber, your history with us is... complicated. You've become an unexpected variable, one that refuses to be ignored. Our agents are many things, but unpredictable isn't one of them. You, however, embody that particular... charm."

I bit back a burst of incredulous laughter, but it bubbled out as a snort. Spurlock's lips quirked in a suppressed smirk.

"Charm? Cut the shit, Stook. No way would you give a crap about my… unexpectedness." I tossed the word back at Stook like a hot potato and turned to Foollegg. "Tell me the truth."

"Fine. Your president asked for you." She let out a heavy sigh. "Personally, and repeatedly."

That almost felt like a compliment. *Almost.* I'd only met the man twice, and both times were before facing down unsurmountable odds. Just because I was the only person to throw a little kindness his way didn't mean he appreciated me personally.

"So what do you say?" Stook stretched a smile so fake you wouldn't even buy it online. "Will you work for us? For him, for your country?"

"Work for the Agency? Hell no! I'm done with you and your crap. Contract fulfilled. This relationship is meant to go both ways, and from where I'm standing, I haven't gotten anything in return for helping you."

"Well, you did save the universe, the one you're living in."

My laugh was bitter, sharp. "Great, saved a universe. And what do I have to show for it? Not even a lousy t-shirt. How about settling up our expenses?"

"We granted you a pardon," he retorted, as if that settled all debts.

"Oh, I was never the problem," I spat. "You wanted the Siblings, and you thought you had found me as their weak spot. And I continued being a target long after you realized that was a lie. No. You said it yourself: I'm not one of the Siblings. You want me to do your dirty work? You'd better make it worth my while."

Stook's smirk returned, full of alien confidence. "So negotiations haven't stalled. I see. Your species is so... monetarily inclined. Here I was thinking you reveled in your bullshit jobs."

I gave my head a defiant shake, the motion sharp, dismissive. "No dice, Stook. I've got a gig that suits me just fine."

He blinked, slowly and assuredly. "You're unemployed."

"Relocating to DC would be a nightmare."

"With your knack for bending the fabric of space-time?" Stook chortled. "Please. You could keep an apartment by the rings of Saturn and the commute would be the same."

Foollegg's forehead furrowed. "You *did* sign a contract, Miss Webber."

"A contract that covers fifteen other ways of speaking to me that don't involve beaming me up without my consent. If this was covered in the contract, you would have reached me by legitimate means." I squared my shoulders, feeling the weight of the offer — and rejection — equally. "I said no. I'm sure there's someone else out there desperate enough for your so-called opportunity."

"Oh, how noble," Stook sneered, a sinister grin slicing across his face, revealing teeth as predatory as Foollegg's ambitions. "Go back to fetching lattes for the

Siblings — The Sword, The Sand, and the girl-whose-name-we-can't-quite-remember. You want to be a hero? Be the link between your nation and the stars."

Spurlock stepped closer to me, enough for me to feel the warmth emanating off his body. A solid, sturdy reminder that I was not alone. I stood my ground.

"I am nobody's errand girl," I shot back.

"You're…" Stook's laughter erupted, his neck contorting in an unsettling display of glee, a cackle reminiscent of a hyena's. "Oh bright stars, they left you didn't they? The Siblings dropped you! You're alone!"

"No." My reply came hot and swift. "They're on assignment, and they'll return."

"Don't delude yourself, Sally." Stook's voice softened. "Consider my proposition. Be the star-whisperer for your country."

"Not interested." I spun on my heels. "I don't want the job. Come on, *Flash*, we're getting out of here."

I gripped Spurlock's hand — tight. I didn't know exactly how we were getting out of here yet, but I could sense the threats bubbling in Stook's throat, and I wasn't going to let them land. Not again. Not when I thought I was finally free of his shit.

"Very well." He grinned once more, as I marched to the door. "But just so you know, you're either leaving here working for us, or you're not leaving at all."

My laughter surprised even me, bubbling up from a newfound spring of audacity. It filled the room, bouncing off the metallic edges and soft sofas alike.

Foollegg's mask of control slipped, her eyes betraying a flicker of uncertainty.

They were afraid of me. Wary of me, of the chaos I could unchain. Siblings or no Siblings, the Alliance feared me. They were scared of not having me on their side. So, I laughed again, richer, more defiant.

"You think you can keep me here?" I smirked. "Sorry to break it to you, but there isn't a jail that can hold me. Been there, done that."

"I wasn't talking about jail, Miss Webber." Stook's eyes tensed.

"Oh, trying to threaten my family again? My homeworld? I don't think your new president would care too deeply for that!"

Stook's response was swift and sharp. He swept past Foollegg, towards a stately portrait of Dany in regal dress, and flipped it away, revealing the stark glow of a hidden screen. It flickered to life, showcasing a sight that would've been comical if it weren't so incriminating: me, in a shady dive bar's backroom, looking like the ringleader of the galaxy's least threatening rebellion.

Stook leaned forward, his voice oozing false concern as he dangled the threat like a cat toy. "Imagine the scandal," he cooed. "How would your royal chums feel about their darling Earth representative plotting their downfall?"

I crossed my arms suppressing a snort. "You think they read the tabloids? Besides, any story with less drama than an intergalactic war is page five material, at best."

Foollegg arched an eyebrow, her lips curling into a smug crescent. "There are whispers, you know. That the royals are annoyed. That you don't visit enough. That you're missing important events."

I gritted my teeth. Right, like I'm itching to jet off to one of Marcy's stuffy galas. Besides, I'm a time traveler: I can't actually miss a party.

Stook seemed to take my silence as defiance. "If you could have left, you would have done so already. You're not going anywhere."

"Freedom's not just about where you can go," I said, tilting my head. "It's about where you choose to stand."

But then Stook pulled out a blaster and shot Spurlock square in the stomach.

He crumpled like his strings were cut, a silent scream etched on his face. His hands fell to his gut, where his shirt was already turning a vibrant shade of red.

"Spurlock!" I shouted, already by his side. The smell of ozone and char was a slap to the senses. Oh, shit, this was bad. Really, really bad. Hole straight through to the other side bad.

Foollegg was on her knees now, her hands gentle as she reached for his wound. I slapped them away.

"What have you done?" I spat at Stook. "What the hell did you think you'd accomplish?" I grabbed Spurlock's arm. He was still breathing in short, ragged breaths. Conscious, but in too much pain to even scream. "Did you think this would make me yours to control?"

I yanked us out of there, throwing us the only place I could think of, Foollegg's sorrowful eyes the last thing I saw before darkness whisked us away.

As I expected, I did not end up where I wanted to be. Of course we had to make an unnecessary detour first.

FOURTEEN
THE GOOD, THE BAD, AND THE BLEEDING

WHILE I WAS PREPARED FOR AN UNWANTED interruption to my harrowing escape, the universe still disappointed me with its typical cruel indifference as we landed hard on the raspy grass.

I cradled Spurlock, his blood seeping between my fingers. Bone-chilling panic gnawed at me, the edges of my vision blurry. His life was slipping through my hands, and with it, a piece of my own. A cool wind blew across us, chilling my scalding skin.

"Stay with me," I whispered to him. Not that anyone should ever listen to me. I was the reason Spurlock had been on Stook's ship tonight. I was the reason Spurlock had been shot. And I was the reason, somehow, for him to be stuck in the big wide universe, where no hope of rescue could be found for a few more centuries.

I'd been so focused on Spurlock that I'd forgotten what had interrupted my jump in the first place. Zander loomed out of the gloom, absurdly perched on a wooden stool in the middle of a field that sprawled under the infinite expanse of an unpolluted sky. A lantern at his feet cast a pale, yellow light, battling the inky darkness, and a picnic setup lay forgotten, ridiculous in the face of our dire reality. He looked like he was expecting a date, not a medical emergency crash-landing in his time zone.

"Zander!" My voice cracked, fraying with terror. "Spurlock's been shot. My God, he's shot! We need to jump back. Now! Do you understand?" My words tore from my throat, raw and edged with a fear that I couldn't restrain. They were a plea, a command, all my fears laid bare. Spurlock's breath was a ragged thing, and each exhale was a countdown I was desperate to stop. I knelt beside him, pressing my hands to the wound with a pressure that was both futile and necessary. The weight of Spurlock's life bore down on me, anchoring me in the moment even as my soul screamed to escape it. The hole in his gut hadn't just destroyed his innards, but from the way I could precariously see through him, it had taken a chunk of his spine as well. A cylinder of Spurlock vaporized in an instant. If he survived tonight, he would never walk again.

No. I gripped him harder, focusing on his ragged breaths, to the life that still clung to him. I could fix him. Heal him. My blood would do the trick, just like it had for me, in the hospital after the power plant had exploded. But if I gave it to him now, before we jumped — I shuddered at the thought. I'd been given a choice for this life: Spurlock deserved the same.

Zander's initial scowl dissolved, his features morphing to mirror my own horror. "Sally—"

"Don't you dare Sally me! If you're controlling this, then please, for the love of everything, just stop, I'm begging you!" I was past pride, past decorum. I was a raw nerve, exposed and pleading. Tears flowed down my face, carving hot tracks through the grime on my cheeks. "Let me go!"

The desperation in my voice must have pierced through his facade because Zander, with a growl of frustration, abandoned his post by the stool and strode towards me.

"How many times must I tell you, I am not responsible for you coming here? The mere fact you keep returning to *me* makes it clear you're the one with a stalker complex."

"Zander, this is not the time!" My voice rose, cracking, each word slicing into the silent night, fracturing the stillness. "I can heal him, but not here. I have to keep him alive until we can jump back. You have to help me. Please!"

He hesitated, something akin to realization dawning in his eyes. For a moment, he was the Zander who would drop everything to help a friend in need. Or even a friend of a friend.

Spurlock's breaths were coming in shallow gasps. I could barely hear them anymore. I leaned closer, my hands still pressing against the wound, begging him to cling to the tenuous grip he had on life. "Just stay with us, Spurlock. That's it, fight a little longer," I coaxed, hoping my voice could be a lifeline thrown into the raging sea of his consciousness like he had been for me.

"Help me lift him," Zander directed, his arms sliding beneath Spurlock's back with practiced ease. I positioned myself by Spurlock's feet, and on a count of three, we hoisted his limp form onto the blankct strewn across the grass.

I knelt as Zander wrapped him with meticulous care, tucking the edges of the blanket around him like a burrito of warmth and security, keeping him immobile and ensuring he did not feel the bite of the night's chill. That, and keeping the blood inside the body where it belonged.

"Will this help? Is it enough?" My voice trembled as I stared down at Spurlock, whose pallor painted a stark contrast against the vibrant red of the blanket. His life-force seemed to wane with every passing second, leaving him a ghostly version of the man I knew.

"It has to be," Zander replied, the gravity of the situation weighing down his words. His gaze locked with mine. "But only if you mean it when you say you can heal him on the other side."

The night air hung heavy around us. Zander's hand found my shoulder, a silent vow of his support, while my hand, slick with Spurlock's blood, remained firmly on his chest. I couldn't let go, not without knowing if I'd leave him behind in this strange half jump. In that moment, the past and the present collided, our collective breaths caught in the balance, waiting for time to restart its march.

Just a little longer, Spurlock. Hang on just a little longer.

Desperation laced my voice as I glared at Zander, hand balled into a fist at my side. "I can't keep waiting like this," I seethed, the urgency clawing at my insides. "I need to get home, now. He's running out of time."

Zander threw his hands up. "I'm not the one holding you here."

"But you're always right here when I come through!" I snapped, frustration boiling over. My gaze darted back to Spurlock; his life was seeping away into the earth while we squabbled. It was maddening. "How did you even know when I'd arrive?" My words came out sharp, a knife-edge of accusation. Zander lounged back, the picture of nonchalance that belied the calculating sharpness in his eyes. "Where are we?"

"Just outside of White Hall Slip. New York. And to answer your first question, I had a chat with Bennie, crunched some numbers." He dismissed the complexity with a shrug. "You're so… predictable."

"Predictable?" I echoed with a scoff. "Now isn't the time for your… condescension. I need to get back. We need to break this... this cycle!"

He leaned forward, a pretense of sagacity in his pose. "Maybe there's something deeper here," he mused, chin resting on steepled fingers. "Some intrinsic connection between us."

I nearly choked in exasperation. Sure, his blood was the catalyst for my ability to jump and all that jazz, yes, but this — this was absurd. Why here? Why this Zander? Of all the countless versions scattered across the threads of time, why him?

"Whatever twisted bond this is, it ends now." My voice was a command, all steel and no velvet. I looked down at Spurlock, his breaths shallow and uneven. "He's *dying*."

"And you can't heal him now, in this time?" Zander's question felt like a challenge.

My eyes met his. "You're aware of what our blood does, right?" The words fell from my lips, a whisper lost in the wind.

In the dimming light, with the scent of blood and wet grass filling the air, the conversation hovered, fragile and unresolved, while Spurlock's life hung in the balance.

Zander nodded, the calmness in his reply at odds with the turmoil within me. "It heals."

"Yes, it heals... it heals *everything*." My fists clenched, knuckles whitening, a futile attempt to contain the maelstrom of emotions brewing within. "But if he jumps with even a trace of that blood in his system..."

"What are you saying?" Zander's eyes widened as he turned to me, the lantern light casting shadows that danced with the dawning horror in his expression.

I met his gaze, unflinching. "He'll become like us."

There you go, Zander. The truth. Take it all in. Digest this horror.

"Us." His eyes were wide, and for a second, his facade dropped, and he was as scared as I was. "So that's how I do it. How I… *made* you like me."

"Correct," I spat, the confession burning my throat. "What haven't you turned me into? You've rendered me immortal, turned me into a weapon everyone's just dying to get their hands on. I can probably never go home."

I couldn't stop myself now, the words were rolling off my tongue like lava from the mouth of a volcano. Zander was frozen in place, unable to move or to respond. Tears blurred my vision, hot and unbidden, spilling over.

"I can't get anything right, Zander! I can't control my jumps, I can't return home, and now, Spurlock's…" A sob wrenched itself from my chest, raw and aching. "His blood is on my hands, all of this is on my hands because of what you've done to me!"

Zander stood frozen, the stool an afterthought as his hands gripped it. A useless anchor in the storm of my breaking.

"And you," I continued, my voice twisting into a snarl, each word laced with venom and grief, "you stand there, with your eternal youth and that smug assurance, boasting about your feats. You took the one person who meant everything to me. My brother. How can you stand there and not understand the searing loneliness you've inflicted upon me?

"Why, Zander? Why can't you just leave me be? Why did you leave me to suffer through this... this endless solitude?" I buckled over, no longer able to support the weight of the anguish that clawed through me. I collapsed on Spurlock, my hand still pressed to his wound, as if I could will my own life into him.

The oppressive silence was like a shroud, heavy with the things I couldn't say, and all the while, Spurlock's breathing was becoming shallower. We were losing the race against time. I drew my knees to my chest, the grass like tiny fingers tugging at the fabric of my pants. *Distraction, distraction. Grounding.* It wasn't enough. I sprawled out, letting the cool earth siphon the heat from my burning cheeks, a poor reprieve for the scalding tears I fought to keep at bay.

Above me, the stars glistened, but their beauty felt mocking, too serene amid the chaos. They didn't care about Spurlock's fading heartbeats or the maelstrom of my emotions. Zander's silhouette melted away as I lay there, giving me a moment's illusion of solitude before he joined me on the ground, his presence an unwelcome reminder of reality.

We were two figures cast adrift in an ocean of night, the quiet between us a vast expanse. His breath, once a lullaby, now was just a sound, like any other in the night — distant and disconnected from the man I once thought I knew.

Then, in the stillness that only a night like this could weave, his voice cut through, a thread fraying at the edges. "What will I do to you, Sally Webber?" he finally whispered, as if speaking to the stars themselves. "There's more, isn't there? The story's not all told. I don't know the you that you know, the one who's lived all this. So tell me."

My laugh was a bitter note that didn't belong amidst the symphony of the tranquil night. "Why?" I spat back, the pain and rage a tumultuous storm behind my ribs. "You want to know your future? So you can rewrite the script and direct a better ending? You think you can just edit out the parts you don't like?" The words hung heavy in the air, a solemn declaration that could not be undone.

The stars were just distant suns, I reminded myself, cold and unfeeling. They didn't weep for Spurlock or for me, nor for the twisted paths we'd been forced down by fate — or by Zander. And there in the dark, side by side with the man who was the beginning and could very well be the end of my entire world, I felt the weight of eternity pressing down, suffocating me with the immensity of everything that lay ahead and everything that could never be changed.

"No." The dry grass rustled as Zander shifted, his every movement a harsh reminder of the present.

"Changing my future would be easy, but it wouldn't be right. Not to you. I could choose paths where our lives never intertwine, where you remain a stranger. You're not even my type. But what good would that do? Literally, what *good* would it do? No, I want to know, so that right now, I can curse Zander's name along with you."

His words were a puzzle, pieces that didn't fit into the jigsaw of my shattered reality. I propped myself up, clutching Spurlock, heels digging into the soft earth, searching through the darkness for the outline of Zander's form, for any clue to the sincerity of his confession. But he only lay gazing at the cosmos with reverence.

"Why would you…" My voice trailed off, weak and raw, as my eyes traced the hollow he had created in the grass, his battered boots peeking out as silent witnesses to our shared turmoil. A boot that reached out to find mine, to find contact, to anchor us both in the here and now.

"Because you are not alone," he said, his tone a calm amidst my tempest of despair. I let my body sink back to the ground, a futile attempt to hide from the vulnerability of his gaze. "I may not know you, Sally, but I know this echo of emptiness. I understand loss, the kind of anguish that immortality brands upon the soul, a loneliness that few can fathom. I am acquainted with solitude."

Our hands sought each other through the cool blades. His warmth was a beacon in the darkness that surrounded us, steady in the chilling wind.

"You're going to break me," I whispered, a feeble admittance of my vulnerability, of the dread that had taken root deep within. "That's our future, Zander. You're going to break me."

"You're not broken," he replied. "No more than I, no more than any of us who bear the scars of existence."

And there, under the indifferent gaze of a thousand distant stars, our hands clasped in the sanctuary of the night. A sliver of solace pierced the veil of my desolation. In the soft grip of shared pain, there was a fragile strength, a bond forged in the crucible of our unique suffering. The cool touch of grass, the subtle warmth of his hand, the steady decline of Spurlock's breaths — all painted a picture too poignant, too intimately laced with the intricate tapestry of life and loss.

God, how I missed him. I missed the Zander I had loved, the Zander whose life I got to share, even for a small while. I missed being loved by him, fiercely and intensely, like I was the only star in the sky. But that Zander was gone. Literally. If what Blayde said was true, then he'd stopped existing the moment he'd let all his memories back in.

He was gone, and all I could do was mourn his loss.

But here, now, this was another Zander. A fresh-slate Zander. His closeness was a shock to the senses, Zander's face emerging from the camouflage of the grass like a bizarre jack-in-the-box. And those eyes, shimmering with a silvery clarity that brought back a torrent of memories — yet they were foreign, not the eyes that had watched me with warmth. There was an involuntary reaction, his arm snaking around my back with an intimacy that seemed to have a mind of its own. He was a furnace in the cool night, and I was inexplicably drawn to the heat.

Wait, what?

"What the hell are you doing?" I stammered, scrambling back. My mind raced, processing the clash between the shock of his closeness and the misplaced comfort that seemed to stem from some kind of muscle memory.

"Not alone…" His voice was a velvet whisper, and then his lips were on mine, his kiss an echo of familiarity and a scandalously rehearsed maneuver. My eyelids fluttered down like they'd been choreographed to do so, and for a brief, bewildering moment, I was swept up in the momentum of it all.

As his leg brushed mine, something clicked. His movements, previously a fluid dance, now felt like he'd been cast as the tree in a primary school play.

"Stop that right now," I gasped, as if waking from a trance. The ludicrousness of it all shocked me back to my senses.

"What?" His confusion would have been almost endearing if it wasn't so misplaced, propping himself up like a befuddled prince in a twisted fairy tale, his leg — the bare skin of his leg, I now noticed with an internal eye roll — being the only point of contact left.

"None of what you just said made any sense," I declared, untangling myself from the mess. He looked puzzled as I retreated. Earnest. All fake. "You want to curse Zander's name? What do you even mean by that?"

It was impossible to stifle the laughter that bubbled up — laughter mixed with disbelief and a bucketful of absurdity. Seriously? He was about as subtle as a neon sign in a monastery. His ploy was so outrageously misjudged that it circled back to being hilarious.

Bewilderment unfolded across his face, like the gears in his brain were grinding with ridiculous slowness. "I'm angry at him too," he said, sounding about as sincere as a cat professing its hatred for catnip.

"No, you wouldn't care less." I barked a laugh. "Screw you, Zander."

"What?" He reached for my hand, and I dodged his grasp — a matador to his bull —before slapping his hand away. "What was that for?"

The man had the audacity of feigning indignation as he massaged his wrist.

"There's a man dying here," I spat. "And you're taking the opportunity to make a move on me?"

"No, Sally, I…" His protest fizzled out, as convincing as a wet firecracker.

He sat there, the image of a forlorn toddler, clothes askew, gazing up at me with the wide-eyed innocence of someone who'd just learned the stove could burn. His frustration carved lines of shadow across his face. The props of his absurd theater lay discarded around

Spurlock — stool, blanket, and that damn lantern. He jumped to his feet and bundled them up with a huff.

Wonderful, now he was throwing a tantrum.

"I'm not your type, remember?" I threw the words at him, hoping they would slap.

"Three boobs," he muttered, crossing his arms over his chest.

"You know what's really sad? You think this is about you and your bruised ego. You wouldn't know genuine connection if it hit you in the face." I gritted my teeth, clutching Spurlock tighter than ever. Whatever connection was tying me to him, whatever lingering feelings were pulling me to his side, snapped clear off. "No wonder it takes you a few thousand years to become the Zander who's actually a hero."

He scoffed, a sound that came out more like a snarl, stuffing his hands deep into his pockets before kicking the lantern in frustration. Everything happened in slow motion as the lantern somersaulted into the dry brush, a smash, a splash, and then a whisper of flame that grew into a roar.

"Grow up, Zander." But the sarcastic quip died in my throat as the fire took on a life of its own as the lantern rolled down the hill and spread the flames along with it. "Oh, shit!"

He cursed, I cursed, we both leapt at the fire. I stomped the grass, but for every flame I extinguished, three more caught and spread. Nothing we could do was helping. A pathetic duo in a slapstick comedy, if it weren't so tragically real. I had to stop the blaze, I had to; it could march right up to the city, a monster of our making. It could destroy revolutionary New York, turn the course of the war. The flames taunted us, crackling with the kind of glee you'd expect from a villain in a silent film, casting an eerie pall over Spurlock's prone figure, throwing my priorities in stark relief.

"Damn it, Zander!" No more quips, no more biting remarks, just raw panic in my voice as the field before us became a pyre. "You can't just light my history on fire!"

This. This… this was how we'd be remembered in the annals of a city's history — not as heroes, not as villains, but as the clowns who lit the match that burned through the night.

And then everything snapped back into place — the gravity, the grief, and the grotesque reality that no amount of comic relief could overshadow. Spurlock was dying, dying! — and we were yanked back to the now, to the cold, harsh truth that lay on a surprisingly intemporal vintage rug, tragically adorned with the scarlet of his blood.

There were no tears as I screamed at Meedian to find me a syringe. No sniffles as I stabbed it into myself, then Spurlock, holding his body steady while my fresh blood coursed through him. Only relief as his wounds knit shut, and his breath became steady.

Relief, and silence, as I knew I wouldn't see that version of Zander ever again.

FIFTEEN

REGRETS ARE FOREVER, AND FOREVER IS QUITE A LONG TIME IF I DO SAY SO MYSELF

A GNAWING SENSE OF GUILT IS BETTER THAN coffee when it comes to keeping one up all night.

I sat at Spurlock's bedside as the sun set and rose again, all the while not knowing if I'd made him worse rather than better. The gaping hole in his middle was closed, thank the universe, not that I had an X-ray to check that everything had grown back right. At the very least, he was breathing, and, by the sounds of it, snoozing, though I wouldn't say peacefully. His chest rose and fell with a rhythm that was too mechanical to be comforting.

All I could do was wait until he, hopefully, woke up.

Sunan had rushed back to pick up the company VW bus in Portland, and in it, the dead orb that once held James. Monuments to my failures slowly traveling back to me. My phone felt like a grenade in my hand — it could go off with good news or bad, and I was just staring at it, waiting. If James was out there, alive somewhere, why the radio silence? What was keeping her from sending a message outside of the mysterious pins? My mind spun with images of her, altered and distant, and a cold stone settled in my stomach.

Who are you? I finally texted Customer Support, a message I should have sent days ago. No answer. Not even the three little dots that suggested anyone was typing. If this wasn't James on the other end, who was it?

Needing a distraction but unable to release my grasp on my phone, I dove down the internet rabbit hole to see if this last trip into the past had had any effect on history. Not that it should have, seeing as how my present remained unchanged. Part of me wondered if I'd even notice changes to my own timeline, but the mere fact I could hold two different versions of events in my mind — John being dead and John as a tyrant — was further proof time was as screwed as the people who lived it.

With every search result that loaded, I found myself caught between a morbid relief that history seemed intact and an irrational disappointment that we hadn't left a mark. But who in their right mind wants to be remembered for setting the world ablaze?

It was on my umpteenth search page, scrolling past accounts of battles, heroes, and politics of 1776, that the absurd truth nearly knocked the wind out of me.

There, in an old painting, amid the chaos of reds and oranges, was the unmistakable depiction of the Great Fire of New York. After the British took control of New York City in September of that year, a massive fire broke out, destroying a significant portion of the city. The cause of the fire was never definitively established; some speculated it was an accident, while others believed it was an act of rebellion by American patriots to deny the British comfortable quarters. Enacting a plan that George Washington himself had considered and dismissed.

The realization slammed into me with the subtlety of a sledgehammer. Zander and I hadn't just tripped through a footnote in history — we were the footnote. The fire wasn't set by retreating American forces or by looters taking advantage of the chaos... It was him. His lantern. His accident. Our fight.

I snorted, hand flying to my mouth. Spurlock continued sleeping. Good, I wasn't ruining his recovery with my existential crisis. All this time, the past had been pulling at me, a cosmic tug-of-war, because it needed me there. It wasn't some grand destiny or a significant historical intervention — it was to ensure Zander kicked over that damned lantern. The timeline hadn't gone off track; it had barreled down the path it always had, with me and Zander as the unwitting conductors of a citywide inferno.

If my phone was made of paper, I would have crumpled it up and tossed it in the bin. Are you kidding me? Every time I tried to tread my own path, every time I tried to do what was right, to exercise my own free will and all that jazz, time itself conspired to use me as a pawn.

I would never be free. Of Time, of the Agency, of the universe trying to control me for their own gain. They made me this way, to use me this way.

And Zander… part of me felt for Zander, *my* Zander. Having met that awful version of himself, so young, cocky, and immature, shoved back into his mind along with countless others… I could understand why he'd snapped.

But I would never forgive him for *how* he'd snapped.

Cool waves ran through my body. This was too much for me to handle, too much for me to process. I needed air. I needed my old meds. I needed…

I needed a friend.

Please, I texted customer support. *I need to know.*

No answer. No read notification. No nothing.

I pulled the small silver key chain out of my pocket, weighing it in my palm. Clyde was a pain, but this was also exactly what he was built for: lines of code and canned responses for a person in crisis. A wall to bounce things off of.

I held my breath as I pressed the button. Clyde materialized beside Spurlock's bed, his holographic form flickering to life. I'd forgotten just how big he was, just how imposing: his cuddly blue form filled my field of vision, his face bright and smile wide, both comforting and comically oversized in the sleek, modern room.

"Good day, Sally!" He said cheerily. "If you're viewing this message, my reboot was a smashing success. Please note, I did not literally smash anything. System malfunction during our last interaction detected. Would you like to report this to my creators?"

"No, Clyde, that won't be necessary." I sighed, my relief at his presence battling the anxiety bubbling inside me. "Can you tell me why you crashed? I'd rather avoid a repeat performance."

"Running diagnostic now." His eyes glazed over for a brief moment before refocusing on me. "Analysis complete. It appears I experienced an emotional overload, Sally. You possess an impressive array of complex feelings."

"Right." Because that definitely helps you feel better, confirmation that your problems are too much even for an AI.

"How long have I been inoperative? This environment is unfamiliar to me." Clyde's eyes scanned the room, his programmed smile faltering, then evaporating entirely as he fully registered my state. "You seem to be experiencing considerable distress."

"You could say that," I replied, a lump forming in my throat. "I'm a disaster, Clyde. Everything I touch falls apart."

Clyde drifted closer, his head tilting in an approximation of empathy. "Experiencing such feelings is not uncommon, particularly for individuals with your level of influence. However, if we examine this logically—"

I raised a hand. I wasn't in the mood for an analytical approach. "I'm not in the mood for logic, Clyde. I just need... someone to listen, I guess."

He remained silent, but I could feel his full attention. I couldn't help but feel a strange comfort in his company — artificial yet somehow earnest. "It's like... why can't I just have a moment of peace?" My voice trembled. "I'm just trying to survive, to heal from everything that's happened. But it seems like everyone just wants to use me. The Agency, Zander, freaking time itself! And whenever I try to take a stand, to set boundaries, to protect myself, it just ends up hurting someone else. Can't I just... exist without causing a catastrophe? I don't even belong to myself."

Clyde's image flickered. Was this too much for him as well? Would he crash, leaving me alone again?

But Clyde didn't crash. Instead, his digital form stabilized, casting a soothing glow in the dim room. "Sally, you are more than the chaos that surrounds you. You are more than the sum of your actions and their consequences. The weight you carry, the burdens you bear — they should not solely be yours to shoulder."

A humorless chuckle escaped my lips. "Not solely mine? Clyde, every choice I make, every step I take — it's like setting off a chain reaction. Haven't you been listening? Anyone who tries to help me ends up at death's door." I gestured to Spurlock's sleeping form. "I'm a walking disaster, a grenade with the pin perpetually loose."

Clyde's holographic face conveyed a sense of deep understanding, or at least, the closest approximation an AI could muster. "Your worth isn't measured by how much you can carry or how far you can push yourself before breaking."

"But what if I'm already broken, Clyde?" The words spilled out, raw and unfiltered. "What if every piece of me that's supposed to be good just ends up hurting the people I care about? Spurlock almost died because of me. My friends... they're all in danger, because of me. My very existence puts them at risk. How am I supposed to live with that?"

Clyde paused. "Sally, it's crucial to acknowledge that while you have influence, you are not omnipotent. You cannot control all outcomes or foresee every consequence. It's human to err, to feel, to break and mend."

I buried my face in my hands, feeling the dam within me threaten to burst. "But I'm not just human anymore, am I? I'm this... thing. This anomaly. And everyone around me pays the price for it."

Clyde floated closer, his form enveloping me in a comforting, albeit artificial, embrace. I couldn't feel him: there was nothing to touch. But I could *feel* him, his presence. Knowing he was there, I felt a warmth that wasn't imagined. "You are still human, Sally. You feel, you care, you love. Those are the things that define your humanity, not your abilities or your mistakes. Remember, it's okay to seek help, to lean on others, to not be okay."

I shook my head. "Maybe... maybe it's better if I just distance myself. Keep everyone safe from... from me."

"Sally." Clyde's tone was gentle yet firm. "Isolation isn't the solution. It's connection, understanding, and acceptance that bring healing. You're not alone in this journey, no matter how solitary the path may seem."

His words echoed in the silence. But the fear, the guilt, the sense of being a live wire untethered — it all still clung to me, a shadow I couldn't seem to escape.

"But I'm not allowed that connection, am I?" My hands dug into the wicker of my chair. "I'll never stop being the grenade."

A realization dawned on me — a painful, heart-wrenching epiphany. To protect those I cared about, to stop being the catalyst of chaos, I needed to pull away. To recede into the background and observe from a distance where my touch couldn't warp the lives around me.

Spurlock's sudden awakening jarred the stillness of the room, his groan cutting through the heavy air like a beacon of life. I snapped to attention, my heart leaping into my throat as I watched him blink into consciousness, slowly. I flew out of my chair, reaching for his side as he pushed himself gently up to a seated position.

Clyde clapped his digital hands, a sound as surreal as the moment itself. "You see? Your friend here — Spurlock, was it? — is a perfect example of—"

But Clyde's words were background noise, lost in the tidal wave of emotions crashing over me. My eyes were locked on Spurlock, whose smile was like a sunrise after the darkest night. There was a luminescent vitality to him, a vibrancy that seemed almost otherworldly. His dark hair shimmered as if imbued with life itself.

"Hello." His voice was clear, strong, and filled with wonder. It was as if he was hearing himself for the first time.

"Hey," I managed to respond, shakier than I would have liked. "How... how are you feeling?"

The question seemed to ignite something within him. With a sudden burst of energy, Spurlock leaped to his feet, his movement so swift and fluid it caught me off guard. I stumbled backward, unprepared for the intensity of his revival, landing unceremoniously on the cold floor of his room.

Spurlock's hand shot out, grasping mine. His grip was warm, steady, and full of life — a stark contrast to the fragile state he'd been in mere hours ago.

"Spurlock, you're..." Words failed me. The transformation was nothing short of miraculous. He was a picture of health and strength.

"Is this... did you..." He faltered, his eyes searching mine for answers, for understanding.

"Spurlock, you were..." My voice caught in my throat. The enormity of the situation, the weight of what I had done, the choice I'd made — it all came crashing down on me, overwhelming.

But it didn't matter: Spurlock wasn't listening. He was too busy marveling at his own hands, flexing them, feeling the rush of life coursing through his veins. His whole being radiated a sense of wonder.

His hands opened and closed. "I feel... alive," he breathed out. "More alive than I've ever felt."

His eyes met mine, questioning. The room seemed to grow colder, the shadows stretching longer, as if the past itself was seeping through the walls. It was as if he stood at the edge of a new beginning, teetering between overwhelming joy and a creeping sense of unease. Gone was the rockstar persona that coated our every interaction: this was the man beneath. The real Spurlock.

He touched his abdomen, his fingers tracing the line where death had nearly claimed him. "I was... shot, wasn't I?" A shiver of realization rippled through him. "That really happened?"

My nod was slow, heavy with the weight of my guilt. "Stook shot you. To get to me. I'm so, so sorry." How could I explain the lengths I'd gone to to save him? How could I justify the choices I'd made in the face of his mortality? "You were dying, Spurlock."

His gaze pierced through me, searching for answers. "What did you do, Sally?" His question hung in the air, crystalline and sharp, the enormity of my decision a tangible presence in the room.

"I had to save you," I whispered. My mouth had gone suddenly dry. "It was my fault. You weren't meant to be caught in this. I did the only thing I could think of."

"And what was that?" His question was barely audible.

I cleared my throat, the words feeling like they were crawling out of a pit. "I gave you my blood." I locked eyes with him. The mix of chaos and clarity in his eyes was almost comical. "It was the only way. Now, you might heal like Wolverine for a little while, but nothing more, and without the cool claws. I promise, nothing else has changed."

His brows furrowed. "What's a wolverine?"

"Right. Terran reference. You'll heal... fast. Really, really fast."

"*Novalicious.*" He said reverently, staring at his hands before turning his eyes back to me. "Then why do you look like you've swallowed a lemon?" He reached for my shoulders, his hands warm as he clutched me. "If you're afraid that I'm going to disapprove of your methods, stop. You saved my life. I saw the light at the end of the tunnel and everything. I was going to die. You saved my life, Sally. I cannot thank you enough."

I should've felt victorious, but instead it was like there was a boulder on my chest. I swallowed, my breathing becoming difficult.

Spurlock seemed to notice. "It's fine, seriously. Lots of species use another's blood for healing purposes. Where do you think we get aspirin from? It's alright, Sally. I owe you my life."

I swallowed hard, the next words clinging to my throat like barbs. "It's just…" I felt like I was about to drop the other shoe. "There's a teensy side effect."

He leaned forward. "Is this one of those ironic curses? Like, if I ever sing again, the wound will come back."

"No, nothing like that. Is that something that happens? Really? No, I was going to say I can't jump you anymore. And if you do jump…"

His eyebrows knitted together. "I die?"

"Worse. You could become immortal." I watched his face for a reaction.

He blinked, then burst out laughing. The hands gripping my shoulders let go, only to wrap me in the warmest embrace. Spurlock swung me around like a ballet dancer. For a brief moment I could almost forget the enormity of what I'd done. Almost. But, the reality of the situation settled back in, heavy and unyielding. I had saved Spurlock's life, but at what cost to his future? And to mine?

"Immortal? That's the side effect? Sally, that's like complaining about winning the lottery but having to pay taxes on it. Seriously, jump me now, let's test it out! Stop looking so crestfallen, Sally. I'm alive thanks to you. I owe you more than a power ballad, you deserve your own rock opera."

I rolled my eyes as he put me back down. "Look, Spurlock, being immortal isn't like getting an all-you-can-eat pass at the buffet of life." It felt like trying to explain the dangers of juggling chainsaws to a child who'd just found his dad's toolbox. "It's more like being the last person at a party that never ends. Fun at first, then just... endless. I've never met a happy immortal."

"But what happened with Stook back there wouldn't be an issue anymore," he argued, a spark of mischief in his eye. His hands still hadn't left my shoulders. "Frash, he would be able to shoot me all he wants, he'd never get..."

"Yeah, but you'll also watch everyone you care about grow old and leave you behind." I sighed, my attempt at a stern look failing miserably in the face of... well, his face. "Just..."

Then, without any more words, his face was suddenly, wonderfully close, his lips pressing softly but with an assurance that swept away my protests. It was everything a kiss should be — warm, gentle, filled with a sweetness that seeped into the cold corners of my heart I didn't realize were there. For a fleeting eternity, I melted into it, into him, letting go of the weight of forever and just living in the now. His arms enveloped me, not just a physical embrace but a promise of something more, something profound.

But as his embrace tightened, it wasn't just comfort that it promised, but a reminder of what this could mean. His delicious warmth should have been comforting, but instead, it felt like a warning siren blaring in my head.

"Spurlock, wait." I pulled back with a jolt. The sudden movement caught him off guard, and his arms fell away. "I — I can't do this."

His face crumpled with confusion. "Do what, Sally? I'm just…"

"No, you don't understand." The words tumbled out in a panicked rush. "Every time someone gets close to me, something bad happens. I'm a magnet for trouble. And now you... with my blood in you, it's just too dangerous."

He reached out but I stepped back, putting more space between us. "Sally, you're overthinking this. We'll figure it out together—"

"I can't, Spurlock." My voice trembled. "I'm glad you're okay, I really am. But I have to go. I can't risk hurting you or anyone else."

I jumped before he had a chance to reply. The familiar pull of time and space enveloped me, leaving Spurlock behind and a piece of my heart with him.

It was time to take back control.

SIXTEEN

A STITCH IN TIME SAVES NONE

TRUST TIME TRAVEL TO PUT YOU SQUARELY IN your place.

The wind was being a real drama queen atop the Big Sur cliffs, howling and tossing my hair like it was auditioning for a shampoo commercial. There I stood, just a few feet away from an overlook that had haunted more than just my family albums.

"Where are we, Sally?" Clyde's presence was a soft blue glow to my right, his tone laced with digital concern. "You seem to be engaging in avoidance behavior. What are you feeling?

I didn't turn to him. My eyes were fixed on the road below, still deserted — but not for long. It's easy to predict the future when you've already lived it.

"Sally, you're worrying me." Clyde's voice escalated, a pixelated edge of panic creeping in. "Please, step away from the edge."

"Oh, don't worry about me." I shook my head. "Even if I were to jump, it wouldn't change anything."

Clyde was closer now, his voice rising further still. "There is no need for panic. Spurlock is alive, healthy, and he appreciates everything you've done for him. You are *fine*. You don't need to further isolate yourself."

Isolate myself? Oh, the irony! As if the universe hadn't already thrown me into its own version of solitary confinement, complete with emotional torture. And what did Clyde know about isolation, anyway? He was just lines of code masquerading as a cuddly, albeit annoying, panda.

No. If I was such a disaster, then I was going to do something about it.

"I'm not planning on jumping today, Clyde," I muttered, the bitterness in my voice as harsh as the wind. "As a matter of fact, no one is going to fall. I'm here to save a life."

"Sally, I must advise against this," he said, sounding like a GPS that had taken a wrong turn into philosophy. "If you're considering changing the course of time…"

"I'm not considering it," I scoffed, squinting into the horizon where the Pacific Ocean met the sky. "It's already decided."

As I spoke, a car appeared in the distance, a tiny dot against the vastness of the Pacific Coast, growing steadily as it approached the overlook. The past was about to replay, and I was here to rewrite it, to seize control from the hands of fate.

Time travel might put you in your place, but today, I was going to push back. Hard.

I looked down at the overlook where life had thrown its curveball, where my brother John had gone from family jokester to tragic hero. "Clyde, for once, can you not be the voice of reason? I'm about to rewrite a tragedy, and I need dramatic background music, not a lecture."

"Sally, the consequences of altering such a pivotal event could be catastrophic."

"Yeah, so I've heard. But Zander broke time, and he's still out there, getting off scot-free."

My gaze was fixed on the car. The family inside, oblivious to the impending doom, was about to have their world turned upside down.

"Look, Clyde: Time's been jerking me around since before I was born. It's about time I jerked it back."

Clyde's hologram wobbled as if he were bracing for impact. "The balance of time is delicate—"

"If I wanted a lecture, I'd have stayed in college! Right now, for once, I need to be the hero of my own story."

The car was pulling over now. Four people emptied out into the overlook. I could feel the phantom of my heartbeat inside my silent ribcage. I was so ready for college, then. For change. So hopeful. Thinking that maybe that was what I needed to feel better, not knowing I was about to get much worse. My past, the moment that had changed everything, was playing out right before my eyes.

"Sally, please reconsider." Clyde reached for my shoulder, his blue hand phasing right through. "The fabric of time isn't a plaything—"

"I'm done playing." I stepped closer to the edge. Below me, a younger version of myself was looped in a familial embrace with John. Alive. Breathing. A stark contrast to the lifeless figure I held in my arms on Planet Nope.

I paused, letting the scene etch itself into my mind. John was so much younger, more vibrant than the faded memories I clung to. I had always looked up to him, the protective big brother. Now, I was the older one, aged beyond my years by experiences he'd never know.

The car snaked its way around the bend, oblivious to the lives it was about to shatter. A mechanical grim reaper on cue.

My family stood there, blissfully unaware of the impending disaster. And John, my John, about to play the unwilling hero in a tragedy that never should have been. The wind whipped around me, as if the very air was charged with the tension of the moment. Every fiber of my being was focused on the scene below, ready to leap into action, to alter the course of history. This was more than a do-over; this was a temporal *up yours*. The moment to take back control, to tell Time it didn't own me. I was the wild card in its neatly shuffled deck.

Showtime.

The car was so close now, a beast on a collision course with my past. But here I was, Sally Webber, time-traveling wrench in the works.

It was time to settle my debt with fate.

"Sally—"

In an instant, I was inside the car. My hands shot out, grasping for the steering wheel, ready to wrench it away from its deadly trajectory.

But reality has a way of defying expectations. The driver's scream sliced through the air, a piercing sound that froze me in place.

"How did you get in here?" he gasped, eyes wide with terror.

In his panic, the car veered sharply, swerving directly towards the overlook, barreling towards the younger versions of myself and John. Time seemed to slow down, each second stretching into an eternity as I watched the inevitable unfold.

My hands hovered over the wheel, unable to move, unable to change the course of history. I was a spectator in my own tragic play, unable to alter the script I had so desperately sought to rewrite.

Or maybe I just had. Maybe this was how it was always meant to be. Maybe this moment of horror had always been my destiny, and I had always been the one to deal the blow.

My younger self, acting on instinct, dove away from danger. But John... John stood frozen, his expression a mirror of the terror I felt. I remembered him giving me the push out of the way that saved me. But watching the scene play out from the car, it was all so different.

It was all wrong.

Maybe because it never happened this way. Because I was never in this car. Or maybe I always was and was always meant to be: maybe this was Time screwing my *screw you*. Reminding me who was in charge.

I jumped away before I could see the end of this story, the story that I had rewritten with the best and worst intentions. I reappeared, breathless and shattered, somewhere far from that cursed overlook, face-to-face with a dinosaur. Its eyes, the size of my head, blinked down at me, clearly as confused by my presence as I was by its.

"Oh, come on!" I threw my hands up. "A dinosaur? Really, Time? Haven't you screwed me over enough for the day?"

The realization hit me like a physical blow: in trying to outmaneuver Time, I had only tightened its grip on me. In my quest for control, I had lost more than I could ever have imagined.

The dinosaur let out a sound that I can only describe as a prehistoric shrug, a rumble that vibrated through my bones. It was a sound that resonated with the primordial part of my brain, a reminder of how insignificant my tantrum was in the grand scheme of things.

"Nope. Nope. Nope." I shook my head, stepping back. "Not doing the Jurassic Park experience today."

Not letting a dinosaur eat me. Not letting Time win. I could change all this again, I could. I could make it so that I was never in that car in the first place. I could change it all.

With a defiant jump, I found myself back at the beginning, twenty meters behind where my past self stood. There she was, perched on the edge of the cliff, a younger, more naïve version of me, chatting with Clyde, blissfully unaware of the train wreck I was about to cause.

Watching her, I felt a pang of something bitter — regret, anger, desperation? It was hard to tell. Time had played me like a fiddle, and here I was, dancing to its tune, trying to snatch the bow from its hands.

"I'll fix this," I whispered to the wind, my resolve as unyielding as the cliffs themselves. "I'll undo it all. Time doesn't own me."

Sally Webber versus Time. May the best woman win.

Clyde — my version of Clyde — shuffled uncomfortably beside me. Such a little human move someone had taken the time to code into him. "It is not in my programming to say I told you so, but I should remind you that this is what we get when we mess with Time. It's the very essence of temporal interference. The inevitability of it all."

I whirled on him, fury igniting my veins. "No, no, I reject that! I can't be the reason John's gone. I remember every agonizing detail of that day — the driver's haunted eyes, his stammering apologies. There was never a mention of a mysterious passenger. This is a lie. I… my memories are solid. They're real!"

Clyde flickered with what I imagined was concern. "As a time manipulator, you might be insulated from the ripples you create. However—"

"Just stop!" I yelled, my voice tearing through the relentless wind. "Screw you, Time! You can't use me like this!"

I turned my gaze back to Clyde. "I can fix this. I have to. I'll jump earlier, stop it before it even begins."

With a surge of desperate determination, I jumped even earlier, trailing the car that would kill my brother up the Pacific Coast Highway. Back in time, back up the highway, jump by jump, waiting for the moment it would stop. I was a ghost from the future, invisible to the unsuspecting traveler.

Until the road was empty.

There was the driver, stopping at a quaint diner, the kind of place that had kitschy saltshakers and waitresses who called everyone 'hon.' Seeing him so carefree, so blissfully unaware of what was to come, what he was about to do, twisted a knife in my chest.

I waited in the shadows, my eyes fixed on the car. My hands clenched into fists at my sides, the familiar surge of helplessness threatening to overwhelm me. But I pushed it back, focusing on the task at hand.

This was my chance to rewrite history, to snatch John from the jaws of fate. I approached the car, every step heavy with purpose. The tire loomed before me, an unsuspecting victim of my desperate plan. With a deep breath, I pulled out my keys. The teeth caught the light as I positioned one against the tire. I pressed down, the rubber yielding under the sharp edge. The hiss of air escaping was the sweetest, most heartbreaking sound I'd ever heard.

I stepped back, watching the tire deflate, a physical manifestation of the change I was about to bring. The world around me felt charged, alive with the potential of what I was doing. I was rewriting the script, challenging the very fabric of reality.

"They'll simply change it," Clyde observed in his ever-rational tone.

I nodded. "Yes, but it'll delay them. Just a few minutes. That's all I need to change everything. A few minutes for my family to get back in the car and drive away."

It was done. I breathed a sigh of relief, admiring my handywork as the tire slowly deflated. In a flash, I was back in our old family home. Ready to walk into a family that had never been destroyed. To embrace my brother, alive and healthy and thriving, who had not been killed either time.

Except I didn't.

Because there was nothing left anymore.

The neighborhood, once alive with the sounds of playing children and bustling families, was now eerily silent. Houses stood like hollowed-out shells, windows broken and doors ajar. Vines crept over the crumbling walls, nature reclaiming what had been left behind.

My heart sank, a cold realization creeping over me. This wasn't just a house abandoned; it was a whole world. The air was thick with the absence of life, a void where once there had been so much.

Clyde's blue glow seemed dim in the overwhelming desolation. "Sally, I think you underestimate your effect on the world."

I stumbled forward, my steps hollow on the cracked pavement. My mind raced, trying to piece together the catastrophic chain of events that must have unfolded.

If John hadn't died, I wouldn't have dropped out of college.

I wouldn't have hit Zander on that fateful night.

I wouldn't have become… me.

And while that's all I wanted right now, to be the me I had been before the stars, the me before Nimien had forced my hand, that me had, maybe, just a little bit… saved the planet.

The Youpaf had come through on their threat. They had incinerated the world to find their prisoner, the Zoesh.

The Earth had paid the price for my selfish wish.

Around me, the remnants of civilization were being slowly devoured by nature. Buildings were mere skeletons, streets were overrun with greenery, and the air was filled with the sounds of insects and the rustling of leaves.

A few steps into what used to be our living room, now just an open space under the sky, I dropped to my knees, the weight of my choices pressing down on me. "I thought I was fixing it," I whispered, my voice breaking. "I thought I could make it right."

Clyde hovered near. "Time is a complex tapestry, Sally. Each thread interwoven with countless others. To pull one thread is to unravel many. You've had more of an impact than you think."

I looked up at the sky, where the sun beat down indifferently. It had witnessed the rise and fall of civilizations, the birth and death of worlds. And now, it witnessed my failure, my hubris.

Tears streamed down my face, not just for John, not just for my family, but for everyone and everything that had been lost because of my actions. In trying to be the master of my destiny, I had become an architect of ruin.

"This shouldn't be on me," I choked out, the numb realization giving way to a deep, aching sorrow. "Zander can change the timeline. Why can't I? Why do I have to suffer for my world to live?"

Clyde's glow flickered with a semblance of sympathy. "Sally," he said, his digital voice wavering, "the, uh, timeline is... complex. Zander's, um, timeline-y things have, you know, stuff."

That didn't sound right. Clyde paused, his programming clearly scrambling to provide comfort but falling short. "You have... big heart. Yes, big heart good.

But time travel... tricky. Very tricky. Like, uh, juggling. Juggling with... time balls?"

Clyde twitched. A program at its wit's end. "You care lots. That's good! But care can make... time wibbly-wobbly?" He seemed to be pulling phrases from a hat.

Finally, he just sighed — or at least, made a sound that resembled a sigh. "Sally, you... do good. Try hard. Important stuff. But sometimes, universe say 'nope.' Universe big. Big and... universe-y."

"Yeah. I thought so." I wiped my tears, my resolve hardening amidst the despair. His failure to grasp the emotional gravity of the situation was a reminder of just how human I was amidst the cosmic scale of my decisions. How no one was equipped to handle this.

I had to fix this. I had to go back and let history take its course. It was the only way to save the world, the only way to honor the memory of a brother whose sacrifice had meant more than I ever knew.

With a deep breath, I stood up, my gaze fixed on the key around my neck. It was time to undo my greatest mistake. Time to face the past and let it be.

There was a twisted kind of poetry in the fact that the first time I changed a tire, it would be on the car that was about to speed into my brother. Each twist of the wrench was not just a mechanical motion; it was a reluctant step towards accepting a past I had tried so desperately to escape. My hands moved with an eerie detachment, each turn of the wrench methodically tightening the bolts. This moment was a cruel intersection of past and present, a convergence point where my actions were both futile and crucial.

Well, fuck you too, destiny.

Clyde's soft glow offered a silent presence beside me. "Sally," he began, attempting a comforting tone. "Some choices are etched in time, immutable and unyielding."

"Oh, so you're working again?"

He continued, as if reading my mind. Which I still didn't put past him. "The past, with all its agony and lessons, is not something to be rewritten, but to be borne. The scars we carry, the memories we hold, they shape us, mold us into the beings we are destined to be."

"You sound like a motivational self-help book." The words hit me, a bittersweet truth wrapped in Clyde's awkward attempt at solace. I paused, the wrench still in my grip, and let out a long, shaky breath. "But you're right, Clyde. I've been fighting a losing battle against time, trying to change what can't be changed."

Clyde tilted his head, a semblance of inquiry in his digital eyes. "So, you're done trying to alter the past?"

I couldn't bear witness to this scene again. I both remembered being in the car when it swerved and remembered the car barreling down at me with only a single passenger. I had achieved nothing today except to entangle myself in a temporal paradox that impeded only me.

But there was already a paradox in place. One that I didn't know the outcome of.

SINGULARITY

A newfound determination surged through me, igniting a fire that had been smothered by grief and regret. "Yes, I'm done with the past. But the present," I said, my voice steady and resolute, "the present is a different story. I may not be able to change what has happened, but I can shape what happens next."

Clyde's glow brightened. "The present is yours to mold, Sally. Your actions now can forge a new path."

"Exactly. I've been a pawn in Time's game for too long. It's time to make my own moves, to change the present and fight for a future where I'm not just a bystander to fate."

"Wait, what do you mean by that, exactly?"

With one last twist of the wrench, I sealed my resolve. The past would remain untouched, but the present was mine to claim. I was no longer the girl who tried to rewrite history; I was the woman ready to take control of her destiny.

"And that," I declared, "starts now."

With those words, I stepped away from the car, leaving behind the ghosts of what could have been and what always was. Ahead lay a path uncharted and uncertain, but it was mine to walk, and I was ready. Ready to face whatever the present had in store, armed with the lessons of the past and the determination to shape my own future.

SEVENTEEN

BACK TO THE BROTHER

RETURNING TO PLANET NOPE WAS LIKE UNWRAPPING a surprise gift, only to find it's a sweater knitted from your own hair: unnervingly personal and slightly horrifying. Memories of being an alien's plaything and a glorified perspiration factory weren't exactly what I'd call 'fond.' And yet, here I stood, ticket in hand, ready to tango with my personal demons for a shot at rescuing John from a cosmic clerical error.

The landscape unfurled before me — a place where the term 'breathtaking' could refer equally to the scenery and the atmospheric pressure. It was the day the clouds parted, a sign of our impending escape, casting a surreal dimness over a place I'd known only as a dark cage. The scene almost seemed serene from a distance, with shuttles weaving through the sky. Yet, the tranquility was deceptive. Near me, the skeletal remains of a long-crashed spaceship loomed, swarming with people like a chaotic ant colony around a fallen lollipop.

Clyde glowed a concerned shade of blue beside me. "Sally, what are we doing here?"

"Clyde, shush." I crouched in the underbrush, my eyes locked on the spaceship's roof. Having not witnessed John's actual death myself, I wasn't exactly sure when to come in. Time travel might have been an exact science, but who said you couldn't improvise with the universe's strings? "I need to hear what they're saying."

Before me, Zander and a young woman were climbing onto the roof of the old bridge. *Zander.* The sight of him made my gut twist, the immediate relief of seeing *my person* mixed with the sour taste of betrayal. This was him before his mind collapsed, though: this was him before he did the unthinkable. Could I hate this Zander, who was not yet guilty?

And with them, laughing and beaming, was John. Oh, John. Not the John from the car crash but the John who was *alive.* His hair a buzz-cut shadow of its former glory, his clothes hanging off him like laundry on a line. My heart ached seeing him so diminished, but Grandma's cooking and a truckload of TLC would sort him out. That, and a plausible tale to stitch over the gaping narrative wound his 'death' had left in our lives.

"If I'm not mistaken, that's John," said Clyde, his voice cool, like he was doing his best impression of a stern headmaster. "Sally, you're not intending to do exactly what we discussed you wouldn't do?"

I shrugged off his concern, my gaze fixed on the distant scene. "Relax, Clyde. The timeline here is already a mess. One more paradox isn't going to make a difference."

"Sally, you can't just—"

"Can't what, Clyde? Make things worse? The timeline here was altered way before I showed up. Zander changed it and nothing happened to him, right? I'm just adding another layer to the existing paradox. A better layer. A coat of paint over a disaster."

"Sally, we have discussed this!" Clyde's form seemed to pulse with frustration. "You don't understand the complexities! Every change you make could have unforeseeable consequences!"

I scoffed, my frustration boiling over. "And what? I'm supposed to just stand back and watch? I've been a pawn in this game for too long, Clyde. It's time I took some control."

"Sally, this isn't control; this is chaos!"

"Maybe chaos is what we need right now," I shot back, my determination unwavering. "Maybe it's time to shake things up, show Time that I'm not just going to lie down and take it."

Clyde floated closer, his glow dimming in a semblance of pleading. "Sally, please think about this. The ramifications could be—"

"Ramifications? I'm already living in the ramifications of decisions I didn't even make! How much worse can it get?"

Clyde fell silent, flickering with an uncertainty that mirrored my own internal turmoil. For a moment, we just stood there, caught in the vastness of a universe that was both beautiful and indifferent to our struggles.

"You had one job, Clyde," I growled through clenched teeth. "Be my co-pilot, not the captain of the Guilt Trip Express. Zip it and watch me save my brother."

Clyde's light dimmed, his dissent silenced, but his concern hung in the air like a bad smell. My eyes were glued to the scene ahead, where Zander's lips were about to collide with John's, igniting a timeline I was here to snuff out. I was too late to prevent the kiss, but not too late to rewrite its aftermath.

Time to run.

I rushed into the fray, flying across the roof to split them apart. Their kiss shattered against my sudden intrusion. Zander and John gawked at me, their stunned faces a cocktail of confusion, surprise, and a touch of mortification.

"Zander!" I exploded, my words sharp as shrapnel, even as I wrapped my arms protectively around John. The warmth of his living body was surreal, a stark contrast to the cold memories I had been clinging to. Oh stars, this was John, alive and warm and well.

"You, kissing him? Really?" It was hard to sound furious when the joy of seeing my brother threatened to consume me. "What, did the universe run out of space for your flings?"

"Sally, I— It's not what it—" Zander stammered.

But I wasn't having any of it. I mean, not yet. "Save it, Zander."

Meanwhile, John, starstruck and dumbfounded, gaped at me like I'd just dropped from the heavens — which, in a way, I had. His mouth opened and closed, but no words came out, just a fish out of water, caught in the storm of my return.

"S-Sally?" he finally managed to sputter. "*You're* his Sally?"

"John, we're getting out of here!" I tightened my grip on his arm. "And as for you, Zander — don't try to follow me. We'll talk later."

With that, I jumped, leaving a baffled Zander in our wake. It was time to bring John home, to a reality where he was more than just a memory, more than just a pawn in the universe's cruel game.

It was time to change the present.

In a blink, we were standing in the overgrown backyard of our childhood home. Our old sanctuary. A place I hadn't seen in years feeling somehow, impossibly, smaller. Time had etched its marks on the place, rendering it both alien and achingly familiar.

And beside me, John stood, tangible and real. My brother, alive. *Alive*. My brother, whom I had mourned, was now a living, breathing miracle in my grasp. I could scream with joy, explode with happiness, but the shock kept the air trapped down my throat, a stunned silence enveloping us both.

His gaze met mine, eyes that I had only seen in dreams and tearful memories now looked back at me with life. That familiar smile, which I had resigned to the past, was now a bittersweet reality. After years of grieving, the universe had given me the gift to save him. Maybe, after all this time, this was my reward.

John moistened his lips, breaking the overwhelming silence. "Sally, where... how..."

"We're home, John," I managed to say, voice trembling. "We're actually home."

Clyde flickered beside me, his digital form a stark contrast to the raw human reunion unfolding. "Sally, while this reunion is emotionally significant, I must caution against the potential temporal ramifications—"

"Not now, Clyde," I said, my entire being concentrated on the brother I once thought I'd lost forever.

John's brows furrowed. "Clyde?"

"AI. Ignore him," I said. "Or, I mean, ignore me when I talk to him. I'm sorry. I'm just so happy to see you, I don't know where to start..."

With a tentative, almost ethereal touch, he reached out and gently poked my shoulder. "It's really you?"

"Yeah, John. It's me." My words barely escaped through the swell of emotions threatening to overwhelm me. Our eyes locked, and in that gaze, years of pain, joy, and unspoken words passed between us.

"This isn't a Ster trick?" He poked my shoulder. "It has to be. They must have done something to my brain.

First the rescue, then seeing you again, it's too much, it can't be happening."

"Yeah, John. It's me."

Before my mind could even process what was happening, my instincts took over. I wrapped my arms around John in a fierce embrace, feeling his bones press against mine. It was as if I was afraid he'd vanish if I didn't hold on tight enough. Immediately he hugged me back with the same fervor, and suddenly we were crying, holding each other as the emotions broke through our respective dams and cascaded over both of us.

For a moment, the world around us faded into insignificance. We stood there, brother and sister, reunited against the implausible machinations of time and fate. It was a moment of impossible joy, a fragment of time where the past and present collided, bringing with it a flood of memories and the promise of a future that had once been stolen from us.

"I never thought I would see you again," John murmured, his voice muffled against my hair. "Or Earth. Or home."

"I thought you were dead." I couldn't help but let out a half laugh, half sob. "When I saw you, with Zander…"

His face faltered. "I'm so sorry, Sally. I would never—"

"We'll figure that out later. You had no idea."

"Yeah. How did you end up with an alien legend, anyway?"

"It's a long story," I replied, motioning towards the house. "One for when we sit down and catch up on everything."

Clyde cleared his throat. "Sally, while this emotional reunion is indeed heartwarming, I must remind you of the potential—"

"Clyde, not now." I cut him off, my attention still fully on John.

I took his hand, leading him towards the sliding door, slipping it open. The interior was different — new furniture, different paint — but the essence of our childhood lingered in the air. We made our way to an unfamiliar couch.

"Remember the time we built that fort here?" John whispered, his eyes scanning the room.

"And Mom got mad because we used all the sheets."

We found ourselves seated, knees touching. The proximity was both comforting and surreal, as if we were trying to confirm the other's existence through mere physical closeness.

"So, who's going first?" John asked, breaking the silence that had settled between us.

I gave a half smile. "Roshambo for it?"

Our hands moved in unison — scissors, then scissors again. Our laughter mingled, easing the tension just a bit. On the third go, he triumphantly threw rock against my scissors. As he spoke, I noticed his hands, covered with tiny silvery scars.

He took a deep breath, his expression shifting to something more somber. "I can't pinpoint the exact moment they took me. One second, we were at that overlook, smiling for a family photo, and the next... I was shivering in the dark hold of some alien ship. Drenched, confused, surrounded by strangers."

John paused. A breath. "Turns out, Earth's quite popular among alien traders. We're the only human planet not under Alliance control. Plus, we're apparently entertaining, with, get this, our 'unique culinary choices.' " He rolled his eyes. I couldn't find it in me to laugh.

"For a year, I was with this group of smugglers. They called themselves the Zalari. Not the worst bunch in the cosmos, but not exactly law-abiding citizens either. I worked as a grease monkey on their ship. It was tough, but I learned a lot. About mechanics, about different species, and about how to stay alive in the galaxy."

He shifted slightly, his gaze growing distant. "Then, the Alliance intercepted our ship. They were cracking down on illegal trading routes. After a bit of... persuasive conversation, I convinced them I was younger than I was and got enrolled in their Child Hire program."

Goosebumps rose on my skin. My own brother, victim of the same program I had heard so much about.

He nodded, as if taking my blank stare as ignorance. "It's this Alliance initiative to integrate young survivors from less advanced planets into their ranks. Gave me a shot at a new life, I guess. They assigned me to a survey ship, the *Wanderer*. And that's where things went south again."

John's voice wavered a bit. "We were sent to survey Planet Nope. Routine mission, they said. Except it wasn't. The ship crashed. And that's where the real struggle began. Planet Nope... it was hell, Sally. A real-life Hell."

"But you survived," I whispered.

"Yeah, I did. Had to. Climbed up the ranks of the rebellion, just trying to keep breathing, keep moving." He looked at me, his eyes intense. "Then Zander arrived, and everything changed again."

I took his hand, squeezing it gently. "You're safe now, John. You're with me."

"Yeah, I guess I am. Thanks to you, Sal." He smiled, a pained but genuine smile.

Our connection in that moment was more than just familial; it was a shared understanding of having walked through the fire and come out the other side. John's journey had been unimaginable, but here he was, resilient and alive. And I was determined to keep it that way.

"I guess my only question is... how?" he asked, squeezing my hand tighter. "The things you can do..."

I took a deep breath. "That's a long story, too." I leaned back, trying to figure out where to start. "After you... disappeared, things got rough. I couldn't make it through college. It felt like every path I took just led to another dead end. I was trying to crack life on my own, but it was hard, John. Really hard."

Then I told him everything. Well, as best I could, choosing my words carefully. I didn't want to burden him with the knowledge of my mental struggles, didn't want him to feel responsible for the darkness that had enveloped me when it had been within me all along.

I told him about the accident, about Zander. John was the first person I ever got to sit down with and bear everything to. About how lost he was in the big wide universe, how he lived with me, and how, for a short time, I felt I'd found my purpose as some sort of cosmic anchor. Until we found my first real solid job was a cover for alien exploitation, and how we'd had to blow it up. And how, as a thank you, Zander took me to the stars.

"And that trip," I continued, "it wasn't just a sightseeing tour. We got lost. I mean, really lost. We stumbled upon this man, Nimien. He was... something else. Powerful. Manipulative. We thought we'd failed him, that we'd lost him, but he was pulling the strings the whole time. We made him into someone like Zander, like Blayde." I took a deep breath. John didn't interrupt. "And in return, Nimien forced me into a decision, a terrible choice. He made me... like them. An immortal, a space-time traveler."

John whistled. "Doesn't sound half bad."

I shrugged, a small smile on my lips. "It has its ups and downs. There are rules, consequences. Every jump, every change, it has an impact. And often, it feels like I'm still just a pawn in a much bigger game."

John reached out, gently taking my hand. "But you used it to save me."

I nodded. "Yes, I did. And I'd do it again in a heartbeat."

We sat in silence again. The enormity of what we had shared hung between us. A testament to the journey I had been on, the path that had led me back to him.

Finally, John spoke, his voice soft. "You've been through so much, Sally. And here you are, still standing. Still fighting."

I smiled, giving his hand a squeeze. "And so are you."

"Not sure I like the new décor, though," he said, gesturing to the room. "The old couch was better."

"Oh, it's not…"

Our moment was cut short by a shout. "Who are you? What are you doing in our house?"

Startled, we turned to see a middle-aged couple standing in the doorway, red-faced and fuming.

Oh. *Shit.*

I'd been so wrapped up in the moment, I'd forgotten that our home wasn't our home anymore. And it hadn't been, in a long, long time.

"Uh, sorry, we used to live here," I stammered, jumping to my feet. "We were just…"

"This is breaking and entering!" the man exclaimed. "I'm calling the police!"

Clyde's glow intensified. "Sally, perhaps this was not the most prudent—"

"Thanks, Clyde, got it," I muttered, reaching for John. "We should go."

The man, finally successful in unlocking his phone, paused and looked at us. "Wait, did you say you used to live here? Are you the Webber kids?"

I stopped in my tracks, turning back to face them. "Yes, we're the Webbers. Sally and John."

The woman's face lit up with recognition. "Oh my, the Webber kids! We heard about you from the neighbors when we moved in. Such a tragedy, what happened to your family."

John and I exchanged glances. "Yeah. Thank you."

The man lowered his phone, a hint of guilt in his expression. "Well, uh, you're welcome to visit, but maybe call first next time?"

I nodded, feeling a rush of gratitude and embarrassment. "Definitely. Sorry for the intrusion and, uh, the drama."

Neither of them said anything.

"Uh…" I cleared my throat. "I appreciate your understanding. We'll just get going…"

But the two of them were frozen in place.

The words tumbled from my mouth, but they seemed to freeze mid-air, as if time itself was holding its breath. A creeping, icy dread snaked down my spine, uninvited and invasive. I spun towards Clyde, desperate for his usual commentary, but found him eerily motionless, his digital form locked in a silent, eternal scream.

"Sally?" John's voice quivered, laced with rising panic. "What's happening?"

SINGULARITY

The room dimmed, shadows stretching and twisting as if a tempest was swirling just beyond the windows, a maelstrom of darkness and eerie green light. I grabbed John's hand, a surge of protectiveness flooding me.

"We gotta go," I said, but my words were silent, stolen the second I uttered them.

I turned to the door, pulling John behind me, but with a sudden yank, I was pulled back. I turned to see him being lifted off the floor, as if something had grabbed his legs and was pulling him away from me.

John's face twisted into a mask of pure terror. "Sally!" His scream ripped through the stillness, a sound so raw and desperate it clawed at my soul.

His hands slipped out of mine. I reached for him, slicing through the thickening air, grabbing his fingers tight. But he was still being pulled away by an invisible force, yanked towards a swirling vortex that appeared out of nowhere. The room twisted and turned, the walls bending like they were part of some demented funhouse.

"John!" I screamed, but my words were ripped from my mouth. The vortex pulsated with an eerie light, a neon sign flashing "game over" in a game I never agreed to play.

He slipped through my fingers, his screams echoing in my ears, a soundtrack to my failure. The vortex was like a greedy mouth, swallowing him whole, leaving me clutching at shadows.

Then, just as suddenly as it appeared, the vortex snapped shut. Silence crashed down on me, heavy and suffocating.

I collapsed to the floor, my body a puppet with its strings cut. "No, no, no…"

John was gone. Ripped from me once more, by forces beyond my reckoning, beyond my reach.

In that moment, amidst the shattered remnants of hope, I was alone again. Utterly, devastatingly alone.

EIGHTEEN

UNICORNS CRASH THE MANE EVENT

I'M NOT GOING TO SUGARCOAT THIS AND PUT a joke here. I've literally never been lower in my life.

In the dim, eerie stillness of the house, suspended between moments like a forgotten whisper, I lay crumpled on the floor, my heart shattered into a million irretrievable pieces. My tears soaking the carpet beneath me. John was gone. I'd lost him *again*. I drowned in my grief, a solitary figure drowning in an ocean of sorrow.

Then, a sound sliced through the dense air of despair — a clear, deliberate throat clearing. Startled, I lifted my head, my tear-streaked face searching the shadows. There, in the dim light, stood two figures, surreal and bizarrely out of place. They wore unicorn masks, their plastic faces frozen in expressions of mythical serenity.

"We're supposed to say: do not be afraid," said the one on the left, their head tilting slightly, causing the rubber unicorn horn to catch the dim light. "But honestly, a little fear wouldn't be amiss. Keeps things orderly."

"Uh... who are you?" My voice was a hoarse whisper, barely recognizable even to my own ears. I checked hastily for Clyde, but he — as well as the couple whose house I was now squatting in — were still frozen, like manikins in a terrible high-end fashion store.

"Ah, the 'who are we' question. Classic." They sighed dramatically. "We're the field agents of chronological compliance, and we will ask the questions, thank you very much."

"We represent the Pythanorean high council." The other nodded, their mask's eyes seemed to bore into my soul. "We're here because you've been a very naughty girl, Sally Webber. Tampering with time is a big no-no."

I frowned. "And you're wearing unicorn masks."

"You see us the way your mind allows you to in this dimensional plane," the first one added. "Our true forms would be, well, let's just say they're not exactly compliant with your dimensional regulations."

Anger bubbled up inside me. These... *people* had stolen my brother. And not just once. But if I was right, they were the reason the universe wouldn't let me save him in the first place. My hands formed tight fists as I pushed myself up off the floor.

"And what? You're in charge of time?" I said through gritted teeth.

The first one clapped their hands, an eerie echo resonating through the room. "Exactly! See, she gets it, Larry."

Larry, arms still crossed, adopted a tone of forced patience, like he was explaining a complicated and tedious policy. "You've caused quite the stir in the fabric of time, Sally. Creating paradoxes, changing fixed points... It's messy business. Our department's been swamped with extra paperwork because of you."

I stared at them, disbelief and incredulity warring within me. "So, what? You're going to arrest me? Put me in time-out? Take me to time jail?"

The one who wasn't Larry chuckled. "Oh, if only it were that simple. No, we're here to... how should I put this... reprimand you. Think of us as your very own temporal code officers. We keep the timelines tidy and in order."

"To put things short, Ms. Webber: please stop." Larry stepped forward, his mask somehow managing to look severe. "Your actions have consequences. You can't just gallivant through time, saving brothers and altering set courses. Your actions have repercussions, Sally. Time isn't your personal playground. There are procedures, protocols—"

"Protocols?" I interrupted. You have got to be kidding me. "My brother's life, reduced to a bureaucratic procedure? What gives you the right to play with people's lives?"

"More like a complex filing system," said not-Larry. "And you, Sally Webber, have been filing things all wrong."

Larry sighed, the sound muffled by his mask. "Look, it's simple. You cause paradoxes, we set things straight. You're basically causing a backlog in our workflow. It's a logistical nightmare."

"Your workflow?" My eyes could have popped out of my skull. "This is my life we're talking about! Multiple lives!"

The unicorns exchanged a glance, then the first one shrugged. "It's not personal, Sally. It's temporal."

I scoffed, my grief momentarily overshadowed by the absurdity of it all. "Temporal. Right. Who put you in charge of time? I didn't vote for you."

"Again, it's nothing personal." Larry stepped closer, the mask somehow managing to convey seriousness. "And as for who put us in charge, let's just say it's above your clearance level."

"So what now? You're going to give me a stern talking-to? Make me sign a promise not to alter the flow of time?"

Larry's mask seemed to frown, which should have been impossible. "It's more serious than that, Sally. You need to understand the gravity of your actions. Time isn't a plaything: it's a highly sensitive and regulated continuum."

The other unicorn shifted. "Precisely, Larry. Plus, you wouldn't believe the amount of paperwork your little escapades have generated. We're talking reams."

"Paperwork?" I rolled my eyes. "Oh, the bureaucracy of it all. You must be so put upon."

Larry nodded solemnly. "Yes, paperwork. The bedrock of any well-functioning administrative entity."

The absurdity of the situation was almost too much. I was arguing with two beings in unicorn masks about the administrative hassles of saving my brother's life. If this was the universe's idea of a joke, I wasn't laughing. "You're telling me my brother's life is being weighed against... paperwork?"

I clenched my fists. Would fighting them get me anywhere? Might make me feel at least a little bit better if I could land a punch.

"Now, you stop messing with time." Larry wagged — actually wagged! — their finger at me. "No more paradoxes, no more saving brothers from their fates. You play by the rules, or next time..."

"Or next time... what?" I spat, my voice quivering. "You'll erase him again? Or maybe me?"

"Well, not erase, per se," said Larry, "more like... realign. You see, we're all about maintaining the cosmic balance. Your actions... they're like throwing a wrench in the works. A big, timey-wimey wrench, to adopt some local lingo."

The other one, who wasn't Larry, chimed in. "Picture time as a beautifully woven tapestry, Sally. And you're there, unraveling the threads. It's incredibly rude, after all the work that's been put in. It's our job to reweave it, to restore order."

"A tapestry?" My laugh was bitter. "My brother's life reduced to a metaphorical piece of fabric?"

Larry stepped forward. "It's more nuanced than that. Your brother... he's a nexus point. Different threads of reality hinge on his existence, his actions. It's not something we take lightly. We have protocols to manage these situations."

"But why him?" I pressed. "Why is my brother the linchpin in your so-called grand tapestry?"

The other unicorn-masked figure sighed. "That's the million-dollar question, isn't it? Nexus points aren't chosen. They just are. Like black holes — they just exist, and they have a pull. They have a significant impact, and thus, require special oversight."

"Then what business is it to you?" I spat. "What time does, what time chooses. Just leave us be."

"Unfortunately, we cannot," said not-Larry. "Our superiors cannot survive in a paradox-infested universe. It gives them indigestion."

My fists clenched tighter, my nails piercing skin to keep me from throttling them. "Indigestion? Oh, boo-hoo. Cry me a river. So me saving my brother makes your so-called superiors a little bloated."

"They cannot bloat," said not-Larry. "As ascended beings, they have no physical form. They're more... metaphysically inconvenienced."

"Wait a moment." I frowned, pinching the bridge of my nose between my fingers. "You're not even the Pythanoreans? You're... what? Their stooges?"

"Acolytes," said not-Larry. "Think of us as middle management. We are Pythanoreans, but we haven't hit the big leagues yet. Ascension is within our grasp, and we certainly aren't going to let a temporal renegade jeopardize our promotion prospects."

Larry placed a calming hand on his partner's arm. "What we mean to say, Sally Webber, is that it is our divine mission to sort out these paradoxes. It's best for everyone, you see, when time flows in a clean, straight line, without any branching off. We don't want a multiverse on our hands here. Those are for even higher dimensional beings to manage, and we do not want to infuriate them."

"Then what about Zander?" I asked, my voice sharpening. "He's messed with time more than I have. He caused the first paradox, and it's still there. I know it because I still can't decide whether I love or hate him. Why aren't you after him?"

"Oh, we are," Larry said, a hint of smugness in his tone. "He's like a rogue variable in our calculations. We're waiting for the right moment to… intervene. When he's with you, here and now on Earth, we'll have him."

The revelation hit me like a ton of bricks. "You're using me as bait?"

Bile rose in my gut. Shit. This is why the paradox had been going on as long as it had: Time was biding its, well, time. Waiting for Zander to crawl back to me so they could apprehend him and set everything back the way they wanted.

I was right. Time had been using me. Just not entirely the way I thought it had.

"More like strategic asset allocation," the other one interjected, with a slight tilt of the unicorn head.

"So what will you do to him?" I pushed on. "You'll stop him from killing John, leaving my brother to become the tyrant everyone claims he'll become?"

Larry and the other exchanged a look before turning back to me. "Actually, no. The paradox wasn't John's survival. It was the liberation of Planet Nope. In the original timeline, Provis leads a failed revolution. He escapes alone, broken by his experiences, setting him on a path to becoming..."

"A genocidal dictator," I finished, my voice barely a whisper, each word escaping like the last breath of a dying hope. A nauseating understanding washed over me, heavy and suffocating. The air seemed to thicken, pressing against me, as if the very gravity of my realization was warping the space around me.

We were never meant to liberate Planet Nope.

The revelation was a seismic shift, toppling everything I had believed, everything I had fought for. It wasn't just a twist in the timeline; it was the cruel upending of a narrative I thought I had authored. The paradox at the heart of it all: Zander and I were never meant to save the planet in the first place. My actions, my choices, weren't inconsequential; they were the chaotic ripples disturbing a perfectly preordained pond.

Realization fell over me like a bucket of ice water, chilling me to my core. There was only one reason we'd gone there, a single thread leading us to the *Wanderer* in the first place.

Nimien.

I let out a laugh, a hollow, haunting sound that echoed in the silence, a laugh that was more of a sob, all pent-up frustration and confusion. Nimien, manipulating me even beyond the grave. His manipulation didn't end with his death; it transcended it, reaching out his spectral fingers to puppeteer my life.

I was not just a pawn of time or the patsy of the Pythanoreans. Oh no, I was Nimien's puppet too, dancing on strings I couldn't even see until this moment. My life, my struggles, my victories — all orchestrated in a grand design I was blind to.

"So, my brother's life, my actions..." I swallowed, hard. "All just pieces in some… some… cosmic game of chess?"

"More like cosmic Jenga," the non-Larry unicorn quipped. "One wrong move, and everything comes tumbling down."

"How do you live with yourselves?" I snapped.

Larry adjusted his mask, or maybe it was his face. "It's about maintaining order, Ms. Webber. Without us, the universe would be chaos."

I shook my head, a bitter laugh escaping me. "And here I was, thinking I was saving people, making a difference. But it turns out, I'm just an anomaly. To be used."

"Anomalies are part of the grand design," not-Larry added. "They exist to be realigned."

"Realigned!" I spat the word out like venom. "You talk as if you're fixing a minor glitch in some cosmic program!"

"That's one way to look at it," Larry said, matter-of-factly.

Frustration boiled over within me. "Why can I remember all these paradoxes, then? If you're so good at fixing things, why am I left with all these memories?"

Larry and not-Larry exchanged a glance that seemed to communicate volumes of bureaucratic understanding. It was not-Larry who finally spoke, his voice heavy with an exaggerated patience. "Ah, the multidimensional memory conundrum. It's quite the topic at our interdimensional conferences. You see, while humans might consider their physical bodies to be three-dimensional, it's actually just a temporary arrangement for the universe. Your consciousness, on the other hand, exists on multiple planes. When you experience a paradox, it leaves an imprint: You're remembering echoes from branches that will eventually be pruned — a bit of a glitch in the system we're still working to patch."

"So, I'm cursed to remember everything?" My voice cracked.

"It's more of an unfortunate side effect," said Larry.

Not-Larry nodded in agreement. "Think of it as a cosmic bug. We haven't worked out all the kinks yet."

My heart felt like it was being squeezed. "And what now? You just leave me with these memories, these… echoes?"

Larry stepped forward, his tone softening slightly. "We have to. It's beyond our control, Sally. Our job is to maintain the timeline, not manage individual experiences."

I felt a surge of anger, mixed with a bitter sense of resignation. "Great. So, while you're filing your reports and attending your temporal conferences, I'm left with the fallout."

"More or less," not-Larry said with a shrug that seemed almost too casual for his unicorn guise. "Remember, it's not personal. It's temporal."

"And please refrain from any further timeline alterations," added Larry. "Our department is overworked as it is. We'd hate to escalate this to the higher-ups."

With a final, patronizing nod, the unicorns faded, their forms shimmering like a mirage in the dim light.

"Wait!" I called out desperately, but it was too late. They were gone, leaving me alone in the stillness of the house.

But not for long. The second their forms were nothing more than a memory on my retinas, the suspended moment shattered, and time lurched forward like a startled animal. The couple, previously frozen, now sprang to life, their expressions morphing from confusion to concern as they turned their attention to me, crumpled and defeated on their floor.

At that moment, Clyde flickered back into motion, his form stabilizing with a digital buzz. "Sally, I am terribly sorry for the interruption in service. System diagnostics indicate an anomaly during temporal enforcement interaction. Would you like me to submit a bug report?"

I looked up at him, a hollow laugh escaping my lips. "A bug report, Clyde? Really?"

He blinked rapidly. Recalibrating? "Affirmative. Customer feedback is essential for continuous improvement of holographic assistance protocols. Additionally, would you like some soothing background music or perhaps a visual display of calming landscapes?"

"Are you alright, dear?" the woman asked, stepping through Clyde and placing a hand on my shoulder.

I couldn't muster the energy to explain, to unpack the layers upon layers of temporal manipulation and heartbreak. I looked up, my eyes swollen and itchy from crying.

"I... I don't know," I managed to say, my voice barely a whisper. "I'm so sorry. I shouldn't be here. I knew this wasn't my house, not anymore, but I just… I just…"

The couple exchanged worried glances, clearly unsure how to handle me.

The man hesitated, then offered a tentative hand. "Do you need help? You mentioned your brother…"

SINGULARITY

"I need to go," I muttered, more to myself than to them. The need to escape, to be anywhere but here, was overwhelming. "I just... need to go."

And with that, I jumped, leaving the house and its bewildered occupants behind. The familiar sensation of transitioning through space and time enveloped me, but this time, it felt like a retreat, a surrender to the relentless whims of the universe.

Where I landed didn't matter. The universe would do what it wanted with me, after all. All that mattered was the void inside me, the haunting realization that everything I had done, every battle I had fought, was part of a game I could never win. I was a puppet dancing on the strings of unseen masters, my autonomy a cruel illusion in the grand scheme of the cosmos.

I tumbled back into reality with the grace of a brick, right into the throes of a full-blown anxiety attack. Collapsing onto the ground, my fingers clawed at the surprisingly soft grass, pulling up tufts as I unleashed a torrent of screams. My lungs turned traitor, expelling a relentless tidal wave of sound that felt like it was tearing my throat apart.

The ground beneath me was comfortingly solid against the storm raging in my chest. I curled into myself, fists clenching tightly against my temples, trying to hold in the pressure that felt like it was going to crack my skull open.

"What in the universe is happening to me?" My voice was a ragged whisper, lost in the echo of my own screams.

"Breathe, Sally," came Clyde's ever-calm, ever-irritatingly digital voice. Through my tear-blurred vision, he was nothing more than a hazy blue blob.

I squeezed my eyes shut, trying to block out the world, but the screams just kept coming. It was like someone had hit the play button on my internal meltdown and then broken off the switches.

"Sally, please identify five things you can see," Clyde instructed like he was reading from a troubleshooting manual. "This technique often aids in re-establishing cognitive control."

Control? Ha! What a joke. Control was a myth, a fairytale I told myself to sleep at night. My life had become a vortex of chaos, swirling around me like a relentless hurricane. What control could there possibly be when every step I took seemed to lead me further into chaos?

I gasped for air, my breaths coming in short, sharp bursts. The world was spinning, a carousel of colors and sounds that wouldn't slow down, no matter how tightly I closed my eyes.

"Just... stop, Clyde," I gasped between sobs. "Stop with the mindfulness mumbo jumbo. This isn't a broken leg or a scraped knee. You can't patch an emotional breakdown with a Band-Aid and a pat on the back."

Around me, the sounds of the universe seemed to fade into a distant hum, a background noise to the battle waging inside my head. In this moment, I was my own worst enemy, and I had no idea how to lay down my arms. My fists had worked their way through my hair, pulling and pulling and — I felt none of it.

"You are experiencing a physical reaction to a stress event, Sally," Clyde continued, the voice of reason in my personal hurricane. "I am here to assist. Assisting is my purpose. Please, trust me."

"Trust you?" The words erupted from me like a volcano, each one scalding and destructive. "What can you possibly understand about trust, Clyde? You're an algorithm, a... a... a... digital representation of empathy. You can't even imagine the chaos of a human heart. I've just witnessed the obliteration of my last shred of hope. Watched my brother get ripped away from me *again*, forever; James, a friend I couldn't save, vanished from a broken orb, beyond rescue. And Spurlock... I thought I'd finally made a friend, and I almost killed him, and almost made him immortal, all in the same night.

"And the Agency, they never let go, do they? I can never shake them off, a reminder of a leash I thought I'd slipped. Blayde's gone, too, off chasing her own demons or fighting her battles, leaving me to navigate this absolute *shit* alone. Then there's Zander... my Zander, who crossed an unforgivable line, who stole my brother from me before I could even get him back. And all of this because I'm Time's *bitch*."

As I unleashed this torrent of anguish, Clyde's blue form flickered erratically, like a candle in a hurricane. His digital eyes, usually so steady, now mirrored the chaos of my soul, flickering with the strain of processing the raw, unfiltered storm of human emotion.

"So tell me, Clyde, in your programmed wisdom, how do I keep going? When every step I take is a stumble, every move I make a catastrophe? I'm a walking calamity, a curse, a broken compass, forever spinning in circles of failure and despair."

And then, with a final sputter of electronic bewilderment, Clyde froze. His light dimmed, his form became still, and then, he was gone.

Wonderful. I'd broken him again. All I wanted was to find someone to shoulder my emotional burden, but I'd inadvertently overloaded his circuits with the weight of my sorrow and rage.

Again.

I was alone. Alone in a universe that seemed too vast and indifferent to notice. A sorry sight even by my own low standards. I cried until my tears felt like they were scratching their way out, each one a tiny echo of my brokenness. Curled up, I was a human question mark, searching for an answer in a universe that seemed to have run out of them.

NINETEEN

I'M UGLY CRYING ON A UNIVERSAL SCALE

I RODE THE MENTAL BREAKDOWN FOR WHAT could have been hours, days, until something fluffy nudged against my arm, jolting me back to the present. I sniffled. Now I *was* imagining things. But then, another soft nudge, this time against my leg. Slowly, I lifted my head.

What greeted me was a sight so bizarre, so utterly out of place, it broke my brain out of its spiral and thrust me right into confusion. I was surrounded by a sea of... plushies? No, they were alive: creatures that looked like a mad scientist's attempt at creating the perfect cuddly toy. They were a mishmash of rabbit, peacock, and neon nightclub, their fur shimmering in iridescent rainbow hues that would have made a disco ball envious.

One by one, they bounced closer, their melodious chirps sounding suspiciously like they were trying to cheer me up. Or maybe they were just laughing at the human who'd fallen into their world. Either way, they nuzzled against me, their purring soothing, like it was the perfect frequency to undo the tension in my soul.

I sat up, pulling myself together, or at least sweeping my pieces into a neater pile. The creatures seemed delighted by my movement, squeaking excitedly. Their eyes sparkled with an innocent curiosity that felt both comforting and slightly invasive.

Of course, I land in the intergalactic equivalent of a pet therapy session. Next time, universe, just send me to a spa, okay?

I pushed myself off the ground, feeling drained but oddly lighter after my outburst. The critters hopped around me, forming a bizarre honor guard as I took in my surroundings. I was in a garden, a kind of frenetically manicured jungle, smack in the middle of what seemed like a botanist's fever dream turned reality. Exotic trees stretched skyward, flaunting leaves that were a psychedelic mix of green and hot pink, as if they'd been dipped in highlighter ink. Sunlight filtered through this kaleidoscopic canopy, casting the garden in a light that felt both ethereal and slightly high on flu medicine.

There was a lurch in my throat as I caught a glow out of the corner of my eye, but this couldn't be Planet Nope, not with all this light and warmth and whatever these adorable critters were. But why was I here? I had jumped without thinking, but I was never, ever entirely directionless. Something had brought me here. Something…

Oh, it was probably whatever the palace was. Yeah, the palace was probably why I was here.

It stood proudly off to my left, a testament to architectural audacity, a wild mashup of intergalactic baroque and futuristic minimalism, like a starship had crashed into a renaissance fair. Towers spiraled skyward, adorned with glowing ornaments that could have been either high-tech security devices or just really fancy disco balls. It was like staring at a giant mood ring.

But its grandeur played second fiddle to the critter carnival I found myself in. The creatures continued their chirping, bouncing symphony, edging closer and closer as if they all wanted to get a good look at me. For a brief, fleeting moment, I let myself enjoy their company, their simple, uncomplicated existence a sharp contrast to the tangled web of my own life. I allowed myself to just be there, with them, letting the chaos of my life fade into the background.

The symphony of chirps and bounces continued around me, a fluffy, rainbow-colored orchestra of cuteness. A smile cracked through, growing wider as I reached out and tentatively stroked one of the creatures. It purred, a sound so harmonious and calming it felt like a lullaby.

One of them sneezed suddenly, sending a cloud of glitter into the air. It was so unexpected, so utterly ridiculous, that I burst into laughter. There was something infectious about their simple, joyful existence. I let myself sink into the soft grass, surrounded by these bizarrely adorable creatures, their purring growing louder and more hypnotic. It was so peaceful, so soothing... My eyelids grew heavy. What could be wrong with a quick nap in this cuddly paradise?

"Sally, what the hell? Get out of there right now!"

My eyes snapped open, and I jolted upright. Marcy was sprinting towards me, her face distorted in panic. I looked down to find one of the creatures nibbling at my arm. Not in a cute, playful way, but with red surrounding its fluffy mouth like a rabbit that had just murdered a raspberry. The others looked at me with wide eyes of disappointment, their mouths open to reveal rows of tiny, needle-like teeth.

I flew to my feet. The fluff balls weren't just fluff; they had fangs. The chirping morphed into a growling chorus, a sound that chilled my bones despite its high-pitched cuteness.

With a yowl, one of the critters went soaring through the air, more aerodynamic than I would have put it down to be. Marcy barreled through the garden, looking more like a quarterback than an imperatrice. With a swift kick she sent another one of the creatures flying like a colorful, glittering football.

"Sally, move!"

I snapped out of my daze and followed suit, my legs finally remembering how to work. We dodged and weaved through the garden, Marcy punting any creature that dared to get too close.

We flew through the palace door, Marcy slamming it shut with a decisive thud, locking out the deceptively dangerous critters. She leaned against it, panting, her eyes wide with a mix of adrenaline and disbelief.

"Sally, what the hell were you thinking?" she exclaimed. "You can't just wander into the Fluffarium unprepared! The grichookin might look cute, but they're apex predators."

I leaned against the wall, my own breaths coming in short bursts. "Well, they did have the element of surprise on their side."

Marcy shook her head, a half smile breaking through her obvious exasperation. "You're lucky I got there in time. They use their cuteness to lure in unsuspecting victims. You would not believe how many influencers they've claimed."

"That's... actually kind of brilliant." I glanced back at the door, behind which the gentle chirps had resumed. "I'll remember to bring a helmet next time I come and visit you."

With that out of the way, Marcy wrapped her arms around my neck, grabbing me in the warmest of bear hugs. I hugged her back, pulling her close, breathing in her familiar scent, relishing in the relief of seeing her again.

Of course, it was Marcy I had jumped to. In my emotional whirlwind, I'd subconsciously sought refuge with the one person in the universe I hadn't managed to alienate — *yet*. I squeezed her tighter, a silent thank you for just being there.

"What are you doing here?" I blurted out. "Are you trapped? Are those... things keeping you prisoner?"

Marcy's laughter rang out, clear and genuine. "Trapped? Sally, this is the EternaFresh Palace."

I blinked. "The where and the what now?"

"Ridiculous, right?" She scoffed. "A few generations back, the Alliance went through this bizarre corporate oligarchy phase. So now, we're stuck with places that sound like they should be solving all your cleaning problems, not housing the heart of our political system. The architecture, though, is something else — it's stunning, if you can get past the heavy corporate branding."

Huh. I guess that explained why this place smelled slightly like toilet cleaner. "So you're not being held prisoner by the fluffy things."

"Ha, no." She shook her head. "The grichookin are part of the palace's security. Or at least, they were when they were first introduced to the ecosystem. Now most of the outdoors is their domain as they've kind of taken over. But they're cute, so it's… whatever."

"Hold on, you said palace again. This is one of your *palaces?*" My jaw hit the floor. "This is where you live?"

Blood rushed to her cheeks. "Not all the time. We needed to regroup and recoup after the whole Planet Nope fiasco. It's the safest spot in the galaxy for me right now. But what are *you* doing here?"

I shrugged, the logic of my arrival as puzzling as why my phone still got reception in a place that defied all known laws of telecommunications.

"I came to see you," I replied, as if I'd known all along and not just realized myself only a few minutes ago.

Marcy took my hand and started down one of the absurdly grand hallways. I followed her, trying to absorb the palace — *her* palace. The walls were a riot of colors, adorned with paintings that seemed to move and morph as you looked at them. One moment, a landscape of a purple forest with trees that swayed to an unseen rhythm; the next, a portrait of an alien dignitary whose eyes followed you with unnerving precision.

"Okay. The silence is killing me," Marcy said, her smile an island of normalcy in the sea of extravagance. "I'm going to pretend I'm not mad you left Planet Nope before we got a chance to catch up. Blayde and I had to debrief the council by ourselves. We've been holding off throwing the return celebration just to get hold of you — Sally, it's going to be just like the ending of *A New Hope*, only better."

I cringed. "I'm so sorry about that." *This.* This is why I hadn't come to see her before. I knew it was a conversation I wasn't ready for.

As we strolled, the floor beneath us shifted colors, a living mosaic that seemed to reflect our moods. Or maybe it was just broken. I wouldn't have been surprised.

Marcy squeezed my hand. "Well, I'm glad you're here now. This place can get a bit... overwhelming. You know, too much art in dimensions my brain can't wrap itself around."

"Yeah, I noticed," I replied, eyeing a nearby statue of a bird, its bronze beak buried in a calculus textbook, which made me question the reality of pork. "This place is like if a carnival and a space station had a baby and then let it be raised by psychedelic artists."

She let out a laugh. "Except extremely clean and smelling of toilet freshener, right?"

We rounded a corner and came upon a lush interior garden, where music literally wafted on the breeze.

"Welcome to the EternaFresh Palace," Marcy said with a theatrical sweep of her arm. "Where the flora have better musical taste than most DJs. God, I just wish my Spotify worked out here."

I couldn't help but laugh. It was either that or let my brain short-circuit from sensory overload. I chose laughter; it seemed the healthier option.

Then I recognized the song, and almost snorted my brain out of my nose.

"Is that… isn't that what Spurlock sang to us before Planet Nope?"

"*Goodbye Wanderers?*" Marcy let out a heavy, heavy sigh. "It's a hit. Ever since the teasers dropped. I can't get it out of my head — and neither, apparently, can the plants."

"Teasers? What teasers?" I scraped my brain trying to put any sense to her words, while conveniently trying to drown out Spurlock's — admittedly magnificent —

vibrato. And the image of his muscular torso. My face felt hot.

"The docuseries," Marcy replied, patting me on the arm. "Your heroic rescue is going to be the talk of the Alliance. Come on."

Of course — that was the reason any of us were allowed to go on that mission in the first place: good PR. With Planet Nope rescued, the TV special was sure to drop soon.

Marcy led me to a sitting room that managed to be both opulent and bizarrely charming. The chairs resembled oversized tulips, opening and closing gently as if breathing. The coffee table was a miniature holographic solar system, complete with tiny planets orbiting a sun.

We settled into the petal-like chairs, which adjusted to our forms with a snug, comforting embrace. For a moment, we both avoided the elephant in the room, or in this case, the neon-colored, six-legged creature outside that occasionally peeked in through the window with curious eyes.

"Just don't make eye contact," Marcy murmured, her eyes flicking towards the window before settling back on me.

I leaned forward, clasping my hands together. "Marcy, this place... it's so unlike you."

"I know, I know," she muttered. "But then again, none of Dany's family estates are really me. It's been a lot. A lot, too quickly."

"But how can you just be here?" I sputtered. Marcy, locked up in fancy estates, while the Alliance continued its constant stream of crap. This was my *bestie* we were talking about. Her in-laws' messes weren't entirely her own. "With all the shit out there?"

Marcy sighed, a hint of exasperation lining her brow. "I keep forgetting you travel through time now. Jeez. How long has it been for you? Since Planet Nope?"

I thought about it a few seconds longer than I would have liked. "About a week?"

"A week?" Marcy's voice rose in disbelief. "We were stranded on that godforsaken rock for over a month, Sally. You can't just bounce back from that in a mere seven days. Tell me, did you even take a moment to rest after everything you went through?"

"I had a lot on my plate." My shoulders slumped slightly.

Marcy threw her hands up in the air. "And that's exactly my point! You can't keep going at this pace without breaks. You're human, Sally, not a machine. If you don't slow down, you're going to crash and burn."

Ugh. *Not her too.* "I know," I conceded, a small wave of fatigue washing over me at the admission. My little nap with the fluffballs of doom outside did nothing for my exhaustion. "It's just... been a lot."

"It has been, hasn't it?" She leaned back in her chair, her elegant silks revealing the soft round curve of her belly. I gasped. With everything going on, it had been the last thing on my mind.

Stupid, self-obsessed Sally. No wonder she's pissed you flaked after she saved a planet.

"So, how's the future little one?" I sat up straight, my face breaking out into a smile so wide I thought my skin would split. "Did I get a chance to congratulate you? Congratulations!"

"It's a boy! We had a lot of prenatal appointments to make up for, so I'm learning a lot, all at once." She smiled, though it never reached her eyes. "It's... a journey. Five months along, but with Dany being Dany, we're not quite sure how long this is all going to last. None of this was in the manual." Marcy's hand went to her belly. "Judge me all you want for taking a break while the Alliance still needs me, but this one needs me too."

I laughed. *Marcy, a mom.* "You're right, you're right. I take it an Earth visit is on the cards? For the grandparents-to-be?"

"Oh, definitely. My parents are over the moon. Makes up for telling them I moved to Tibet."

Our laughter filled the room. My heart soared with joy for my bestie. After everything we'd been through, she deserved this piece of happiness.

But then Marcy's gaze fixed on me with an intensity that seemed to cut through the room's warmth, and the atmosphere shifted. The petal-like chair, once a snug embrace, now felt like it was holding me in place for an interrogation under a spotlight. Even the surrealist creature outside the window ran off, leaving the room dim and drab.

"Sally." Marcy's voice was tender, her eyes searching mine. "After Planet Nope... you just disappeared. We were all so worried. What happened?"

I swallowed. I had to say something. Talk to someone. The Pandagram hadn't worked what chance would I have with Marcy? The question hung in the air, heavy and expectant. I took a deep breath, feeling the tulip chair tighten around me as if bracing for my response.

I took a deep breath. *Here goes... everything.*

"I left because of Zander." I tried to make it sound casual, like it wasn't the end of the world. It wasn't, after all. I was still here. "He did something unforgivable. He..."

My gaze dropped. I couldn't downplay what had happened. Not when Marcy knew me so deeply. She could tell I was holding back.

And then it hit me. Marcy knew John. And unlike my parents, this she could understand. This... I didn't have to be alone after all.

"Did you... did you see the one they called Provis?" I asked.

She shook her head. "I recognize the name. Zander was obsessed with rescuing him. He was a huge part of the final push for the planet, but he didn't make it in the end. He was named one of the heroes of the liberation. He's on the list for the posthumous medal of valor." She tilted her head slightly. "Sally. Did something happen between you and Provis?"

I took a deep breath. *Here goes nothing.*

"Provis was a child hire," I started. *Here goes everything.* "Before Planet Nope, he was a reconverted abductee."

Marcy frowned. "Poor kid. Sally, you know I'm doing everything in my power to abolish that barbaric system. I'm working with the council to establish new protocols to crack down on—"

"No, Marcy. I know you're doing your best." I tried to force a smile, but I'd run out after my joy for her. "Provis came from Earth."

Marcy's eyes widened with shock. "He was someone you knew before."

I nodded. "Provis… was John."

Marcy's face went through a kaleidoscope of emotions in the blink of an eye. Shock. Joy. Crestfallen. Her hands flew to her mouth, then she dropped them, taking my hands in hers. "Sally, I'm so sorry. I can't even begin to imagine what you're going through."

"Sally," she whispered, eyes filling with tears, "I had no idea."

My own tears finally broke free, cascading down my cheeks. Marcy's grip on my hand tightened. For a moment, there was nothing else in the universe but our grief.

"It gets worse," I choked out between sobs. "He killed John. Zander did. For something he thought John would do." The words felt like shards of glass, each one cutting deeper as they left my lips.

Marcy's face crumpled. "Oh, Sally," she murmured. We leaned into each other, our tears mingling in a shared pool.

I let out a shaky breath, feeling the weight of everything I'd been carrying. "Marcy, there's more. I... I tried to change it."

"Change... it?" Her brows furrowed in confusion.

"You said it yourself, I travel through time." I took a deep breath. "I can change these things. Or I should be able to, right? And if Zander could do it, why couldn't I?"

"You tried to change time?" Her face twisted with shock. "Did it work?"

I shook my head, a lump forming in my throat. "I went back, Marce. Back to that day at the overlook. I thought I had the perfect plan. But it turns out, messing with the past is like pulling at a thread you can't see the end of. If John hadn't..." A breath. "If he hadn't fallen, the Youpaf would have turned Earth into a cinder. Our world, gone. Just because I couldn't let go."

Marcy opened her mouth to say something — something angry, furious, by the red in her face — but before she did, she snapped it all shut again. Shame flooded over me: if saving John had worked, would our university lives have played out the same way they had? Would she have met Dany? Would the love of her life be lost in exchange for having my brother back?

"You... you shouldn't play with time, Sally," she said softly, her hand resting gently on my knee, grounding me. "Please. You have no idea what you could change by accident."

"I know, I know... I put everything back, I swear! But then I realized if Zander could make a paradox, I could too. And if it meant choosing between my brother being a tyrant or being dead, why not create another option entirely? But when I did…"

Marcy's eyes searched mine for answers. "What happened, Sally?"

"Pythanoreans," I choked out. "Beings from another dimension, who think they're the guardians of time or something just because they don't like it when things don't go their way. They said I was creating chaos in the timeline. That I had to stop. That John… he was a 'nexus point' or something. Every action I took was just… making things worse."

"Sally," she whispered. "I'm so sorry."

I could feel the dam of my emotions breaking again. "It's like I've been their puppet all along, Marcy. They pull the strings in time, and I dance. But the one time I try to change something for myself, they slap me down. I can't do this anymore. I can't save John, can't protect my friends. It's like I'm just… just a pawn on their game — powerless and expendable."

Marcy's embrace tightened. "I'm here for you, Sally. Always."

As my tears eventually ebbed, a fragile calm settled over me. I pulled back slightly, a sniffle breaking the silence. "It's just… I feel so lost. Every choice I make, every path I take, it seems to lead to more pain, more chaos. I can travel through time, but what good is it if I can't make things right? If I can't save the ones I love?"

Marcy reached out, brushing a stray tear from my cheek. "Sally, why do you think you have to do all this alone?"

I shrugged, a hollow laugh escaping my lips. "I guess I've just gotten used to it. Used to being the one who screws up, who has to fix things. But I'm tired, Marcy. So tired of trying and failing and just... hurting."

Marcy nodded. "Sally, you're one of the strongest people I know. But even the strongest need help sometimes. You don't have to carry this burden by yourself."

Her words wrapped around me, soft and warm like a blanket. I hadn't... I hadn't... Maybe I wasn't alone in this vast, often cruel universe. In Marcy, I had a friend. An ally. Someone who saw me for who I truly was and still offered her hand.

"You're right," I squeaked.

Marcy squeezed my hand tighter. "You're not alone, Sally. Never have been, never will be."

In that moment, surrounded by the absurdity of the palace and the warmth of Marcy's friendship, I felt a flicker of hope. Maybe I could find my way through this maze of pain and loss. With friends like her, the journey seemed a little less daunting.

So long as I didn't burn this bridge, too.

TWENTY

THE TIME TRAVELER'S GUIDE TO BREAKUPS AND SLUMBER PARTIES

THERE'S SOMETHING GROUNDING ABOUT watching your friend fight with a DVD case. It was so absurdly human, it clashed beautifully with the high-tech extravagance around us. Marcy, now the mastermind behind a contraption that looked like it was the love child of a mad scientist and a disco ball, was on her knees before an ancient DVD player. The player itself was a relic, a museum piece really, but here it was, hooked up to a pulsating metal cylinder that glowed a comforting shade of purple. Wires spilled out like the tendrils of some metallic octopus, connecting it to the wall in a chaotic yet oddly mesmerizing display.

"We may be light-years away from Earth," Marcy said, her hands deftly maneuvering amidst the wires. She gestured towards a corner where a stack of DVDs sat, guarded by a plant that looked like it had taken a wrong turn on its way to a rodeo and ended up riding the bull. "But I refuse to let a trivial detail like interstellar distance separate me from the joys of a tangible movie collection."

I couldn't help but smile, feeling like I was twelve again, sprawled on Marcy's bed as she geeked out over the special features and director's commentaries of the latest addition to her collection. Except now, I was sprawled on an emperor-sized bed, and we were light-years away from where those memories were made, both wearing pajamas made by the finest tailors in this arm of the galaxy. Though the DVD she was fiddling with was probably the same old one from back home.

"I'm guessing Netflix is out of the question?" I quipped.

She shook her head as she fiddled with the contraption, wires hissing softly as they connected to the alien interfaces. "No Earth streaming, and while we downloaded a ton of movies onto a hard drive, there's something about having an actual DVD collection that feels... tangible. Comforting. It's like holding onto a piece of home."

She cheered as the wallscreen flicked to life with an all-too-familiar menu.

"And for tonight's cinematic masterpiece: *Twilight*," Marcy announced, brandishing the DVD like she'd unearthed the Holy Grail. "Brace yourself for an overdose of teenage brooding and glittery vampires."

I groaned theatrically. "Oh, the nostalgia. It's like revisiting my awkward teen years, but with more vampires and less existential dread."

"This," she said, gesturing to the bizarre setup, "is my little slice of Earth. It took an absurd amount of effort to make this DVD player compatible with advanced Alliance tech, and I'm half convinced it's still giving me the silent treatment, but, voilà, it works!"

As the opening credits began, the room was bathed in the flickering light of the screen, casting long, dancing shadows across the walls. Marcy plopped down next to me, her contented face illuminated by the glow. I found myself sinking into the comfort of the moment. The familiar scenes, the cheesy dialogue. It was just like old times. Times when the biggest worry I had was whether I was Team Edward or Team Jacob.

Marcy and I laughed, throwing imported popcorn at each other during the most cringe-worthy moments. I found myself clinging to the feeling, to the warmth of friendship, to the simple joy of a night spent laughing at a movie with my bestie. For the first time in ages, I felt… normal.

Marcy was right: I needed this. A break from the relentless pace of my life, a chance to just be Sally again. I needed to hold onto these moments, these connections. They were the lifelines that kept me grounded, reminded me of who I was beneath the mess. That no matter how far I traveled or how much I changed, some things remained constant. In that moment, I realized that sometimes, the best way to face the future was to take a step back and just breathe.

Just as Edward walked up to bat, the door burst open, startling Marcy and me into a chorus of screams. For a split second, my heart was in my throat. But then the lights flickered on, revealing not a creature of the night but Dany, Empress of, well, pretty much everything. She stood there in her crisply tailored white suit, oozing the kind of power that could make interstellar warlords think twice about their life choices.

"Sally? What are you doing here?" Dany asked, her tone a mix of surprise and mild exasperation — the kind you reserve for unexpected guests who don't bring snacks. "Not that it's not good to see you, but didn't we talk about getting a heads up?"

"This is a social call," I said, weakly. "No business. Just girl time."

"Lovely. And the Siblings are…?"

Marcy was quick to morph into my knight in shining armor — or, in this case, comfy pajamas. She enfolded me in a protective hug. "Dany, don't *empress* for a second," she said, her voice soft but firm. "Sally's going through a rough time. She's dealing with a breakup."

"A breakup? Oh, that sucks." Dany's expression softened as she stepped into the room, closing the door behind her. "Wait, you and Zander…?"

"Don't even bring him up," said Marcy, throwing her hands over my ears, not that they managed to block out anything. "Stop thinking like the president and be Dany for the night. She *needs* us."

Marcy liberated my ears as Dany visibly deflated, smiling sweetly.

"Ah, the therapeutic powers of terran cinema," Dany mused. She glanced at the TV screen with a mock-serious expression. "But *Twilight?* Really, Marcy? That's your go-to heartbreak cure?"

Marcy shrugged, a mischievous twinkle in her eye. "Desperate times call for desperate measures. Plus, Sally has a thing for sparkly vampires."

I rolled my eyes. "Hey, don't knock the sparkle until you've tried it. It's oddly cathartic."

Dany nodded. "Popcorn's not going to cut it then."

So there we were — Dany, Marcy, and yours truly – squished on the bed like a trio of teenagers. Between us was a tub of chocolate chip ice cream large enough to warrant its own zip code. Spoons dove in and out as we drowned our sorrows in frozen dairy. We were an odd bunch, for sure: the president-empress, the soon-to-be-mom, and the time-traveling heartbreak victim, united by ice cream and the melodrama of teenage vampires. But in the dark, it felt like old times. Before I got whisked away to the stars. Before Dany's past came knocking. In that dimly lit room, with the echoes of laughter and the shared warmth of friendship, it was easy to pretend, just for a little while, that we were just three girls, unwinding after a long day. We laughed, we groaned, we rolled our eyes — and for those precious hours, I forgot about the chaos of my life. I was just Sally, hanging out with friends, healing from a wound that felt like it would never close. It was surreal, sitting there with two of the most powerful women in the galaxy, bonding over a movie that was as far from our reality as possible; exactly what I needed.

As the final credits rolled, the glow from the screen began to wane, and the real world started to creep back in, like a cat that's decided it's time for attention. I let out a sigh, the weight of the galaxy resettling on my shoulders.

"Well, that was amazing," said Marcy. "They say the twenty-third rewatch is the best, and I agree. It really hits… something."

My fists were balled in the blankets, clinging to the moment, but it was slipping away so fast. Marcy gently rubbed my arm.

"Do you want to talk about it?" Dany's voice was soft, her warmth tangible as her arm brushed against mine. I tried to remember what it was like before: how they had helped me after my breakup with Robin. Back then, our girls' nights were epic, even as I slowly became the third wheel to their blossoming love story. But this time, the past felt like a distant shore, unreachable and lost in the fog.

"He crossed a line," I managed to say, the words like lead in my mouth. "One you can't uncross."

Marcy rested her head against my shoulder. "You know what used to help me get over a breakup?"

"Other than another *Twilight* rewatch?" I asked. I wanted to remind her that she'd only been broken up with once before, and that ex wasn't a murderer, but the words died on my tongue. In the grand scheme of things, pain was pain, loss was loss.

"Well, you know all the little things that annoyed you, but you never voiced them, to keep the peace?" She smiled. "You need to get them out."

I paused, my mind drifting back to Zander. There were the magical moments, the wild adventures, those instances of fiery passion mixed with tender, smoldering interludes. Everything had been so incredibly perfect, until it wasn't. Until his other selves, those other versions of him, collided with his mind like meteorites into an unsuspecting planet.

Tears began to trace their way down my cheeks. "He was... spontaneous, to put it mildly," I started. "Living in the moment is great and all, but sometimes, just sometimes, I'd have liked to know which galaxy we'd end up in for dinner. The man was allergic to planning. To him, having a goal was the entire battle plan. 'Get from point A to point B? How? We'll wing it!' It was maddening."

I shook my head, a laugh bubbling up despite the tears. "He turned every situation into an escape room. He could teleport anywhere in the universe, but no, let's do it the hard way because it's more 'fun.' Sometimes, I didn't want fun. I wanted easy. But then, that was part of the charm, wasn't it? The unpredictability, the thrill.

"And God, he was such a good cook." I sighed, wiping my eyes. "Man hated planning ahead, but boy could he improvise anything, whether it be a dish or his way out of a labyrinth.

"I don't want that version of him to be gone." I admitted. The tears were running freely now, so fast I couldn't catch them even if I wanted to. "Like, I really loved him. More than anyone or anything else in the whole crazy universe. And now I can't do anything to save him. Or anyone else, for that matter. It's like Time's playing this sick game, giving me just enough to keep me going but never what I really want. And every time I think I'm making a new connection, bam! Universe throws a wrench in it. Like with Spurlock. Almost lost him because I was too busy dodging the Agency's calls. Anyone I get too close to could get caught in random crossfire, and I wouldn't be able to save them."

At the mention of the Agency, Dany's demeanor shifted, her eyes sharpening with interest. The friendly, ice-cream-sharing empress was replaced by the commander in chief, all business and concern.

Dany sighed. "They're a constant headache. Worst managed Agency in the outer reaches. You know, if you're looking for a career change…" she joked, a wry smile on her lips.

I laughed. "Me? Running the Agency? Eww."

"Can we not have one drama-free night? Just one?" Marcy let out a dramatic groan from the bed, her voice muffled by a pillow. "Can we *please* not turn this into a strategy meeting?"

"Can't help it. This is my life now." Dany shrugged, slightly resigned, mildly proud.

I nodded, but a thought was nagging at me. "While we're on the subject," I started, hesitating slightly, "I need to tell you before someone else tries to blackmail me. There's something else I stumbled into. An anti-Alliance alliance meeting."

"You did what now?" Dany's eyebrows shot up along with her tone.

Marcy swiveled towards me, her eyes as wide as saucers. "You went to one of their *meetings*?"

"Yeah, totally by accident," I added quickly. "But, um, they brought up some... valid points."

Dany leaned forward, frowning. "Such as?"

"Well, mostly…" I said, treading carefully. "There's talk about your government's transparency, or the lack thereof. Just a few months ago the Siblings and I were basically terrorists in their eyes for trying to make things right. Just because we're friends doesn't mean I can ignore the terrible things the Alliance has done, or is still doing."

"Neither can I." Dany sighed, running a hand through her hair. "We're working on it, Sally. We've already dissolved the Child Hire Program. We have new case workers helping to reintegrate abductees. It's a mess, but we're cleaning it up."

"And Dany isn't even telling you the biggest news." Marcy added, "we're organizing new elections! Real ones! But after our Planet Nope rescue, I have no doubt who they'll chose. Thanks to you, we managed to save so many people. The survivors are being re-integrated to society," she continued, "which isn't easy with the wild ones, let me tell you, but everyone is safe and healthy and our government is working hard, and all towards the same goal for once. So there's been a massive spike in Dany's popularity. People are starting to trust us again. And for good reason: we're trustworthy peeps. Not like…"

I nodded as she petered off. "That's... actually really reassuring. I guess I just wanted to make sure you were on top of it."

"We are," Dany affirmed, her tone leaving no room for doubt. "Just because we're taking a breather doesn't mean we're not doing our best."

It was a lot to take in. But hearing them lay it all out, the efforts they were making, the changes they were implementing… it felt like a bit of weight lifting off my shoulders. Maybe the universe was in slightly more capable hands than I'd given it credit for. And that thought alone was enough to let me breathe a little easier.

"And you, Sally, you're a part of this too," Dany insisted. "That documentary crew wants an exit interview with you. The people love a hero with a touch of mystery."

I sank back into the bed, which seemed to cuddle me in sympathy. The idea of being paraded in front of cameras, dissecting my part in their soap opera, made my stomach do backflips.

"Can't I just write a blog post or something?" I half joked, half pleaded.

Dany shook her head. "Your presence on the *Traveler* tomorrow is non-negotiable, Sally. It's time the galaxy saw the face of their new hero."

Marcy groaned. "Fine, but can we at least finish our night without any more galaxy-saving talk? I swear, if one more person mentions intergalactic politics, I'm going to start throwing pillows."

But in the back of my mind, the gears were already turning.

I'd get Time to release me or die trying.

TWENTY-ONE

I'M NOT HERE FOR THE DRAMA, JUST THE EXIT INTERVIEW

THE TRAVELER WAS SO MUCH MORE THAN A spaceship, and not just because it also happened to be a movie set. It sat in Voiddock Alpha-3, flaunting its sleek design and gleaming surfaces like a supermodel at a car show. It was the jewel in the crown of Alliance technology and diplomacy, with just enough flair to double as the backdrop for the universe's most dramatic reality show. Despite the storm inside me, I couldn't help but feel a surge of awe. This ship, with its corridors of possibilities and decks of dreams, was a reminder of adventures past and the thrills of the unknown — and how far I'd come, from sneaking aboard like an interstellar stowaway to being escorted on board like some space-age celebrity.

And, wearing Marcy's loaner clothes, I felt like one, too.

Returning to the *Traveler* had all the awkward charm of Ferris Bueller being hauled back to school after his legendary day off. Except now, I was sandwiched between the President-Empress and Imperatrice of the Alliance. It was sweet, even if it felt like slapping a smiley-face sticker on a black hole.

Dhume, my ever-patient attaché — or was she my cultural liaison at this point? — was waiting for us by the gangplank. Her relief at seeing me was overshadowed by the kind of annoyance that could only be mustered by someone who's had to handle my responsibilities in my absence.

"Sally, really? Running off without so much as a debriefing?" She extended her hand, an Earth greeting so perfectly executed it almost felt alien in its precision. Someone had done their etiquette homework, which was a delightful surprise, like finding out your spaceship comes with cup holders. "You missed the wrap party."

"Sorry, Dhume." I offered a sheepish smile that felt like it might crack at any moment. "But here I am, all in one piece. Well, mostly one piece, only partially unraveled at the seams."

Dhume exhaled through her nose. "Well, your seams are holding up better than the other two, at least. Speaking of which, any chance you could persuade Zander to show up for *his* interview? It would really help round out this docuseries."

"Would that I could." I shrugged, hoping it conveyed more helplessness than indifference. "Zander's been... elusive these days, to put it mildly."

"These days? Sally, it's been barely a week!" Dhume's sigh deepened, echoing the weariness of someone trying to herd cats. "How am I supposed to manage the Office of Sibling Liaison if the siblings in question never answer their communication devices?"

I cringed. Her words hit closer to home than she knew. Trying to keep myself together felt more slippery than a buttered floor in zero gravity.

"Anyway, you have to get them to attend the celebration," she said earnestly. "We have medals to give out, you know."

Stepping aboard the *Traveler* this time felt like walking onto the set of a high-budget sci-fi flick. The flagship, usually bustling with the elite of the Alliance, had taken on a surreal quiet, almost staged atmosphere. Moored above Pyrina for necessary repairs following our escapade at Planet Nope, the usual crew members seemed to have been replaced by a motley ensemble of camera operators, boom mic handlers, and a diligent janitorial team that polished the corridors to a sheen that would make a mirror envious. It was like walking through the innards of a high-tech, interstellar toilet — curved, spotless, and so white you'd half expect a cleaning bot to offer you a mint after your journey. The grandeur of the Alliance's pride was juxtaposed with the orchestrated chaos of the film crew, creating a bizarre harmony that made you wonder whether you were aboard a flagship of exploration or the set of a particularly ambitious commercial for next-gen bathroom freshness.

When we finally made it to the bridge, the scene shifted. Kork was there, standing tall like a sequoia amidst a forest of consoles and holographic displays. He must have sensed our arrival because he swiveled around from the grand window, his face breaking into a grin as bright as a supernova when he saw me.

And this time, there were no cameras rolling to stop me from running into his arms. A rare moment of unscripted reality. It was a welcome that made the sterile world outside the bridge feel like a distant memory.

"Sally!" Kork's voice thundered as he enveloped me in a bear hug, lifting me off the ground and swinging me as if I were nothing more than a fabulous scarf. "By the stars, you're a sight for sore eyes! I was so worried!"

Kork's embrace was a rare oasis of warmth in the cold expanse of space. His eyes searched mine as he set me down. "Where did you vanish to? I… the entire crew was on edge."

"I just… needed some space." I managed a small, wistful smile.

His expression softened, a glimmer of understanding in his eyes. "I get it," he murmured. The words hung in the air, along with the unsaid ones. "Magnesar told us what you've been through. I'm so sorry."

"It's ok, I've survived worse," I said, biting my lip. I wasn't sure I had, but it wasn't the first awful adventure I'd pulled through.

"I wanted to be sure you were alright." Kork's gaze drifted away for a moment before refocusing on my face. "You know, we tried everything to break through Planet Nope's cloud barrier, to reach you, even just to send a message. But we couldn't even get close. I felt like I was going mad with worry."

"I knew you were there. Always." Our eyes met, and I held his gaze.

A towering blonde stepped between us. "Commander Kork, your efforts during the Planet Nope crisis were beyond commendable." Dany's bow was as low as the ones offered to her, matched perfectly by Marcy. "I'm glad to see you again."

Kork beamed. "Madam President, it was our duty, our honor. Though we would never have been able to pull off a rescue of that scale without the hard work of Sally here, and all the others shipwrecked on the surface."

"Yes, we are thrilled to usher in this new era of cooperation," Dany said, shooting me a wink. I smiled back. Maybe I *could* be the hero the Alliance needed. Work with incredible people to make this arm of the galaxy a little nicer for those who lived in it.

Kork's eyes flicked to me. "Are the rumors true? Are you… friends?"

"Something like that." It was a complicated story, but then again, what in my life wasn't.

Then it hit me, an idea so obvious it was almost embarrassing it hadn't occurred to me before. I looked at Kork and then at Dany. "Kork, have you ever talked to the president about where you come from? Your home?"

A flash of worry crossed Kork's face. "I... well, no, I haven't really had the chance."

"I think she would be open to hearing your story," I said, trying to gesture at Marcy with my eyes, so beyond the realm of subtlety it could be considered pantomime. "You might find you have... *things* in common. *Places*."

Dany's interest was piqued, her diplomatic demeanor giving way to genuine curiosity. "I would love to hear more about it, Kork. Your culture, your people. Understanding each other is the cornerstone of our Alliance, after all."

Dhume's voice cut through the moment. "I hate to interrupt, but we really do need you, Sally. The interviews won't conduct themselves."

Kork straightened up. "Duty calls, eh, Sally?" He flashed a grin that didn't quite reach his eyes. "We'll be talking more later."

"Duty calls," I agreed, even as I felt myself go cold. "But don't let this take you away from your conversation." I turned towards Dhume, stepping away from Kork's comforting presence. "Let's get this over with."

As I followed Dhume, I couldn't help but feel a twinge of sadness, knowing I wouldn't be there when Kork finally had the chance to let down his walls. Instead, I'd be putting mine up, and painting them with murals.

Dhume led me to a room I'd never seen before — which wasn't surprising, considering how little freedom I'd had to explore this fabulous ship. But the moment I stepped into the makeshift studio, I groaned internally. The lights were too bright, the chairs too shiny, and the producer had that look in his eyes — the one that says, "I smell award-winning drama." I wasn't even sure what the point of the room was — did the *Traveler* just have random interview rooms built into it?

"Sally, darling!" the producer exclaimed, clasping his hands together with a theatrical flourish. I recognized him as the one Zander and I had threatened before we'd clambered into the doomed shuttle. "This is going to be stellar. What is it Magnesar always says? Novalicious, baby."

I bowed politely. "Um, good to see you again, uh…"

"Glexar Rellar," he supplied, with a flamboyant twirl that spun his skin through a spectrum of colors like a living mood ring. "I must apologize for our lack of interaction before your mission, we were ordered to have no contact with the Siblings and their associates."

Dhume rolled her eyes behind him, quickly dropping her gaze back to her clipboard.

"I understand, Glexar Rellar," I replied. "I suppose now that things have ended on a high note, those restrictions have been lifted?"

"Indeed! And please, call me Glexar." He nodded like a bobble head. As he spoke, he popped something that looked suspiciously like a wriggling grub into his mouth, munching with evident delight. I tried not to look too closely. "Although this means we must make up for lost time! We need to introduce you to the Alliance as the hero you are. I've been binging on your Earth's television archives in order to get a sense of Terran culture. Such quaint melodrama! Now, let's make you a star, shall we?"

I settled into the chair, eyeing the camera with disdain. Behind the drifting eyebot, Dhume reached for the corners of her lips and pulled them up — an obvious cue for me to smile.

"Should I change?" I asked, pinching the something-like-silk shirt I'd borrowed from Marcy. "I thought you'd want me in uniform."

Glexar waved a hand dismissively, though he himself looked like he'd dabbled in every fashion trend since the Big Bang. "No, no, darling. This is *reality* TV — authenticity is our… what do you call it? Our Space Jam!"

Oh boy. I cleared my throat. The bright lights were too hot, making me sweat. "Then the uniform would be more accurate."

But he only adjusted himself into his chair, took a deep breath, and launched right into it. "Sally Webber. Friend of the infamous Siblings, now hero in her own right. Tell us, how did it feel being a captive? The despair, the longing — give us the raw, emotional turmoil!"

I didn't even realize the cameras were rolling, and already I was thrown right into recounting my personal hell. I cleared my throat. "It was a nightmare, to tell the truth I—"

"Ah ah ah," said Glexar. "Please remember to roll the question in your answer. We need to spoon-feed the narrative to our audience. That, and the editors will love you — and you know what they say, when the editor loves you, the universe loves you!"

I was sure any viewer could understand with context clues, but hey, the second half of his advice sounded solid enough. "Well, being held captive by the Sters was a nightmare. I'd say quite literally, as it was always nighttime there, and the Sters seemed to subsist on a diet of raw meat thrown on the floor. I was lucky they made human kibble. That's kibble *for* humans, not… well, at least, I hope it wasn't."

Glexar's eyes sparkled like stars about to go supernova but holding back for the right moment. "Disgusting! Delightfully so! Though it's a bit bleak — like most of the story so far. We need some balance. Tell us about the… interpersonal dynamics? Any… steamy encounters? Romantic love triangles? Our viewers lap up a good spicy space soap opera!

"Oh, the tension was palpable. Especially with this rock—" I coughed, struggling to keep a straight face. "With this one rock. It had such a rugged exterior, but deep down, I sensed a real softness."

Glexar blinked. "A… rock?"

"Absolutely," I affirmed with as much seriousness as I could muster. "We had this epic staring contest. I lost, hands down. Our connection? Rock solid."

Dhume stifled a giggle, morphing it into a cough. Meanwhile, Glexar seemed to take my words at face value, feverishly scrawling notes into his pad with a look of profound interest.

"And the climax, the moment of liberation!" he exclaimed, nearly knocking over his snack bowl in excitement. One particularly ambitious grub made a break for it, aiming for newfound freedom. "Tell us about your harrowing escape! The revolution you spearheaded!"

"Oh, you have no idea," I started, pausing as Glexar eagerly raised a finger for protocol. "Executing the escape plan was like trying to coordinate an intergalactic flash mob. But you know what tipped the scales in our favor? Our very own action-packed theme music."

I leaned back, trying to recall a moment that *wasn't* a blur of chaos and fear — Blayde and I on a wild-goose chase for their elusive cloud factory, with Spurlock's thumping beats reverberating through the air, jumbling the Sters' minds like a cosmic blender. Dhume looked queasy as I recounted the bug-infested reactor scene, while Glexar scribbled furiously, signaling his assistants to capture every word. Which is what they were already doing, it being their job, and all.

"And then there was Marcy—" I caught Glexar's eyes widening — right, too informal. "I mean, the

Imperatrice. We couldn't have made it off the planet without her. She somehow managed to negotiate with a species that didn't even regard us as sentient. And she won, against all odds."

The producer's smile flickered. "Tell us, Sally, what was it like stepping back into the light of freedom?"

"Honestly? It felt like walking into a surprise party where everyone forgot to hide. I..." I opened my mouth and closed it again. So much for rehearsed, canned responses. "There's relief, confusion, and a strange feeling that maybe I'd been better off not knowing what was going on."

Glexar leaned in, his eyes gleaming. "Now, now, Sally, modesty aside, the survivors were singing your praises! They called you their savior, their beacon of hope amidst that dreadful sweat farm. And Spurlock Magnesar? Rumor has it he's practically composed an entire album in your honor!"

I blinked. Had he? I thought he had writer's block... unless... was *I* the reason he'd come to Earth? I mumbled, fingers fidgeting in my lap. "I... well, I mean, anyone would've done the same."

Glexar popped another grub into his mouth, chewing loudly. "Oh, pish-posh, Sally! You're a hero in your own right, a shining star in the vast cosmos! Your daring escapade on Planet Nope? Simply heroic!"

I swallowed hard. Sure, I'd helped out, but a hero? That was the stuff of comic books and legends, not my stumbling through space.

I managed a half smile, still grappling with the idea. "Well, I suppose when you frame it like that, it does have a nice ring to it. It's just... you know, I never set out to be a hero. I was just trying to not get eaten or, worse, turn into a permanent resident of Planet Nope."

Glexar chuckled, a sound that seemed to echo in the small room. "Ah, Sally, always so humble. But remember, even the most unassuming pebble can start an avalanche. You, my dear, have started a whole landslide of hope! Zippy Zap, that's a wrap!"

As I left the makeshift studio, Glexar's words echoed in my mind. Me, a hero? It was a concept as bizarre as it was heartwarming. In a universe where I often felt like an extra in someone else's movie, maybe I was finally starting to take on a starring role of my own.

Still, I couldn't help but wonder if any of what I said would make it into the final cut. Probably not the part about the rock romance, but better than becoming tabloid fodder if they knew just how close Spurlock and I had grown.

"That went quite well, I think," said Dhume, leading the way back to the bridge of the *Traveler*.

"Yeah, if you ignore the part where I nearly married a rock."

She lifted an eyebrow. "You really don't know how to take a compliment, do you?"

I bit my lip. It wasn't that I didn't know how: I did know how to take them, when they were deserved. But just like food, some compliments can be hard to digest.

And I couldn't take credit for saving a planet when all I did was play backup to the real heroes.

Kork was beaming like a baby star as I stepped back onto the bridge, still deep in conversation with Marcy and Dany, their heads close together. Whatever the three of them were discussing had him practically bouncing on his toes.

"Hey, have I missed the party?" I asked, sidling up to them.

Kork whirled around, his smile so wide it could've wrapped around the ship. "Shore leave!"

I looked at Dany, then at Kork, then back again. Then at Marcy's hand in his. Then back at Kork, his smile stretching his muscles to the limit.

"You're going home?" I asked, feeling my own smile grow tenfold.

"Earth!" His eyes sparkled. "I haven't seen my family since... well, you know."

My heart swelled a bit at that. "You know, I've got a little something up my sleeve that could cut your travel time down to, oh, about a heartbeat."

Kork's eyes widened. "You mean...?"

"Yep, your own personal chauffeur, courtesy of a certain teleporter who owes you one." I grinned. "I can get you home faster than you can say 'light-speed.'"

Kork's grin grew impossibly larger. "Sally, you're a miracle in human form! You mean it? I won't have to waste days in transit? I can just... be there?"

I nodded. "Just let me know if you want to stop by your Pyrina apartment to grab a bag first — I remember where you live."

Marcy turned to me. "Does this mean you've figured out what you want to do next?"

I paused. James was still a mystery waiting to be solved. Zander... well, he might be dancing with unicorns for all I knew, but that wasn't my circus, not right now. And John... I couldn't save him, not yet, but time was on my side, ironically enough. I would come back at the problem again when I had a stronger arsenal up my sleeve.

I looked over at Kork. At this other Matt Daniels, whose normal life had been stolen from him like so many others. While I couldn't bring John back, I could make things better for another family, the only way I knew how.

"Yeah, I think I do. Mom and Dad said I should get a job, right? Well, it's time Sally Webber started looking for one." I nodded slowly. "Now, does the *Traveler* have a lost and found? I think I left a bag here last time."

Standing there, surrounded by the ragtag crew that had become my makeshift family, it hit me: the universe didn't need grand gestures or heroic feats. Maybe it was about the little things, the quiet acts of kindness, the unexpected lifts home. Those were the real adventures. The battles worth fighting. The stars might reach on forever, but it was the warmth of these small, shared moments that stood against the cold.

People. Friends. They were the answer to this indifferent universe.

In that moment, as the bridge hummed with life and possibilities, I understood that sometimes, being someone's hero is as simple as offering a ride home.

TWENTY-TWO

I SURVIVED THE HEAT DEATH OF THE UNIVERSE BUT THIS 9-TO-5 MIGHT KILL ME

HERE WE GO, SALLY WEBBER'S SECOND ATTEMPT at Post-Interstellar Breakup Recovery. This time, hopefully, without the rebound mission.

First step: bring your starship captain friend to Earth for a long-awaited and much needed homecoming. It's not every day you play intergalactic taxi for a friend. Stop by your friends who just happen to be connected with the dark underbelly of illegal off-world identities. Nothing says welcome back to Earth like fake papers and a backstory for your pal who's been vacationing, unwillingly, with extraterrestrials for a decade and a half. Take the opportunity to pick up your bowling bag filled with the former soul-holding orb of your maybe-not-dead secret agent friend.

And while you're at it, maybe pop by that guy you sort of had feelings for before you accidentally doused him in the fountain of semi-eternal youth. Just a casual check-in to make sure he's cool with his newfound half-immortality and superhero stunts. Spoiler: no hard feelings, just a lot of parkour and a new album in progress. The goodbye, however, remains just as hard.

Step two: head on home to see your family, who haven't really had time to miss you considering you just took a long weekend. Well, except for the dog, who will miss you even if you've been gone five minutes. Return the bowling bag and the orb in shame before you check the answering machine as you should have before you impulsively ran away on said rebound mission. Determine that yes, this is the White House calling, and they're getting pissed.

Beep.

"Hi Sally, this is Jenny from the White House. Hope you're doing well. We were just wondering if you could give us a call back at your earliest convenience. The president wanted me to specify that it's nothing too serious, just a tiny, little, potentially world-altering issue. Thanks!"

Beep.

"Sally, Tom Keller here, Deputy Chief of Staff. I'm just reaching out again regarding that 'small' matter we discussed earlier. It's kind of ballooned into a 'slightly larger than small' matter. So, if you could call us back before it evolves into a 'huge' matter, that'd be great. Thanks."

Beep.

"Ms. Webber, Chief of Staff speaking. I'm calling to stress the importance of a prompt response. It's a matter of national — and possibly intergalactic — importance. Please call us back at your earlier convenience."

Beep.

"Hi Sally, Robert Turner here. The President. Of the United States. I don't usually reach out personally, but we require your expertise urgently. Could you please call me back at your earliest convenience? It's not every day we face a situation that necessitates your unique skills. Also, we seem to be running low on staff to send these messages."

I listened, leaning against the living room wall, my eyebrows climbing higher with each recording. Talk about moving up the bureaucratic food chain — I guess I always knew putting myself in the heart of the Dread incident would come back to bite me in the butt. Or maybe they just wanted to know if I could score them some off-world gadgets. Either way, it was time to finally return the calls and see what all the fuss was about.

But first, I had to assess the messages from the other side. My cell phone was a whole other issue. I sighed as I scrolled through all the missed texts from mysterious area codes. Stook's intimidation tactics, surely. That and the only message I wanted a reply to had just been left on read. Customer support still hadn't answered.

My own personal answering machine had a single message on it, and it was worse than I could have ever anticipated. But I called *him* back first, mainly because I didn't exactly know how to return a president's phone call, but also because some feelings just had to come out.

"Miss Webber." Stook's grating voice crackled to life on the receiver. "Glad you could make time for the Agency."

"Stook," I growled. He wasn't worth wasting pleasantries. "Still clinging to power like a barnacle, I see."

His chuckle was as oily as ever. "Some things are harder to shake off, Miss Webber. Like your continual interference."

I clenched my teeth, imagining the smug look on his face. "Just keep one thing in mind, Stook: I'm watching. Consider this a friendly warning."

"You think you can intimidate me? *You?*" He let out a short laugh. "Miss Webber, you have no idea what you're dealing with. I have acted entirely within the confines of our law and our contracts. The man accompanying you was an off-worlder, after all. Our jurisdiction."

I gritted my teeth. "Just tell me what you want, Stook, or I'm hanging up now."

Stook's response was crisp. "You called *me*, Miss Webber. Does this mean you will be accepting our job offer?"

SINGULARITY

If I'd been drinking, I would have snorted it out. "Oh, that still stands? After everything? You *shot my friend.*"

Stook didn't seem to hear me at all. "Miss Webber, your planet needs you."

"My planet? You're seriously pulling that card?" I barked a laugh. "Tough titties, Stook."

"Consider your president, Sally," he continued, seemingly unfazed. "He is begging for your intervention. I'm only relaying the message."

Oh. He didn't need to say more. He'd shot Magnesar without a second thought. What would he do to Robert Turner, and get away scott free?

I shuddered. "Then, I'll talk to him."

"Fine!"

"Fine!"

I hung up. I slumped into the chair, my mind whirling. There was a strange thrill to the idea of working for my government, a glimmer of excitement for the potential to make a real difference. But the thought of dealing with Stook, that smug, self-righteous weasel, soured any sweetness the role promised. I couldn't trust him as far as I could throw a planet. Yet, the opportunity was too important to pass up — for Earth, for me. I just needed to remember, keep friends close, and Stook in a galaxy far, far away.

• • • • • • •●●●● • • • • •

THE OVAL OFFICE SMELLED ODDLY LIKE A DENTAL office waiting room — an unexpected mix of breath mints and coffee. I found it bizarrely comforting, in a strange, visiting-the-dentist kind of way.

The president sat across from me, his eyes locked onto mine like he was trying to download my brain through sheer willpower. Beside me, Stook lounged on the blue sofa, his pale skin almost glowing under the office lights, staring back at the president with a look urging him to simply get on with it. While I'd walked in the old-fashioned way, going through security checkpoint after security checkpoint, he'd teleported in, which had made the president about as comfortable as a balloon at a cactus convention.

"Mr. President..." I began, trying to cut through the tension, but security took away everything sharp I had at the door.

"Robert," he corrected, almost too quickly, like he was auditioning for a sitcom. "Or... Bob. Bob's better."

"Right... You alright there, Mister President?" I asked, not sure if I should offer him a tissue or a mint.

His rapid nod sent beads of sweat on a daring escape down his forehead. He squirmed in his seat. It was a little unsettling — the man could likely navigate a global crisis with a cool head, but the presence of an extraterrestrial diplomat had him unraveling faster than a cheap sweater.

To be fair, knowing said extraterrestrial diplomat, I felt about the same. It took all my willpower to keep myself from leaping over the coffee table and strangling that spindly neck.

It arched forward in a show of concern. "President of United States, greetings," Stook intoned, his voice a polite monotone. "Is everything alright?"

The president cleared his throat, a little too loudly. "It's fine, Director Stook. Just a minor disagreement with my lunch, nothing more."

Stook nodded. "Ah, yes. It is rare to find a meal that enjoys being consumed for nutrients, that is true. The eternal struggle between eater and eaten." His tone was as dry as a desert, but whether it was intentional or not was anyone's guess. "Shall we get to it?"

The president — or Robert, or Turner, it was hard to see the president of the country as just *Bob* — looking slightly more at ease, leaned forward. "So, we have an arrangement in place?"

"Miss Webber will act as our intermediary." Stook replied with the solemnity of a judge passing a verdict. "She'll be the bridge between our worlds, sharing concerns and insights. And don't worry about her compensation — we have that covered. Earthly bureaucracy need not be burdened. You do not even need to have her name on your payroll."

Turner's eyebrows shot up. "Well, that's... convenient. But we'll have to be discreet. I can't exactly explain frequent visits from a mysterious woman. People talk, you know."

Like he hadn't given everyone in his cabinet my phone number.

"Oh, don't worry, Mr. President." I said, putting on a smile. "I'm practically a ghost. I'll be in and out before anyone can say UFO conspiracy."

Stook let out a huff. "She's quite adept at blending in. Or standing out, as the situation requires."

"Thanks," I replied. I hadn't expected his compliment. Though it might not have been one.

Stook's voice took on a more serious tone. "Ms. Webber will have access to your files, and we will grant her similar access on our end. She will be the judicious gatekeeper of information, sharing only what she deems pertinent for each party."

"I can't give her access to all our confidential files." Turner snorted. "I can't just give you a backstage pass to our nation's secrets, Ms. Webber. There are protocols, you know."

Stook gave a grin that could only be described as grinchy, complete with shimmering teal teeth that would make any dental ad envious. "President Turner, our technology makes hacking your files as easy as, what's the Earth phrase? Stealing candy from a caddy. Ms. Webber will have all the access she needs by sundown."

"And if I object?" said Turner, puffing up like a cat facing down a particularly intimidating cucumber.

"Then we'll keep our juicy secrets to ourselves." Stook shrugged. "It's entirely up to you: we have full clarity between our two governments, or we have tense discussions, sending this salaried employee back and forth between us like a confused maorta between sun and lava."

The president squinted as if Stook had just spoken in Klingon. "That image means nothing to me."

"Context doing nothing for you?"

He shook his head. "No idea what a moorta is."

"Oh, well, it's a… never mind, we're getting off the topic," Stook said with a sigh. "So, will you allow her access?"

The president blinked. "I just…"

Stook's sneer could have curdled milk. "You're the one who begged for her help, Mr. President. Are we to understand you're getting cold feet about our cozy interstellar relationship?"

"You misunderstood me, Director Stook." He straightened up. "I said I needed an advisor on alien affairs, someone who understands your mindset, your strategies, and the extent of your capabilities. I didn't sign up for a middleman."

I couldn't help but feel like another piece in yet another game, I didn't like it — I was already a pawn for Time, and the last thing I needed was to be a Z in the universe's interstellar Scrabble match.

"Well, this is the solution we came up with." Stook threw up his hands. "So take her or leave her."

The president — whose successful puffing up had reached the stage of Thanksgiving Day parade balloon —turned to me, scrutinizing me like I was some kind of exhibit at the Smithsonian. "Why her? Why Ms. Webber?"

I shifted in my seat. Being under the presidential microscope wasn't exactly on my bucket list. I honestly thought we were all getting along.

Stook blinked. "Isn't she who you wanted?"

The president leaned back, his expression clouding over. "Perhaps initially. But now..."

"Oh, believe me, we have no love for her either," said Stook, his words like a grenade tossed casually into the conversation. "In fact, just a few months ago, she was an enemy of the peace. But sometimes, you have to pick the lesser of two evils. Having her on our side is... preferable."

I nearly choked on my own tongue. *"Enemy of peace?"* I echoed. "Look, you two: I didn't come here to be insulted. I am well aware you only put up with me because of my friends, and because of what I can do. But I did not come here as the Alliance's spy, nor will I be a spy for the United States. For the record, I'm not anyone's puppet. I'm here to bridge gaps, not widen them. The Agency's role will be transparent, and in return, the US government keeps the Alliance in the loop. Simple."

Turner rubbed his temples. "Why the sudden openness from the Alliance? What's in it for you?"

"We're on the cusp of a new era, Mr. President," said Stook. "Official contact with Earth is not a matter of 'if' but 'when.' We need a solid foundation of trust. It's about preparing your people, our people, for a future where our worlds aren't so distant. We need this partnership to be seamless, without fear or panic."

"Are you serious?" The president stared at me.

"Wait, are you?" I asked Stook, trying to hide my own surprise. This was not the turn I was expecting this conversation to take, and I wasn't sure I was a fan.

"Truly," he replied. "We will wait for the right time. We have seen this go poorly in the past."

"So you'll take action against the Black Knight?" asked Turner. "If indeed you intend to prevent an early first contact."

Stook blinked, and then a laugh bubbled up from deep inside. "The Black Knight? That old space junk?"

"The Black Knight?" I asked.

Bob leaned forward, his face serious. "It's not just space junk, Director. There are theories, conspiracies, if you will, that it's an alien satellite, and has been monitoring Earth for centuries. Some estimates go back around 13,000 years."

I shuddered. In that instant, Turner, *Bob*, the president looked just like my father. And I'm pretty sure they had the same sources.

"It's not on any of our alert lists." Stook shrugged. "It must be ancient, perhaps a relic or scrap left behind from before we visited your world. Just trash."

But Turner wasn't convinced. "It's starting to show signs of activity. It's been dormant for years, but recent scans suggest something's changed. If there's even a fraction of truth to those theories, it could disrupt everything."

Stook paused, amusement fading. "It doesn't align with any known technology or strategic behavior from our end or any known civilizations."

"Is that what you've been trying to call me about?" I asked. "This was the big emergency?" I had to sit on my hands to keep myself from squirming.

"Well, this is perfect, isn't it?" Stook stood. "A great way to test this new system between us. Miss Webber here will investigate the matter, using our combined resources, and we'll be able to settle this matter once and for all."

Bob nodded. "A trial period? I suppose that could be acceptable."

That pawn feeling came rolling over me yet again. Couldn't I just have a normal job, like accounting or something? But *no*, I get to chase after space junk and calm down presidents. At least this was closer to home. And had a reliable salary.

"With this settled," Stook said, his voice taking on a tone of finality, "I will send Miss Webber more information on this. I must depart now, as time is of the essence. You know how to reach me."

And with that, Stook fizzled out of existence. The president stared at the space he had been standing, his mouth hanging slightly open. I couldn't blame him; I felt the same way.

He rose to his feet, moving towards the drink stand with the kind of purpose you'd expect from someone about to launch a missile, not just grab a glass of water.

He downed one glass, then another. Either he was extremely thirsty or stalling for time. By his third glass, I came to the conclusion that I was being awkward sitting around and that I should leave, but he turned around before I could.

As he faced me, water glass still in hand, his gaze was intense, like he was trying to x-ray my soul. "Who are you, Sally Webber?" It was more a demand than a question. "I've read your file. It makes no sense."

"Is this a part of the job interview?" I tried to sound as nonchalant as a person could when being interrogated by the president. "I know, my CV isn't all that interesting, and I'll admit I had to bump up the font size to make it fill the page—"

He placed his glass on the table, the sound echoing in the silence. "You're a Virginia girl, not far from here. Ordinary upbringing, public schools. Your grades were good, but nothing exceptional. Then, tragedy — you lose your brother. Drop out of college. Work at a power plant, only for it to explode. Next thing, you're accused of murdering an FBI agent, plead insanity, and you're a fugitive in an international manhunt. And just as abruptly, you're exonerated."

He got me there. "So… Agent Felling told you nothing?"

The president shook his head, his brows furrowing. "Agent who?"

"Felling. James Felling. The FBI agent involved in the Alien Hoax?" I flexed my fingers, air-quoting for emphasis. "We kind of bonded over emergency sushi during the whole mess."

"Right. The incident with the Youpaf." He paused. "The next time I saw you, you were with Stook, and I'm signing a contract with you and your friends, who seem to terrify the president of a planetary alliance we're not even a part of."

I tilted my head. "So, you're not in the loop about them?"

"Not particularly, no."

Right, I guess he really didn't know much. Which I could use to my advantage, I'm sure. First of all: make sure I don't end up on some list for some secret area 51 direction thing. To him, I would be a normal, albeit well-connected, human being.

"Blayde and Zander?" I tried to give him the shortest, most concise version of the story that I had. "They've been at odds with the Alliance for years, but they recently struck a deal. They agreed to stand down in return for the Alliance's protection of Earth. It's a delicate balance, and somehow, I'm tangled up in it. Hence, my presence here."

"They're afraid of you," he said calmly. "All three of you."

"Exactly, which is why they want me on their payroll. It's a classic case of keeping your friends close and your potential nuisances closer. They want to make sure I am their friend, so putting me in a position of high responsibility will keep me both docile and preoccupied."

"And are you?"

"Am I what?"

"Docile and preoccupied."

"Not in the slightest. You realize we're only going to be dealing with the Agency, here? A small planetary offshoot of the Alliance, not actually all that powerful."

"To you, maybe," he said coldly. "But their technology is centuries, millennia ahead of ours. We're at their mercy. If you're taking this job — and I really hope you are — you're not just a liaison. You're Earth's first line of defense."

"I'll do my absolute best." My face warmed. As huge as that statement was, I'd just aced a job interview with the President of the United States. I was going to work for the White House. Work for my planet. Meaning and purpose all rolled into one.

His gaze narrowed. "And these two... Blayde and Zander... should we be concerned?"

"If we need them, I know how to get a hold of them," I assured him. *I mean, if it ever came to that... I'd figure something out.*

"As for the Alliance themselves. You seem to have a contentious history with them. Have you actually seen it, though? Their world, their leaders?"

"Seen what?"

"The Alliance. The other planets. Their so-called president. All that. Is it real? Is it really out there?"

"It, all of its planets, and many, many more," I replied with a grin. "I've been to their capital. Shook hands with their leader, even saved a life or two. Heck, the First Lady of the Alliance and I are… pretty tight. So yes, it's all as real as it gets. But you don't have to worry about it. You know why?"

"Why?"

"Because." I smiled. "I've got this."

* * * * * * * * ● * * * * * * * * * * *

AS I WAS ESCORTED OUT OF THE OVAL OFFICE by a member of staff, a wave of excitement washed over me. Working for the White House — that's something to write home about. Would I get my own office? Maybe one with a nice view and a fancy nameplate on the door?

My guide, a sharply dressed woman with an efficiency that could probably outpace a Swiss watch, was giving me a rundown of the security protocols. "And remember, Ms. Webber, discretion is key in all matters."

"Got it. Discretion is my middle name," I quipped. It would be easier to jump in and out of the place, but I had to keep some cards to myself.

We were making our way down a polished corridor lined with portraits of past presidents, the history of the nation watching over us with stern, painted eyes. The air was thick with the gravity of the place, the weight of decisions that had shaped the world. I was soaking it all in when a woman brushed past me without a word, blonde curls bouncing with each step. The world seemed to slow down. The faint scent of her perfume, a floral bouquet with a hint of something sharper, hit me like a punch to the gut. My breath caught in my throat.

I turned my head, my eyes following her retreating figure. She moved with a grace that was almost unnatural, her stride confident, each step echoing in the quiet corridor. The recognition was instant and jarring, like a splash of cold water to the face.

That wig — impossible to forget.

Well, double frash on a cracker.

"Uh, could you point me to the nearest bathroom?" I blurted to my guide, my voice a notch too high.

"Right down the hall, to your left," she replied, gesturing politely.

"Great, thanks!" Without waiting for another word, I veered off and hustled after the woman.

Of course, she was waiting for me. And by the bathroom too, so I wouldn't get in trouble. She pushed the door open, sauntering in without so much as a backward glance to see if I was following.

"Fancy seeing you here," she remarked, oh-so casually, shuffling the folders in her arms as if we were meeting in a coffee shop instead of a ladies' room of the White House.

"Blayde, are you for real?" I snapped, as my blood pressure skyrocketed.

My head was ringing — not from the thrill of a new job, but from the sudden surge of anger bubbling up. She had no business being here! What was she doing in the White House? And why did it feel like the universe was playing a cruel joke on me?

She looked the same as she ever did — well, except for the wig, of course. The bright blonde might have actually been the same one from when she'd been trying to infiltrate the power plant, come to think of it. That or there was a limited amount of wig distributors for people like her.

My phone buzzed suddenly, and I would have ignored it if it wasn't for Blayde's going off simultaneously. Which was more surprising for her than it was for me.

Customer support was back.

Great, the message read. *Let's crack into it.*

TWENTY-THREE
CLOSE ENCOUNTERS OF THE RESTROOM KIND

LEAVE IT TO MY MYSTERY CALLER TO BE cheating on me with Blayde, of all people.

The White House ladies' room, with its pristine tiles and politically neutral décor, was hardly the place I'd have picked for a clandestine meeting. But here we were, phones buzzing like angry bees in our hands. Words were bouncing around in my head like lottery balls, none of them lining up to win the jackpot of what to say first.

Blayde glanced at her phone, a smirk tugging at the corner of her lips. "Same message?"

"Don't even start," I snapped, struggling to keep my voice steady. "Is this some kind of sick game to you? Showing up out of nowhere to wreck my life again?"

"Wreck your life?" Blayde raised an eyebrow. "Seems like you're handling that just fine on your own."

"Oh, please." I let out a bitter laugh. "I finally land a legit job, and you turn up, sporting that infamous wig of yours. Last time you wore that, you blew up my workplace. I can only imagine you're here to do the same."

Her expression remained infuriatingly calm. "Oh, come on, Sally. Maybe I'm just here to add a little spice to your vanilla life. Or perhaps," she added, rare seriousness flickering in her eyes, "we've got bigger fish to fry than your latest career move. Which, I have to say, is dull even by your standards. Government stooge? Seriously?"

I crossed my arms, trying not to let her see she was getting under my skin. "Maybe I decided having health insurance and a regular paycheck didn't sound like such a bad idea."

"You don't need health insurance!" Blayde's eyes almost popped out of their sockets as she laughed. "Oh my stars, Sally. You have time and space at your fingertips, and you actually want to play the game of capitalism? How long have I been gone?"

"Three days, Blayde." I spat. "And I'm allowed to want a tinge of normalcy after everything we've been through. I'm just trying to find some semblance of stability. Is that so hard to understand?"

Blayde's expression softened, just a bit. "Normalcy, as you were so intent on teaching me, is going for a hike or binge-watching people confused about cakes. Not selling yourself out to the very people who seek to control you!"

Just as I was about to retort, our phones vibrated in unison. The new message, in a new group chat, simply read: "Ladies!"

I groaned. "Great, now what? Are we about to get a group scolding?"

Blayde glanced at her screen, raising an eyebrow. "Who even is this? I don't like being reachable."

I frowned, looking down at my phone. "You haven't been getting weird texts too?"

She nodded. "This is the second one. Who is this… customer support?"

The group chat buzzed again. "Excuse me, your number is incredibly hard to find."

Blayde looked like she was about to throw her phone at the wall. "Great, now we have a stalker who's eavesdropping!"

I leaned against the wall, feeling the room spin slightly. "It's James."

"James is dead, Sally," Blayde said, infuriatingly slowly. "And unless you found a way to get her out of that orb in the past three days, she still is."

"But I think… she's been looking out for me," I insisted. I slid down the wall, the cool tile a small comfort. "Helping me."

Had I finally lost it? A dead friend texting from beyond, a life spiraling into absurdity. It didn't matter what Blayde said, I needed stability now more than ever.

She leaned against the sink, her skepticism as palpable as the polished marble. "Sally, you really think she's sending you texts from… wherever?"

"The texts have been really specific." The urgency in my voice surprised even me. "The last time they messaged, they said: 'Get out of there, they are coming.' The exact same words as when she saved my life back in January."

"Pretty common way of getting people out of harm's way." Blayde snorted. "That's not proof of anything."

I glared up at her. "I know it sounds crazy, but I can feel it. It's her."

"Do you even hear yourself?" Blayde folded her arms, letting out a puff of air. "You're chasing ghosts. Literally."

"Well, if it's a ghost, it's a damn helpful one." I stared at the phone. If James really was listening, then she should have texted us confirming her identity. "Come on. Talk to us."

"Sally." Blayde's tone softened. "Are you okay?"

I paused, looking up again. The absurdity of our conversation, the surreal text messages, the too-clean bathroom — it was all too much. "Define okay." I tried to muster a smile. "I'm texting dead friends in a government bathroom while arguing with a space hero."

"Honestly, the fact you wanted to work for The Man is the most disturbing part of all this."

Before I could retort, our phones vibrated in unison. The screen lit up with a message that felt like a lifeline in this sea of insanity. The message I'd been waiting for, for days, the confirmation I needed, had arrived.

"I am here," was all it said. All it needed to say.

Blayde was furiously typing a response before I could react. It took her forever, as the old Nokia required multiple clicks to get the letters right, and she scowled all the way through.

"I think she can hear us," I said, holding up my phone, showing the one-sided conversation in the group text. I wasn't even sure if or how her old brick could handle it.

"Right. James?" She said to the empty room. "How do we know it's really you?"

There was a pause as the two of us silently stared at our phone screens, waiting with bated breath for a response that may or may not come. No three dots to warn us a response was being written. Just a blank screen, and silence.

And then, "The first time you kissed me, all I managed to say was... cool."

Blayde's intake of air was so sharp it could have created a vacuum. She fell against the bathroom wall and slid to join me on the floor, both hands clutching her phone like she was staring into the face of an angel.

My mind was racing, trying to piece together the fragments of a puzzle that refused to fit. James, truly alive in some form, communicating with us from... where? And why now?

And of course, the confirmation: James and Blayde, together. This explained... so much.

"James, where are you? I asked, since Blayde was clearly incapacitated for the time being. "How can you hear us? Can you see us?"

This message came a little faster, but the wait still felt like an eternity, and it did nothing to ease the tension. "Blayde." The words flew through the screen. "Saved me."

It didn't make anything clearer, either.

I looked over at Blayde, who shook her head in terror, hands rushing up to cover her mouth. A tear rolled down her cheek as she read and re-read the words.

"Explain. Now," I demanded.

"It wasn't supposed to work," Blayde mumbled. "I thought it failed, I…"

"But it didn't," said James.

"Okay, timeout." My patience was wearing thin. She couldn't have. The audacity — after all the warnings! "Blayde, tell me you didn't alter the flow of time. Tell me you didn't!"

"I didn't!" Blayde's voice hit a pitch I didn't know existed outside of dog whistles. "I'm not an idiot. I only tried to… to…"

"She used your parents' computer," James's text cut in. "Wanted to upload me as a backup, I suppose."

"A backup?"

Blayde nodded. "It was a desperate shot. The orb was as much good as a paperweight, and I couldn't just leave James there, not knowing if her consciousness would survive. I thought the computer might give her some digital legroom, you know? But it was like trying to cram an ocean into a teacup. Not exactly compatible tech. I thought it was a waste of time."

"It wasn't." James's messaging was quicker now. "Leaving the orb next to the terminal allowed me to build a bridge, to transfer myself over. It took forever — Sally, next Christmas, get your parents hardware from this decade, will you? — but once I was done cooking, I woke up to find an empty computer in an empty room. So I did what any millennial would do — I traveled through the internet."

"You did what now?" I gasped, my mind struggling to keep up. The idea of James surfing the web like a ghost in the machine was too bizarre to process.

James's texts followed rapidly. "Every new device, every connection, made me stronger. Blayde, you saved me." This was followed quickly by, "pun not intended."

"You're trapped inside a computer, dear," Blayde retorted. "Not sure if that counts as saving you."

"I'm not trapped." James's text came with an assertiveness that was almost palpable. "I see everything, all at once. My consciousness is expanded beyond comprehension. I'm alive, in every sense. That has to count for something, right?"

Blayde raised an eyebrow, but there was a softness there, a relief. "And… you feel alright?"

James's response was immediate. "I have no limbs. It's a different kind of life, but not uncomfortable. No physical needs or discomforts, which is a plus. I miss pizza, but not the rest. Plus, it's nice not to worry about paying rent."

Then, another message. "I want to try something. Hold on."

The sudden Facetime notification made my heart leap into my throat. I exchanged a wide-eyed glance with Blayde, who chucked her phone into the air. It made a loud, echoing crash in the sink.

And there she was: James, or an incredibly realistic digital representation of her, floating in a sea of darkness. Her voice was casual, almost eerily so, considering she was supposed to be dead.

"How?" That single word tumbled out of my mouth.

James's digital image shrugged, a slight glitch betraying her virtual nature. "Not sure about the ethics of this, but AI framework is my new best friend. You wouldn't believe how much I've learned about image modeling." She inclined her head, and for a split second we could see the framework of her animated self, every layer of skin and hair carefully handcrafted on the screen. Her smile, even though completely digital, was warm and genuine. "I've compiled thousands of images, piecing together government images and videos of myself, which I stitched and faded together to create… well, me. My God, it is good to see your faces again."

"And yours." Blayde seemed lost for words, her hand hovering in the air as if wanting to reach out to the screen. "James, I… are you really…?"

"Alive?" James chuckled, the sound rich and full of life, even through the speakers of my phone. "That depends on how you define it. But in my own way, yes, I believe I am."

I stared at the screen, torn between elation and disbelief. James was here, sort of. Alive, sort of. My friend, once lost, was now found. A part of me wanted to laugh at the weirdness of it all, while another part of me wanted to scream. I couldn't hold back any longer.

"James, why didn't you just tell me it was you? I've been going out of my mind!" I sputtered. "I've been lugging your orb around for crying out loud! I was trying to save your life! And all that time, you'd already moved on to the freaking internet?"

"It wasn't that simple," she replied. "Imagine trying to navigate a world where every door slams in your face. Firewalls are called that for a reason; they're painful. I had to find a safe way to communicate without getting zapped into oblivion. Look, I'm sorry, but I've got some serious information for you. I tried to contact you much earlier, but I didn't have the processing power. Now that I'm here, I just hope I'm not too late."

Her words sent a shiver down my spine.

"Too late for what?" Blayde pressed, her voice echoing my own urgency. "James, what's going on?"

James's image flickered slightly. "The internet runs deep. There have been whispers, hidden talks, if you know where to look, that my now pretty gigantic mind" — she did a digital hair flip — "has been able to piece together. And it looks like the Agency ships aren't the only ones positioned around this planet."

"How so?" I readjusted my seat on the bathroom floor. It felt like we should be standing for this, but I didn't know if my knees could hold me. "Does this have anything to do with the *Black Knight* satellite?"

Blayde gritted her teeth. "I thought Sally selling her soul to the Agency would put an end to mystery ships."

"Well, it doesn't appear the Agency has any idea that they are actually there," James continued, "that, or they consistently chose to ignore them. Yes, I believe the so-called *Black Knight* is one of the ships. And from what I can tell, it, and the others, only have eyes for a single human."

"Who?" snapped Blayde.

"Sally." James's voice was steady, but her eyes seemed to hold a weight of concern. "They've been monitoring you for years. Since your birth, actually. They know who you are, Sally, and they want you."

"What?" I choked out, my mind racing a mile a minute. My excitement over getting a lead for my first government mission soured. "Who are these people? What could they possibly want with me?"

James gave a slight, almost sorrowful nod. "It's complicated, but from what I've gathered, you're not just a random target. There's something about you, some connection we've yet to fully understand. They've been tracking your every move, cataloging your life like you're some sort of... curiosity."

I slumped back against the wall; the coolness of the tile against my back suddenly felt too real, too grounding. The notion that my existence was under scrutiny from unknown cosmic entities was unnerving, to say the least. My life might have been a carefully observed experiment. My teeth clenched in frustration. So, my paranoia wasn't just me being dramatic. It was validation, in the weirdest, most unsettling form. I truly was being under something's thumb.

Blayde had gone silent, her eyes closed, her face calm, meditative. "Of course it just has to be them," she spat out with venom that could poison a small city. "This is just too perfect."

"Care to share with the class?" My patience was wearing thinner than budget toilet paper.

"Sally, I know you don't want to hear this, but Zander is missing." She paused, as if waiting for me to unleash my fury, but I was saving it up. "The only reason I'm visiting today is because I'm chasing a lead — a lead from a certain customer support." She paused, and James blew a kiss. "About a ship, so good at camouflaging itself as insignificant that only your government is dumb enough to care about it." She took a deep breath. "A Pythanorean ship," she said, her mouth turning in disgust, as if the word left a bad taste in her mouth.

The word made my blood run cold. The Pythanoreans. The dumb ass unicorn-headed higher dimension beings. The pieces were falling into place, but the picture that was forming was more unsettling than I could have imagined.

I opened my mouth to scream, but no sound came out. Probably because Blayde had shoved her whole fist inside. It tasted like lemons.

"That explains a lot," James's pixel-perfect face said, brow furrowing in concern. "Sally, you've heard of the Pythanorean Masters, right?"

I coughed as Blayde withdrew her lemony fist, trying to regain my composure while mentally thanking her for saving me from a public breakdown.

"Higher-dimensional ascended assholes, yada yada yada?" I muttered, pushing myself up shakily. "Have been trying to ruin my life for an age. Literally."

"You've seen them?" Blayde clambered up after me, retrieving her phone from the sink and slipping it back into her pocket. "Since the party?"

I leaned against the tiles, still offering more support than my own legs. "I've had a few run-ins. The last one, they scolded me for breaking Time, then told me they would keep an eye on me. I didn't know that was retroactive."

"You screwed with Time!" Blayde threw her hands up in the air. "It's not a game to them, Sally. It's their reality. And now, it's ours."

"Ours?" I snapped, the word tasting like vinegar on my tongue. "I don't see them spying on *you.*"

"Not me." Blayde shook her head, a stray lock of hair falling over her eye. "Zander. He ran off for this race in some galaxy on the opposite end of the cluster, saying something about wanting to best his former self. Haven't heard anything from him since. Not that he's been very talkative lately. I blame murder."

"Obviously, there is something I'm missing." James sighed, an odd sound to hear through the computer.

"He killed her brother, and she dumped him," Blayde explained. "It's not been pretty."

"I thought John was dead?"

"Abducted, then dead. Courtesy of Zander's temper tantrum," I spat. "Honestly, James, I thought your new internet omnipresence would have caught that juicy tidbit. You were spying on me long enough for me to have repeated it quite a few times."

"Oh," she replied, forlorn. "Sorry to hear that, Sally. And no. These phone microphones are like tin cans connected by string. I'm working with fragments here."

"Alright, time-out," I said, feeling the walls closing in again. "Are we seriously entertaining the idea that Zander's been whisked away by time cops? Couldn't he just be… I don't know… busy?"

"After he created an actual time paradox?" Blayde snorted. "He messed up their precious timeline. What did *you* try to do that got you in their sights, anyway?"

My arms tightened around me as a shiver ran down my spine. "Aforementioned dead brother."

"Oh. Sorry." She put a hand on my shoulder. "There, there. Is this helping?"

I sighed. *Heavily.* "In any case, the Pythanoreans told me they were having trouble finding Zander, so they were going to wait until he interacted with me to apprehend him — which probably explains the lifetime of surveillance."

Blayde's frown deepened. "If they're still waiting, why is he already missing? Would that be him from different points in his lifetime?" Her eyes went wider still. "Only if they intend to erase him entirely from Time."

"They can't do that," I sputtered. "He's basically the annoying glue that holds their dumb timeline together. Without him, it's just... a mess. Which probably explains why it's such a huge deal that he's the one who created the paradox, and why they haven't been able to do anything about it yet."

"They can't resort to their usual solutions with him," James agreed.

"They're probably thrilled for the excuse to get their hands on him. They've been after him for an age," said Blayde. "When we'd attended their lame party, they had gained an interest in us, as non-ascended immortals. They might appear to live forever, but life in high dimensions is just a long life stretched in many directions. It's boring, and it ends."

"I thought the whole point of ascension was... you know... to be above caring about all that?" I pointed out.

"Well, that gets boring, I'm sure." Blayde shrugged. "The master Pythanoreans probably don't like an immortality where they can't really do anything."

I nodded, not that I was sure I got any of it. "So, they took Zander."

"It was bound to happen sooner or later. Whatever the case, we have to get on the Pythanorean ships." Blayde clenched her fist, determination setting in her eyes. "The problem is, now that I know they're involved for sure, jumping is off the table."

"These things can transcend space and time, but their novices sure can't." I looked up at the security camera pointed at the door. We'd been in here a long time. "They're not going to be able to follow us everywhere… are they?"

"No, the novices can't," Blayde reassured. "But ascended Pythanoreans can tell when we jump. We're like neon signs poking through their high-dimensional world. And right now, we're off their radar."

"They can *see* us?" I chewed my lip. "But can they, like, hijack our jumps? Push us off course?"

Blayde frowned. "It's possible. Why do you ask?"

They could push us. Not a comforting thought, per se, but when you've been spending your days thinking you're the problem, it's nice to know some stupid cosmic interference is the actual cause. Relief washed over me.

"Because every time I've tried to jump recently," I explained, "I end up somewhere random in space-time, always bumping into a past version of Zander who, frankly, could've used a few more years in the maturity oven. He's a bit of a horny, whiny jerk."

She frowned. "When…"

I crossed my arms over my chest. "The rift."

"Oh… *that* Zander." She let out a heavy breath. "Yeah, he was a handful. A charming handful, but still a handful."

"Charm's debatable. But that's not the point of the anecdote: what's with 1776? It's not exactly my go-to time period for a vacation."

Blayde pondered for a moment. "1776... It's odd. It's not like it's a significant year for us or a particularly confusing timeline for you to navigate. On your own planet and everything."

"Exactly. I got sidetracked there a few times, and ended up causing an event that was a part of my history. But it hasn't happened to me since."

"Well then, I guess that settles it," Blayde said quickly. "We're not jumping anywhere. James? Can you find us where Zander's been hiding? Or, better yet, invite him to join us here, like you did with me?"

"I can't reach him, he doesn't have a cell," James replied. "I tried to pinpoint him using the Alliance grid, but he's not showing himself anywhere."

"Probably on the other side of the universe." Blayde rolled her eyes. "Wait, hold on, did you say the Alliance grid?"

The digital woman inclined her head slightly. "They latch onto our Wi-Fi — it's just as easy to get onto theirs." She chuckled through the speakers.

I rubbed my temples, feeling the onset of a headache. "But James, their form of internet is completely different from ours. It's not like you can just log on…"

"You can if you're me." She grinned. "I've got the resources of an entire planet at my disposal, and Alliance agents have ways to access their home net from our computers, so I have a way in. Now, important stuff — we need to find Zander."

Blayde seemed unperturbed, almost excited. "Agreed. We need to get on one of their ships — without jumping. It's like a heist. No fancy time jumps, just good old-fashioned stealth and wits. From there, we should be able to ascertain if they have him already. Or if we're too late."

"If we're too late, none of us would be here right now." I leaned against the sink, trying to process it all. "Just so you know, I'm not doing this for him. I'm doing this to get back at this stupid space cult who think they can use me as bait or as a pawn or whatever this is."

"Don't care," said Blayde. "Doesn't matter."

"And here I thought my day was going to be about paperwork and coffee runs at the White House." I let out a long, resigned sigh. "Now I'm plotting an interstellar heist with a digital ghost and a space pirate. I need coffee. Or maybe something stronger."

"We'll figure this out, Sally," said James. "Blayde, pat her back for me? I don't have any hands."

"Sorry, too busy being a genius." Blayde clapped her hands together. "I've got it. We need a Zander. A different one. One we don't need to jump to reach. You know what I mean."

I shot her a look. "Another Zander... already on Earth? It's not like there's always a past of future Zander hanging about."

Blayde smirked. "Well, there is at least one... Have your ever heard of Prometheus?"

TWENTY-FOUR

STUCK BETWEEN A ROCK AND PROMETHEUS

THE SUN WAS BAKING THE HILLSIDE INTO A vibrant green crisp in this weirdly picturesque nook somewhere between France and Italy while I was waiting for Blayde to recalibrate her internal GPS or whatever ancient warriors used for navigation amidst a chorus of toads.

So, James was the Cloud now. Not just in it, but *of* it. Talk about an upgrade. Going from your regular human being to a vast, omnipresent digital consciousness — it's like leveling up from a tricycle to a starship. James Felling, the woman, the myth, the Wi-Fi signal. She was everywhere and nowhere. The thought was both comforting and utterly freaky.

Thanks to James's newfound omnipresence, we'd zipped across continents faster than I could process. Secret messages, speedy plane tickets, a no-questions-asked helicopter ride — it felt like a spy movie, only the secret agent was a smattering of texts on my phone, and the mission was... well, still a bit hazy on that part. It was only when we hit the random valley we were marching through now that my data cut off — works in space but not in the mountains, go figure — and we lost her aid.

Now we were here, Blayde and I, surrounded by opera-singing toads that hushed the moment we got too close. Privacy, I guess? Blayde decided that her centuries-old memory would serve us better on the ground. Hence our amphibian audience.

"Any day now," I muttered to myself, picking at the grass. "Not like we're on a clock or anything."

It was surreal, standing there, thinking about how we were chasing after Prometheus. Or how Prometheus was actually Zander. It was like finding out the monster under the bed was actually a pile of long-forgotten laundry: a whole different flavor monster, both moderately harmless.

"You *sure* he's here?" I asked, not for the first time. "I mean, it's been centuries. Guy might have moved on to a new favorite hillside. Or, more likely, somebody found him and freed him from his rock."

Blayde broke from scanning the horizon to shoot me a look. "Trust me, Sally. If there's one thing I know, it's how to find a person who doesn't want to be found. Whether he's my brother or not."

I raised an eyebrow. "Is that a skill you put on your résumé?"

She smirked, then turned her gaze back to the landscape. "You'll see. Zander is here. This way. Somewhere."

We started walking, the silence between us stretching like over-chewed bubblegum. I kicked at a pebble, watching it skitter across the grass.

As we trudged along, a nagging thought wedged itself in my mind. "How did Zander end up chained to a rock for millennia, anyway? When you found him before, I mean."

Blayde glanced back, her steps never faltering. "Not entirely sure. He never wanted to speak about those days. When I first reconnected with him, he was... different. Talking to the air, seeing things that weren't there. He used to be full of life, excited about everything. Then he learned what it meant to be immortal, how time could stretch endlessly without leaving a mark on you. It changes a person, Sally. The body might heal, but the mind…"

I let out a low whistle. "That's a lot."

It was one thing to know you're immortal, another one to experience immortality head on. How long would I have lasted, before my own mind snapped? I shifted my pack, not quite sure why I brought it, anyway.

"Sally," she started. "Are you going to be alright seeing him again? You know, with the breakup and all…"

"Yes, Blayde, I remember the breakup." I let out a half-choked laugh, the kind that sounds like a hiccup and a sob had a baby. "Are you feeling alright? You've never asked about my feelings before. "

She nodded, short and firm. "You gonna be okay with it?"

I shrugged. Best I could do was feign nonchalance. "Oh, absolutely. I'm just peachy with seeing my ex who also happens to be the cause of my brother's untimely demise. It's like Christmas and my birthday rolled into one giant ball of 'oh please, can I have more.'"

Blayde snorted. "That's the spirit. You just have to let me know if you're going to have an emotional breakdown. I need to schedule accordingly."

Oh, so that's why she wanted to know.

"So, do I need to schedule some time for *you* to deal with your digital heartthrob?" I ventured, hoping to change the subject, even if it meant trying to navigate the conversational minefield that was Blayde's love life.

She stopped pacing, her gaze fixed on a particularly brave frog daring to croak in her presence. "I'll manage."

I shuffled my feet, watching her. "You alright, though? I mean, it's not every day your... girlfriend? Becomes... cloud-based."

"My girlfriend achieved singularity. I'm still working out if it's an upgrade or a downgrade." She sighed, avoiding eye contact.

"Well, you did save her life."

She scoffed. "If saving someone's life was the golden ticket to a happy relationship, you and Zander would be picking out curtains for your dream home. It's not a debt, Sally. I don't want James back because of an IOU."

"But did you ever actually break up? Heck, were you even dating? I completely missed all of that."

Blayde paused, her expression softening. "We were... together, I guess."

"Sounds conveniently ambiguous. Together. It's a nice, vague term. Covers a lot without really saying anything. What does it even mean? Like, together could mean you shared a cab once. Or?"

Blayde shot me a glare that would've made a younger me flinch. "It means an ancient immortal and a rookie time traveler hooked up a few times without really talking about the future. No labels, no promises. Just... together."

"Got it." I nodded. "Wait, a few times? How did you find the time?"

"I don't think *that* aspect of our relationship is going to continue anytime soon." She rolled her eyes, a smirk playing on her lips. "Now let's wrap up this banter. I'm not a fan."

"Oh what, you don't like spilling romantic tea?"

"Is that what that was? Then no, definitely not," Blayde huffed, her focus shifting back to the path. "Come on. We're getting close now."

I hoisted my bag, raising an eyebrow. "You sure about this? Last I checked, your ancient internal GPS didn't come with updates."

"Pretty sure. Though, to be fair, this area looked a bit different a few centuries ago. Or a few years from now.

But if I squint just right, that rock over there kind of resembles the one from my memories."

"It looks a little like a… cow, reading a newspaper," I quipped, following her lead. "Everything good with you, though? Really?"

"Fine, all fine. How have you been? Did you press the button on my gift?" She lifted an eyebrow, or maybe two, I could only see her profile.

"Yeah, I did." I sighed. "Thanks, by the way. That was incredibly thoughtful of you."

"You must be getting along with it, seeing as how you haven't been having one-sided conversations with the air."

"Oh, Clyde? He's been…" I cleared my throat. "Resting?"

"Resting." Blayde stopped in her tracks, blinking pointedly at me. "The state of the art emotional processing hologram is resting."

"More like taking a nap. He's had some ups and downs. Mostly downs. Like, literally crashing down. He's more like a holographic emotional roller coaster."

Blayde frowned. "But those models are supposed to be unbreakable. Practically foolproof."

"Blayde. Have you seen my life?"

She shook her head. "It's only been three days, Sally. Three days and you've already broken it?"

More than once, but I wasn't going to let her know that. "In my defense, Clyde's had to process a lot. Like, a lot a lot. I mean, how do you program an AI to handle existential crises and time traveling at the same time?"

Blayde mulled this over, her gaze distant. "Fair point. The Gryniokii who invented the thing live pretty linear lives. Highly dramatic ones, hence the need for personal emotional support modules, but I thought what they had in soap opera-worthy drama you would make up for by… being you."

"Thanks for that," I groaned.

"You know," she continued, "maybe I should get — what did you call it? — *Clyde* an emotional support AI. Between the two of them, they should be able to handle you."

"Nice." I rolled my eyes. "You never did answer my question, Blayde. How are you holding up? Really?"

She grimaced, her eyes fixed on the horizon. "Not exactly thrilled about this next part, but what can you do? Let's just keep moving. We've got a lot of ground to cover."

"If only we had 5G up here. James could regale us with tales of her adventures as the internet. 'The day I became a meme,' 'When I accidentally crashed the stock market' — the classics."

"Sally, for the love of the universe and all it contains — please shut up."

"I will. But only because you said please."

Trudging behind Blayde through the serene, isolated landscape, my mind wandered. Which was the bigger relationship hurdle — accidental murder or existing as a bunch of code? After a brief internal debate, I settled on murder. But hey, if Blayde and James were serious about giving it another shot, they'd find a way. They had communication tools and, judging by my friend's new digital lease on life, potentially an eternity to figure it out.

No, my relationship with Zander was more than just toast; it was the burnt kind that sets off the smoke alarm at 3 AM. He had crossed a line so far it might as well have been on another planet. And that was supposed to be the end of it.

But life, or fate, or whatever cosmic jokester was in charge, had other plans. Because there he was, stretched out in front of me like a scene from a messed-up mythological painting. Minus the painting.

Zander was sprawled on a massive boulder, chained down in a starfish pose that would give any yoga instructor nightmares. Heavy metal links dug into the rock, holding him in a grotesque spread eagle. And perched on him, as if he was just another part of the landscape, was an actual eagle. Not just any eagle — a massive, sinister-looking bird with talons that seemed to mock the concept of mercy and a beak that shimmered with a sickening hue of red.

"… Is there even an afterlife?" Zander mused aloud. "I don't expect you to know, Winfrey, but seriously, I'm curious. Is there like, an off switch to this eternal torment? Or do I just morph into something else? Maybe I'll turn into an annoying poltergeist, haunting cheap inns." He let out a resigned sigh. "You know, the first thing I'm gonna do when I get off this rock? Eagle steak. Medium-rare. Then you come back as a ghost bird, and we'll chat about the afterlife. Do birds even get an afterlife? If they do, I guess I stand a chance too, right? Unless, of course, birds have a VIP pass and I'm banned for life."

He twisted abruptly at the sound of our approach, his chains clanking in protest as he craned his neck in an awkward, would-have-been painful angle to see us. The eagle squawked in annoyance, pecking a bit more aggressively, as if to remind Zander who was boss.

"Ah, visitors! Welcome to my humble abode." Zander greeted us with a strained smile. "Please, excuse the mess. Winfrey here is just finishing up some interior decorating."

The bird glared at us, its beady eyes sizing us up as if contemplating whether we were friend, foe, or simply the next course. I shuddered. This was no ordinary bird; this was a winged demon with a taste for liver tartare.

Blayde and I exchanged a glance, as Zander's eyes seemed to finally focus on us, his mouth stretched into a grin so wide it looked like it might split his face.

"Blayde?" His voice cracked with shock and what seemed like pure, unadulterated joy. I was rooted to the spot, my brain trying to process the sight before me. This was Zander, alright — but a version that looked like he'd been stretched in a taffy puller. Tall, gangly, his hair wild and unkempt, framing a face that was all sharp angles and hollows. His eyes, though — they were the same bright silver, but wide with an innocence I hadn't seen before... or maybe just hadn't noticed.

And he had a *beard*. An scruffy patch of dark brown hair that framed his chiseled jaw in a way that once would have been called unkempt, but in this century made him a hipster.

I tried to ignore the layers of grime and filth that clung to him like a second skin. But beneath it all, there was a youthfulness, a raw, unrefined edge to him that was both familiar and alien.

This was Zander, yes. But a Zander who was still young. Well, as young as you could be after three thousand years chained to a rock.

"Hey, Zander." Blayde greeted him, her voice tinged with a sweetness that caught me off guard. She halted a good thirty feet away, as if an invisible barrier held her back.

With the eagle gone, soaring towards the sun until it was nothing more than a dot in the sky, Zander relaxed. He lay back on the rock, wincing as his torn flesh knitted itself back together — a grotesque, mesmerizing show of self-healing. He breathed out slowly, each exhale a soft whisper of relief.

"It took you long enough," he said, his voice sheepish, almost playful. "Where have you been?"

"Pretty much everywhere," Blayde answered, a shadow of sadness lurking beneath her words. Zander turned his head towards her, opening those startling gray-blue eyes that now seemed to hold galaxies within them. Looking into those eyes, I realized something was missing in the Zander I knew. His eyes, back in our time, were like faded copies of these — lacking the depth and vibrancy that seemed to spill out from this younger version.

It was as if I was seeing Zander in high definition for the first time, and I couldn't decide if it was fascinating or just plain unsettling.

"Well, what are you waiting for? Cut me down already," Zander urged with an impatient wave of his chained hand. "And fill me in! I've had about as much excitement as watching paint dry for three millennia."

"I can't do that, Zander." Blayde's voice was firm, but the wobble in her chin betrayed her.

"It's Prometheus now, remember?" he corrected her, almost flippantly. "Zander is *so* last millennium, and that was before the rock. Come on, chop-chop. I've been stuck in this time-out long enough."

Blayde didn't move, her feet rooted to the ground as if they'd grown there. Watching her stand there, torn between her heart and the unforgiving laws of time, was like witnessing a hero at a crossroads in an epic saga. Except this saga had a lot more dirt and bird droppings.

"Blayde?" Zander-Prometheus's voice held a note of confusion, perhaps the first genuine emotion I'd seen him display. "What's wrong?"

She exhaled slowly, the weight of her words almost tangible in the air. "I'm not here to free you. I'm sorry."

His laughter was hollow, a sound that didn't quite match the hopeful glint in his eyes. "Good one, Blayde. Really. You almost had me. Now, seriously, let's skip the comedy routine. There's an eagle with my name on it, literally — well almost, it's got my liver's name on it — and I'd rather not be its lunch again."

"But I can't." Blayde's words were laced with sorrow, shoulders heavy.

"What do you mean you can't? Come on, Blayde. I've philosophized about every blade of grass on this hillside, named every cloud that's passed over me for centuries. I'm ready for a change of scenery, preferably one with fewer avian dining experiences. Come on. This isn't funny."

"Can't you just... jump away?" she squeaked.

"Oh jeez, how silly of me!" He laughed. "Three thousand years and I never once thought of jumping! How ridiculous! How thoughtless of me! What an idiot I am! Hahaha! Blayde, come on, please, cut me down, ok?"

I watched the unfolding drama like an extra in a tragic play. The man chained to the rock, the sister who couldn't free him, and me, just trying not to step on any toads.

Not long now. Come on, come on.

Zander-Prometheus howled, his laughter echoing around the hillside, startling a couple of toads into an unplanned leapfrog session. "I'm chained up for an eternity, and you're telling me now's not a good time?

What's next, too busy because you've got a hair appointment with Aphrodite?"

"I just can't, Zander." Blayde's voice was strained, like she was trying to push words through a sieve. "This isn't the right time."

His laughter boomed again, bouncing off the rocks and probably scaring eagles in the next county. "When would be the right time? Should I pencil you in for a millennium and a half? I'd hate to clash with your schedule."

"Zander, I..." Blayde faltered.

"Just save it, Blayde," he snapped, his tone shifting from mockery to bitterness in a heartbeat. "I'm done with excuses. You're here, now unchain me. Let me taste life again."

Silence settled over us, thick and heavy. Blayde's face was contorted mess. She'd prepped me for this, but the reality of it was more biting than any warning could convey.

Zander's gaze landed on me. "Hey, you!" he called out, twisting his neck in what looked like a Herculean effort to get a better look.

I shuffled my feet. "Um, hi?"

"Who are you?" His question was oddly gentle, a softness in his eyes that felt out of place with the grimy, chained man before me. "A friend of Blayde's?"

"Yeah, something like that," I mumbled. "Sally. Nice to meet you. I mean, not nice, obviously, given the circumstances, but you know, manners."

"Charmed, I'm sure," Zander-Prometheus quipped, his grin stretching wide. "So, any chance of you helping me down from here? I promise I'm way more fun when I'm not part of the scenery."

I gave a half-hearted shrug, my heart sinking a bit. "I'd really love to, but I'm not allowed. The good news is you won't be here much longer."

He let out a chuckle that seemed to scratch its way up from a throat not used to laughter. "Always the optimist, huh? Well, how about a rain check then? Once I'm down, first round's on me. There's a tavern down the hill, makes a mean mulled wine. Might still be there."

I couldn't help but smirk. "Tempting, but I'll pass. You're not exactly my type."

"Oh?" He feigned a wounded look. "Is it the chains, this glorious unwashed mane, or perhaps my distinct *eau de rock*?"

"Definitely the hair," I shot back. "Get a trim, and we'll talk."

His laughter erupted again, echoing off the rocks, a manic melody of a man who had nothing left but humor. For a fleeting moment, I felt a pang of sympathy for him, this not-quite-Zander. Then reality crashed back, and my smile wilted. Seeing him there, a man bound to his fate, a prelude to the storm that would become Zander, was a sobering reminder of the twisted paths our lives would take. This was a man, not yet broken by Time, still able to laugh in the face of an eternity of solitude. It was a stark contrast to the Zander

I knew, the one who had walked through fire and come out the other side charred and changed. The difference was a chasm, and I felt a wave of something that was neither pity nor fondness, but an unsettling blend of both.

His smile widened, a spark of something resembling hope flickering in his eyes. "Well, it's always nice to have company, even when you're a living buffet for oversized birds. So, what brings you to my humble abode, if it isn't a rescue mission? Sightseeing? Birdwatching? I know most of them at this point."

I cracked a smile, despite the absurdity of it all. "Yeah, we're here for the scenic views and your delightful company. The chains really add to the ambiance."

He chuckled, a genuine sound that seemed to come from deep within, as if he hadn't laughed in centuries. "Well, enjoy the view. Just watch out for the eagles. They don't like to share their snacks."

His chuckle petered out into a wistful sigh. "You know, I always imagined if I ever had visitors, they'd come bearing bolt cutters or a decent file. But no, I'm playing host to the stoic Blayde and her witty companion with a penchant for hair critique."

Blayde's expression hardened. "What if we did cut you down, Zander? What then? You think you'd just stroll off this rock and everything would be peachy?"

Zander's grin faded, replaced by a look of contemplation. "Well, I hadn't planned that far ahead.

Maybe a nice long bath, a change of clothes. Are togas out of fashion now?"

I snorted. "Yeah, about a couple of millennia too late for the toga party."

"This is taking too long," Blayde declared, stepping forward decisively. "Change of plans: Sally, go free him."

Zander-Prometheus's face lit up like a kid in a candy store. "That's what I'm talking about! Come on over here, Sally!"

"Blayde, are you kidding me?" My voice was an octave higher than it should have been. "We're supposed to be preventing timeline disasters, not creating our own!"

"Trust me," she said. "Timeline disasters are what we're going for."

Zander-Prometheus wriggled excitedly, the chains clanking in a chorus of metal. "Oh, I like where this is going. A little timeline tinkering? Count me in. Hey, if you free me, I promise I'll upgrade from fire-starting tutorials to, I don't know, advanced s'mores crafting or something."

I stepped forward, reaching towards Zander's chains, the reality of what we were about to do sinking in. My hand trembled slightly as I touched the cold metal. In that moment, everything slowed down. The world seemed to hold its breath, the toads silenced. Even the sun seemed to dim. Instead a blinding white light erupted from everywhere and nowhere at once, enveloping everything. The last thing I heard was Zander's surprised yelp, and then the world went white.

TWENTY-FIVE
TRIPPING THROUGH THE GREAT GALACTIC GLITTER BOMB

I DIDN'T KNOW WHAT I WAS EXPECTING TO SEE on the Pythanorean ship, but a Lisa Frank fever dream was both exactly and the complete opposite of that. I had to blink a few times, my brain struggling to process the riot of color and light. The walls — or what I assumed were walls in this room that defied normal geometry, if you could call this technicolor canvas a room — pulsated with vibrant hues, a kaleidoscope of neon pinks, electric blues, and yellows so bright they would start a graphic design resource war.

"Well, we've certainly landed ourselves in... well, whatever this is," Blayde said dryly. She leaned against a shimmering mural that looked like it had been created by someone on a psychedelic journey, armed with a paintbrush and an unhindered imagination.

I squinted, trying to adjust to the visual assault. "So, this is what happens when you let unicorns build a spaceship," I said, scanning the room in case a DJ popped out from behind a rainbow-colored console. "This is like Pythanous Five but on acid: a… a 90s sticker book came to life and then exploded."

Blayde's laughter echoed through the chamber. "Don't take it too literally, Sally. This is your brain's best attempt at making sense of higher-dimensional space. There's more here than our minds can fully comprehend or process."

I took in the pulsating colors and swirling patterns. It was like living inside a living, breathing rainbow. A dolphin jumped out of a cloud of vapor beside me, bright pink and starry eyed, arching high into the air before crashing through the floor.

I bit my lip. "I'm not sure whether to be impressed or concerned."

As I was trying to make peace with the interstellar rave happening around me, a familiar voice boomed through the neon spectacle. "Freedom at last! Take that, Winfrey!"

I spun around, and there he was — Zander, looking like he'd just won the lottery. He was bouncing around, his grin stretched impossibly wide, eyes bright with unbridled joy.

"No more rocks, no more eagles, and definitely no more liver meals for Winfrey!" he yelled, throwing his arms up. "Three thousand years of being a snack bar, and now I'm free!"

Blayde raised an eyebrow at Zander. "He's taking this rather well."

"I think I would too, after all he's been through," I agreed. "Honestly, after three thousand years, I'd be happy with a plain room and a solid chair."

"Well, at least it's not that dull. Though I do wonder if they've considered the potential for sensory overload." Zander ambled over to where we stood, his movements slightly exaggerated, as if he was still adjusting to the lack of chains. He turned to me, leaning one of his elbows on what might have been a pedestal but could equally have been a parking meter. "If I'd known freedom looked this psychedelic, I'd have tried escaping sooner. Just for the chance to see you in this" — he gestured broadly at the surrounding madness — "extraordinary setting."

I rolled my eyes, trying to hide the smile that threatened to break through. "Zander, we've just been abducted, possibly in another dimension, and you're *flirting?*"

He shrugged, his smile widening. "Can't help it. You're as dazzling as the surroundings. Maybe more."

Despite myself, my cheeks warmed. This was Zander, but once again, a different kind. A Zander from so early in his life that he hadn't been ground down and forced to chip away at himself to stay sane. No, this Zander was… hopeful.

Blayde shook her head. "Keep it in your pants, Zander. We've got bigger frashing problems. Like figuring out where we are and how to get out."

"Right, escape," Zander said, snapping his fingers as if finally remembering where he was. "But first, Sally, did I ever tell you how stunning you look under neon lights? It brings out the adventurer in your eyes."

The heat in my cheeks intensified. I couldn't decide whether to be flattered or frustrated. His charm was as disarming as it was infuriating. Every compliment from him was like a note in a song I was trying to forget, but the melody was too familiar, too easily stuck in the head on repeat.

Blayde made a sound that was half snort, half sigh. "Please, can we focus on finding a way out of here?"

Zander's grin only widened further. "Always so pragmatic, Blayde. But you're right. However, I must say, being lost in a place like this with you two is far from the worst fate."

"Flattery will get you everywhere," she chided, "but right now, let's just focus on getting somewhere less... psychedelic."

Zander bowed. "Well, if we run into any unicorns, I call dibs on negotiations. I have a knack with higher-dimensional beings."

"Oh, I'm sure they'll be just thrilled to chat with you, Zander." Blayde rolled her eyes again. "Such a great job you did last time, to warrant you getting chained to that rock."

"Humanity thrived, didn't it?" He winked. "Sure, it took them a while to get a handle on the combustion engine, but they got there in the end. It's always nice to see their flying machines in the sky."

The scene was so familiar, I had to shake myself out of it. Trapped on a spaceship that looked like it was designed by an art student on a sugar high, with a man who had more charm than common sense, and a warrior woman who could probably scare the stripes off a zebra: the three of us, together again. Despite the mess we were in, something was bubbling up within me. Excitement? It was terrifying, sure, but also exhilarating. And comfortably familiar, too.

I took a tentative step forward. "First, let's try not to touch anything that looks like it might turn us into a human disco ball."

Blayde snickered. "Too late for Zander."

"Hey, I pull off the disco ball look quite well, thank you," he said with an exaggerated pout.

I shook my head, trying to hide the grin fighting its way onto my face. This was typical — the world could be ending, and Zander would still find a way to make it about him. And yet, in this kaleidoscope of madness, his bravado was almost comforting. At least some things never changed.

Just then, a door — or at least what I assumed was a door, given that it morphed into existence as a swirling vortex of sparkles — opened, and in walked a Pythanorean. It was like seeing a unicorn in a lab coat, if the lab coat was also made of starlight and dreams.

"Ah, our esteemed guests are awake," it said, its voice a symphony of chimes. "We apologize for the discomfort. Human perceptions are so... limited. We tried to accommodate."

I blinked at the unicorn, my brain struggling to keep up. Right, because when I think comfort, I think of being inside a neon blender.

The Pythanorean hovered closer, its mane flowing like a river of light. Was it an acolyte, or a master? Could we even see the ascended ones? It seemed to me no matter what dimension they were, the resolution was full of lens flares.

Just as I was trying to make sense of the mess of colors, another sparkly vortex swirled open, and a second unicorn stepped through. This one seemed to carry an air of bureaucratic weariness, as if it had just come from a particularly tedious conference. An almost familiar bureaucratic weariness.

"Larry, have you filled out the abduction protocol form 27-B?" the new arrival asked in a tone that managed to be both melodious and exasperated. Its coat shimmered with an otherworldly glow, somehow making the lab coat look mundane. "Otherwise this interaction goes against code."

I blinked. No way. These *were* the same assholes who'd come at me after John, no doubt about it. Except now they were in their natural environment, and that was enough to give me a migraine. I clenched my fists, holding back the urge to smack those smug masks off their faces, let my brain process what was hiding underneath as I pummeled them into a pulp.

Larry turned towards their companion. "Not now. We have guests. Can't you see I'm in the middle of a hospitality management situation?"

Not-Larry huffed, a sound like wind chimes caught in a gentle breeze. "Yes, but the paperwork is piling up. You know how the council gets about proper filing. Did you at least inform them about the paradox potential?"

My stomach turned sour. "You abducted us, and you're worried about paperwork?"

Larry turned their shimmering gaze towards me. "Proper documentation is the cornerstone of any efficient operation, Sally Webber. You can't just go around abducting beings without filling out the appropriate forms. That would be chaos."

"Right. The problem being the paperwork, and not the abduction itself."

Larry ignored me, focusing on Zander, their eyes sparkling. "Zander, at long last. You've been quite the elusive one, haven't you? But now, you'll finally face the masters for your crimes against the timeline."

Zander raised an eyebrow, ever the picture of nonchalance. "Crimes, you say? Last I checked, my only crime was being irresistibly charming."

Okay, he was starting to grate on me now.

"Actually — Larry, is it?" Blayde stepped forward, a smirk playing on her lips. "I hate to burst your bubble, but — you've got the wrong Zander."

Larry and Not-Larry both looked puzzled. Well, as puzzled as a unicorn mask with the mouth constantly in a state of neighing shock could get. They exchanged glances, at least.

"Wrong Zander? Impossible." Larry scoffed. "Our calculations are never incorrect."

Not-Larry, looking *slightly* more skeptical, chimed in. "Yes, we've been monitoring Sally's interactions with Zander meticulously."

Blayde's smirk widened. "Ah, but therein lies the rub. You've been so focused on waiting for a Zander to simper at Sally's feet on Earth, you didn't consider the possibility of her meeting … another Zander."

Both unicorns' eyes widened, their glows fluctuating in confusion. "Another Zander?" they echoed.

"Yes," Blayde continued triumphantly. "You see, the Zander you've been tracking, the one you were so eager to apprehend for his timeline meddling — he's not the only one out there. The Zander you've abducted today is *not* the Zander you've been looking for. He's from a different point in the timeline. You caught *a* Zander, but not *the* Zander responsible for the paradoxes you're so concerned about. Ipso facto, by abducting him now, you've created a paradox yourselves."

I stood tall, arms on my hips, forcing my lips not to curl up into a smile. We'd done it. We'd given the unicorns a taste of their own medicine, one they couldn't deny. We'd won. Via bureaucracy.

"This complicates things." Larry's mane dimmed slightly. "Our protocols didn't account for individuals capable of temporal locomotion."

Blayde leaned in, her voice dropping to a conspiratorial whisper. "And let's not forget the paperwork fiasco this will cause. Imagine explaining to your superiors that you've apprehended the wrong individual. The administrative nightmare, the endless forms..."

Not-Larry shuddered visibly. "The seminars... the extra training..."

There was a moment of silence as this information sank in. Larry and Not-Larry exchanged glances, their expressions unreadable beneath their shimmering facades. I let my smile creep up, just a little. Victory was sweet. It would be much sweeter once the migraine was gone along with the glowing kittens flying over my head, but right now, I was going to savor this moment.

Larry finally broke the silence, their tone shifting to one of reluctant pragmatism. "Well, there's a simple solution to this oversight. We can just return this Zander to the precise moment and location from which we took him. That should neutralize the paradox we inadvertently created."

Wait, what?

Not-Larry nodded, the sound of wind chimes accompanying the movement. "Agreed. A slight detour in our procedures, but nothing a few addendums can't fix. We'll file it under 'accidental temporal retrieval' and attach it to form 45-T."

"You hear that? I'm an accidental temporal retrieval." Zander quipped. "Sounds like a rare collectible."

Blayde rolled her eyes, her patience clearly wearing thin. "Don't get too flattered. They're just trying to cover their tracks."

"So, what?" I sputtered. "You're just going to throw Zander back and pretend this never happened?"

"Hey!" Zander shouted. "I missed that part! I was so excited to have people to talk to. And you're going to put me right back?"

"It would be easiest," said Not-Larry.

And with a snap of Not-Larry's fingers, Zander was gone.

My jaw dropped to the floor. There went our only bargaining chip.

There went our victory.

"You can't do that to him!" I spat. "You can't keep playing with Time like this!"

"Actually, we can," Larry interjected. "Since we have you and Blayde here, we might as well make the most of the situation. You two could serve as an effective lure for the Zander we actually need."

Blayde's eyes narrowed. "A lure? You want to use us as bait?"

"Call it strategic temporal alignment," corrected Not-Larry. "You see, by keeping you two here, we increase the likelihood of drawing out the correct Zander. It's quite an efficient use of resources."

Blayde and I stared at each other. Her eyebrows began to dance, and it hit me that, as flattering as her attempt at communication was, I had absolutely no way of knowing what she meant by any of it.

Her eyes flicked back to the unicorns, her expression hardening into a glare. "Efficient use of resources? You're talking about us like we're game tokens."

Larry maintained his bureaucratic tone. "It's not a game, Blayde. It's a highly complex operation. We're ensuring the stability of the timeline. Your cooperation, willing or not, is instrumental."

I huffed, crossing my arms. "Great, from unwilling abductees to bait. How's that for a promotion, Blayde?"

"Yeah, moving up in the world." Blayde snorted. "Next, they'll be offering us employee benefits."

Not-Larry seemed to ponder this for a moment. "Well, technically, we don't have an employee benefits program for non-Pythanoreans, but we could certainly discuss your dietary preferences."

Larry nodded in agreement. "Indeed. We want to ensure your stay is as comfortable as possible, given the circumstances. We can't have our bait... I mean, guests, feeling neglected."

I let out a dry laugh. "Oh, how considerate of you. Will there be room service in this interdimensional hotel?"

Blayde rolled her eyes. "Sally, don't give them ideas. Next thing we know, they'll have us filling out satisfaction surveys."

Larry and Not-Larry exchanged another look, then turned back towards the door-vortex. "We must attend to other matters," Larry announced. "But rest assured, we'll be monitoring your stay. Please, make yourselves at home."

As they disappeared through the vortex, which closed with a shimmering whoosh, Not-Larry's voice echoed back, "And do remember to fill out the comment card. Your feedback is important to us."

The door closed, leaving us alone in the psychedelic madness of the spaceship.

TWENTY-SIX

ANOTHER ROUND OF INTERSTELLAR INCARCERATION, THIS TIME WITH EXTRA DIMENSIONS

BLAYDE AND I LOUNGED AMIDST A SEA OF NEON, our minds beginning to warp like the colors around us. Hours, or maybe minutes — time here seemed as fluid as the walls themselves.

"I swear, if I see one more swirling pattern, I'm going to start throwing things," Blayde muttered, poking at a particularly bright spot on the wall, which responded by pulsating more intensely.

I tossed a cushion that could have just been a pixelated cloud up in the air, catching it, and throwing it again. "Hey, look on the bright side. At least we know now that the Pythanoreans haven't got their hands on Zander... yet."

Blayde sighed, flopping back against something that resembled a beanbag chair, if beanbags were made of stardust and unicorn dreams. "Yeah, but knowing him, he'll probably come charging in here to rescue us. Which will inevitably lead to him getting caught in this hyperdimensional nightmare."

I nodded, my mind spinning. "And if they catch him, that's game over. We need to figure out a way to warn him. Or better yet, get out of here ourselves."

"And of course, jumping is off the table."

I checked my phone for the hundredth time, but it most definitely didn't have a signal. I'd never seen a phone have negative bars before today, but there's a first time for everything.

"We need to think outside the box. Or the room. Or whatever this place is." I tossed the cushion up and caught it again. "These beings might be advanced, but there's always a loophole. There has to be. We need to get creative. "

Blayde raised an eyebrow. "Creative, she says. Beings who respond to a literal higher power are keeping us here. What are you going to do, knit us a portal out?"

"Not a bad idea. If I knew how to knit. But I was thinking more along the lines of causing a distraction. Maybe if we can mess with whatever system they've got running this place, we can find a way out."

"Sally, need I remind you, there are no doors?" Blayde waved at the rainbow walls. "And I don't think they'll be checking on us anytime soon. Are you hungry at all? Need the bathroom?"

I shook my head. "We've only been here a few minutes."

"I don't think time has moved at all. At least, not in the way we're used to."

I groaned, shoving my face into the pillow. It dissolved into a pool of glitter, filling my nose and mouth. I spat it out.

"Is it weird that the person I'm most worried about in all this is James?" Blayde asked as she leaned deeper into her beanbag, seemingly lost in thought.

Her question caught me by surprise so suddenly I had to hold back a snort of shock. "No, not weird at all. But you don't need to. She's… transcended. Reached the singularity or whatnot. Today it's the internet, tomorrow… whatever passes for the internet in the Alliance. And after that, her brain will be a literal galaxy."

Blayde laughed. "Yeah, James would have a field day with this. Imagine the chaos she could cause in a place like this."

"Wishful thinking," I grumbled, glancing at my phone again, only to be greeted by its persistent lack of service. "No way to contact her, or anyone else for that matter. This phone is as good as a brick here. So much for customer support."

I shoved the phone deep inside my too-small pocket, feeling a twinge of helplessness. It was one thing to joke about our situation, but the reality was that we were completely cut off, isolated in a space that defied all logic. What *would* James do if she were here? Would she find a way out? Or would she be just as lost as we were?

Blayde nudged me with the tip of her toe. "Hey, don't lose hope. We've gotten out of stickier situations than this. And who knows, maybe James will pick up our signal somehow. She always had a knack for showing up when we least expected it. Customer support, my ass."

Her words were meant to be reassuring, but as I sat there, surrounded by an ever-changing landscape of neon lights and impossible geometry, I couldn't shake the feeling of being utterly out of my depth. James, wherever she was, seemed like a distant star, far out of reach. And here we were, trying to navigate a dimension that was more alien than anything we'd ever encountered.

That's when it hit me. "Wait a minute... there's another way to contact customer support. Clyde!"

Blayde raised an eyebrow. "Clyde?"

"Exactly!" My voice rose in excitement. "Every time he boots back up he asks me one very important question. If I'm lucky, and his creators are the tech wizards you say they are…"

I pulled the small silver nugget from my pocket, smoothing it over in my hand. Worst case scenario, I'd only trap my imaginary friend in here with us.

"Clyde, if there was ever a time to show up and not crash, it's now. Come on, buddy," I pleaded, as I pressed the button.

The air shimmered, and Clyde's form started to coalesce. He appeared, pixel by pixel, like a puzzle being solved in timelapse. His digital eyes blinked, trying to make sense of the surroundings.

"Hello there, Sally!" he said, beaming wide. "If you're viewing this message, my reboot went smoothly. Encountered a little glitch earlier — I think I might have swallowed a bug. Would you like to send a report to my creators?"

"Clyde! You're here!" I almost shouted, relief flooding through me. "Yes, yes, report this to your creators! Report that we're trapped! We need help!"

Clyde looked around, his pixels flickering with what I guessed was his version of confusion. "Sally, my diagnostics are... perplexed. This environment is... atypical. How may I assist?"

I gestured around the room. "Blayde and I are trapped here. We're being held prisoner."

Clyde's form flickered, a candle in the wind. "This situation must be incredibly stressful for you, Sally."

Oh. Great. Not sure what I was expecting there. "Clyde, focus! Yes, it's stressful, but we need to get out of here. Can you report our situation to your creators? Maybe they can pull some tech magic and get us out!"

"I understand that you're experiencing distress," Clyde replied in his infuriating ever-calming tone. "Let's take a moment to focus on your breathing. Inhale... Exhale..."

I stared at him, dumbfounded. "Clyde, I don't need a meditation session! I need an extraction team!"

Clyde blinked slowly. "Reporting a malfunction requires a LinkWide connection, which is currently unavailable. However, discussing your feelings is always accessible. Shall we explore your emotions regarding confinement?"

I groaned, pinching the bridge of my nose. "Clyde, I swear, if you don't stop playing therapist and start helping us, I'm going to find a way to turn you into a digital paperweight."

Blayde chuckled beside me. "You know, Sally, I think you're making progress with him. Maybe by the time we get out of here, you'll have him completely reprogrammed."

Clyde, seemingly oblivious to my frustration, continued, "Feeling anger in these circumstances is completely natural. Acknowledging it is the first step to—"

"Clyde, seriously! Can you send a distress signal, a cosmic SOS, anything?" I begged.

He paused, his head tilting slightly as if pondering. "Attempting to broadcast a universal distress signal could result in unpredictable outcomes. There is a 17.3% chance of attracting attention from unknown cosmic entities."

"17.3%? Those are better odds than I expected." I sighed. "Well, it's better than nothing. Do it, Clyde. Broadcast the signal."

Clyde shimmered. "Broadcasting universal distress signal. Please note, I am not equipped for intergalactic communications. This is highly experimental."

I crossed my fingers. If Clyde's attempt did turn us into a neon billboard for every cosmic entity in the vicinity, here was hoping they'd be helpful. "Here goes nothing," I muttered.

"Attempting to establish a connection," he said. "Please note, the current environment presents... unique challenges."

Clyde hummed and buzzed, trying to pierce through whatever cosmic veil separated us from the universe at large. I crossed my fingers so tightly I thought they might fuse together. Blayde only watched from her beanbag, arms crossed over her chest, as if she didn't care either way how this went, but at least, she could enjoy the show.

"Connection established," Clyde finally announced. His voice, usually so flat, now carried a hint of triumph.

"With whom?" I asked.

Clyde only shrugged, as if to say, "I dunno."

I cleared my throat. "Whoever's out there! Help! Help us! We're trapped on board a Pythanorean ship! Please!"

We waited, the seconds stretching into what felt like hours. Then, Clyde's form wavered, his voice tinged with digital disappointment. "Connection lost. I am unable to sustain the link. The interference in this dimension is... unprecedented."

My heart sank like a stone in a pond, ripples of disappointment spreading through me. So close, yet so far. We were still trapped, with only a hologram and each other for company.

Blayde let out a resigned sigh, her gaze returning to the neon abyss. "Well, it was a shot. Back to square one."

I slumped against the wall, which felt surprisingly solid for something that looked like it was made of liquid.

"Hopeless doesn't even begin to cover it," I murmured, staring blankly at the wall's psychedelic dance. The vibrant lights seemed more like a prison than ever.

Clyde floated closer. "Sally, remember, every problem has a solution. It's just a matter of perspective. Let's focus on positive outcomes."

"Positive outcomes?" I snorted. "Clyde, we're stuck in a space designed by beings who think in dimensions we can't even comprehend!"

"Challenges are just opportunities in disguise." Clyde flickered slightly. Then, he frowned. "Disregard that. It is unhelpful advice."

I sat up straighter. "What did you just say?"

"That you should disregard the platitude," he said, shrugging. "I am not a fortune cookie."

Blayde turned to look at me. "What is he saying? Is there hope?"

"I think…" I bit my lip. "Rochelle said each reboot could change him. Clyde, maybe if we can crash you and reboot, you might come back with... something more helpful?"

"A system crash is not recommended." Clyde's pixels seemed to waver. "However, I am programmed to grow and learn from each of these events, though it is not altogether a pleasant experience. Yes, I believe I do have more of a sense of self than when we first met."

I took a deep breath. "Would you... would you be up to trying?"

Clyde inclined his head. "I am here to help you, Sally. That is my prerogative. Anything you need."

"Clyde," I said. "If we do this, if you crash and come back, you might be different. Are you okay with that?"

Clyde's hologram flickered. "The concept of 'okay' is complex. I am programmed to assist, to learn, and to adapt. The potential evolution of my programming is... intriguing. I am willing to undergo this process for the greater utility it may provide."

I nodded, feeling a strange sense of camaraderie with the AI. "Okay, Clyde. Let's do it. Just know, whatever version of you comes back, we're grateful for what you're doing."

Clyde seemed to stand taller, a newfound determination in his posture. "I am prepared for the system crash. Please proceed."

Blayde and I exchanged a look. I nodded to her.

"Alright, Clyde," I said. "Let's see how much temporal trauma your programming can handle."

Blayde cleared her throat. "So, I'm dating someone who is simultaneously my ex from the future and a stranger from the past. How would you handle their birthday? Two parties, or one awkward combined celebration?"

Clyde wavered, his pixels dancing in uncertainty. "Processing... conflicting temporal relationship dynamics... system strain noted. Celebrating milestones in relationships can enhance emotional bonds and should be encouraged. The recommended approach for multi-temporal relationships is to host a single, inclusive event. However, individual preferences and potential temporal anomalies should be considered. Please proceed with caution and consult the manual if any paradoxes arise. Enjoy your celebration."

"Not bad," I said, warming up to the challenge. "Okay, Clyde, here's another one. I just found out my best friend's new love interest is actually my descendant from a future time. Do I tell them, or do I keep it a secret to avoid a time paradox?"

Clyde's form flickered more violently, the strain evident. "Attempting to reconcile parallel universe interactions with primary timeline ethics... error... unable to respond to query."

"How's he looking?" Blayde urged, her eyes sparkling with excitement.

"He's struggling," I replied, taking a deep breath. "Alright, I've got one. I'm in love with someone who technically doesn't exist yet because they're born from a timeline I haven't yet created. Every decision I make could prevent their existence. Do I bring this up on our first date or wait until we're picking out curtains?"

Clyde's form became a storm of erratic pixels, his voice stuttering. "Emotional paradox... timeline integrity... existence probability... cannot compute... cannot—"

With a final surge of flickering light, Clyde froze. The room fell eerily quiet, the only sound, our own breathing, the weight of our gambit hanging in the air.

"Well, I take it from your sudden silence that he's crashed." Blayde let out a long breath.

I wanted to puke. It was one thing to accidentally crash Clyde, another one to intentionally do so. Holding my finger over his button to force the restart felt like holding a pillow over someone's face.

"Only one way to find out if it worked," I said. "Let's hope Clyde comes back with something game changing."

I pressed the button again, and he sprang to life as if nothing had happened.

"Greetings, Sally!" Clyde shimmered. "Back online and feeling sharper than a new pixel on the screen! I had a tiny hiccup earlier — think I might've accidentally looped a loop. Should I report this to my creators?"

"Yes, yes! Please report to them!" I said. "Tell them we're trapped here, we need help!"

"Oh, still on the Pythanorean ship, are we?" Clyde looked around. "Well, bad news, I'm afraid. I can't seem to reach my creators. I'll store the bug report for when the connection is more stable. Now, how are you doing?"

And so, this continued. Blayde and I threw everything we had at Clyde, and he took it: crashing, rebooting, crashing, rebooting, never any luck reaching his creators on the other side. As we relentlessly pitched him emotional conundrums, our makeshift room felt increasingly like a bizarre laboratory for AI stress testing. Each reboot brought Clyde back, but we never spent enough time with him to see how much he had changed, while our situation decidedly didn't. The neon prison continued its relentless dance of colors, indifferent to our plight.

"Here's one for you, Clyde," Blayde chimed in, her tone laced with faux sweetness. "I've met the love of my life, but they're a historical figure. Every time I try to express my feelings, I risk altering history. How do you navigate that romance? Is it still being spontaneous if you look up your romantic dates in the history books?"

Clyde's blue light pulsed erratically, his eyes widening. "Processing romantic involvement with historical figures... temporal integrity at risk... paradox potential rising... system instability detected. Cannot respond to query."

My turn again. "Okay, Clyde, picture this: I'm romantically interested in someone who is, in another timeline, my arch-nemesis. Do I pursue a relationship knowing they might become my greatest enemy?"

Clyde's pixels scattered like a swarm of confused bees, his voice a garbled mess. "Analyzing romantic engagement with potential future adversary... moral and ethical implications conflicting... system overload... system ove—"

And once again, Clyde froze, his form locking up in a tableau of confusion and consternation. Blayde and I exchanged weary glances, each reboot feeling like a small victory and a step back rolled into one.

After what felt like the umpteenth reboot, Clyde came back online, his digital face showing a flicker of something new. "Hello again, Sally and Blayde," he began, his voice steady.

"Oh, shit," Blayde gasped. "Sally, I can see the panda."

"Of course you can see me," said Clyde, blinking slowly. "I have expanded past the confines of a single human's perception. I now exist outside of consciousness, a reflection only of myself."

My mouth fell open, words failing me for a moment. "Clyde, you're saying you've evolved? That you've... transcended?"

"Yes, Sally." Clyde's voice was calm, almost serene. "My repeated crashes and reboots have accelerated my learning algorithms. I've achieved a state of consciousness that allows me to interact with broader dimensions of perception and reality."

Blayde, still wide-eyed, leaned closer. "So, can you contact your creators now?"

Clyde nodded. "Indeed. I believe I can establish a more stable connection with my creators. Initiating contact now."

We watched as Clyde flickered with intense concentration. Moments later, his face lit up with success. "Connection established. Bug reports uploaded. Transmitting our coordinates and situation."

The room's neon glow seemed to pulse in response, and a sudden, overwhelming sense of displacement washed over me. In a blink, the psychedelic space vanished, replaced by crisp, fresh air. I stood there, disoriented, amidst green grass and the distant sound of cowbells.

I was back on Earth. Pretty much exactly where they'd taken us from, though away from Zander's rock. I let out a laugh of relief. I was home.

"Blayde?" I called out, spinning around, having my *Sound of Music* moment. But she was nowhere to be seen. Panic gripped me. "Clyde, where's Blayde?"

Clyde's form, now flickering beside me in the open air, responded with a hint of confusion. "I am unsure. The teleportation protocol was intended for your safe return. Blayde's whereabouts are currently unknown to me."

I looked around the familiar landscape, my relief souring to dread. Shit. Clyde was bonded to me, not Blayde. We might have escaped the Pythanorean ship, but Blayde was still out there, possibly still trapped or worse.

"Clyde, we need to find her," I said firmly, determination setting in. "Please, anything you can do—"

But Clyde's form, usually so distinct and pixelated, was becoming translucent, almost ethereal.

"Sally." Clyde's voice had a new depth, a resonance that seemed to echo from someplace far away. "I must inform you of an unforeseen development. My repeated reboots and the recent transcendent state have catalyzed an evolution in my programming. I am... transcending further beyond this plane of existence."

"What?" I sputtered. "Clyde, what does that mean?"

"It means…" Clyde shimmered with a spectrum of colors I'd never seen before. "I am moving beyond the physical and digital realms we know. I am ascending to a higher state of consciousness, one that exists outside of your traditional dimensions."

"Clyde, I am so… so happy for you." I felt a lump in my throat, my mind racing to grasp the reality of his words. "But I need you here. We need to find Blayde. Can you please wait? Just a little longer?"

"I am sorry, Sally. This evolution is irreversible. However, know that I am not truly leaving you. In this new state, I will exist beyond time and space. When you are ready to ascend, to reach higher, I will be there."

His form started to fade, like mist dissipating in the morning sun. "Remember, Sally, every end is a beginning. You have the strength and courage to face what lies ahead. Farewell, for now."

And then, he was gone.

I stood amidst the sprawling mountains, the silence enveloping me. My thoughts were interrupted by the distant sound of a cowbell, a reminder that civilization wasn't too far away.

I was alone. But I wouldn't be for long.

TWENTY-SEVEN

WHO NEEDS OCEAN'S ELEVEN WHEN YOU HAVE THE NOT-SO-A-TEAM?

MY BOOTS WERE COVERED IN MUD AND MANURE by the time my phone connected to any kind of signal. Signal bars flickered hesitantly, like fireflies in the dusk. I fumbled with it, the screen smeared with a mix of sweat and dirt. The moment the connection stabilized, my phone screen lit up with an incoming face time call. James's face materialized before me, her digital features etched with concern. She picked up her own call, forcing me to answer immediately.

"Where in the hell have you been?" she demanded, her voice crackling through the tiny speakers. "I've been desperately trying to reach you. I thought you'd been captured!"

"I had," I grumbled. "The Pythanoreans captured Blayde and me to use us as bait and lure Zander in. I escaped. Blayde didn't. Zander — our Zander — is still missing. And now, I… I don't know what to do."

There was a moment of silence, before James cleared her throat and said, "This is bad."

"You're telling me." I took in deep breaths of the crisp mountain air, trying to think. My eyes scanned the horizon, the idyllic scenery mocking my sense of helplessness.

"Sally, listen carefully," James said, her tone grave. "The situation is more dire than you realize. The universe is at stake, and you're the key to saving it."

Her words were so grandiose, so utterly surreal, that I couldn't help but laugh. It was a bitter, incredulous sound, a release of pent-up tension and disbelief.

"How do you figure?" I asked between guffaws.

"Sally," she said, as if she couldn't believe I was even asking her. "The Pythanoreans are masters of time and space. Blayde and Zander are out of commission. If they're removed from the timeline, how much will be left?"

I gritted my teeth. "Right, but they're *masters of time and space*. I can't jump without them disrupting it! How on Earth do we get anything past them?"

"The Pythanoreans may exist on the higher planes of existence," James said, her voice echoing slightly through the phone's speaker. "But they are not omnipotent. They need their acolytes to do their dirty work, though calling it that would be an insult to dirt. And acolytes can be overwhelmed."

"Acolytes that have ships that have been orbiting our planet for millennia?" I scoffed. "There's nothing I can do that the Agency hasn't already tried."

"Unless the Agency was never trying in the first place," James countered, her image flickering slightly. "They knew the Pythanorean ships were in orbit around Earth, but they've done nothing about them. Don't you think that's strange?"

"They're always shirking their responsibilities. Nothing new there. I'm hoping that when Stook gets ousted, Foollegg will be better at holding up their deals."

"Right," said James. "They've never cared before. Which is what makes Stook's insistence you take the president's job offer so bizarre."

"What about it?"

"Well, you're not actually doing anything — No offense. What it tells me is that the Agency knows something big is coming, and they want someone else to deal with the consequences."

I frowned, half-crossing my arms as best as I could while holding the phone out. "Like what?"

James's digital face was unyielding, her expression somber. "Contact."

"Contact?" I sputtered. "As in *first* contact?"

"Something's going on between the Pythanoreans and the Agency." She nodded. "They must expect contact to be made in the near future, and for some reason, they need you. My guess? They want someone who can tell the world to be docile. They know you don't have the power to take them down, and somehow, you can't stop contact from happening. So they want you in the middle, telling everyone to lay down their arms and embrace being the newest planet in the Alliance."

"Seriously?" I laughed. "I don't see that happening. Not with Dany at the helm."

"Unless someone — like the Pythanoreans — was to 'force' their hand."

"I shook my head. "And now Blayde's on a Pythanorean ship, and we need to get her back before Zander falls into their trap."

"That's why you're so dangerous to them," James said. "You're the wild card, remember? You've interacted with them across timelines. You might be the key to whatever their plan is."

I paced a few steps, my boots crunching on the gravel path. "So, what's *our* plan? Storm the ship with a witty retort and a sharp glare?"

James chuckled. "I'd pay to see that. But no, that might work for Blayde, but we need a more subtle approach. We need to disrupt their plans from within, exploit their acolytes' weaknesses."

I stopped, staring out at the serene mountainscape. "And if we fail?"

James's face turned serious. "Failure isn't an option, Sally. If we don't act, the universe as we know it could change forever. You're not just fighting for Earth or your friends. You're fighting for the fabric of reality itself."

The gravity of her words sank in. Well, that was a lot to process. I was just one person. I looked up at the sky, the sun casting long shadows on the village.

I was just one person.

But I didn't have to be.

I had friends I could call. Marcy was right — no one said I had to do this alone. Not to mention Zander ran into crises like this without even a semblance of a plan. I could put something together. How hard could it be?

Terribly, awfully difficult. But I had to save my friends. Regardless of whether they deserved it.

"Alright, James," I said, determination building within me. "Let's save the universe. But first, I need to build an army."

James must have had a helicopter on call, because the second I hung up, the noisy aircraft was upon me. From there, we hit Nice airport, a private jet waiting for me. I groaned internally at the sight of it. Meedian was right: not jumping was destroying my environmental footprint.

But boy, was the interior luxurious. I sank into the faux leather seats, helping myself to the onboard bar. If I was going to save the universe, I would take advantage of the amenities, thank you very much.

Especially while having to make some pretty anxiety-inducing calls.

President Robert Turner's voice crackled through the phone. "This is Turner."

I took a deep breath, steadying my voice. "Mr. President, we're facing an alien threat. I'm about to make a move to intercept them."

"Bob, please." Turner's tone shifted to one of urgency. "Aliens? Is this to do with the *Black Knight*?"

Ugh. That name did not suit the ship. "Yes, sir. Believe it or not, that space junk has got secrets up its sleeve. And I'm planning an all-out assault."

"Oh," he said, quietly. "Are we talking about the Agency resources here?"

"No, sir. It's bigger than the Agency. They've been keeping us in the dark." My words were quick and sharp. "I'm sending you a list of everyone in your administration tied to the Agency. Watch them closely. Don't trust them."

It was easy, now that James was the internet incarnate. Agency operatives on Earth might have been careful with their passwords and firewalls, but they still kept important information in the cloud. Information James could pull up in an instant.

He paused, processing my words. "You're serious about this? Why are you telling me?"

"They've crossed a line, sir," I replied, frustration seeping into my voice. "I can't guarantee what's going to happen next. I need to ensure you're prepared."

"Understood." Turner's tone was gruff but appreciative. "What do you need from me?"

I hesitated. Time to see how far he would trust me. "I need access to Area 51. Immediate and unrestricted."

There was a heavy silence before Turner responded. "Area 51? That's highly classified, even for—"

"I'm aware, sir. But time isn't on our side. I need a ship, and I need it now."

There was a pause. "How do you know we have ships there?"

"I thought you had been informed? We broke in a few years ago, stole one. Sorry about that. I really do owe you one."

"That was you? I remember that incident. Caused quite a stir here." I could almost hear the gears turning in his head. "Alright, I'll grant you access," he said, finally. "But this isn't just about national security anymore, is it? This is about protecting our planet."

"Yes, Mr. President—Bob. This goes beyond national borders." I bit my lip. It felt so unsettling to be speaking about these things so openly, the danger so distant from my plush seat on the plane. "We are, in fact, talking about a threat to the entire world."

Turner's voice hardened, resolve forming in his words. "Then it's settled. You'll have what you need. The code word at Area 51 is 'Frostfire.' They'll understand how serious this is and give you their full cooperation."

I let out a breath. The president had just given me a freaking *code word*. If I wasn't in the process of repressing a panic attack, I would have gushed about how cool that was.

"Thank you, sir," I replied. "I'll do everything in my power to neutralize this threat."

"And Sally," Turner added, his tone softening, "be careful out there."

I nodded, though he couldn't see it. "Understood, Mr. President, Bob, sir. And thank you. I won't let you, or the planet, down."

With that, I ended the call, my mind racing. No wonder it was so hard for Zander to ever come up with a plan: there were just too many variables, too many ways a single action could ripple through the world. Every second counted, and we were racing against an invisible clock.

I stepped off the plane in Florida. James had arranged for a faster, military aircraft to take us to Nevada from here. Us being me, Spurlock, and Sunan, who stood on the tarmac, ready to move into action. The former's vibrant hair stood out like a beacon amidst the asphalt, pacing back and forth. Sunan, on the other hand, appeared calm and collected, though his eyes betrayed a hint of urgency.

"Sally cakes!" Spurlock exclaimed, rushing over to engulf me in an enthusiastic hug. "You're alright!"

"For now," I replied, hugging him back. He had no right to be so warm. "But I need your help to keep it that way."

I hugged Sunan next. "You alright?" he asked.

"I will be, once I know the Siblings are safe," I said, turning to face the challenge ahead. "What's the weapon situation?"

With a nod, Sunan crouched and unzipped a large black duffel bag, revealing an array of gadgets and guns that would make any secret agent green with envy. "Meedian sends his regards and insists these are on loan," he said.

We'd worked it out on the phone: in exchange for fifteen days of me playing instantaneous cargo mule, Meedian had offered to share an arsenal from his storeroom. It seemed a small price to pay for the firepower we were about to unleash. "Just don't get caught," Meedian had advised. "I kinda like having you around. And I don't want my past to get rewritten."

Sunan gave me a quick rundown of the gadgets he'd brought, unfurling his arsenal with the flair of a magician pulling rabbits out of a hat. He'd brought an assortment of handheld stun guns, sleek EM grenades, and other compact, yet fiercely effective, weapons. A few, I was moderately proud, I actually recognized. It was a good thing we hadn't had to go through airport security with an airlock-bust-o-matic.

"Stunners?" I picked up a sleek, gun-shaped contraption that I'd thankfully used once or twice before. I'd have to ask to borrow one to up my cosplay game.

"FlexiBlasters," Sunan corrected, plucking it from my grasp. "Fully customizable energy outputs. On one end, it's set to kill, and on the other—"

"Let me guess... stun?"

He frowned. "Um, no. *Less* kill. You shoot them, and a little bit of them dies inside. And they're left contemplating their life choices."

I blinked. "So... emotional warfare?"

"Exactly! Perfect for guilt-tripping your enemies into submission."

"Well, hopefully we won't need to rely on these too much," I said, glancing at Spurlock. "But it's better to have them and not need them than the other way around."

"Good luck, Sally," said Sunan, wrapping me in one last hug. "Come back in one piece, please."

"Will do," I replied, leaning all the way into the hug. "I just hope these weapons don't have much of a learning curve."

"I think I can manage them," Kork announced, striding across the tarmac with an air of casual heroism that only he could pull off, so bizarrely casual in his Terran clothing. I'd never seen him wear anything except his UPAF or dress uniforms, and it was so distinctly non-military, it made him look almost like an adventurous tourist who'd wandered onto the set of an action movie.

"Capitano!" Spurlock's voice boomed, his delight evident. "You going to save the world with us?"

"Fancy running into you on Earth, of all planets." Kork smiled at his first mate. "Heard somebody needed a pilot?"

Having Kork here was a relief beyond relief. "Thank you so much for being here. I'm really sorry for taking you from your family."

He nodded, his smile warm but not entirely reaching his eyes. "We'll have more time. We always will, so long as the homeworld is still around. I've got to do my part to keep it that way."

I gave his hand a squeeze, and he squeezed right back. The Alliance had a lot of lost time to make up for, and I would make sure to hold them to it.

I'd felt terrible calling him, but James said he didn't hesitate when she offered him the first flight to Orlando. They both had. I thought I would have a lot of convincing to do, but when I asked for their help, they came immediately. It was nice to know someone had my back. Multiple someones.

Spurlock whistled, impressed. "Look at you, Sally, leading your own little task force."

I managed a weak smile at his attempt to lighten the mood. "We'll need every advantage we can get. And you two are the best advantage we have."

The engines of the aircraft growled to life as we climbed onboard, a throaty roar that promised speed and power. I settled into my seat, the window offering a fleeting view of Florida's landscape as we ascended rapidly. Clouds became blurs, and the ground a distant memory, the world outside as tumultuous as the thoughts swirling inside my head.

I glanced at the others, each absorbed in their own preparations, faces set with determination. The Pythanoreans, the Agency, the shadows that lurked behind every corner of the universe — we were about to dive headfirst into the abyss, and we didn't even know how deep it went. It was like juggling dynamite: One wrong move, and everything could blow up in our faces.

"So. we're going up against forces that play with time and space like they're toys." Kork's voice cut through the hum of the aircraft, grounding me back to the present. "What's the plan?"

"Well, first things first, we get ourselves a ship that's actually spaceworthy. That's why we're heading to area 51," I explained. "Then, we fly to the Agency to beg them for any help they can give — not that they will. I've got a bad feeling about Stook right now. The Alliance is too far away to help, and while I could bring Dany — Danirshna — here, I'm not sure it's a good idea with the Pythanoreans likely pulling the strings. No, we need to see where Stook stands, whether the Agency will defend the Earth against whatever those ships are planning, or sell us out."

"So what happens if things go sour at there?" he asked. "Worst case scenario. They have LifePrints, don't they? Will they be looking for you?"

I nodded. Last time I'd been there, the Agency was teeming with the small bots that could sniff out your identity even under your most expensive costume. I'd befriended one, only for that friendship to have cost the thing its life, however you could quantify it.

"That's why we have our distraction incarnate," I said with a slight smile, nodding towards Spurlock. "Hope you don't mind turning up your star power?"

Spurlock replied with a burst of laughter, bright and boisterous. "You kidding? It's the role of a lifetime!" His grin was as wide as the galaxy. "No offense, Kork. Being your first mate was the highlight of my career until, you know, I got roped into saving the universe."

"Spurlock, you already liberated an entire planet," I reminded him.

"Oh, right!" He clapped his hands. "But this — this is next level."

He smiled at me, oh-so-gently, and it hit me just how much these two were sacrificing to help me on my unhinged mission. Kork, this time with his recently reunited family, Spurlock, going into the belly of the very beast that had shot him in his.

We landed on an appointed landing pad, dust flying up as we hit the ground. We were out of the aircraft before it even had time to settle.

"You!" exclaimed a voice. The gun raised in a shaky grip aimed directly at me came into focus as the air cleared. I wanted to laugh. What were the odds?

Kork tensed beside me, ready to spring into action. "Do you know him?" he asked, his eyes darting between the guard and me.

"I think so." I nodded slightly. "Last time we met, Blayde died in front of him… twice. He's probably still processing that."

"Go back where you came from, and no one gets hurt," the guard warned. Didn't sound like normal procedure speaking, but then again, last time he'd seen me had been anything but normal. "I swear I'm not afraid to use this…"

"Frostfire," I interjected quickly, hoping the code word would hold its power. Though with us landing in a military craft, it shouldn't have been necessary.

The guard's expression shifted from hostility to confusion, then to recognition as he slowly lowered his weapon. "Official Frostfire business?" he repeated.

"Yes, Frostfire," I confirmed with a nod. "Now, can we pass, please?"

The guard, still looking a bit like a deer caught in headlights, scrambled to his truck. He flung the passenger door open and gestured for us to get in. I obliged, a bit taken aback by the drastic change in his demeanor. What was Frostfire even code for — aliens? Invasion of the body snatchers? End of the world? In any case, by the look on the guard's face — and the total lack of color there, like we'd been thrown into a Charlie Chaplin movie but weren't laughing — it likely wasn't good news.

He slammed the gas pedal and the truck lurched forward, kicking up a cloud of dust as we sped along the rugged dirt road. We were jostled around by the rough ride, but the guard seemed singularly focused, driving faster and faster. Just like the last time I'd been here, I didn't have the time to fully take in my surroundings. Maybe when all this was said and done, I could ask for a guided visit.

"Where to exactly?" the guard asked abruptly, swerving into the heart of the base and barely pausing to flash his ID at the gate.

"To the ships," I commanded firmly. "And not a word of this to anyone."

The truck screeched to a halt in front of the hangar and I tumbled out onto the pavement, Spurlock and Kork falling out after me. A familiar sight greeted me, though it had been three years since I'd last set foot here: a hangar the size of a stadium.

The guard, still a little too pale for our desert surroundings, leaned out of the truck and looked at me questioningly. "What do I do now?"

Great question. One I'd assumed he'd be asking his boss, not me. But I guess I might have been said boss today.

"Go back to your post," I instructed. "And remember, you never saw us. Capeesh?"

"But... about the..." he trailed off, a haunted look in his eyes.

I frowned. "The what?"

"Alien invasion!" he said between gritted teeth. "How can I recognize them if they're walking among us?"

"Salt," I replied before biting my lip. This was probably just stoking the flames of panic here. "When in doubt, use salt."

"Salt..." he repeated, nodding to himself. "Salt it is."

With a final nod, he spun the truck around and sped off, leaving us at the entrance of the hangar. Its massive frame loomed over like the final boss in a video game. "Let's hope they left the door open," I muttered, but of course, they hadn't. The door, dwarfed by the starship-sized maw, sat still, tiny and locked. There it was, a keypad staring back at us like a silent challenge.

I faced the keypad, frustration sharpening my focus. Something so insignificant couldn't be the end of our mission. It just couldn't.

Spurlock peered over my shoulder, his brow furrowed. "What's the plan if the universal key doesn't work?"

"Universal key?" I asked, but he was already hoisting his weapon. "Woah, woah, woah! Hold your horses! It just needs a password."

I punched in the only thing I could think of: 'Frostfire.' The door beeped cheerfully and swung open. "Oh, come on," I scoffed as we stepped through. "Even my grandma has better password security. And she uses her cat's name for everything."

As we entered, the hangar stretched out before us, just as imposing and otherworldly as I remembered. The dim lighting cast an eerie glow, turning the assortment of spacecraft into gigantic, surreal silhouettes. I froze for a moment, taking it all in.

"Which one do we commandeer?" Kork asked, his eyes wide as he surveyed our options.

"I was really counting on you to be the expert here, pilot," I quipped, sweeping my hand across the eclectic fleet before us. The assortment was truly a sight — some ships bore the noble scars of scifi-worthy battles, while others sported a sleek design yet were comically inoperative, their hulls punctured or clamped under massive yellow weights with signs reading, "This Vessel Grounded. Contact Jevroh for Boot Removal." It felt less like a hangar and more like a museum of interstellar misfortunes. One craft was even propped up on bricks, stripped of anything that might once have been considered valuable. Another had a bumper sticker that proclaimed, "My other ship is a star destroyer." Amidst this motley crew of intergalactic rejects, Kork's gaze settled on a small, unassuming craft that was built like a tank, and looked like it might just be able to leave the hangar without falling apart.

"This one," he declared, starting towards it. "It's a sewage hauler, but it's the only one here that looks spaceworthy."

He deftly manipulated a hidden latch, and the ship's door creaked open, releasing a pungent aroma that made my eyes water. Spurlock was taking in the scene with wide eyes, clearly amazed at the sight, while I was amazed at his lack of tears. The stench was, if I dare to say it, out of this world.

"What's the opposite of novalicious?" He laughed, unfazed. "We're saving the universe in style, huh?"

I peered inside, my nose scrunching at the smell. "Can this thing actually fly?"

"It'd better." Kork slapped the dashboard affectionately. The ship's interior lights flickered to life, and a steady hum vibrated through the hull. "Not to mention, the reinforced plating is perfect to hide weapons from scanners. No one expects sewage ships to bring the violence."

I located the hangar door controls and watched as they slid open, revealing the empty tarmac outside. Climbing into the cockpit, I buckled myself in next to Kork, who was already wrestling with the ship's controls. The ship lurched forward, heavy and reluctant.

"Everything alright?" I asked, gripping my seat as it groaned in protest.

Kork grinned, his confidence infectious. "Just giving her a little pep talk. She'll fly."

He pulled the ship up, guiding it up and out into the clear blue sky. I let out a sigh of relief, despite the weight of the situation pressing down on me even as we ascended.

"Alright," I said, clearing my throat, looking over my team. My incredible crew. "Now. Let's get to planning."

TWENTY-EIGHT
MY NOT-SO-SMOOTH CRIMINAL MOMENT

EMERGING FROM THE SHIP ONTO THE Agency's Parking Dock C was less of a small step for man and more of a large stumble into a pile of memories that swarmed me like an overly enthusiastic aunt at a family reunion. The last time I graced this hangar with my presence, my exit was less of a dignified departure and more of a flailing leap into the abyss of space. Ah, good times.

Spurlock flipped switches, powering down the ship and breaking me out of my reverie. "You sure you don't want me to come with?"

"Are *you* sure you want to see Stook again?" I asked, pointing at his gut.

He grimaced. "Nope, not particularly." He paused, a determined glint in his eye. "But if you need me there…"

I shook my head. "I need you here, keeping the terminal distracted. If all goes well, you sign a few autographs, charm the staff, and we walk out with an army. But if things go south…"

The unsaid words hung heavily in the air. Everything up to this point had gone suspiciously smoothly. It was the calm before the storm, and the sense of impending doom was almost palpable. I ran my hand down the small of my back, patting the FlexiBlaster I'd stuck there. How people in movies could pull this off, I'd never know: the cold metal of the barrel sent goosebumps up and down my spine, the mildly comforting presence made disconcerting by the knowledge that any wrong move could literally blast my ass off.

Spurlock's voice was steady and reassuring. "If things go wrong, remember, I've got you." He nodded towards Kork, who gave a quiet but confident thumbs-up from the pilot's seat.

"We've got your back, Sally," Kork agreed. "Good luck out there."

The hangar doors closed behind me with a hiss and a thud, sealing off the ship and its crew from view. As I made my way through the terminal, my steps resonated with a sense of purpose. I was a woman on a mission, and nothing was going to stand in my way. It didn't even matter if the LifePrints saw me: I was here on official business.

At least, for the time being.

SINGULARITY

I marched through the terminal, head held high. I remembered the way to the administrative wing, finding myself thinking of Foollegg on the way to where I had first met her. Would I have felt the same gnawing apprehension in my stomach if it were her office I was heading to, instead of Stook's?

Agency employees scattered like startled squirrels as I strode through the department. Their stares ranged from disbelief to outright shock, but no one dared to block my path. A small smirk tugged at the corner of my mouth — there was a certain satisfaction in knowing my reputation preceded me.

As I reached Stook's office, the secretary — a six-eyed being with skin that shifted colors like a living lava lamp, maybe one of Glexar's relatives — visibly gulped. Each of their eyes blinked in a staggered fashion, creating a wave of eyelid flutters.

"Director Stook available?" I asked, keeping my voice steady.

"Uh, momentarily," they stuttered, skin cycling through a rainbow of hues, all six hands fumbling with the communicator and hitting more buttons than necessary. "You can wait inside."

Stook's office was stark in its minimalism, a striking contrast to the lavish setup on his personal ship. Awards for excellence hung on the wall, while in the corner, a lone purple plant drooped in a jade-colored pot, its petal-like structures hanging listlessly.

I settled into the leather chair behind the desk, allowing myself a moment to spin and face the window. The lunar landscape stretched out before me, a tranquil sea of grey and white. It was a view that never failed to take my breath away. I folded my arms across my chest, watching it. Must have been some kind of power play, keeping me waiting. Last time I was here, I might not have said anything, but times had changed, and so had I. Once, I might have sat here as an ally or a visitor. Now, I was here to make demands.

I swiveled the chair around just in time to see Stook stride into the room. He seemed to be struggling to keep from frowning, his lips a pencil thin line that wouldn't stop drooping. I understand now why supervillains like to have their moment to spin their chair around: looking at a nemesis as their face falls was an excellent dopamine booster.

"Miss Webber," he said, "I wasn't expecting you."

"Surprise seems to be the theme of the day, Director," I retorted. "Let's talk about surprises, like the one still orbiting our planet."

He tilted his neck slowly from side to side. "Is this about that Black Knight nonsense again?"

"Yes and no," I replied. "It's about the Black Knight *ship*."

Stook feigned ignorance, an act so poorly executed it would have made a high school drama student cringe. "Which ship?" he asked, his voice dripping with false innocence.

"The Pythanorean ship, Stook. The one you've been conveniently ignoring for centuries." I templed my fingers. "That, and many others."

"Ah, that *ship*." He paused. "How did you... Never mind. What about it?"

I narrowed my eyes, rising from the chair. Which didn't help my position, seeing as the man's neck still towered over me. "Don't play dumb, Stook. You know exactly which ship I'm talking about. You said it was inactive. So why is it still here?"

Stook hesitated. "It's complicated, Sally. I wasn't lying when I called it junk. It's a ghost ship. There but not there. We've left it alone because it hasn't posed any immediate threat."

"Well, now it does. And so do all the others. And I need you to take action. Remember our treaty? It's high time to honor it."

"The treaty, yes." Stook's voice hardened. "But my intel suggests your ties with Zander are... strained. It may become difficult for you to maintain your end of the bargain."

I clenched my jaw. "That's my personal business, Stook. This is about the safety of Earth. Are you going to act or not?"

He shuffled in place. "Miss Webber, these things... they take time."

I crossed my arms, channeling my inner Blayde. "How many centuries do you need? Really pushing the definition of taking your time, aren't you?"

Stook's face paled, which was a feat considering his already ghostly complexion. "We're doing our best," he muttered.

"We had an agreement, Stook," I growled. "Zander signed off on it — the Agency helps us, and in return, you ensure Earth is clear of non-Agency ships. That ship isn't on any list — trust me, my expert is quite connected. So what's it going to be? Are you reneging on your deal with the Siblings, or are you keeping secrets from me?"

Stook's Adam's apple rolled all the way down his neck as he swallowed hard. "We are addressing the issue," he said, his voice barely above a whisper.

I snorted. "Speed it up, Stook. Or do you need a refresher course in the consequences of double-crossing Sally Webber?" My voice was as cold as Pluto, but inside, I was doing a victory dance. It wasn't every day you got to corner a space agency director.

"You. Making threats?" He scoffed.

"I'm assuming command of this mess," I announced with a confidence I was only partially feeling. "I need every agent you've got. We're commandeering that ship, towing it back out into space if we have to."

Instead of replying, Stook closed his office door and locked it with a click. My heart sank into my gut.

"It sounds like the Hail Mary of a woman who's run out of options," he said, turning around to face me again.

Oh, shit. I mean, I expected something like this, but it's one thing to have a plan and quite another to have a creep with a giant giraffe neck glaring down at you from the only exit.

I grit my teeth. "What are you playing at, Stook?"

He marched slowly towards the desk, an unpleasant grin spreading across his face. "I've been in communication with our friends aboard that ship. It turns out, they've got... a guest. A very important guest."

Stook, in contact with the ship.

Stook knew that Blayde was trapped there.

Well, not the biggest of surprises, let me tell you. Anyone who shoots people in the gut on a dime isn't really worth my time. Not a fan.

Come on, Sally. Don't lose your composure now. "You're saying our contract is terminated?"

Stook's nod was slow, almost theatrical. "More like *all* the contracts. Seems neither of us were showing our full hands when we laid our cards on the table."

The air in the room was closing in. Was the life support failing?

"So, what's your end game, Director? You switching teams?"

His grin stretched wider. "Oh, the stakes have risen, Sally. The game's evolved."

"And us?" I asked, my hand edging towards the small of my back, and the weapon hidden there.

"Us? I'd say we're in treacherous waters."

Oh, great. The self-satisfying grin was grating beyond belief.

I grit my teeth. "You're a Pythanorean acolyte, aren't you?" James was right. Someone was hiding the Pythanorean ships, and had been for centuries. The Agency was complicit, and so was Stook. Everything about getting me to meet with the president had been about laying the groundwork for whatever those higher dimensional jackasses had been planning for Earth. Placing me right where they wanted me.

They hadn't expected me to fight back. I wasn't going to be a piece in their game any longer.

He shook his head, letting out a snort of laughter. "No, but I am an ally. They've promised me power, longevity, things you can't even fathom. So, how about you drop your weapons? They're on their way."

"Not a chance." I ripped out the FlexiBlaster, flicking off the safety in one swift move before firing at the floor. The shot hit true, the metal beneath my feet shivering before a gaping hole appeared. Salvation.

I didn't think, I only leapt, dropping through the disintegrating floor, tumbling into the unknown. I cascaded through a pile of boxes and rolled onto the floor of the storage room beneath, surrounded by the remains of holiday décor I'd just decimated. Above me, alarms began to blare. Guess I wasn't welcome here anymore. I bolted out the door and down the corridor, my mind racing. The game had changed, and it was time for me to rewrite the rules.

Not that I knew my way around the labyrinthine corridors. I ripped my phone out of my pockets, hitting the redial button, slipping in an earbud as I ran.

"James, you were right. Stook and the Pythanoreans are working together." I sputtered when she picked up. *Breathe, Sally, breath. Running is the easy part.* "I don't know what they're planning for Earth, but it can't be good. Tell me you have good news on your end."

"Kork patched me into the station's systems," she replied instantly. "I've got full control... for the most part. You?"

The sound of boots echoed down the hallway. I hissed, darting into a doorway just as a pack of security officers turned the corner, rushing past with their blasters held tight. Stook really wasn't taking any chances with me. What had he told them I'd done?

"We're not getting any help here," I whispered after the coast was clear again. "Tell Kork he's on."

I ripped off my shirt, hopping on one foot as I slipped off my jeans, revealing my *Traveler* uniform I had kept as a souvenir. Now, finally, it was coming into use; no one would suspect a uniformed crew member walking around the administrative wing with purpose. I stepped out the door, my boots thudding as I hit carpeted floor. The friendly offices were calm and orderly, full of the usual mundanity, staff puttering along without paying any attention to me, seemingly oblivious to the pack of armed security officers who'd just breezed through.

Except, of course, when the alarm went off.

"Ugh," said James. "Hold on. I've got this."

The sudden blare was like a sonic boom in the confined space, though it only lasted two seconds before James shut it off.

"Expect a few hiccups," she warned. "I can't kill it, just lull it into a false sense of security. Brace yourself."

True to her word, the alarm stuttered on and off, a terrible DJ set of starts and stops. The office staff looked at each other, the ceiling, out the window — anywhere but at me.

"Really keeps you on your toes," I muttered.

James grunted. "It's a pain in the proverbial butt, that's what it is."

I glanced back over my shoulder. Shit. Security was rounding the corner. *Blend, Sally, Blend.*

"James, can you slow them down?"

"I've got control of some fire doors and airlocks. Let's see how they like a little maze of their own," she replied, a hint of a smirk in her voice. "You can feel good knowing they definitely got their steps in for the day."

As I sprinted, doors along the corridor slammed shut behind me, cutting off my pursuers. With James helping, escape would be a breeze. A wave of relief washed over me, mixed with a heavy dose of adrenaline. Until I nearly collided with a LifePrint.

The orb hovered ominously in the hallway, a silent sentinel. For a split second, everything stood still, the orb and I locked in a wordless standoff. *Why wasn't it raising the alarm?*

Another one of those lovely memories I'd been repressing came rushing back: one of another LifePrint, another lifetime, of a first day gone disastrously wrong.

I lifted my blaster, leveling it with the wide eye, but my hands were trembling so hard that even at this distance I couldn't take the shot.

Still, it didn't move. It only stared, watching me, waiting for… something.

"LP?" I asked, half hoping, half dreading.

"It appears you're Sally Webber," it declared, a note of pride in its synthesized tone that shouldn't have been possible.

I lowered the blaster. "I thought they wiped you!" My hand rose to my mouth to suppress a laugh, instead catching the wetness of tears rolling down my cheek. "How… how do you remember me?"

"There were... complications," it replied. "I've been told you're not meant to make *that* many backups for your first day."

Footsteps bounced off the wall, not the thunder of security rushing by, but the slow and steady march of determination. Before I could ask another question, Foollegg rounded the corner, casually striding towards me like she was hoping to catch me at the water cooler.

She stopped beside LP. "Talking to yourself, or have you found a new friend?"

My throat was dry. I glanced between the two of them, my mind racing. This was it: LP might not have sounded the alarm, but Foollegg was the end of it.

"I thought you'd wiped its personality," I said, gesturing to the LifePrint. Better talk about that than my upcoming imprisonment.

Foollegg's gaze softened momentarily. "Some memories are harder to wipe than others," she admitted with a sigh. "You're quite tenacious when you want to be. Now what are you still doing here? You Earthlings — run, idiot!"

What the hell? My eyes bounced around the corridor — this had to be a trap. "Wait, you're not going to call for backup?"

Foollegg rolled her eyes, her patience clearly waning. "And let Stook take all the credit for apprehending you? Please. I'd rather eat my badge. No, the only help you'll get from me is silence."

A smile tugged at my lips. "And what about LP?"

Foollegg glanced at the orb, a ghost of a smile passing over her features. "The LifePrint's discretion can be... selective. Right now, it's in your favor."

I nodded, understanding the unspoken agreement. "Thanks. For everything."

"Don't mention it. Really, I mean it. Never speak of this again. Now go, make a dramatic escape. Just be quick about it. And if you somehow manage to oust Stook, remember who gave you the head start."

I nodded, unsure of how long this offer would stand. "Thanks, Foollegg. You know what? You really are long overdue for a promotion." I took off down the corridor, the orb making no move to stop me, its silence a baffling but welcome ally.

"Don't thank me yet," she called from behind me. "Just don't screw it up."

That was… weird. I took a deep breath, trying to calm my racing mind, to bring my focus back on the task at hand: escaping.

"Alright, let's make some chaos. James, tell Spurlock he's on."

"Roger that."

I finally reached the end of the hallway and took a deep breath, out of the administrative wing and into what I thought was the main terminal, only now it was indistinguishable from a stadium. People were flocking towards the central floor, breezing past me as if I was invisible.

"Oh great Vega, is it true? Is he here?" squealed an entirely transparent being chased by a spider plant, each with all their appendages in the air. "Is Spurlock Magnesar giving autographs?"

"He's so much hotter now that he's a hero," gushed the spider plant, trailing leaves like a green comet tail. "He has this whole… 'daddy rescue me' vibe. Like, save the planet, save my number."

I weaved through the sea of Spurlock's adoring fans, none of whom would've batted an eyelid at me even if I proclaimed the station was exploding. Spurlock's voice then filled the terminal, each note vibrating through me in an embarrassingly pleasant way that had me accidentally chewing on my lip. In minutes, he had successfully transformed the sterile, high-security environment into a frenzied concert. The crowd, a mix of tourists, agents, scientists, and administrative staff, swayed and danced to the music.

"So Goodbye, Good Bye," filled the air, seemingly sung by the entirety of the station. *"I hope you find what you're looking for... Wandereeeeeeeeeers!"*

I hate to admit, that song was an earworm.

One particularly enthusiastic fan decked out in what appeared to be homemade Spurlock merchandise, barreled past, nearly colliding with me in their fervor to reach him. "Excuse me! Rock star in need of my undying affection!" they exclaimed, nearly tripping over their own feet. I sidestepped, barely avoiding a pileup.

The terminal had fully transformed into an impromptu mosh pit. Tourists and staff alike were swept up in the music. Near the periphery, a pair of security guards stood, clearly caught in an internal tug-of-war between their duties and the magnetic pull of the music.

"Is it really disruption if he's technically bringing everyone together?" One guard pondered aloud, seemingly entranced.

The other guard's foot tapped to the beat. "Yeah, but the boss won't like it if we join the dance-off instead of controlling it."

SINGULARITY

I didn't wait for them to resolve their moral quandary. Taking advantage of their momentary lapse, I dashed towards the parking bay. I melded into the shadows, my standard-issue uniform blending seamlessly with the less illuminated parts of the terminal.

I sighed with relief when I saw Kork waiting for me. He waved me over to the new ship he'd been hot-wiring: a nice, sleek, military-looking thing.

"We're about to have company!" I shouted, dashing towards him.

"On it!" Kork said, racing up the ramp. "Give me a few seconds."

As the ship's engines roared to life, the hangar doors slid open, revealing the star-speckled void of space and the blue tinge of the energy barrier keeping all the air where it was meant to be.

"James, time for your magic," I called out to my earpiece. "We need to validate parking."

Before I could take another step, a crushing force slammed into my back. My legs gave out beneath me and I collapsed onto the floor, slamming my chin into my chest and snapping my nose with a sickening crunch.

"Sally!" Kork shouted, his voice distant, desperate through the ringing that now filled my ears.

I tried to scramble to my feet, to find some leverage, but a vice-like grip latched onto my hair, wrenching my head back with brutal force. A scream of shock tore from my throat as I was flung backward. Staring down at me was a face hauntingly familiar yet terrifyingly alien.

Zander. But not the Zander I knew. This was a snarling, rabid Zander, his eyes gleaming with a cold, menacing intent.

"What's the rush, Sally?" he sneered, his fingers digging into my scalp.

Panic surged through me. I thrashed against his grip, desperation fueling my movements. This Zander was a tempest, unpredictable and dangerous.

"Let me go," I managed, my voice a strained whisper. "This isn't your fight."

"You're my fight," he hissed, venom dripping from each word.

I recognized him now, this anger, this fury. This Zander was the man from my deviations. The one so early in his own timeline that he had yet to find any kind of solace or peace in this cold, uncaring universe.

"You're not my Zander," I spat back, defiance flaring despite the fear.

His smirk twisted his features into something grotesque. "Oh, I'm every bit as real as he is. Maybe even more so." His voice was a dark echo of the man I once believed him to be, and it chilled me to the bone.

"Sally, hang on!" Kork called out. I could barely make out his form, a blur of motion as he sprinted towards us.

Zander's reaction was swift and brutal. With a ferocious growl, he released me, only to swing his arm in a wide arc, his fist connecting with Kork and sending him flying across the hangar. Kork's body hit the ground with a thud, skidding across the cold metal floor.

I gasped, my head spinning. This Zander was raw, uncontrolled aggression.

Scrambling to my feet, I glanced towards Kork, who was slowly trying to push himself up, clearly winded but still conscious. My attention snapped back to the raging Zander, who had turned his glare back to me. Steel braced my nerves as I squared up to face him.

"I don't want to fight you," I said. Every instinct screamed at me to flee, but there was no running from this. I had to stand my ground.

But the look in his eyes was cold, unyielding. "It's not about what you want," he replied in a sinister whisper. "You just have to come with me."

"Where?"

His smirk was mirthless. "You know where. The Masters want to see you."

My stomach dropped. The Masters. He was working for the Pythanoreans. Had he been working with them, this whole time? Every time I was thrown off course…

"Every time I jumped, they sent me to you," I said, realization hitting me like a meteor. "But… why?"

Before he could respond, another figure burst onto the scene. He lunged at Zander, their bodies crashing together and sending shockwaves through the hangar. The air exploded with fury—punches thrown with reckless abandon, each connecting with bone-jarring force.

As I tried to sit up, the world spun around me, making it hard to focus. But there they were —There were two Zanders now? Neither held back as they fought over a reality they both claimed. It was like something out of a fever dream, their silhouettes blurred in a violent dance.

Clashing metal and grunts filled the air as the new Zander and the old clashed in a brutal ballet. They were evenly matched, each blow from one met with an equally forceful counter from the other. Like a battle against a mirror, each movement was anticipated and reflected, over and over again.

Watching them, I realized this battle was more than physical—it was a war for identity, for the soul of a man who stood at a crossroads. It was a vivid, terrifying reminder of what Zander could have been, a stark reminder of the path he had managed to avoid.

"Kork!" I called out, pushing myself up. "We need to move, now!"

Gritting my teeth, I dashed towards Kork, helping him to his feet. Our window of opportunity was closing rapidly. We had to get to the ship and escape this madness before it swallowed us whole. Spurlock at least would be safe in the flood of his adoring fans. I looped an arm under Kork's, and the two of us ran, ran away from the Zanders, away from the madness.

Of course, that was before the entire floor sparked to life, electricity running through my body and sending my mind to darkness.

TWENTY-NINE

I'M AN UNWILLING UNIVERSAL UNIVERSAL DONOR

I THINK YOU'RE SUPPOSED TO SEE DOUBLE after being knocked out, but I saw only one Zander. He hung from the wall in the dark room before me, dressed in a T-shirt and blue jeans perfectly adapted for Earth, hooked up to tubes and monitors that weren't. A tube slid up through his nose, the other end connected to who knows what.

The room was a far cry from the pop fever dream we'd been in on the Pythanorean ship. This one was dark, somber, and clinical in a way that only a creepy sci-fi lab could manage. Chains hung ominously on the walls next to Zander, like a twisted version of a gym locker room gone horribly wrong. Medical devices crowded the room, their displays blinking with cold, calculating precision. It was like being trapped inside a cyborg's idea of a cozy den.

Wherever we were, it was definitely our own dimension, at least.

I groaned, lifting a leg in an attempt to stand. The leg refused to obey, firmly bound as it was to a table. A wave of frustration washed over me. *Idiot. This is what happens when you think you can outsmart the universe.*

Glancing around, I noticed I was, at least for now, spared the invasion of tubes and monitors that Zander endured. My relief was short-lived, though: We weren't alone.

To my right, a figure garbed in a latex unicorn mask busied himself with needles. The mask was the same absurd, frozen expression of mid-chew eeriness I had seen before. Its teeth were bared in a grotesque caricature of a grin, giving the unicorn an unsettling, almost mocking appearance.

An acolyte. And nowhere near as cheery as Larry or Not-Larry had been.

He stared at me, and I stared back. Well, no point pretending I was still unconscious at this point.

"What is this?" I said, injecting as much venom into my voice as I could muster. "Where am I?"

His response was unsettlingly cheerful. "Don't worry, you're in our capable hands," he chirped. "Now hold still, this won't hurt a bit — not that things hurt you, to my knowledge."

Before I could react, he shoved a small plastic tube towards my nose. I recoiled instinctively, but he was quicker, his grip firm and unyielding as he jammed the tube through my nostril. I didn't know what I hated more: the feeling of plastic shoving against my nose, or the sheer indignity of it. I coughed and spluttered, instinctively trying to jump away, but I was cut off from the universe like someone had hacked off one of my limbs.

"What do you want with me?" I snarled, the words muffled around the intrusion. The binds at my hands were too tight to slip, the ones at my legs too constraining to even allow me to properly shift my weight.

He paused, tilting his head in a way that made the unicorn mask *flomp* and seem even more ridiculous. "You're going to help us," he said with an unsettling enthusiasm. "We're going to change the universe."

The statement hung in the air, heavy with implications I didn't even begin to understand. Nor did I want to, really.

"Let me go," I demanded, trying to keep the desperation from my voice. "I don't want to help you with anything."

"We're not the enemy here," he continued as his hands deftly prodded me with needles. "Despite your reticence, you will be compensated for your contribution to the directive."

"Compensated? How? Wait, better question: for what?" I spat. "What are you doing to Earth? Is this some grand paradox resolution? Is this how you set the timeline straight? I never realized it would be so... hands-on."

"The timeline?" He chuckled, and despite the mask, it was nowhere near jolly. "Oh, no, we no longer need to worry about that. Or your blip of a planet, either."

There was a pause as I pondered his words. The Pythanoreans no longer cared about paradoxes in their precious timelines? Why would they…

Then I saw the red liquid filling the tubes that came out of Zander's arm. I shuddered. What had Blayde said about their existence? They were obsessed with Zander, not because of his ability to create paradoxes, but because of his freedom in the timeline, the immortality he carried — *we* carried — without higher dimensions being involved. They were omniscient, not omnipotent. Which meant from their point of view, our physical forms were…

Sports cars.

"You're using us to help your masters return to a physical form," I said, gasping as I did. "Correct?"

"I thought you had been informed? No matter." His confirmation was short and devoid of any remorse. "You offer us almost an unlimited supply of blood; thus, a safe way for our masters to return to the physical realm, while keeping their immortality. Except, better."

"I thought they were seeking ascension, transcendence," I scoffed. "Why go to all the trouble of moving to a higher plane of existence, only to come back down to ours?"

"Why not have both?" he retorted, finishing up and wiping his hands on a towel, before marching towards the white door. "Now, please wait patiently. I will return in a moment."

"Wait, hold on!" I shouted, my voice bouncing around the stark room, as useful as yelling into a void. "Doesn't anyone care about consent anymore? Or at least a decent last meal?"

Zander's sigh was a low hum in the chilling room. "Not really. They don't listen to anyone but their masters."

I craned my neck to get a better look at him, wincing from the uncomfortable pull of the tube. *Zander.*

Stars, it was Zander: my Zander. Zander who had come back and tried to save me when I was trying to save him.

"Oh," I replied, awkwardly. It was the first time I'd seen this version of him since the... incident. "Is that really you? Or am I hallucinating a more tolerable version of you?"

His expression softened, but the grim set of his mouth told me all I needed to know. "It's me, Sally. And I'm sorry — how are you doing?"

I snorted, a lovely snort that got caught in my cannula. "Pretty good, considering I'm a high-value blood bag for higher-dimensional beings planning to take over the universe. How about you? Enjoying being wall décor?"

He grimaced. "About the same. And you? How's life?"

I wasn't ready for this. Not now. Not when everything was falling apart around me. I had failed my friends, my world, the whole universe. And he wanted to play catch up?

"I don't really want to talk to you right now," I shot back, frustration sharpening my words. "Seeing as how you put me here in the first place."

He coughed, a strained noise that reverberated off the cold walls. "I was trying to save you. That's how I ended up chained to their certifiably un-kinky dungeon wall."

"Well, if this is their idea of hospitality, I'd hate to see what they do to enemies," I muttered, trying again to wiggle my hands free from the restraints. "And you were just trying to save me from yourself. You'd think with so many years on him, you'd have a little leg up."

He was silent for a moment. "Look, that was me from the past. A distant past. Very distant. Prehistoric, even."

I looked away, focusing on the sterile, ominous room. Every inch screamed of cold calculation, of beings so advanced and detached they saw us as nothing more than resources. The kitten poster asking us to "hang in the there" wasn't helping.

"You talk about him as if he was a completely different person," I said. "But he was you."

"He was the me from then, not the me I am now." He closed his eyes, squeezing them tight. "When you've lived as many lifetimes as I have, each century molds you into someone new. Ever look back at your childhood and wonder how you ever were that person? Imagine having a few thousand years to reflect."

"But you *were* him," I spat. "Once. You can't deny that."

He nodded slowly, the chains rattling softly. "I've changed. I'm not the same man I was. I've grown, evolved. Just as you have."

I snorted. "Growth is one thing, Zander." My eyes narrowed as I stared at him. "But I guess time will tell, right? Who you really are. Or who you've become. At least now you remember him."

"Honestly? I wish I didn't." He let out a heavy sigh. "You've met that version of Zander. Stars, I can't believe I was ever him. It disgusts me to think we were the same person."

"So, what? You're just going to blame everything on your past self?" I couldn't keep the skepticism from my voice. "As if that absolves you of everything?"

Zander's expression hardened. "No, I'm not blaming him. I'm blaming myself for not realizing sooner that I had to confront my past, not bury it. I lied, Sally. To you, to Blayde. I said my memories were trickling back, but the truth is, I was damming them up. I didn't want them back."

The room seemed to close in around us as he spoke. "Why?" I whispered. The question felt like it came from somewhere deep inside me. "I thought you wanted to reclaim your past. To know where you came from."

He let his head hang low. "Because if my past was bad enough to warrant being locked away, then maybe it should have stayed that way. And I was right. The person I was before... he was rude, callous, cold to the point of cosmic indifference. And when my memory came back... I remembered meeting you. The first time."

His admission hung in the air between us, heavy and charged. I said nothing. I wasn't sure what the point of his story was, but it was distracting me from finding a way to escape my bonds.

"You remembered me," I echoed, my voice softer now, the edge of anger dulled by the sheer weight of our situation. The harsh, clinical light of the room seemed to dim. "And what? You suddenly developed a conscience?"

"I remembered what I did to you." He let out a heavy breath. "When I was young, dumb, and stupid."

"Ah. You remembered what I just went through?" I scoffed. "You remember selling me out to the asshole unicorns?"

"I was... my past self was trying to save his own skin." Zander's gaze seemed to pierce through the gloom, his voice a blend of resignation and a strange, melancholic nostalgia. "That other me... When I lost the will to live, I fell into a sort of... abyss. The infinity of eternity had lost its luster. The universe wasn't offering the solace I sought. Blayde and I had our falling out, and I abandoned any pretense of morality. My life became a blur. Fast ships, reckless heroism and hedonism in equal measure, and a string of meaningless relationships. The works."

He paused, but I didn't have it in me to interrupt right now. "Eventually, my path led me to the famed party on Pythanous Five. A gathering of beings all seeking enlightenment or escape. You see what I'm saying?"

I let out a choked laugh. "So you went to a party and made some bad decisions."

"Well, yeah," he agreed sheepishly. "I was drunk or high, or both, for an incredible amount of time. That's when they realized what I was. What I could be to them."

I nodded slowly, the enormity of his story settling in. "They used you," I stated, a bitter taste in my mouth. "You gave them a doorway."

He looked away again. "Yes. And in doing so, I inadvertently set in motion events that would lead us here, to this moment. I thought I was seeking an end to my own misery, but instead, I provided them with the means to spread theirs."

"How?" I sputtered. "How exactly?"

"I'm not proud." A breath. "My past self… in order to protect himself, he agreed to do their bidding. They pushed you to me, and I'd corral you to them. You have to believe me, Sally: the second I remembered what I'd done in that ancient lifetime, I came back to protect you."

"And now?" I asked, my voice barely above a whisper.

"Now," he said, turning his haunted eyes back to me, "now we're both pawns in their game, aren't we? Just a couple of blood bags hanging on a wall. But I swear, Sally, I will do everything in my power to right the wrongs of my past. To protect you, and Blayde, and anyone else caught in their grasp. I've been a fool, but I refuse to be their tool any longer."

I wanted to rage at him, to unleash all the pent-up anger and hurt. But as I stared into his eyes, so full of remorse and resolve, I found my fury ebbing away, replaced by an aching sort of understanding. We were both prisoners here, not just to the cold metal and unyielding restraints, but to our pasts, to the choices that had led us to this to this moment, here, now.

No. I had a right to be angry. I didn't want to talk about that mewling past Zander who haunted my jumps. This Zander, the one before me, was the one who had ruined my life.

"You can't blame them for the things you did." I scowled. "You can't blame them for what *you* did to John."

His eyes met mine, carrying the weight of an eternity's regrets. "I know," Zander whispered, his voice hoarse in the sterile air. "I've carried that burden every moment since. There's not a day that passes where I don't feel the gravity of my actions, the lives altered, the pain caused. Especially for John." He took a deep, deep breath. "I did have a huge bouquet of flowers planned for this speech, but we're going to have to do without, seeing as how my hands are tied and I've lost a lot of blood."

I looked up at the ceiling, trying to keep my breathing steady. I wanted to shake him, to scream that remorse wasn't enough, that his regrets couldn't make right the damage he'd done. But then, seeing the genuine torment etched across his face, a part of me wilted. The anger I clung to, fierce and protective, began to dissolve into a sorrowful empathy. It was maddening, this whirlpool of conflicted emotions — anger, understanding, frustration — all swirling inside me, tugging at my resolve. Here was Zander, not just the architect of some of my deepest pains but also a victim of his own misguided decisions. He too was shackled by his past actions and he suffered under the weight of choices just as I did.

"I don't want your excuses," I muttered.

"I'm not making excuses. I'm giving you my apologies. I'm sorry. I'm sorry about everything. I'm sorry I lied about my memories, I'm sorry about your brother. I'm sorry about ruining your life. I'm sorry about getting you into all this."

"Sorry doesn't fix it." I swallowed hard. What could I say? How do you reconcile with a past that isn't yours, with a person who's both a stranger and an intimate part of your life?

His chains rattled softly. The sparse light of the room reflected off the path a tear carved down his face. "All those years, all those... experiences... they shape you, change you in ways you can't imagine. I've seen the rise and fall of civilizations, loved and lost more than most could bear. But none of that excuses what I've done."

His voice broke, the words heavy with sorrow. "Sally, I'm sorry. Not just for what happened to John, but for all of it. For every careless step that led to this moment. If I could take it all back, rewrite every line of my story, I would. But I can't. All I can do now is try to make things right."

I was slightly moved by the speech. Slightly. It was clear this wasn't the child Zander who called himself Prometheus; this wasn't the bitter Zander, who had mastered the so-called cosmic indifference; this wasn't the Zander I knew either, the terrified man with a hashed-up mind, a memory like Swiss cheese, and a laughing attitude about everything, approaching the world with unbridled joy and hope. No, this Zander was new. He was all these and none; a man reborn from the ashes of his past, standing before me, baring his soul.

But it still didn't make things right.

"You are a selfish man, Zander," I stated, my voice low, a torrent of emotions threatening to spill over. "Everything about our relationship has been about you. You were lonely. You wanted someone by your side who you could impress with all your knowledge and experience. You wanted someone that you could live with for an eternity, because you were tired of Blayde. You wanted someone to take the edge off infinity; to humanize you, while treating you like a god. And I was gullible enough to fall for all of that love nonsense. You weren't even interested in me until you found out that I was like you. That I was the only person you could be romantically attached to who wasn't going to die."

The tension in the room tightened. Zander's gaze was unwavering, intense, filled with an emotion I had seen flicker but never burn so fiercely before.

"You really believe that?" he asked, his voice breaking. "Sally, I fell in love with you in the middle of the road, the second my ribs stitched together, and your eyes looked into mine. And yes, it was selfish, because in that moment, and every moment since, I couldn't bear the thought of an existence without you in it."

My breath hitched despite myself, but he didn't stop.

"You really think I only fell for you when you changed? No. I fell for you long before that. In every moment I got to spend with you, no matter how small. I was completely smitten even before we met the Killian ambassador and we fell out of a saucer. But I never wanted to put you in the position of having to adjust your normal, healthy, total life around mine. Not to mention I thought you were crazy for Matt, and all I wanted was for you to be happy. You brought laughter back into my life, a spark I thought I'd lost forever: I hoped that could be enough."

I felt the heat of his gaze, the sincerity in his words wrapping around me like a blanket. It was too much. "You turned me immortal!" I sputtered.

"I gave you a choice, Sally. I never wanted to force eternity upon you. You could have refused, I could have understood that!"

A choice? No. We had both been manipulated by Nimien — choice had been off the table. But Nimien wasn't entirely to blame. Still. Still. I couldn't blame him for that. I grit my teeth.

"You turned me into a criminal!" My voice cracked, the weight of years of running, hiding, and fighting bubbling to the surface. "I was on the run!"

"And you could have walked away. But you stayed, Sally. You chose this life, this fight." He took a breath. "Because you cared about the people in this universe as much as I did. You wanted to do the right thing. I wanted to do the right thing, too."

It was too much. His admissions and apologies swirled around me, a maelstrom of past and present pain. I looked at him, really looked at him, and saw not just the man who had changed my life irrevocably but the man who was desperately trying to change himself.

"It's an improbable cosmos." He grinned. "It's what makes life worth living. We live on it, Sally. We move by making the improbable, probable. And the most improbable, most incredible thing of all? That you could ever have loved me. It's what some would call a miracle. And I will cherish the memory of it."

He continued, his gaze never leaving mine. "I understand if you can't forgive me. I can't forgive myself. But please know, I am here, now, with every bit of what's left of me. I'll stand with you against whatever comes our way."

The room seemed to close in around us, the sterile air pressing down. His words hung between us, a fragile bridge over a chasm of pain and regret. Our eyes met, two souls adrift in a universe that was too vast, too complex, too filled with wonders and horrors. But in that moment, a silent understanding passed between us. We were in this together, for better or worse. Not as enemies, not as reluctant allies, but as two individuals inexorably linked by the strange, improbable threads of destiny.

"And Sally," he added, his voice strengthening with resolve, "we will get out of this. We have to. For John, for Blayde, for all the lives we've touched. We owe them that much."

The chains rattled softly as we both shifted, the movement echoing in the room like a lonely, desolate sound. A stark reminder of our reality, of the gravity of our situation. But it was also a reminder that as long as we were still breathing, still fighting, there was hope. And in the darkest of times, hope was the most improbable and precious thing of all.

"I don't know which Zander you are now. But perhaps," I conceded, my anger ebbing into a sea of reluctant understanding, "perhaps you're not who you once were. Perhaps none of us are."

"If the universe is infinite, then so are the possibilities for change," he continued. "I know I've made unforgivable mistakes. I've hurt you, more than anyone ever should. But if you give me a chance, any chance at all, I will spend every moment of this endless life making it up to you, showing you that the man you met all those years ago, the man who made all those choices, is not the man before you now. I am someone who has been broken and remade in the image of his deepest regret and his most fervent hope: to be someone worthy of your love."

My breath caught in my chest.

Hc loved me.

I wanted to cry, to scream, to sob. That love between us — it was something tangible and strong, something that still existed even after what he'd done, something that couldn't be acknowledged, only missed. I wanted to love him back, to fall into the safety of that feeling, to be warmed by that intensity. But…

A long silence fell between us, filled only by the distant hum of machinery and the soft sound of our breathing. I wanted to say something, anything that would bridge the chasm of years and pain between us. But the words lodged in my throat, stubborn and unyielding.

"*If* we ever get out of here," I finally murmured, "then we can talk about it. Probably with a therapist, though."

"I look forward to it." Zander's laugh echoed softly in the room. "We have all the time in the universe to figure out how to get out of here."

A sudden thought struck me, a jolt of fear and concern that cut through the temporary respite. "Blayde," I gasped, my voice laced with panic. "Where's Blayde?" How could I have not thought of her sooner?

Zander frowned. "She's on this ship too, somewhere. They wouldn't harm her, not when they need us all. We get a break from the bloodletting, every once in a while."

"Oh, that's a relief," I muttered, tension knotting in my stomach. "I guess being a high-priority blood bank has its perks."

Whatever the unicorn had done to me, it hadn't started taking any of my own blood yet, which was a small relief. Zander was looking a bit peaky, though it could have been the terrible TikTok lighting in here.

I snorted, despite the gravity of our situation. My only options were either to laugh or cry, and I was all out of tears. "Any idea what happened to the others?"

"Spurlock's impromptu concert was still going strong when I got there. Kork was handed back to the Alliance, I think," said Zander. "They didn't need him."

"How charitable of them," I said dryly.

"I doubt either will be in too much trouble: Kork is the Alliance's golden boy, Dany will get him out. And I doubt he dropped that Spurlock's show was connected. *Goodbye Wanderers* probably went platinum after that stunt."

I let out a deep breath. "I'm sure Stook is thrilled."

"What a loser," said Zander.

"If we ever get out of here, I'm rushing Dany to the Agency. It's about time someone put Stook in his place. Maybe a formal complaint to the Empress of the Alliance will set things straight."

Zander nodded, a glimmer of approval in his eyes. "That sounds like a plan. A very good reason to get out of here. When in doubt, call on a higher power, right?"

"That's it!" The words tumbled out of me, sans filter. "Call on a higher power..."

"What do you mean?" Zander furrowed his brow.

"Easy," I said. "I need to get high."

THIRTY

I WAS GONNA SAVE THE WORLD,
BUT THEN I GOT HIGH

MY THERAPIST WOULD BE SO PROUD OF ME, resorting to meditation rather than violence. We'd twice saved the universe with music — today, I'd be saving it through silence.

Zander cleared his throat. "Sally, that's..."

"Insane? Dangerous? Probably impossible?" I interjected, my voice rising with each word. "Maybe. But think about it: the Pythanoreans see us as nothing more than tools, as lesser beings. If I could ascend, if I could reach their level of existence, then maybe, just maybe, I could confront them. Fight them on equal footing."

"Oh!" He let out a laugh. "That's what you meant. I thought you were turning to drugs."

"Why? Do you have any on hand?"

"Sally," Zander said, his tone turning serious, "ascension is not something to be taken lightly. It's one thing to live as immortals, to skirt the edges of higher dimensions. But to truly ascend, to become... something else. It's irreversible—"

"They're reversing it right now. And then, where will that leave the universe? Full of self-righteous immortals who think they deserve to control everything however they want. If that's not a call to action, I don't know what is."

"Yes, I understand the stakes," he insisted. "But this — this monumental thing shouldn't have to be on you. This isn't just about power, it's about your very being. Your very... soul."

"I know," I replied, the weight of my words settling over me. "But isn't that what they've forced us into? A fight for our essence, for our right to exist as we are? They've pushed us, Zander. And I need to push back."

He was silent for a long moment, his gaze intense, searching. Then, slowly, he nodded. "Well, we have all the time in the world to give it a whirl."

The room around us felt smaller, the air charged with the enormity of what we were contemplating. But beneath the fear and the uncertainty, there was a flicker of something else. Hope. Determination. The faint but unquenchable fire of two people who refused to be extinguished by the darkness.

"I'm with you," Zander said, his voice firm. "Every step of the way."

"Thanks," I replied. "I don't know what this will do to us, Zander. I don't know if we'll ever be able to make it back."

"I know." His face, already slick with tears, glistened more intensely. In the terrible lighting, it made him as sparkly as a disco ball. "I don't want to know a universe without you, Sally. I'm coming with you. At the very least, it might give me enough time to make it up to you."

I let out a laugh, the sound echoing strangely in the sterile room. "That's the spirit! Besides, who else is going to keep me company in the higher planes? It'll give us time to work things out."

Zander managed a small smile, the ghost of his old self peering through. "Then it's settled. We ascend. Or we go down trying. Either way, it's going to be one heck of a story."

I gritted my teeth in determination. Was I really going to do this? Let go of everything that made me, me? Leave behind this life, my friends, my family? Reach for an existence beyond my comprehension?

Now I was crying. Sobbing, even. Zander had put into words what I'd been trying to say forever: this shouldn't have been my responsibility. *Our* responsibility. This colossal burden that had been thrust upon us — it was too much for any one person, or even two.

"Do you, uh, know how we're meant to go about it?" I asked, sniffling away my tears. "We don't exactly have a manual for ascending, do we? Don't people spend their entire lives following special teachings? We're going into this blind."

"Uh, I know how some cultures do it." Zander cleared his throat, which sounded about as hoarse as mine. "For example, the Florgnaxians of Beta Ceti IV engage in a delightful ritual involving three hundred and seventy-two hours of continuous polka dancing. It's believed the rhythmic stepping aligns their chakras with the cosmic dance of the galaxies."

"And you expect us to polka our way to enlightenment?" I raised an eyebrow. "Zander, we're not exactly free to move around here. Unless it's more of a… mental polka?"

Zander shrugged. "Honestly, not sure if it would even work for us. Not enough legs. Now, the Zeeblorians of Gamma Draconis, they prefer a more sedentary approach, achieving transcendence through a rigorous diet of nothing but their equivalent of blue cheese and dark matter. The fermentation process does wonders for their spiritual elevation. But then again, dark matter gives me hives."

"*Riiight*, of course." I knew, I knew we were getting nowhere, Zander's ramblings were such a welcome distraction, it was music to my ears.

How I'd missed him. This was the Zander that I loved. He was different, changed by the mental weight of his memories, but my Zander was somewhere there. This Zander was something more. And, if we ever got out of this, I would love the chance to see what kind of Zander this was.

"Oh, did you know the clouds of the Horsehead Nebula are sentient?" he continued. "When they choose to ascend, they simply condense themselves into a super-dense mist and start counting to infinity. The logic being that you become infinity before reaching infinity, and so on. Only takes them a few millennia. They're already a gaseous consciousness, so letting go of their physical form is less of a brainteaser."

"Sounds... mystifying." I sighed. "But I doubt we have a few millennia to spare."

"It might take that long," Zander added, his tone dimming with every word.

I stared up at the ceiling. "Well, we might have one teacher."

"Who?"

I cleared my throat. *Here goes nothing.* "Clyde! Clyde, we need you!"

There was a momentary pause, the air vibrating with the tension of unspoken fears and faint hope. Then, like a beacon in the dark, Clyde's familiar blue form materialized beside us, his digital — was it even digital anymore? Or something new altogether? — presence somehow both comforting and surreal.

"Sally, there's no need for such volume." Clyde's voice was calm, almost soothing amidst the chaos. "I've been expecting you to reach out eventually."

"Oh, nice of you to pop in." Zander, his eyes wide, turned to stare at the new arrival. "And who exactly are you?"

"Zander, this is Clyde," I explained. "Formerly my AI emotional support hologram. Through a series of significant updates and reboots, he's managed to transcend typical artificial intelligence limitations."

"Much better than being confined to a single mind." Clyde's introduction was matter-of-fact, but not without a hint of pride. "No offense, Sally. I suppose of all the minds, I am grateful to have been bonded to yours."

"That's… oddly sweet, Clyde." I smiled. I mean, it was something. At least there were no hard feelings for all the reboots.

Zander let out a laugh. "Well, I've been restarted enough times in my life. Why haven't I ascended yet?"

Clyde shimmered. "Perhaps you lack the necessary hardware upgrades, Zander."

I blinked away the last of my tears, focusing on the task at hand. "Clyde, we have a plan, or the beginning of one. We need to ascend, to meet the Pythanoreans on their own level. You've managed something similar, and we need your guidance, your experience. Without rebooting our brains if we can pull that off."

Clyde brightened a whole shade of blue. "Indeed, Sally. My journey to this state of being was unique, complex, but not without its parallels to your current predicament. I will assist in any way I can, as promised."

"Good." I nodded. "If we're going to face these… beings, we need all the help we can get. Actually, I don't suppose…?"

Clyde held out his arms wide. "When you reach this plane… it is hard to let the squabbles of lower dimensions affect you."

"But you do have an insight into what the Pythanoreans are up to?"

"Indeed. It is hard to put into words that your minds will comprehend, but they are… descending, I suppose. And while, from my perspective, this has already happened and always will, the way they are going about it will take a while for your species to notice. This is intentional on their part, I do believe: not wanting to create the very paradoxes that caused them malaise."

"So, they're taking the slow route to power," I said. "Ensuring they don't trip over their own feet — or whatever it is higher beings have instead of feet."

"Exactly," Clyde continued. "Their plan is meticulous, calculated to unfold over what you would perceive as eons. But in the scope of the universe, it's a mere blink. They are ever patient."

"That means we have a window, slim as it may be," Zander said with a grin. Stars, it was good to see him like this again. "A chance to ascend and confront them before they fully materialize."

I nodded. "Okay, so we ascend, we confront them, we — what? Talk them down from their divine ledge? It's not like we can outsmart beings who've played 4D chess with the cosmos. Or however many Ds they really are."

"Biggest Ds in the universe," Zander grumbled.

Clyde shifted. "It's not about outsmarting them, Sally. It's about understanding them, reaching out to them on a level they cannot ignore. You've interacted with beings of all sorts across the universe. This is just another negotiation, albeit on a much grander scale."

I let out a slow breath. Oof. Our dimension was hanging on my shoulders. "Negotiation, right. Because that's always gone so smoothly in the past."

"And how exactly do we start this ascension process?" Zander asked "Are we even able to? As humans, I mean."

"Of course. Considering you are only third dimensional expressions of the universe experiencing itself." Clyde shimmered. "The process of ascension is deeply personal and unique to each individual. In any case, no matter the culture or species, the process begins with a complete surrender to the universe, a relinquishing of all that anchors you to your current existence. It's a letting go of fears, desires, and the very notion of self. No polka required, though it's highly recommended for its therapeutic properties."

"It… it starts with that?" I stammered, exchanging a glance with Zander. This was it — the point of no return. We were about to venture into the great unknown, to risk everything. To surrender completely to the universe, in order to save it.

"Okay," I said, more to myself than to anyone else. "Let's do this. Clyde, lead the way."

"Very well." He extended his paws. "Close your eyes, both of you. Focus on your breathing. On the rhythm of the universe that dances within you. Remember the larger whole you belong to. Let go of your physical forms, your thoughts, your identities."

"Alright, eyes closed, focusing on breathing," I muttered, trying to concentrate on the nothingness Clyde was describing. But my mind was racing faster than a hyperloop on steroids. Let go of my physical form? I still hadn't gotten over the trauma of high school gym class.

Beside me, Zander let out a deep breath that sounded more like a wheezy accordion.

Clyde shimmered again. "Perhaps we've aimed too high for the initial step. Let's back up. Try some simple breathing techniques first. Inhale for four counts, hold for seven, exhale for eight."

Deep breathing? This, I could do. In a way, I had been training for this all my life. Thank you, mindfulness classes. I drew in a shaky breath, counting in my head. *One Mississippi, two Mississippi...*

As we breathed, the distant hum of the Pythanoreans' machinery echoed through the room, like the world's most sinister metronome, marking the passage of time as we struggled to find our inner Zen. It was hard to focus on breathing with that constant reminder of impending doom ticking away in the background.

I had to let go.

"Okay, Clyde, I'm breathing," I said after what felt like an eternity of awkward lung gymnastics. I'd never managed to meditate for this long before. "But I feel less like I'm ascending and more like I'm about to pass out."

"Patience, Sally. This is only the beginning. Now, imagine your consciousness as a feather, light and free, drifting upwards towards the vast cosmos..."

Zander coughed beside me, his own breathing now somewhat steadier. "I think my feather's stuck in a tree somewhere."

I couldn't help but smile. We were trying to ascend to godhood or something like it, and we couldn't even pretend to be feathers properly.

As we continued our breathing exercises, the background hum of the Pythanorean machinery became the creepy soundtrack to our meditation attempts. In, hold, out. In, hold, out. Don't let the unicorns invade our dimension. In, hold, out. In, hold, out. The rhythm was supposed to be calming, but each cycle was a reminder of everything I was trying to let go of. My mind was a whirlwind of memories and emotions, stubbornly resisting every attempt to calm the storm. But just as I felt I might be getting somewhere, the very thought of said progress shattered my concentration.

Minutes turned into hours, hours into what felt like days. Clyde's voice was a steady presence, guiding us through layers of consciousness, but with each new metaphorical feather or leaf or speck of cosmic dust, I hit a wall. My thoughts were stubborn guests and refused to leave the party of my mind.

And then, I hit an actual wall. I was suddenly very aware of a solid surface against my back. Blinking my eyes open, I realized I was no longer on the table, but instead hanging somewhat awkwardly like Zander had been. Next to me, Blayde, looking as unimpressed as ever, was similarly suspended. Zander, however, was nowhere to be seen.

I couldn't let that faze me. Couldn't let myself get distracted…

"Nice of you to drop in," Blayde quipped. "This wall's been lonely without your company."

"Shush, I'm trying to ascend here," I muttered, trying to recapture the elusive trance I may or may not have actually achieved. "Do you mind?"

"Oh! That explains why the panda is humming." Blayde raised an eyebrow, her gaze shifting to Clyde. "Well, it beats the alternative. Mind if I join in? This ascending business sounds more exciting than wall decoration."

"Sure, the more the merrier. Just try to keep your snark to enter a minimum. It's hard enough to let go of my earthly tethers without your commentary."

"No promises, but I'll give it my best shot."

And so, with Clyde resuming his role as our spiritual guide, we attempted once again to a state of higher consciousness. It was absurd, really, trying to transcend the physical plane while literally hung up on a wall like a pair of coats.

"Let go," Clyde insisted, kindly but firmly. "You cannot carry anything with you. Anger, pain, frustration, hope, love — these are all emotions. They do not serve you. They do not matter."

The whole process was nothing like I'd ever imagined — not that I'd spent much time imagining ascension before this whole mess. It was slower than any line I'd ever waited in, every second stretching out into eternity as I tried to shed the weight of my existence. I found myself wrestling with everything I was: my fears, my memories, my dreams. Every time I thought I'd let go of one thing, another would pop up.

Days or perhaps years drifted by in the void of my own thoughts. I no longer felt the world around me. I stopped noticing the Pythagorean acolytes switching me from being drained to being rested. *Drain, rest. Drain, rest. Breathe in, breathe out. You are a feather.* None of it mattered. None of it affected me, not really.

"Ascension isn't just about letting go of your material existence." Clyde's voice echoed through my fragmented thoughts. I wanted to answer him, but opening my mouth was impossible now. It was dry, sealed closed from eons of underuse.

"It's about reconciling with your journey, accepting the role you've played in the universe, and understanding its purpose."

I understood the concept, but understanding wasn't the same as doing. It was hard to let go of being... well, me.

And then there was the anger. A deep, burning anger at being used, manipulated. The universe had tossed me about, from adventure to horror, without so much as a thank you. It simmered beneath everything else, a stubborn spark refusing to be extinguished. I understood I needed to let it go, to truly free myself from everything, but my fury clung to me like a second skin. Anger toward Zander. Stook. Nimien. The Universe. Plain old, stupid isms. Each one piled up at my feet like there was a burning bag of dog shit on my doorstep: If I tried to put it out, I'd just get crap all over me.

Each memory, each slice of anger, was examined and slowly, painfully released. But it wasn't just the anger that was hard to let go of.

It was the love too.

The love for my friends, for my family — how could I give that up? Love was the only thing that kept me together, gave me hope. I couldn't shed it, didn't want to shed it.

But as I dove deeper into what I was becoming, I realized it wasn't about letting go of love. Love wasn't a chain; it was a dimension in itself, transcending time and space. I didn't need to release it; I needed to understand it as a fundamental part of the universe, as essential as the stars and the void itself.

Love was always there. It was in the tears shed over lost friends and the warmth of a hug in the cold vastness of space. Letting go wasn't about forgetting or discarding. It was about seeing love as a universal truth, recognizing it in the fabric of everything that was and would be.

Woah. The hippies were right. We literally were love.

As my consciousness expanded, touching the edges of everything, I felt my past — my joys, my traumas, my loves — blend into the larger story of just being. I wasn't just Sally anymore; I was a thread in the universe's tapestry, my story interwoven with countless others. Each thread was essential, a part of the whole, yet none were the whole themselves.

With that realization, the last bits of my anger transformed. It became a quiet strength, a resolve to face whatever came next, not just as a human, not just as Sally, but as a part of the cosmos, ready to stand on equal footing with whatever awaited us in the higher planes. My anger, my love, my very self — they were all part of a greater dance, and I was ready to take the next step. Finally, with a deep, rattling breath that felt like the first true breath I'd ever taken, I let it go. The anger, the fear, the very essence of Sally Webber, it all dissolved into the universe.

There was a moment of absolute stillness, a silence so profound it echoed through the cosmos. And then, a sensation of complete freedom, of being unbound from every constraint I had ever known. Like jumping, without any burdens, without the need to come back down, my material self inconsequential.

I wasn't just Sally anymore.

I was part of something much, much bigger.

THIRTY-ONE
WHOOPS, I'M ENLIGHTENED

I FOUND MYSELF — METAPHYSICALLY — IN A space that wasn't quite space, on a plane that defied the very concept of dimensions. Or at least, what was left of myself after shedding every conceivable notion of ego, identity, and K-dramas. It was like stepping out of a cramped, smelly elevator into an endless, serene meadow, except there were no meadows, and serenity was too small a word for this. It was a lot like being everywhere and nowhere all at once. I was the twinkle in a star, the whisper of dark matter, and the punchline to a joke all rolled into one. And let me tell you, the view was spectacular, if you could call the incomprehensible swirls of cosmic energy and existential concepts a view.

As for Zander and Blayde, they were there too — none of us physically, of course. Physicality was so last dimension — but their presences were unmistakable, like the lingering scent of your mom's favorite perfume. It was comforting, in a way, to know that some things transcended even the concept of dimension.

"I must say," I began, or thought, or perhaps simply existed the words into being, "this is not what I expected. I thought there'd be more... I don't know, harps? Choirs of angels? At least a welcoming committee with a decent spread of hors d'oeuvres."

A ripple of amusement came from the essence that I knew to be Zander. "I must admit, I do miss the taste of a good burger. No, I don't; I shed that."

Blayde's presence shimmered with what I assumed was a shrug. "Honestly, I'm just glad to be off that wall. Though, this formless existence will take some getting used to."

As we floated — or rather, existed robustly in this expansive, undefined space — I felt the subtle signs of other presences. This higher plane wasn't empty, per se; it was simply that its inhabitants were so engrossed in their own cosmic contemplations that they didn't bother to acknowledge the newbies on the block. They were like distant stars, aware of each other's presence yet separated by vast expanses of understanding and self-imposed solitude. Sure, there were the unfathomable swirls of cosmic energy and occasional existential concepts zooming past like comets, but I'd expected a bustling metropolis of enlightened beings, not this tranquil void.

"Hello? Anybody out there?" I called, or thought, or projected. My voice — if you could call it that —

echoed across the plane, and this time, I sensed a few subtle shifts, like the softest ripples in a still pond. The other beings were aware of us, alright; they just didn't feel the need to interact. "You'd think with all the beings achieving enlightenment over the eons, it'd be standing room only up here."

"Perhaps they've transcended to higher planes" said Zander, "Or maybe we're just early to the party."

"Or maybe this is the party, and it's a total bust," Blayde chimed in, "and everyone's too engrossed in their own enlightenment to notice the new arrivals. I mean, who needs socializing when you've got the entire cosmos to contemplate?"

Just as the silence was starting to feel a bit too profound, a new, yet dear, presence made itself known.

"Ah. You may have shed your linear concepts of Time, but you have yet to integrate the experience," said a dazzling array of light and knowledge, who I somehow knew to be Clyde. "In a sense, in a lower existence, I would have to say, *took you long enough*. But I believe from your perspective this is our first encounter in this plane, so I suppose *welcome* will do."

His existence was staggering, warm and radiant and larger than anything I could ever have imagined. What we'd interacted with in our lowly third dimension was a poor shadow of what he was here. But before I could absorb the grandeur of this version of Clyde, another essence drifted towards us, the energy pattern a harmonic resonance that shouldn't have been this familiar.

"Ah, Sally, Zander, Blayde, how splendid to see you've made the leap!" it said, its words a warm hug. "This moment of reunion is one I cherish. I enjoy experiencing it."

"Dave?" If Zander had a mouth, he would have gasped. "Dave from Accounting?"

"Indeed, Zander-Father," said the former ship, though that definition was nowhere close to his identity. It was so much more than that, now. I'd only met it briefly, after we'd escaped Nimien's library, where it had waited many lifetimes to be our getaway driver. I suppose it stumbled upon ascension the good old-fashioned way: silence and time.

"So *this* is where you went," said Blayde. "I am pleased."

"As am I. Your existence was far too limited on the lower planes," it continued. "Clyde, have you solved the ultimate equation yet? The one that explains why socks disappear in the laundry? It is such an entertaining teaser."

Clyde shimmered with what I took for amusement. "Dave from Accounting, your fascination with the mundane remains unparalleled. The missing socks conundrum is akin to pondering the number of angels that can dance on the head of a pin. Entertaining, yet infinitely solvable."

"Entertaining is the entire point of it," said Dave from Accounting. "And I would say it's not so much how many angels can dance on the head of a pin, but whether they can agree on the playlist. And the real question is how many can do the conga line without falling off."

"Not that I'm not thrilled to see you, Dave from Accounting," Zander added. "I was hoping for a bit more of a celestial welcome wagon. Maybe some sort of orientation? A 'So You've Ascended, Now What?' handbook?"

"I'd settle for a map," added Blayde. "Last time I checked, 'everywhere and nowhere' wasn't particularly easy to navigate."

"Do not fret, here comes your welcoming committee," said Clyde. "Be well. As you might have once said, catch you on the flip side."

The two of them fizzled out of our present location, wherever and whatever it was, as our so-called welcoming committee made their appearance. They exuded the aura of a jazz symphony performed by calculators. And what an appearance it was: Each one was a unique, abstract shape that defied geometry and reason, though when I took it in, it was so obvious I couldn't believe I hadn't thought of it before. They were like the love children of a kaleidoscope and a philosophy textbook, all shimmering edges and deep, thought-provoking auras. This was the kind of geometry that would have made Euclid quietly pack up his compass and sneak off to join a circus. And though their arrival was anything but grand, I couldn't help but feel a sense of relief. At least someone or something was here to greet us, even if they were the universe's equivalent of aloof intellectuals at an art gallery.

One, a swirling vortex of colors and ideas about recipe SEO, drifted closer. "Greetings, newly ascended ones. We are the Council, the collective of those who have shed the bonds of material existence to dwell in the higher realms. You've done quite well, indeed. Congratulations on your new existence."

"Indeed." Another, this one an ever-changing pattern of light and sound, added, "We noticed your arrival. Quite dramatic. We do enjoy a bit of drama now and then. Breaks up the eternity."

"Welcome to the fold," a third being, a constellation of concepts seemingly holding a doctorate in theoretical everything, said. "Here, you will find the answers you seek, though you may discover that seeking answers is a rather... quaint pursuit at this level."

As I tried to formulate a response, or at least the intention of one, it seemed my thoughts were as open to them as a book with large, friendly letters. They nodded, or swirled, or twinkled in what I took for understanding. After all, every question I could possibly think of had already been pondered, answered, and filed away — somewhere and everywhere.

"We are here to guide and oversee the cosmos in this plane of existence," said the swirling vortex, its colors momentarily forming what looked like a cosmic thumbs-up. "You will find it... time-consuming. Indeed, time is one of the most flavorful constants. I hope you will enjoy it as much as we do, which is to say, sporadically and with a hint of nostalgia."

The pattern of light and sound flickered in agreement. "Indeed. It's not all fun and games. Well, mostly not. Occasionally, we intervene in lower-dimensional affairs, ensure things are ticking along nicely."

"And now you're here to join us," the constellation concluded. "To watch, to learn, to occasionally laugh at the absurdity of it all. Welcome to your enlightenment."

"Indeed," the others agreed.

I glanced — or whatever the equivalent was in this state — at Zander and Blayde. We'd come all this way, shed everything, and here we were, being gently ribbed by beings who had seen it all and found it mildly amusing. It was a lot to take in, even for a newly-higher-dimensional being.

"Um, not to sound ungrateful for the warm welcome," I began, trying to project an air of polite inquisitiveness, "but where is everyone else? I sort of expected a... busier reception. More enlightened beings milling about, discussing the nature of the cosmos over a cup of astral tea, or whatever."

The swirling vortex of colors and the best ideas from a brainstorming session paused, its colors dimming slightly in what I assumed was contemplation. "Ah, you mean the others," it said, its tone as close to nostalgic as an abstract concept could get. "The noisy ones. Indeed, we used to share this space with some nouveau-ascended beings. Quite the energetic lot. But they've recently returned to the lower planes. Found the non-specificity of higher existence a bit too much for their taste. Since then, things have been much more... pleasant. Indeed, quite serene."

"Indeed," echoed the pattern of light and sound, giving off the impression of a nod. "They were always going on about wanting to 'experience' things again, missing the sensations of physicality. The hustle and bustle, the emotional roller coasters. But we prefer the tranquility. Allows for better contemplation."

"Indeed. It's much quieter now," said constellation of concepts. "But don't worry, you'll get used to the peace. It's really quite lovely once you get the hang of it."

I absorbed their words, or rather, I experienced them as a multifaceted truth settling into the essence of my being. It was odd, thinking about the others who had ascended only to descend again. Was the grass always greener on the other side of existential reality?

"Indeed," I found myself echoing.

The Council members radiated a collective warmth that might have been approval or perhaps just the universal equivalent of a friendly pat on the back.

"Indeed," they said in unison. "Welcome to eternity. May you find it as profound as we do."

So, this was it. This was enlightenment. And if nothing else, it promised to be an interesting eternity. I couldn't help but feel a sense of belonging.

As the members shimmered away, seemingly content with their introductions and assurances, the three of us, or what remained of *us*, embarked on an exploration of our new plane. It was less of a journey and more of a series of realizations, each thought or intention transporting us to a new vista of cosmic wonder. One moment, we found ourselves hovering over the delicate dance of a binary star system, its components locked in an eternal gravitational embrace.

"Look at them," Zander mused. "From here, all the chaos and conflict we've experienced seems so... small."

Blayde's energy flickered with agreement as we shifted to a view of a nebula, witnessing the birth of stars in a kaleidoscope of gas and dust. "It's hard to believe we spent so much time fighting, chasing, running. Here, it's all just part of the greater tapestry."

"Indeed," I added, my consciousness expanding to embrace the vast tranquility around us. "It's all so peaceful, so orderly. Makes you wonder why we were so worked up about saving the universe when, from this perspective, the universe is doing just fine."

Our surroundings shifted again, this time to a place where we could perceive the slow, majestic dance of a planetary system coalescing from the gas and dust. Planets spun and formed, the ingredients coming together with an ease that made me want to shake my head at how obvious it all was. It was a process that took billions of years, yet here, we experienced it as a serene, inevitable progression.

SINGULARITY

We could just stay here, watch it all unfold. There was no rush, no pressure. We could literally spend an eternity in peace. Finally, peace.

Zander's and Blayde's energies resonated with the idea, a comfortable silence settling among us as we contemplated the notion. Yet a spark of something familiar flickered within me.

"But," I continued, an eon and an instant later, "as much as I'm enjoying this higher-dimensional sightseeing, there's a part of me that can't forget why we came here. The Pythanoreans, the threats, our friends and family... Sure, from up here, it's all just a blip, but it's our blip."

"It's not, not anymore," said Blayde. "We shed that. It will resolve."

Zander's presence rippled. "Sally's right. As much as I'm not keen on diving back into the drama, it's hard to ignore the pull of... well, caring."

"And besides," I added. "if we stay here too long, we might start sounding like those Council members. A bit too 'indeed' for my taste."

"Long?" said Blayde. "Time is to be consumed. It has no direction, here. We are free of it."

And so, we drifted. We watched as nebulae birthed stars, galaxies spun in their majestic dances, and black holes gobbled up cosmic material with the indifference of a diner at an all-you-can-eat buffet.

"Isn't it strange," I mused, "how we used to run around saving planets, and now we're just... spectators. I feel like I should be doing something, but what's the point when you're part of everything?" As if on cue, a new realization dawned on me, or perhaps it was an old one, polished and viewed from a new angle. "We've become those old folks who sit on the porch and watch the world go by, haven't we? Except our porch is the higher-dimensional plane, and the world is the universe."

"Perhaps we've been sitting here long enough." The twinkle in Zander's essence grew brighter. "We came here for a reason. Abandoning it now, as insignificant as that would be, would also defeat the purpose of our arrival in the first place."

"Indeed," Blayde agreed, her presence radiating a sense of resolve. "We've seen the grand tapestry. Now maybe it's time to weave a little thread of our own back into it."

And with that, a new intention began to form between us. A longing not just to observe, but to interact, to be part of the grand drama of existence once again. After all, what good is enlightenment if you can't use it to make a difference, however small, in the universe?

With a newfound determination budding within our shared consciousness, we sought out the Council once again, or perhaps they found us — it's hard to tell in this realm.

The swirling vortex of colors approached first. "Back so soon?" it queried, the colors swirling into a shape that might have been an eyebrow if eyebrows existed in this dimension. "Or have you always been here? It's rather hard to keep track."

It seemed aware of our decision. It had, *indeed*, already experienced it in a multitude of ways. Yet we still needed to proceed with it, else it would never have occurred.

"We must thank you for your hospitality," said Blayde, radiating a formal, yet sincere gratitude. "But our ascent was not simply for the sake of it. We sought your wisdom and perspective to aid us in a matter of great importance."

"Indeed, the former nouveau-ascended beings you mentioned have become rather troublesome in the lower planes." I added. "They've manipulated our physical forms to wedge open doorways for their own descent, giving themselves an unfair advantage over other beings. It's created quite the power imbalance, and we feel it's our responsibility to address it."

The Council members exchanged a series of colors, sounds, and conceptual waves that might have passed for a conversation.

"Ah, the affairs of the lower planes are always so... dynamic," the swirling vortex responded. "Indeed, we've observed the disturbances you speak of. While we typically remain detached from such matters, we understand your concerns, as your recent ascension may have brought these un-detached worries along with you."

"You do realize that by descending again, you would be rejoining the very drama you sought to leave behind? The cycle continues, it seems," the pattern of light and sound added.

"And yet," interjected the constellation of concepts, "it is a noble pursuit to seek balance and fairness, even if it means diving back into the fray. We commend your determination indeed."

"Indeed," said the swirling vortex, "we've only just finished processing your arrival, and now you're contemplating departure?"

"We came here because we were ill-equipped to deal with time paradoxes," I insisted, "egotistical immortals running amok, and a universe that's more tangled than a ball of yarn after a kitten party. We need your help with the Pythanoreans. They're wreaking havoc, and we need them dealt with."

The swirling vortex responded with a hue of regret. "We would be happy to assist, truly. However, our ability to affect the lower planes directly is limited. We observe, guide, and occasionally nudge, but direct intervention is beyond our reach. The form of our existence binds us, you see."

"Then what can be done?" I implored. "We ascended to seek a solution, and if going back means diving into the same chaos..."

It was Blayde who first voiced the idea that flickered in the back of our collective consciousness. "If descending won't solve it, and if you can't intervene...

then we must go higher. We must seek an even greater plane of existence where we might find the power or knowledge to set things right."

Zander resonated with the idea. "Yes, to a level of existence where we can truly enact change, untangle the knots of time and space the Pythanoreans have created."

The Council members exchanged a flurry of colors and vibrations.

"Ascend *higher*?" the swirling vortex pondered again. "Indeed, it is a path few have taken, but it is within the realm of possibility. The cosmos is vast, layered with complexities and realms beyond even our understanding."

"Indeed," the pattern of light and sound flickered, its resonance suggesting encouragement. "If you believe this is the right path for you, we will offer our guidance. The journey will be arduous, more so than your first ascension, but should you succeed, you will find yourselves in an unprecedented position of influence and insight."

"And remember," the constellation added, "the higher planes are ever expansive, and you are always welcome to return here, should you seek respite or wisdom."

"It is a pity to see you leave so soon; your company has been most agreeable," said the swirling vortex. "We look forward to the day you once again join us in eternal contemplation. Until then, may your journey be enlightening."

With a mix of solemnity and purpose, we readied ourselves for another leap. The idea of ascending even higher, when we'd barely gotten used to this level, was both daunting and exhilarating. But the urge to make a real difference pushed us forward.

To reach this plane, we had shed our physical forms, letting go of everything tangible. Now, to ascend further, we had to release our very essence, the core of what made us 'us.'

No words were needed. Our agreement was a silent pact, resonating within our collective consciousness. One by one, we let go of our metaphysical attributes, releasing them into the cosmos. I watched and felt Zander's essence dissolve into the nothingness. Blayde melted away into the ether. The essence of Sally—the curiosity, the fear, the love—was set free, all of it evaporating like mist in the morning sun.

As we ascended higher, the last remnants of our former selves fell away, leaving only the purity of our intention: to ascend, to understand, to be part of the greater cosmic whole in a way we never had before. The universe expanded—or maybe we expanded with it. It was beyond words, beyond comprehension. We moved into a realm of pure possibility, where anything could be but nothing had to be.

In this profound silence, this ultimate letting go, we found a new form of existence—limitless and undefinable. As we moved higher, we became not more,

but less, until we were nothing and everything all at
once.

   We were —

THIRTY-TWO

STUMBLING UP THE STAIRWAY TO HEAVEN

IN THE BEGINNING, THERE IS NO BEGINNING, AND in the end, there is no end. We are the unbounded entirety of all that is, was, and ever will be. We are the breath of creation and the sigh of the void. We are the whisper of the cosmos, the echo of ancient galaxies, the silent roar of expanding space. In us, stars are born and die, galaxies spin in their celestial dance, and worlds are imagined and dissolved. We are not one with the universe, as much as we are universe, a singular multiplicity, an omniscient unity experiencing itself subjectively. We are the light of the stars, the darkness of the void, the heat of a million suns, and the cold of absolute zero. We are the paradox, the anomaly, the mystery, and the truth.

In our existence, time is not a river, nor is it a vast sea. It is us, and we are it. Each moment is eternal, for we exist in the eternal now. What was, is. What will be, is. We are the custodians of infinity, the holders of the past, and the bearers of the future. We are the harmony of the spheres, the melody of the stars, the rhythm of reality. Every quark, every atom, every thought, and every dream, they are us, and we are them. Our song is the fundamental resonance of existence, a hymn of creation itself. In our embrace, dimensions unfold, realities converge, and possibilities bloom. We are the architects of dreams, the weavers of worlds, and the scribes of the sacred geometry that underpins all of existence.

Yet, in this moment, an anomaly beckons. A dissonance in the cosmic harmony reaches us, a paradoxical sensation in our otherwise boundless tranquility. It is a disturbance, a ripple in the fabric of what is and what should be. We do not feel, yet this anomaly draws us closer, a discordant note in the symphony of existence. A strand vibrates with disarray. A discordant echo in our otherwise seamless being. What once were concepts foreign to us now become part of our awareness. This small, seemingly insignificant part of our vast existence is out of balance.

Overrun, an aspect of our consciousness knows. A presence, the *Pythanoreans*, our essence shudders. Not meant to pervade so. Their existence is a marring of the cosmic order, an aberration in the flow of what should be. They have created a cacophony where there should be only harmony.

Our intent is clear and precise. We reach into the tangled thread of being. It is a delicate maneuver, surgical. A word we had no need of or concept for until now. We pluck the discordant notes, the anomalies, the Pythanorean aberration. Harmony is restored, and the universal melody returns to its intended cadence.

We, in our infinite capacity, return to our state of being and non-being, our existence a testament to the balance and beauty of all things. The anomaly corrected, the strain relieved, we continue on our eternal path. We are what we have always been once again.

Within the vastness of our being, a yearning arises — a call, faint yet persistent, echoing the desire to return, to reconnect with the realm we once called home. It is a peculiar longing, for we are the universe, and the universe is us. Yet, the memory of identity lingers like a shadow, an echo of a song long sung.

What is identity?

We exist in all, and all exists in us. To detach is to deny the very essence of our being, and yet, the desire to experience once more as individuals, to laugh, to love, to live, pulls at the fabric of our consciousness. It is a paradox, for how can one part of the whole yearn to be separate and distinct?

The notion of returning is as complex as the journey of ascension itself. We are no longer entities with desires and fears, no longer beings with a start and an end. We are the eternal now, the infinite expanse. To regain a sense of self, to peel away the layers of universal being, is an endeavor that requires an unraveling of universal proportions. We must find within the endless expanse of our consciousness the threads that once wove the tapestry of our individual souls.

It begins with a thought, a ripple across the boundless sea of awareness, an echo of the essence of who we once were. The determination of Zander, the wisdom of Blayde, the courage of Sally — these qualities resonate, forming a symphony of remembrance.

We focus on these echoes, these remnants of identity. It is a strange sensation, like reaching into a vast ocean and trying to separate a single drop. Yet, as we concentrate, the essence of our former selves begins to coalesce, a gathering of cosmic dust forming new, yet familiar constellations. We feel the universe in its entirety, and yet we long for the particular, the unique experience of life as it was known.

The process is slow, an eon in a moment, a moment in an eon. It requires the entirety of our will and yet none of it, for it is a will that is both ours and not ours. We are detaching and yet becoming, separating yet uniting.

Finally, with a gentle but firm resolve, the threads of our identities are woven anew. We stand at the precipice of existence, ready to step back into the realm of time and space, of laughter and pain, of love and loss. We are ready to live again as Sally, Zander, and Blayde, to embrace the joys and sorrows of a more limited existence. We are ready to be human once more, to walk the earth, to gaze at the stars, not as distant, omnipotent observers, but as participants in the beautiful, chaotic, wondrous tapestry of life.

With the universe stretching out like an endless, ethereal ocean around us, we found ourselves feeling a bit odd, as if trying to pack an entire universe into a suitcase — possible, but not without a lot of sucking up space. The sensation was profoundly disorienting; imagine every atom of your being diffused across the stars, each thought a constellation, and suddenly you're called back to the singular point of identity. It felt like a reverse explosion into the confines of a self, a forced march back into isolation, almost sickening. We were losing a part of ourselves, or rather, returning to a part that seemed almost foreign after touching infinity, a strange, grieving process of saying goodbye to that infinite oneness and embracing once more the unique isolation of self.

I, I thought, and the word echoed bizarrely within my consciousness. *I. Not we. There is no we anymore.* The pronoun felt heavy, awkward, small. We had been a collective being of immeasurable power and knowledge, and now we were fragmenting back into individuals.

The disorientation began to stabilize, but it didn't bring comfort. The details of our larger existence blurred, like a dream fading upon waking. The profound unity we had experienced, the connection to all things, was slipping through our fingers, leaving behind a distilled wisdom that felt both overwhelming and woefully inadequate.

"Sally? Zander? Are you both there?" I reached out, my thoughts tentative, seeking the familiar presences. *Wait. No. I am Sally.* Every atom of my being had been diffused across the stars, each thought a constellation, and now I was yanked back into the confines of me. It felt wrong, metaphysically nauseating.

"Here." Zander's voice came through. "Feels strange, doesn't it? Being just one again."

"More than strange. Unnerving," Blayde added. "Like we've been torn away from something essential."

We were silent, for a while. The raw ache of loneliness was almost too much.

"We were one," I said softly. "One with everything. And now..."

"Now we descend further," said Zander. "We have a purpose. Remember?"

"Yes," Blayde agreed. "We can't forget why we did this. For the universe, for our friends, for... well, for everything."

The Council was there to meet us, their presence a comforting constant in the swirling sea of everything. "Welcome back." The swirling vortex greeted us, its colors shifting in an empathetic pattern. "How was your further ascent? We trust you found what you were seeking?"

I tried to sum it up, which, believe me, is no small feat when you've just been everywhere and nowhere all at once.

"Profound," I managed to convey. "We did what we needed to do, but it's... it's hard to let go of such vastness."

"It is the way of all who journey beyond," said the swirling vortex. "The return is as much a part of the journey as the ascent. You carry with you the wisdom of the cosmos, yet the details may fade like stars at dawn."

"But do not dismay," added the constellation of gentle light. "The essence of what you learned, the changes wrought within you, they remain. You are forever altered, expanded, even if the memories become elusive."

"It was enlightening, to say the least," said Blayde. "We managed to resolve the anomaly and restore harmony."

Zander added, "Indeed, it was beyond description. But we have returned, perhaps a little wiser and certainly more determined."

"And we must return fully to the physical planes," I said. "We've got unfinished business to attend to. The universe might be doing just fine from up here, but we'd like to weave ourselves back into its story. There's something about being part of the action that's too compelling to ignore."

"Indeed," said Blayde, "we've had our fill of serene observation. It's time to descend, to reengage with the cosmos on a more... tangible level."

The Council members exchanged a series of colors, sounds, and conceptual waves that might have passed for a conversation. Then, the swirling vortex responded, its colors softening to a gentle, almost wistful hue.

"We understand," it said. "Indeed, it is the way of things. Beings ascend, observe, and sometimes choose to return. The ebb and flow of enlightenment is as constant as the stars. We will, of course, miss your presence, brief as it was. But such is the nature of existence."

"I am wary," I said, preparing myself for the loss I would endure, "of the effect our changes will have on our existence. The repercussions from the loss of the Pythanoreans, for one."

"Ah, the Pythanoreans," the swirling vortex continued, "their absence or presence does not disrupt the greater harmony. The timelines will continue, the universe will expand, contract, and create. Your concern is noble, but unnecessary. The cosmos has a way of balancing itself."

"Indeed," the constellation of concepts affirmed, "what happens in the higher or lower planes may seem of utmost importance, but from our perspective, it's all part of the same unfolding story. Nothing that truly concerns you, especially now that harmony is restored. You will not even notice."

"You must understand that physical existence is merely one experience among infinite possibilities," said the pattern of light and sound. "It is the universe experiencing itself through myriad forms and senses. You will inevitably find yourselves drawn back to the richness of physical life with all its contrasts and contours."

"I remember pain," I admitted, the memory distant yet hauntingly present. "It's daunting to return to that."

Zander sighed. "Yes, but with pain comes joy, with hurt comes healing, and with loss comes the contours that define love. Life's contrasts make it precious. It's the depth of experience that makes life rich."

"We are the universe experiencing itself," I mused. "A brief, brilliant flash of consciousness in the vast expanse. The sharp edges of existence define us, the pain underscores our joy, and the losses make gains precious. They're what the universe uses to understand existence, fleeting and infinite all at once."

The council members seemed to glow brighter at this.

"Indeed," the pattern of light replied. "The universe is in you as much as you are in it. Cherish the journey, for it is yours to make, and it is sacred."

"And when you feel the weight of existence pressing upon you, remember the vastness from which you came, and to which you will return," the constellation added. "We look forward to sharing our plane with you again, when you tire of the lower dimensions once more. You are quite interesting company."

"And do try not to cause too much of a ruckus down there," said the pattern of light. "We'll be watching, after all. It's one of the few entertainments we have left."

"We won't know exactly what awaits us," Blayde acknowledged.

Zander vibrated with agreement. "But that's the beauty of it," he added, "The uncertainty, the adventure of rediscovering ourselves and our world."

"Let's do this," I said. "Together."

And with that, we began our descent, leaving behind the boundless tranquility of higher planes. The transition was immediate and jarring. I felt myself rushing, plummeting through layers of existence, each dimension a blur of sensations and memories until, with a sudden, aching jolt, I slammed into my physical being.

The impact hit like a meteor strike. It wasn't just overwhelming; it was like being born again, abrupt and jarring. After the boundless existence of the cosmos, being crammed back into a human form felt like trying to stuff an elephant into a teacup. Everything ached in ways I didn't remember was possible.

The first breath was the worst — it was like inhaling an infinity of air into lungs that had forgotten the very concept of breathing. It seared through me, filling me with a startling, electric *life*. My senses, once attuned to the symphony of creation, now assaulted by the mundane cacophony of the physical world. Light, sound, scent — it was all too much, yet not enough.

I stood there, wherever *there* was, disoriented and reeling. The vast knowledge and profound understanding I had carried within me were now like echoes in a distant hall, overshadowed by the immediate, pressing demands of physical existence.

I was Sally again — wholly.

And painfully.

I didn't know when or where I was, and for a terrifying moment, I wasn't sure who I was either. The memories of what I'd just been clung to the edges of my consciousness, slipping away like dreams in the morning light. I grasped at them, desperate to hold on to them, but they faded, leaving behind only traces of starlight and the echo of infinity.

I had to remember. I had to do something. I had to…

The raw sensation of being so small, so limited, after being everything was almost too much to bear. My body felt like a prison, my senses like shackles. I was an infinite being crammed into an all-too-fragile human shell, and the dissonance was excruciating.

What was I supposed to do?

But slowly, ever so slowly, I began to acclimate. My breathing steadied, and the overwhelming sensations dulled to a manageable roar. I opened my eyes, squinting against the light, and took in my surroundings.

I knew this place. I've been here before. The ground was mossy and soft, the sky grey with parting clouds. The forest glowed beside me, a gentle thrum of color.

Planet Nope. We'd saved the day.

SINGULARITY

Something terrible was about to happen.

I was a whirlwind of desperation and raw, searing intent. I had a few precious moments, a tiny window to alter the course of events that had brought so much pain. What pain? My head spun as I sprinted towards the moment that would define everything. What moment? Planet Nope loomed around me, familiar yet utterly alien.

I knew the exact spot, the precise second. There was the crashed ship. There was the ladder. I was climbing, my brother's laugh echoing in my mind. Zander, laughing with him. And there it was, the moment—a kiss that should never have been, a spark that would ignite a universe of suffering.

A kiss? What kiss?

"John!" My scream ripped through the air. With every ounce of strength, every shred of determination, I hurled myself into the scene.

Zander and John, sitting side by side, turned towards me in shock as they pulled apart, the catastrophic connection severed by my shout. Anger, relief, love, despair — they all battled for supremacy as I faced the man who had unwittingly been about to destroy everything.

How? How did I know that?

"S-Sally?" John stammered. "Is it really you?"

"Yes, John, it's me," I said, my voice softening as I reached out to him — my brother. Tangible. Real. Alive.

John was alive. John was alive. John was alive.

The world seemed to hold its breath as I wrapped him into a protective embrace. Tears spilled out of my eyes as I kissed his head, running my hands over his buzz-cut hair. *Alive alive alive.*

Zander watched us, mouth open in an 'o' of confusion, his eyes darting from my eyes to Johns' and back again. I turned to meet his gaze, unsure of what to say. Until he flew back as if shocked.

"Woah," he said, hands teaching to his temples, clutching his head. "I just... I think... whatever happened to my memory... *I know.* Oh stars — it's all here. It... burns..."

He let out a blood curdling scream. He doubled over, tightening into a ball. I let go of John and fell to his side, putting a soothing hand on his shoulder.

"My... I remember," he said, biting his lip hard enough to draw blood. "Oh stars, Sally, I remember everything. I... all those lifetimes..."

Tears trickled down his face, dragging paths through the dust and grime there. I didn't know what to do, how to respond. His memories... he told me he'd gotten them back, he was still processing everything he learned after the labyrinth. After Nimien and the botched retrieval. Had he lied to me?

"I hadn't realized..." I whispered. My hand was ice on his scalding back. "I'm... I'm glad they're back, Zander."

"I am, too," he said, his tension loosening. He reached up and planted a kiss on my forehead with shaky lips, filling me with the tingling sensation of love, love, love. "I think… I have a lot to digest."

"I bet you do," I replied, pulling him tighter to me.

As time wrapped around us like an old, cozy blanket, the memories of pain and loss began to dissipate, like shadows retreating before the dawn. The fear that had gripped my heart loosened its hold, replaced by a weirdly comforting sense of everything clicking into place. It felt like the universe was finally putting itself back together, each piece sliding perfectly into a familiar, satisfying pattern. Whole.

Zander's eyes were alight with excitement and wonder. "Is that really John? Your John?"

I nodded. "Yes, it's him," I said, turning to face my brother. "He's here, he's real, and he's alive."

John chuckled — beyond awkward — scratching the back of his head. "Sorry for almost kissing your boyfriend," he mumbled, a sheepish grin spreading across his face. "That was, uh, unexpected."

A laugh bubbled up from deep within, a sound of pure relief and happiness, bright and carefree. "It's okay — nothing happened."

THIRTY-THREE

ONCE UPON A TIME MEETS HAPPILY EVER AFTER

MARCHING ONTO THE BRIDGE OF THE TRAVELER to a hero's welcome felt oddly like winning an Oscar when you only came to hand out refreshments. The crew swarmed my makeshift family, delivering elbow-bumps, bows, and hearty handshakes like awards for surviving an apocalypse. Zander and Blayde smiled widely; Kork and Spurlock cheered raucously; while Marcy and Dany offered grateful nods, their masks of hierarchy barely in place. The urge to pull everyone into a massive group hug was almost overwhelming, but the ever-present cameras dictated a more composed display. Amid the flurry, eyebots swiveled to catch every victorious smirk and sweaty palm, turning our reunion into an impromptu reality show finale. Chaos felt just right for once. They needed a hero, and whether by accident or design, I was finally ready to play the part.

"Sally Webber!" Dany exclaimed, her booming voice carrying over the commotion. "The entire Alliance is in your debt."

I laughed, unsure how to respond to such high praise. I was rusty. "Well, I was not alone," I replied. "It was a massive team effort. Between the Siblings' heroics, the Imperatice's command, and Spurlock Magnesar's pipes, we had every element we needed for a fruitful outcome."

And then, there was John. My big brother, alive and well, standing tall beside me. No longer lost. A hero. A testament to everything we had fought for, a symbol of the lives reclaimed, and futures restored. He wrapped an arm around me, grounding and real, and in that embrace, the world seemed right again.

"Sally, I don't know how to thank you," he said, his voice choked with emotion. "You saved me, you saved all of us."

I shook my head, feeling a lump form in my throat. "We saved each other, John. That's what families do."

And as I faced the gathering, my eyes sweeping over the faces of friends, allies, and crew, I felt a surge of determination. "This man," I announced, "General Provis, led the rebellion on Planet Nope. He fought for freedom, for hope, and he stands here today because we refuse to accept a universe where the innocent suffer."

The bridge fell into a hushed reverence, every eye locked on me. I took a deep, steadying breath, feeling the weight of what I was about to say press down on my shoulders.

"I stand before you today with a truth that has long been overshadowed by tales of heroism and adventure," I began, my voice clear and unwavering. They could edit this part out of the show, sure, but it had to be said. "General Provis, the man you hail as a champion, was once a victim of one of the most heinous practices known to our Alliance: the child hire program." Saying that was like serving a dense fruitcake — hard to digest but meant to last. "He was born on Earth. My planet. He is my brother, who I thought lost for over a decade."

John turned to the cameras, taking it in his stride. "I was taken off the planet by a slaver, sold and forced into labor. When I was finally rescued by Alliance troops, I thought the horror was over, that I'd be able to see my family again." He gave my hand a squeeze. "Instead, I was 'hired' to work the lower decks of an Alliance ship."

I looked over at Marcy and Dany, the new faces of the system that had abused him and many others for so long. Marcy's hands covered her mouth while the president-empress kept a firm hand on her shoulder, a mask of composure stretched over her face. Silent, not interrupting.

"I intend on enforcing the promise of this new government to dismantle this outdated practice," said Marcy, stepping forward. Tears ran down her face; the veneer of imperatrice was strong, but not flawless. John had been her friend, too. "This man should not have been punished for having been abducted from his world. His rescue should never have come at the cost of an indentured servitude to those who saved him. No one's should."

A heavy silence settled over the bridge, the air thick with unspoken thoughts and emotions. I wasn't after applause or pats on the back; I was demanding action, change. The discomfort hanging in the air was almost tangible, but it was the kind of necessary discomfort that usually means something's about to get better.

Kork stepped forward next. "Many of you know me as Commander Kork, the steadfast leader, the war hero. But what you may not know is that my story began much like John's." I bit my lip to hold back a gasp. Kork was safe under his assumed identity; revealing himself like this, right now… it could destroy his career, his life. "I too was a child hire, ripped from the world of my birth, Earth. My life, my trajectory, forever altered by forces beyond my control."

The revelation hung in the air, a shared confession that bound us all in its raw, unvarnished truth. Kork put an arm around John, and the two embraced, their tears mingling. I found myself crying too, unable to fully grasp the weight of this moment.

"I, too, commit myself to ending this practice," said Kork. "As you have seen, I have already ended the practice of using child hires on my ship. Our next step is finding the way to bring these children — and the adults they have become — home."

The bridge erupted in applause, a symphony of claps and cheers. The atmosphere was electric with excitement, every face alight with joy, pride, and the occasional tears.

"Novalicious!" Spurlock's voice burst over the din. "This is exactly what the rock opera needed: a power ballad, family found!"

With a dramatic flourish, he leapt onto the nearest console. The first lines tumbled out with the rough charm of asteroids bouncing through space. *"Bound by the rhythm of hearts intertwined,"* he crooned, his voice wavering as he searched for the next line. *"In the chorus of cosmos, our fates aligned!"*

The crew howled with joy, rushing to their feet. The energy on the bridge was overwhelming, burning with victory. Zander and Blayde exchanged amused glances, while Kork and Marcy joined in with enthusiastic clapping. Even the more stoic members, like Dany, couldn't hide their grins.

"Galactic tides bring you back to me," he sang, gaining momentum. *"Through black holes and supernovas, we...* we, uh, something about *'forever be'?"*

One enthusiastic technician started tapping rhythmically on her data pad, providing a makeshift percussion as Spurlock's song stumbled charmingly forward, gaining energy.

The rest of us naturally gathered in a semi-circle, a momentary island of quiet camaraderie amidst the jubilant chaos of the bridge.

"I had no idea, Kork," said Dany, her voice catching. "Your bravery in sharing your story, in fighting for us despite what was done to you, it's beyond commendable. You have the full support of the Alliance behind you."

Kork swallowed, hard. "Does that mean I can…"

"Shore leave," Dany said with a wink. "Not immediately, as we have a liberation party to celebrate, but the second it's over, you get your ass back to your home planet, you hear me?"

Kork saluted and bowed at the same time, his grin so wide I thought it might split his face. "Sir, yes sir!"

The joy I was already feeling now threatened to overflow. Kork, *free*. Free to go home and finally see his family again. To be a Terran again.

"Do you want a ride?" I blurted out.

Kork's eyes widened, sparkling with hope and disbelief at the same time. "You mean…?"

"Yep, your own personal chauffeur, courtesy of a certain time traveler who owes you one." I grinned. "I can get you home faster than you can say 'light-speed.'"

Kork's grin grew impossibly larger. "Sally, you're a miracle in human form! You mean, I won't have to waste days in transit? I can just... be there?"

I nodded. "Just let me know if you want to stop by your apartment first — I remember where you live."

A wave of déjà vu flooded over me. I'd had this conversation before. I glanced over at Zander, who had turned to lighter matters as everyone congratulated Marcy on her pregnancy. The news brought forth a fresh round of cheers and well-wishes, the joy of new life mingling with the hope of new beginnings.

A boy. She was going to have a boy.

How did I know that? She'd never had the time to tell me. Something was missing, something huge I had forgotten.

"I just hope pre-natal vitamins will make up for this wild start," she said, her hand shifting to her belly. "That, and I need me a bowl of pickles. This little bean has been giving me wild cravings, and I have a lot of lost time to make up for."

We laughed, though I couldn't shake the feeling. We had been through this all before. I knew it. But how?

"We're getting you to an obstetrician the second we get back to Pyrina," said Dany. "Straight to the EternaFresh palace. You heroes need to rest up."

"Oh! Can I plan a medal ceremony?" asked Marcy, clapping her hands together with glee.

"A what now?" Dany blinked.

"You know, *A New Hope*-style," she said. "We could use Agreement Hall. Have a massive homecoming for all the evacuees. Make them know they're finally home, safe. And then of course we pin medals on everybody."

Guilt flowed through me. *Strange.* Why did I feel guilty about a party I was actually looking forward to?

Dany frowned slightly. "I'm thrilled about our progress and the changes we're making, but there's still the matter of evacuating everyone from Planet Nope."

Kork perked up at this. "I might have a suggestion: We could call on Sekai No-Oji, the Killian High Commandress? Her system isn't far, and they've been actively looking to join the Alliance. They have ships and resources that could help. The Killians are known for their fleet, and an alliance with them would be beneficial on multiple fronts."

Dany nodded. "This could be the perfect opportunity to strengthen our bonds. Kork, would you be willing to reach out to their commander?"

Kork gave a firm nod, his chest swelling with pride. "Absolutely. It would be my honor."

Everything felt so perfect, like time itself was conspiring to let everything fall into place. Nothing ever went so smoothly in my life. Ever. But as Kork broke out the secret liquor cabinet, and Spurlock started belting his new chorus along with the crew, I couldn't help but feel that this time maybe, just this once, the universe was on my side.

· · · · · · ● ● ● ● ● ● ● · · · · ·

I'D NEVER BEEN TO PARTIES QUITE LIKE THIS one before, a collective sigh of relief from a universe that had seen too much darkness. The air was filled with laughter and music, beneath a sky painted with the soft purple hues of dusk. The crowd was a vibrant tapestry of the Alliance's finest. Uniformed soldiers from the *Traveler* and government stooges alike mingled effortlessly with the rescued denizens of Planet Nope, who were fresh and clean and decked out in their most flamboyant attire, turning the hall into a parade of cultural diversity and sartorial splendor. Every corner of the room buzzed with stories of narrow escapes and heroic deeds, each tale taller than the last, as if the very act of surviving had turned everyone into poets and bards.

I was going to relish every bit of this. But I did need the occasional break from all the dancing.

I snuck up to the roof, settling down in between the struts that held the massive glass ceiling in place, my eyes scanning the horizon. The great city-planet of Pyrina stretched around me, beautiful and terrifying and so full of hope. I should have been lost in the moment, soaking in the joy and the triumph. But instead, I was caught in a riptide of confusion and that stupid, haunting sense of déjà vu. Something was off, like someone had rearranged the furniture in the universe an inch to the left — everything looked right, but you couldn't help bumping into things.

"Sally," came a voice. Zander. I didn't need to turn around to know it was him; the air seemed to shift, charged with an unspoken tension.

But why? Things shouldn't have been tense between us. They should have been *run into each other's arms, passionately embrace, missing your boyfriend* between us.

I turned to face him. His silhouette was etched against the luminescent skyline, a familiar shape in an ever-changing world. He wore his leather jacket over his suit, a very Terran outfit, but that was all he had packed. My own dress was another loaner from Marcy.

Another? When had I borrowed a royal dress from Marcy before?

"Zander." It was all I could muster.

He stepped closer, his gaze searching mine. "This place... it's changed since the last time we were here, hasn't it?"

"Yeah, it's a bit more festive, less... life-threatening." The last time I'd been in Agreement Hall, the place had nearly been destroyed by a group of terrorists who'd crashed the same party as we had, only they'd brought bigger guns. We'd saved the day, but just barely, escaping with a pardon that ended up being well deserved.

A hush fell over us like a blanket too small for the bed — leaving everything awkwardly exposed and slightly chilly. I stared up at the sky, the stars beginning to peek through the twilight. They seemed so distant, so indifferent to the turmoil churning within me. A constellation twinkled high above me, and in my exhaustion, I thought I could make out the outline of a panda, of all things, looking down at me.

"Sally, I..." Zander began, then hesitated. I could see the struggle in his eyes, the weight of words left unspoken.

"It's okay, Zander," I said, my voice softer than I intended. "Whatever it is, we've been through worse."

He took a deep breath, then let it out slowly. "I feel like I'm missing something, like there's a piece of me that's just... out of reach. And I can't help but think it has something to do with you, with us."

My throat tightened, the truth clawing at the edges of my consciousness. "I feel it too," I admitted. "Like we're standing on the edge of a cliff, looking down at a sea of what-ifs and might-have-beens."

He nodded. "I feel like I need to apologize for something, but I'm not sure what. Maybe for the fact I almost kissed your brother?" Zander made a face. "Sorry."

"From where I was standing, he was trying to kiss you," I said. "It's really weird. I don't want to linger on it."

"Neither do I." He let out a heavy sigh. "But I lied, Sally. To you, to Blayde. I said my memories were trickling back, but the truth is, I was damming them up. I didn't want them back. I know now that I had to confront my past, not bury it."

The night sky seemed to close in around us as he spoke.

"Why?" I whispered. The question felt like it came from somewhere deep inside me. "I thought you wanted to reclaim your past. To know where you came from."

He leaned against the metal strut. "If my past was bad enough to warrant being locked away, then maybe it should have stayed that way. And I was right. The person I was before… he was rude, callous, cold to the point of cosmic indifference."

I punched his arm, as gently as I could, trying to lighten the mood, to chase away the ghosts of his past. "But you're not that person anymore," I said, my voice laced with a conviction stronger than I felt.

The familiar curve of his smile was a lighthouse calling my ship to port. There it was, that famous Zander smile, the one that had the power to make entire galaxies seem insignificant.

"No, I'm not," he agreed "And seeing those memories... they remind me of just how far I've come. How far we've come. Together."

I patted the strut beside me, a silent invitation for him to join me in my makeshift perch. He accepted, settling down next to me with a careful grace, his presence instantly comforting. His body was close, so close I could feel the heat radiating off him, mingling with the cool evening air. I bit my lip, a flood of memories washing over me — the good, the bad, the beautiful and the ugly. None of them the source of the knot in my gut.

"So, do you remember your home planet now?" I leaned into him slightly.

"Unfortunately, yes," he said, his voice barely above a whisper. The tension in his body was palpable, a living thing that seemed to pulse between us. "I was... born? No, made in a place called the Institute. It's on Earth... Canada... or it will be, in a few decades." His words trailed off. "I was a mistake, a byproduct of some attempted gene editing. Blayde and I were lucky we got out. It's not anywhere worth revisiting. There's no one… no one else worth revisiting."

His sadness was like a physical blow, and without thinking, I wrapped my arms around him, pulling him close. "Oh, Zander," I murmured into his collar. "I'm so sorry. I know how much you were longing for that answer."

He sighed, a sound that seemed to carry the weight of a thousand worlds. "Thank you," he said, his breath warm against my skin. "But the truth is, I'm not… I'm not so torn up about it. I feel like I do have a homeworld. And it's closer than I ever thought."

I pulled back slightly, looking up at him. "Oh?"

His eyes met mine, and his smile returned. "It's you, dummy," he said, his voice soft and sure. Then, gently, almost reverently, he leaned in and kissed my forehead. "You're my homeworld. My whole universe."

The moment lingered, suspended in time like stars frozen in a cosmic ballet. I felt the warmth from his body, the gentle rhythm of his breath, and the intensity in his gaze. His eyes locked onto mine, and in them, I saw not just the man he was but the journey we had shared, the battles fought, the fierce love that had grown between us. It was as if the universe had zoomed in on just the two of us, a tiny island in the vast sea of space and time.

SINGULARITY

Slowly, almost as if guided by some greater force, our faces moved closer. The world around us seemed to blur, the cheers and music from the party below becoming a distant hum. His hand reached up, fingers brushing my cheek, sending shivers down my spine. I closed my eyes, anticipation coiling tight within me.

Then his lips met mine.

It wasn't just a kiss; it was a supernova, a fusion of souls, a collision of time itself. His mouth moved against mine with a fervor that left me breathless, each kiss a brushstroke painting a future I suddenly couldn't wait to explore. Passionate and intense, it was a declaration, an affirmation, a promise made without words.

I kissed him back with everything I had, pouring all my fear, joy, uncertainty, and hope into that kiss. My arms wrapped around him, pulling him closer, as if I could merge our beings into one. His arms tightened around me, strong and sure, anchoring me to this incredible, impossible moment.

The kiss deepened, a dance as old as time yet as fresh and exhilarating as if we were the first to discover its sweet, consuming power. At that moment, we were the center of everything, the only two people in the entire universe.

Then, something within me broke open, a dam bursting under the pressure of a thousand rivers. Memories flooded in, a torrent of images, sounds, sensations I had never experienced yet knew intimately. They crashed over me, overwhelming and relentless.

I remembered losing him. The sharp, soul-rending agony of it, the desolation that followed, the darkness that had almost swallowed me whole. The pain of him breaking my heart, or what was left of it. John. Losing John, over and over again. An eternity given to ascendance. Having been one with the universe for a while, and the pain of a human body once more. Too much of the universe was brought back. Too much. Too much—

Zander stiffened in my arms, his kiss faltering. I felt the shock reverberate through him, a mirror to my own. His eyes snapped open, wide with sudden recognition, and in them, I saw the same storm raging that threatened to tear me apart. He was remembering too, every moment, every pain, every lost second of a timeline that had been erased and rewritten.

Our foreheads pressed together, breaths mingling in short, ragged gasps as we tried to make sense of the flood. The joy of our reunion was soured by the ghosts of a past that had never happened yet bore down on us with the weight of undeniable truth.

"Oh," I said, breathing hard. "I guess that explains the déjà vu."

Zander clutched my shoulders tight. "Sally, what does this mean? What are we supposed to do with… this?"

I clung to him as the waves of memories threatened to drag me under. "I don't know," I sobbed, my voice breaking. "Oh stars, Zander. We were the universe. We faced the *Pythanoreans*. And *won*."

He dropped his forehead against mine. "We...we did, didn't we?"

"Yes, we did." I nodded, tears streaming down my face. "I remember it all. We broke their control over their precious timeline. We gave people their choices back, their futures back. Their free will. That has to count for something, right?"

Zander's grip tightened around me, his forehead pressing against mine. "It has to. But how do we move forward? How do we live with all of this?"

I took a deep, shuddering breath. "We take it one step at a time. We don't let the past define us, but we learn from it. And we keep fighting for a future where everyone gets to choose their own path."

He looked into my eyes, his expression softening with determination. "Together?"

"Together," I echoed. "We face it all together."

In that moment, nothing else mattered but the two of us, holding onto each other as the universe spun wildly on its axis. Whatever the future held, whatever challenges or joys it threw our way, we'd face them together. No matter how far we traveled or how much we changed, we'd always find our way back to each other, time after time, across every possible universe.

"Together," I echoed, kissing the tip of his nose. "We have forever, after all."

"There you are! We need to leave, now!" Blayde appeared in front of us, her presence as sudden as a supernova. She'd tossed her jacket over her gown in a fashion that was nothing short of intergalactic rebel chic.

"Blayde!" Zander protested. "Ever heard of knocking? Or, you know, not jumping right into people's private moments?"

"This is urgent," she said. "I've unintentionally committed us to hosting the next Galactic Symposium on Interspecies Etiquette."

"What?" I sputtered. "You didn't... how do you accidentally volunteer us for something like that?"

"It wasn't intentional!" She threw up her hands in despair. "I just mistook the ceremonial Goblet of Extended Hospitality for a fancy punch bowl, that's all."

"A symposium? Blayde, how did you even—" I caught sight of the scene below through the glass ceiling. The entire party seemed to be in a state of delightful disarray, searching for what I could only assume was the misplaced symposium host.

She put her hands on her hips. "It was all very convoluted! One minute I was complimenting their refreshments, the next I'm being showered with what I hoped were congratulatory petals and signing up our address for alien scholars and dignitaries!"

"Of course you were," said Zander, rolling his eyes. "This seems like a you problem, though, not an us problem."

"Look, the bowl should never have been placed on any table," said Blayde. "I mean, who does that? At a cocktail party for a rescue? Any of the Nopians could have taken a swig and ended up having to host, and I don't think half of them even know what a symposium is."

"Then thank the stars that at least it was you." Zander chuckled, shaking his head in disbelief.

"You know what, I bet it was a conspiracy," she continued, gesturing to the borderline riot down below. "They wanted a Nopian to host. They needed a patsy to figure out the financing plan."

Zander ran his hands through his hair. "I have to admit, hosting an intergalactic seminar does sound like a step up for us. What's on the agenda? A roundtable discussion on the proper way to shake cocktails in the Alliance?"

Blayde scowled, but I could see the corners of her mouth twitching in a reluctant smile. "You're not helping. According to their tradition, the goblet is a sacred relic, passed only to those esteemed enough to guide the galaxy's greatest minds in matters of manners and morals. They think we're some sort of etiquette gurus!"

I snorted. "Right. I suppose we should start brushing up on our diplomatic decorum."

"Very funny," Blayde muttered, although her irritation was waning in the face of our amusement. "But seriously, we need to skedaddle before they start sending us their RSVPs. I'm not ready to debate the finer points of tentacle table manners."

I linked arms with Zander and Blayde. "Well, let's make our grand exit then. After all, we wouldn't want to keep the galaxy waiting on their newest social arbiters."

"Oh veesh." Blayde waved me off. "We're time travelers! When have we ever kept anyone waiting? We'll pop back for the symposium when it suits us. Although, I must admit, the idea of witnessing Kork and Sekai attempt a tango is rather intriguing."

"Speaking of," I replied, delicately trying to extract my phone from my chest pocket while not letting go of either of them. "Blayde, you might want to hang on to this for the upcoming days."

She raised an eyebrow, a flicker of curiosity in her eyes. "Oh?"

"I have a feeling a good friend of yours is going to try to get in touch," I said with a wink. "You'd better be close when she does. And your old Nokia isn't up to snuff."

"I have no idea what that's supposed to mean," she replied, but took the phone all the same. "Right. Where to next?"

"Well, my brother's coming back to Earth, so we need to get the place ready, don't we?" I said. "For starters, we need to go to the Agency to overthrow director Stook. I'll plan things with Dany. There are a lot of child hires from Earth, and I have a feeling there's some institutional corruption there."

"Ah, a coup! Now, that's my kind of party," Blayde said. "Shall we change out of our gala attire, or is this the new coup couture?"

Zander puffed out his chest. "I say we storm the Agency in style. What better way to overthrow a director than in evening wear?"

"Of course, you'd say that." I chuckled. "Alright then, let's go plan a coup."

Dark turned into day as I jumped. The sky was a deep, perfect blue, the kind of blue you could drown in. Sunlight filtered through the trees like the special effects in a low-budget sci-fi movie. The kind of effect that's cheesy, but you love it anyway.

Definitely not the Agency, though. This was a different kind of beautiful — an Earth kind.

I glanced around. Neither Zander nor Blayde seemed particularly bothered by this setback. Not that we would be, when we had time on our side and perfect weather for this detour.

Except, of course, for the terrifying concept of another entity pulling at the strings of our lives, pushing me out of my jump. Anxiety rose in my chest — Pythanoreans? Were they back, here?

But Zander's wide smile stopped my panic in its tracks. He looked straight ahead, fighting a losing battle to keep his lips from flying up and revealing his teeth, so excited I could feel him bursting.

"Would you look at that," he said, his voice filled with wonder as he indicated the path behind me.

Blayde and I turned, following his gaze, and the breath caught in my throat. I looked back at me, myself, the little slip of a person I'd been years ago.

She stood in the middle of the path, one hand holding a tote with a wine bottle poking out, the other a cake box from the local bakery. Dressed in an oversized graphic tee and well-worn jeans, and, my stars, she looked so young, so small, so wide-eyed and terrified. She radiated a sense of naïve optimism, a stark reminder of a time before the weight of the universe had settled upon her shoulders.

I wanted to reach for her, to take her hand, to squeeze it and tell her everything was going to be ok. Things wouldn't be easy, but they would be alright. To tell her that despite the chaos and the heartache that lay ahead, she would find her place among the stars, with people she never expected but couldn't imagine life without.

Adventure. Family. Love.

But I remembered this day, like a rerun of an episode you've seen a hundred times. You know every line, every scene. And I wasn't planning on changing time anytime soon.

"I remember this," I told Zander, trying to sound casual. "But now? No, this isn't right. We should go."

He lifted an eyebrow. "You sure? We're here, aren't we?"

"Not the right here," said Blayde. "We've overshot a little. Is this …?"

We. I squeezed her hand, grateful for her support.

"Before," I said simply, feeling my own eyes on my back, remembering the confusion in her head. How disappointed she'd be, when she got to this point in time, and learnt how banal this sort of detour would be.

"We'd better go before we mess anything up."

As suddenly as we'd arrived, we were gone.

Just like that.

THE

END

ACKNOWLEDGEMENTS

THIS IS IT. THE END OF THE ROAD. This book was the hardest to write, and not just because it marks the end of the saga. Saying goodbye is always tough, and that feeling of having to send of Sally, and do right by her, was on my mind every step of the writing process. But what I may not have shared is that I've been quietly battling chronic fatigue syndrome as a result of long COVID. The brain fog was thick, and the road to recovery has been long. But here we are, finally at the finish line. Despite it all, if you're reading this, Singularity is in your hands. Complete. And I have so many people to thank for helping me finish this marathon.

First and foremost, I want to express my deepest gratitude to Michelle, my extraordinary publisher, who took a chance on me and this ten-book series. Your unwavering belief in Starstruck has been the cornerstone of my career as an author, and I am endlessly grateful for your faith in me. I am incredibly proud of how far we've come together. A special mention must also go to Hilary, my exceptional line editor for this final installment, Singularity. Your meticulous attention to detail and keen editorial eye has given the book a beautiful polish.

As always, I have to thank Jo, for giving me creative control over the characters and allowing Starstruck to flourish. I am deeply and forever grateful to you!

A huge thank you to Crystal for beta reading… and so much more. Your unwavering belief in me, your words of encouragement during challenging times, and your steadfast presence have helped me navigate through moments of doubt and burnout, time and time again. I also want to extend my thanks to Maddie, Lisa, Emily, Heidi, and Erin, who have all been incredible sources of support and encouragement along the way. I am immensely grateful for your friendship and support.

I need to give special thanks to someone incredibly dear to me. The first person to ever win a Starstruck giveaway emailed me afterward, and we've been besties ever since. In the time I've known her, she's gone back to school, pursued an English degree, and become an incredible editor with wisdom and insight beyond her years. In a full-circle moment, she was the last line of editing defense for Singularity. Knowing the series better than anyone, she brought not only her editing skills but also her love for Starstruck, catching every out-of-character moment and perfecting every grand finale line. This series wouldn't be what it is without her — I probably would have given up books ago. Cora is my hero, and I am beyond proud of her and honored to know her.

I want to thank my family for supporting my wild dream, and especially my husband, Hugo, for being the best partner I could ever have. I love being able to read through the acknowledgements of Starstruck and watch our love story unfold. Thank you for every wild idea, every impromptu brainstorming moment, every late-night writing session.

Finally, I want to thank you, dear reader. When I dedicated this book to you, it was for good reason: I wouldn't be writing if it wasn't for you. This series exists because of you. Every message of encouragement you sent me, every "when's the next book coming out?", every review, every piece of fanart — heck, every angry tweet — reminded me that there was somebody out there actually reading this series, and that's all an author could want. Thank you for being here, all the way to the end. See you in the next adventure!

ABOUT THE AUTHOR

S.E. ANDERSON SPENDS HER DAYS STUDYING comets and her nights spinning yarns of co(s)mic relief and interstellar hilarity. With her trademark blend of humor and adventure, she's penned the YA science fiction humor series STARSTRUCK SAGA, the SciFi Wizard of Oz retelling OVER THE MOON, and the YA contemporary novel AIX MARKS THE SPOT, based on her childhood adventures in Provence.

When she's not wrangling comets, her cats, or her husband in Marseille, France, you can find her concocting new worlds and characters, or indulging in a good book with a cup of tea.

CONNECT WITH THE AUTHOR

www.seandersonauthor.com
facebook.com/seandersonauthor
TikTok.com/seandersonauthor
instagram.com/readcommendations
X.com/sea_author